NIR BARAM was born into a political family in Jerusalem in 1976. His grandfather and father were both ministers in Israeli Labor Party governments. He has worked as a journalist and an editor, and as an advocate for equal rights for Palestinians. He began publishing fiction when he was twenty-two, and is the author of five novels, including *The Remaker of Dreams* and *World Shadow*. His novels have been translated into more than ten languages and received critical acclaim around the world. He has been shortlisted several times for the Sapir Prize and in 2010 received the Prime Minister's Award for Hebrew Literature. His most recent book is a work of reportage, which Text will publish in 2017.

JEFFREY GREEN is a writer and translator living in Israel. He has a doctorate in Comparative Literature from Harvard, and has also published, among other things, a novel in Hebrew, a book of poetry and a book about translation.

GOOD PEOPLE

NIR BARAM

TRANSLATED FROM THE HEBREW
BY JEFFREY GREEN

Text Publishing Melbourne Australia

textpublishing.com.au

The Text Publishing Company Ltd
Swann House, 22 William Street, Melbourne, Victoria 3000, Australia

The Text Publishing Company (UK) Ltd
130 Wood Street, London EC2V 6DL, United Kingdom

First published as *Anashim Tovim* in Israel by Am Oved
Published by The Text Publishing Company 2016

Design by W. H. Chong
Typeset by J&M Typesetting

Printed and bound in Australia by Griffin Press, an Accredited ISO AS/NZS 14001:2004 Environmental Management System printer

National Library of Australia Cataloguing-in-Publication entry
Creator: Baram, Nir, author.
Title: Good people / by Nir Baram ; translated from the Hebrew by
    Jeffrey Green.
9781925240955
9781911231004 (UK paperback)
9781922253576 (ebook)
Subjects: World War, 1939-1945—Fiction.
Other Creators/Contributors:
    Green, Jeffrey, translator.
Dewey Number: 892.437

GOOD PEOPLE

CONTENTS

CAST OF CHARACTERS

vii

PART ONE

PREPARATIONS FOR A GREAT DEED

1

PART TWO

THE ARTIFICIAL MAN

129

PART THREE

THE WORLD IS A RUMOUR

275

CAST OF CHARACTERS

BERLIN / WARSAW / LUBLIN

Thomas Heiselberg, market researcher at the Milton Company

Marlene Heiselberg, Thomas's mother

Johannes Heiselberg, Thomas's father

Hannah Stein, housekeeper and companion of Marlene

Jack Fiske, director and then president of the European department of the Milton Company

Carlson Mailer, Fiske's successor as director

Frau Tschammer, assistant director of the research department at the Milton Company

Hermann Kreizinger, Thomas's schoolfriend and member of the SS

Erika Gelber, Thomas's psychoanalyst

Clarissa Engelhardt, Thomas's neighbour and subsequent housekeeper

Paul Blum, a partner in Bamberburg Bank

Georg Weller, senior adviser to Dr Karl Schnurre in the German Foreign Office

Rudolf Schumacher, bureaucrat in the Ministry of Economics

Hauptsturmführer Bauer, German intelligence officer

Albert Kresling, officer in the *Haupttreuhandstelle Ost*, 'Göring's man in Poland'

Sturmbannführer Wolfgang Stalker, SS officer working under Kresling in the *Haupttreuhandstelle Ost*

Sturmbannführer August Frenzel, commander of the *freiwillige Umsiedlung*, the program for the voluntary deportation of Jews from Lublin

LENINGRAD / BREST

Alexandra (Sasha) Andreyevna Weissberg, literary editor of confessions for the NKVD

Andrei Pavlovich Weissberg, Sasha's father, physicist

Valeria Weissberg, Sasha's mother

Vladimir (Vlada) and Nikolai (Kolya) Weissberg, Sasha's younger twin brothers

Emma Feodorovna Rykova, poet

Brodsky, literary critic

Nadyezhda (Nadya) Petrovna, poet arrested by the NKVD

Konstantin Varlamov, poet

Osip Borisovich Levayev, publisher

Vladimir Vladimirovich Morozovsky, mechanic and poetry lover

Maxim Adamovich Podolsky, Sasha's husband and coworker in the NKVD

Stepan (Styopa) Kristoforovich Merkalov, head of Sasha's department

Reznikov, coworker of Sasha and Styopa

Nikita Mikhailovich Kropotkin, Sasha's superior in Brest

PART ONE
PREPARATIONS FOR
A GREAT DEED

People meet people. That's how the story goes. There's no need to be alone, not until you take your last breath. You see a world bursting with people, and are fooled into believing that your days of solitude are over. How hard can it be? Someone approaches someone else, they were both moved by *The Twilight of the Gods*, and by Gerhart Hauptmann's new play, both invested in Thompson Broken-Heart Solutions ('The heart is the curse of the twentieth century'), and they're allies already. It's a fiction useful to the state, to society, to the market. Thanks to it, lonely people buy clothes, shares, cars, and spruce themselves up for dancing.

Through the parlour window Thomas Heiselberg could see that she was swaddled in the same fur coat she'd worn the last time she left the house. She hadn't gone by choice. After all, the outside world offered her nothing. But his family could no longer afford to employ her. They had let her go and given her a white fur coat that had now turned grey. Parting is a chance to be reborn: something good might happen, another job might turn up, the pall of loneliness might be torn open.

She approached with small steps—she had put on weight, Frau Stein—steps that seemed to say, 'Don't look. There's nothing to see here.' And so you have it, the cunning of history: recent events in Berlin had given Jews like her good reason to hide in the shadows.

He watched her flat face, reddened by the cold air, her delicate neck whose grace was cruelly contradicted by her short body, like a seed of beauty that, in different circumstances, might have blossomed. She was totally alone, that was clear. He had no doubt that, aside from routine exchanges, she had scarcely spoken with anyone in the years since she had left.

A car stopped next to her. Two men sat in the front seat. She didn't look at them, but her every movement indicated her awareness of their presence. She brushed a whitish curl from her forehead and kept walking. Now a stone wall hid her from his view. Thomas watched until the car disappeared in traffic. A moment later, Frau Stein emerged again and, he thought, saw his face in the window.

How his mother had mourned when she left. Frau Stein was one of the family, she had filled the gaps—the sister his mother never had, for example—until they came to terms with the fact that his mother had no sister, and fired her. In the final analysis, when his mother's annuity dwindled under the blows of inflation, and their lives were in danger, blood was blood.

A knock on the door.

'Hello, Frau Stein,' Thomas said.

She nodded with her impatient gaze, pushed him aside. Their eyes met: the years hadn't diminished the hostility between them.

He took some pleasure in her disgrace, which was all over the newspapers, in the law books and on signs in the street. Close up, he could even spot its traces, a tortured urgency in her face. Hannah Stein's soul, just like her stooped body, was waiting for the next blow. Familiar with the house, and all its twists and turns, she hurried down the dark corridor and was swallowed up by her mistress's bedroom.

Thomas didn't move, then he set out after her. She was sure to be plotting something.

By the time he caught up with her, she had managed to hang her coat in the closet and seat herself at his mother's bedside. His mother's eyes expressed no surprise when the woman whom she hadn't seen for more than eight years leaned across and asked whether she needed anything. His mother said no. Frau Stein asked whether she was being well taken care of, and his mother whispered, 'Yes', which was in fact 'No'. Frau Stein took her hand and murmured her name over and over: 'Marlene, Marlene.'

Thomas imagined how she had crossed all of Berlin to see her mistress in her decline. Slightly breathlessly, she told his mother, 'This morning by chance I met Herr Stuckert. He turned away as if he hadn't seen me. I said to myself, very well, I'm already used to old acquaintances behaving like this. In my heart I always wish them well. But there was something strange about Herr Stuckert's behaviour. I stopped and asked, "Sir, is there something you want to tell me?" I didn't say his name. He could always pretend that he didn't know me. He lowered his eyes and said under his breath, "Frau Heiselberg is very ill."'

His mother said something to her that didn't reach Thomas's ears and Frau Stein nodded. He was overcome with disgust: it was all too familiar. The countless mornings the two of them had sat, clinging to each other in the bedroom, sharing secrets. Anyone in the vicinity felt as though he were invading a country where he would never be welcome.

Frau Stein settled the pillows under his mother's head and stroked her hair, then buried her face in his mother's breast. 'Marlene, how did it happen?' she said. 'How did it happen?'

With a kind of lightness the two women made the gap that had yawned between them for the past eight years disappear. It was as if a curtain was opened, revealing an older landscape: here they were again, a dreamy mistress who, on the rare occasions she ventured into the world, remembered its harshness and withdrew, and a housekeeper who had become her good friend and, in taking over her duties, had built the wall that kept her mistress isolated. They were rebelling now against the scraps of time that remained, mourning the years that had passed, and the hours that were slipping away.

Do you still want to protect her, Frau Stein? Thomas thought in anger and turned away. Do you want to protect her from the years she sacrificed, the injustices that stained her wedding dress, the errors of her life? Then you'll have to sketch the figure of a hangman. Here he is: a horrible illness that devastates your mistress's body and shoves her towards death. And you still believe you can do something for her?

Thomas stood in the roomy parlour. Following his mother's orders, the thick velvet curtains were always drawn. He turned on a lamp beside the sofa with its down cushions, and looked at the statuettes— an Auguste Rodin, a porcelain *Arc de Triomphe*, and a little gilded Buddha, a gift she received from a scholar she met when she was young, and under whose influence she had become interested in the religions of the Far East. Above the Buddha, on a shelf, stood a picture of Ernst Jünger, with a dedication: 'To Marlene, whose curiosity is so marvellous.' Artificial plants surrounded the arched fireplace, decorated with Delft tiles that featured silly pictures of lakes and windmills. He always felt dizzy at the sight of this parlour, confronted by the clutter that was intended to reveal the breadth of his mother's thought.

Thomas decided to ignore what was happening in the bedroom, sat at the desk, and made a few last corrections to the presentation he was to give that evening to convince the directors of Daimler-Benz that the Milton Company was the answer to their needs. What a shame little Frau Stein hadn't come across certain articles in the newspapers, where his name was mentioned. What a shame she didn't know about his triumphs.

In his early twenties, while his father and his unemployed friends were trudging the streets of Berlin dressed as tyres, sandwiches or chocolate bars, he had already dreamed up an original plan. About two years after he finished his degree, he read that the Milton market research company was planning to open a branch in Germany. Milton, an American company, with its offices all over the world but only one in Europe—in England of all places—had kindled his imagination even while he was a student. An American friend who was enrolled in economics told him about Milton and its advanced market research, which was at least ten years ahead of Europe. That had been one of the only points of light at the University of Berlin. In the early 1920s he was of course interested in the social sciences, and even considered studying linguistics, but in the end, influenced by his mother, who believed that 'a change would take place in his spirit' if he enrolled at a university that took pride in its intellectuals, he had studied philosophy, which he mainly thought a waste of time. The moment he received his degree of 'Magister' he left.

In the winter of 1926, when he was twenty-three, he travelled to London, where he met an American named Jack Fiske, the director of the European department of Milton. He spent months—with the help of an American teacher he had hired—polishing up his English in preparation for his presentation to Fiske. He sat in a leather upholstered chair in the spacious office of the director, whose wrinkled face and thick moustache impressed him, and pored over a huge blue, red and white map of the world that had numerous flags marking Milton branches pinned to it. Seeing that map, he knew he had made the right decision. He decided to adopt a forthright manner that would put off most German executives.

The director eyed him suspiciously, as if he couldn't understand where this young Berliner had sprung from, with his flashy suit, blue cravat and carnation in his lapel. Thomas crossed his long legs, offered his host some fine Dutch tobacco, lit his pipe and amiably asked what had inspired the choice of a desk in the shape of a pirate ship. Then he plunged in. 'My dear Mr Fiske,' he said, 'I have read about your plan to open a new branch of Milton on the continent, in Berlin in fact, my hometown. First, sir, allow me to congratulate you on behalf of my fellow Berliners. As an experienced market researcher, you will have already studied the opportunities that Europe offers, and learned from your limited success in England. Let's face it: Milton has stumbled in Europe. Sadly, one might say that you haven't even reached the continent. A small prediction: it will be even harder in Berlin. Sir, how do I know? It's simple. Every community has its own system of assumptions, and the parameters of market research that have been applied to the Americans won't do for us Germans. From my sources I've learned that in your meetings with German companies you boast about Milton's scientific methods. But remember: the aura of science is in fact a fiction. You might persuade a few gullible Germans who love to "scientificate" everything, but we both know that in two years even the most naive will realise that your methods aren't effective, and they'll boot you out of the German market.

'My dear sir, the only science that works here is the science of the German national spirit. You don't understand the German essence. You aren't the first and won't be the last. The German essence is hard to understand. Some believe that our tradition, our scholarship, our art and our philosophy have produced a fascinating mosaic of personality types. I am, however, sorry to inform you that the German spirit is much simpler. Sir, you will be surprised to discover how easily this spirit can be deciphered and manipulated. It is not the kind of simplicity that you Americans are familiar with. The educated German bourgeoisie are, for example, nothing like your assertive east-coast Americans. To understand them you have to study them in depth. The last move in a chess game may seem obvious, but it is preceded by intense preparation.'

Fiske stretched out his legs and wrinkled his brow. 'Actually, Mr Heiselberg, Milton has recently made a thorough study of the German market,' he said.

Thomas sensed that their meeting was giving him pleasure, and that Fiske was testing him. 'With all due respect, sir, my mother will hunt down lions in the Colosseum before Americans understand the German mind. Have you read Ernst Jünger? Certainly not. He's a close friend. Do you know Wolfgang Pauli? The yearning for a great light is planted deep in our soul. If you haven't seen the crowd in the Winterfeldtplatz in the late evening, staring at the shining torches of Nivea, you haven't seen Germany. Do you know what *völkish* means?

It's actually a definition of the German essence. And are you familiar with Naumann's theory about the state as a Great Business for the people's benefit? Indeed, sir, you must agree with me that you are hardly an expert on the German mind…

'Now the Reichsmark has stabilised, and the economy has improved, but if you wandered around Berlin a few years ago you would have learned about the true essence of Germany! You would have seen apparently rational people simply printing money and eroding the currency until it wasn't worth a seashell. That's German logic: to gallop, in denial, towards catastrophe.

'The German person is composed of a mass of varying elements. You could say that everyone is like that, and you would be right, but the German essence, the dollop of sentimentality it contains, for example, is unique. I have been striving to discover the formula that will conquer the German market. You may wonder whether I have it already? I believe I do. I have devoted most of my life to the study of the German. Therefore, sir, if you want to do business in Germany, I suggest that we cooperate.'

Jack Fiske was impressed. 'Young man, you don't completely understand the field yet, but you have ability, and your gift of the gab is scary.'

When Fiske moved to Berlin, Thomas became his assistant. A year later he became the director of the new one-man Department of German Consumer Psychology. If truth be told, he believed he was born for the job. Even as a boy he understood that his talent was to pluck the right strings in the buyer's soul. Now he played things well, combining persuasion, research and charm. Fiske asked him to work as a consultant with the American discount chain Woolworth, one of Milton Berlin's first clients. Milton staff were inclined to think that the Germans would not trust a popular chain from a country that remained mysterious to them.

'Surveys that Milton has performed in the major cities show that the Germans don't believe that this merchandise is any good,' announced Frau Tschammer, who gloried in her title of Assistant Director of the

Research Department, though her real job was to hunt for clients. She was a short blonde woman who had lost her husband in the Great War and was bringing up two children on her own, and she always over-estimated the discernment of the German consumer. Thomas saw her as the faint, self-righteous voice of the old world. Frau Tschammer annoyed him, and he intended to chop off her head—professionally, of course—by the end of the year; the stratagems of a grand master were hardly necessary here. Meanwhile, she shocked him by recom-mending that prices be raised in order to increase sales.

Thomas stood up. 'First, I must disagree with Frau Tschammer,' he said. 'Germans are very curious about America. Second, I suggest that Woolworth should burst into the market from above. I remember how excited everyone got when a plane sprayed Persil in the sky, and that was only laundry detergent. A giant company like Woolworth should buy the skies of Berlin for a month. We'll wipe out every other company. You won't be able to look up and see anything that isn't a banner, a beacon or Woolworth skywriting. And if we have to, birds, too. We'll rent all the Zeppelins, the planes, anything that can take wing. And if our competitors get hold of an aircraft, we can intercept it for all I care.'

The Americans loved it. From the books he had read and the movies he had seen, he concluded that Americans liked daring statements that expressed an adventurous idea and promised a decisive blow against the enemy. 'Let's do A, and we'll show them! Let's do B, and we'll wipe them out. Let's do C, and they'll lose so much they'll be selling trinkets in the street.' The more uninhibited his ideas, the more they were convinced that he was 'a man after our own heart'. They had to believe he was prepared to burn down Dresden to sell a teapot.

'Our lights will shine from every truck,' he went on, 'from every building, shop window and windshield. Product and price. Product and price will constantly change.'

'Sounds mighty good,' enthused one of the directors of Woolworth Europe.

'I happen to know the people who work for Paul Wenzel,' said Thomas.

'The ones who registered the patent for a plane that changes advertisements?' asked Frau Tschammer.

'Exactly,' he confirmed. 'Really incredible guys. They have a lot of other patents up their sleeve. I suggest that Woolworth buy that patent.'

'Do we really need a plane that will change advertisements twenty times on every flight? We're just one chain,' another Woolworth director objected.

'I already explained,' said Thomas, fatherly affability glowing in his green eyes. 'We're not going to go crazy or lose our heads, which is what people do in this city. First we'll advertise a product and its price, and in the second phase we'll advertise the chain.'

'Interesting. Can you set up a meeting with Wenzel's people?'

'Of course,' Thomas said merrily. 'They're close friends.'

His rise in Milton was vertiginous. Very few of its employees ever became partners, certainly not in such a short time. The meeting tonight with Daimler-Benz, which he'd been working on for the past month, could cap off a very good year; ever since the merger of Daimler and Benz, he had been dreaming of how he could snare their new brand, Mercedes-Benz. But the finale of his presentation didn't please him. Too artificial. The muffled whispering from his mother's bedroom was keeping him from concentrating.

As a child he used to sit with a notebook on the floor outside the closed door and write down the things that his mother and Frau Stein said, but he never managed to distinguish between their hushed voices. So his notebook was filled with phrases stitched together into one long monologue. At night, in his room, he would study each remark, deciding whether to attribute it to his mother or Frau Stein, until he had his own version of their conversation. He would celebrate a small victory every time he heard one of them say something that reminded him of a phrase he had decided was hers.

The whispering died down. Heavy steps were heard. He rose, but Frau Stein beat him to it and went around him, leaving thin muddy footprints as she hurried to the bathroom. She evidently still believed in the cold towel method.

'Frau Stein, haven't we developed more sophisticated remedies by now?' he asked, but actually he wanted to say, 'Frau Stein, haven't you heard that the Department of German Consumer Psychology at Milton is me? I'm a managing partner now. You must want to hear about my enormous progress. After all, we're not strangers.'

Frau Stein came back carrying a towel. Her dress was stretched tight over her protruding belly. As her eyes met his, he saw the indictment in them, her shock at how sick her mistress was. How dare she accuse him, even in thought. But she narrowed her eyes into two resolute slits, as though to proclaim: 'Yes, the cold towel method is the remedy I trust.'

Frau Stein had a marvellous ability to organise events into a story that she devoutly believed. 'Men against women' was one of her favourite narratives. When she had worked in the house, she had placed herself between the evil of the father and the son and the weak mother and wife. Erika Gelber had interesting things to say about this. In his imagination, he imprisoned Frau Stein in Erika Gelber's clinic: he laid her down on the stiff couch and forced her to answer the psychoanalyst's questions, to confess her dreams, to confront the distressing fact that there were other points of view. A woman like Frau Stein—who always laid claim to the whole truth—would never let anyone else in the world show her anything new. In her view, everything she didn't know formed a single grand despicable lie. Good people, who were few, spoke the truth and never betrayed you, and all the rest were liars. That was why his mother's betrayal had floored Frau Stein. When the subject of letting her go had come up, his mother had asked Thomas to contribute to her wages, but he had refused, claiming that Milton didn't pay him enough. 'And anyway, Mother, Frau Stein has worked here for more than twenty years. You have to know how to leave people behind…'

At the end of 1930, Frau Stein had left their house and entrusted his mother to him, and now, eight years later, she came back to find Marlene on her deathbed. She was doubtless convinced that if she had stayed none of this would have happened. It was interesting that she still felt the need to protect the woman who had fired her. Perhaps Frau Stein did possess a rare degree of loyalty, and maybe certain people could never free themselves from old habits.

'Frau Stein,' he called out cheerfully, his eyes sparkling—even Frau Tschammer admitted that their clarity was captivating—'have you heard that your faithful servant has been made managing partner at Milton, and that he is the director of the Department of German Consumer Psychology, including our offices in Paris, Warsaw and Rome? I set those branches up. Now the Frogs want to do it their way. Frau Stein, if you were in my shoes, would you let those Frenchmen have their heads? To be part of Milton, they have to fit into our systems, don't you agree? I told them, "There's no way the French office can keep thinking it's still the last century." And that's presuming there is such a thing as the French spirit anyway. Perhaps the passion for fine but meaningless formulations *is* the French spirit, this weakness for style at any price.'

'I don't buy products from advertisements,' Frau Stein said.

'I could have guessed that, of course.' Thomas always enjoyed chatting to her. That was one of the strange things about the connection between them: she acted as if his prattle disgusted her but often listened. In fact, part of Frau Stein marvelled over his doings, as if she couldn't believe that a person like him truly existed.

'All of our research has shown that the German working class is hostile to advertising, and the reasons are clear. Advertisements are aimed at people with money or at people who envy people with money or at people who believe that one day they'll have money or at people who pretend to have money.'

'Frau Heiselberg has asked me to stay with her for a few days,' Frau Stein said.

'She's dreaming. That's completely impossible, and you know it,' he sputtered. How he hated people who denied the simplest facts. Now he remembered that he had to avoid mood swings in front of strangers; people might lose faith in his cordial nature. But, he consoled himself, it was only Frau Stein.

'I won't go out of the house,' she said.

'That doesn't matter. People talk. Somebody might have seen you climb the steps. Actually, you have to leave now.'

'Your mother asked for my help. And I intend to give it,' Frau Stein declared.

'Frau Stein, the subject is not open for discussion! I don't have time to stand here and quarrel with you. Your towels are getting warm. Please put them on my mother's forehead, and then you have to go. I'm in a hurry. In two hours, at 7 p.m., we have a meeting with Daimler-Benz.'

He heard his mother calling his name from the bedroom. He hurried to her. 'Thomas,' she mumbled, raising her head with great effort. 'Thomas, I want Frau Stein to stay here for a few days.'

'Mother, that is impossible. The woman is putting us in danger.'

'Thomas, my dear, I've been in danger for a long time now,' she said and stretched out her hand. He took it and stroked her thin fingers. Pain swelled in his body along with the memory of their old ritual: he, a young boy, standing in front of her bedroom mirror, always drawn to its wooden frame and the soft, flattering light. His mother lying on her bed, Frau Stein on the chair next to her. They would talk about him as if he weren't there. 'All day long the boy stands in front of the mirror and imitates the hairdos of good-for-nothing movie stars. We gave him everything! Philosophers and musicians taught him, and especially for him I invited Ernst Jünger here, one of our most eminent authors, and the boy asks him if he's been to America…I offered him the best values in the world, and one day he will sell his soul to Pluto. Look at him, fussing over his hair like a girl, roaming the streets all day with Hermann Kreizinger, the son of that crook who sells fake trinkets. They do all kinds of shady deals with the delinquents on Oranienburger Strasse, who sell their bodies to diplomats and Frenchmen.'

The mirror had wings you could move to the right or left and arrange in a kind of triangle that multiplied your reflection. He loved to fold the wings. Here are the faces of the two women becoming molten and distorted; a face like a swollen balloon; a face as small as a coin; rubber faces that stretched from one side of the mirror to the other; faces as thin as pencils or as broad as the base of a mountain; Frau Stein's eyes next to his mother's lips; the snow-white forehead next to pink cheeks, bristling eyebrows under hair like a fox's fur. He liked to place the wings of the mirror at an angle that would set as many faces dancing as possible, twenty-seven.

'Dear Thomas, I won't ask for anything more.'

He couldn't bear the floating touch of her fingers, the memory of the caress that would never happen again. 'I'm hurrying to a meeting, Mother. The customers have made a list of demands that we can't meet. Times have changed. People are hoarding money, afraid of war...' The urge to flee quivered in every muscle of his body.

His mother seemed to understand. She gave him a distant look that pinned him back in the position of the scorned child—once again he was gathering up motherly gazes like a beggar—and she closed her cold fingers on his hand. Now the release would be even harder.

'At least let Frau Stein stay until you get back. I don't want to be alone.'

'If there's no choice, Mother,' he conceded.

Happiness rose in her face. She released his hand; her eyes were already dismissing him.

'How elusive your mother's love is,' Erika Gelber once said to him. He left her bedroom and Frau Stein passed by him again, hugging the towels to her chest. Water dripped onto the floor. He looked at it with annoyance. Nothing in Frau Stein's face showed satisfaction, but they both knew that, rather than celebrating her victory, she was elated by his defeat.

...

Thomas ordered his driver to park in front of the Milton building, so the clients would see the company's new Mercedes-Benz when they arrived, and he skipped up the steps. He extricated his thoughts from the trap laid by Frau Stein and thrust them into the meeting. (Erika Gelber didn't believe he was capable of controlling his mind, or could summon up the focus to make a firm decision about anything. 'You psychology people don't have enough faith in a person's willpower,' he once scolded her in response.) He removed his coat, handed it to the doorman and gave him a warning glance: this is not the time to ask for a raise, or to tell me again how your daughter is getting married and needs an apartment.

Meanwhile he went over his presentation: sales of luxury cars were expected to be flat in the coming months. Daimler-Benz needed a new project, a prestige vehicle that would appeal to those who yearn for something stylish but would speak to the masses too. In short—they had to invent the people's car for the coming decade.

Thomas stood in his office—he preferred to spend most of his working hours on his feet, a position that filled him with a sense of vitality and strength—and called for his two secretaries. A week earlier he had announced to all the staff that today they would be required to stay in the office until evening. A clear message had to be conveyed to the Daimler-Benz people: Milton will be at your service day or night. He started dictating letters to the company's various European directors, inviting them to the traditional New Year party in Berlin. Each letter was seasoned with a more or less personal tone, depending on the branch's achievements. Then he called in an underling, who was preparing their presentation to a smallish client, gave him ten minutes to run through the outline, made his comments and asked for a finished document by the end of the week. While the employee was gathering up his papers, Thomas spoke on the telephone with his friend Schumacher from the Ministry of Economics, listing several ideas and the names of companies to which Milton might offer its excellent service. After taking care of a few other bits and pieces, he stood in front of the mirror, straightened his hair, smoothed some creases in his jacket and headed for the boardroom.

Frau Tschammer was in the hall in front of the directors' offices, between framed letters of appreciation from Piaggio and the Wedel chocolate factory in Warsaw, hiding behind a newspaper. The letters had of course come from clients of the branch offices Thomas had established. Her face, pink and heavily made up, emerged. She approached him, fiddling with the front of her light blue dress.

'Frau Tschammer, you're prettier than ever tonight,' he called and kept on towards the boardroom. 'It's time to finish with all the petty details of work and celebrate with one of your many admirers.'

'But you asked us to stay late today,' she complained.

'Of course, but it's clear that we didn't mean you, Frau Tschammer. You're in a class of your own.'

'Did you hear?' She blocked his way.

'Of course I heard,' he hissed. Frau Tschammer was an expert at wasting other people's time with trivial matters.

'Vom Rath is dead.'

'So tell Elisabeth to order a wreath and draft a letter. I'm rushing to the meeting.'

'What kind of letter?' Frau Tschammer asked in surprise.

'Frau Tschammer, what kind of question is that? We don't turn our back on our clients even when they die. We'll be working with the Richard Lenz Company for many years.'

'Thomas, that's not funny. Vom Rath didn't work with us. He was the Third Secretary of the German Embassy in Paris.'

'I'm quite familiar with the matter, Frau Tschammer,' he interrupted. 'For two days now, people have been talking about nothing else. Maybe you don't remember, even though it's your job to remember, but Richard Lenz has a manager named von Kraft, a not dissimilar name.'

Her astonishment amused him. Once again she had failed to understand how he dared to undermine her with some ridiculous remark dressed up as an unassailable truth. Frau Tschammer, like his ex-wife Elsa, insisted on speaking to him like a schoolmarm, despite his own flippant approach to things: *The world is a game; it's pointless to search for truth or lies, so don't complain, play!* He had already heard that she secretly scorned this teasing behaviour as 'Heiselbergian Ethics'.

'By the way, I have a lot of respect for companies and people who have finite dreams, like Richard Lenz,' he added. 'Not everyone is destined to conquer the world, Frau Tschammer, as you well know.'

He hoped that the Vom Rath affair wouldn't ruin the meeting. The streets were teeming, feverish, as if yet another rowdy march was about to invade the city and keep people from working. Earlier, when he had driven by Kurfürstendamm, he had seen some hopeless types from Hermann Kreizinger's old gang. Hermann himself, who now wore a shiny SS uniform, had stopped running around with them a long time ago.

'Thomas, people say hard times are in store,' Frau Tschammer nagged him, worried.

'I have to get to the meeting.' For a moment he was distracted. Fifteen years earlier, in the summer of 1923, a week after his father was fired by the Junkers aircraft company, he sat with him in the back of a café in Unter den Linden. His father complained about the madness that had gripped Germany. Those had truly been strange times: their whole world was being stuffed into a straitjacket and people were muttering about the end of days, while the hungry masses were staring at the advertisements that glowed in the skies of the city. Banknotes were printed with the paintbrush of imagination. People carted off salaries in the millions in wheelbarrows, but by evening those piles of paper weren't enough for a beer and a sausage.

Suddenly, Hermann's gang burst into the café. Thomas greeted him with a nod, as usual, but Hermann pretended he hadn't seen him, which was how he had behaved ever since finishing school. Once Thomas had met him by chance and said hello, but Hermann only gave him a strange look, as if Thomas's voice itself had made him feel ill.

Thomas didn't understand the meaning of such behaviour. After all, they had until recently been close friends. When Hermann's father had committed suicide, leaving his wife and children penniless, Thomas had been the one who sold their property for them, and at a fantastic price. He had taken Hermann under his wing.

That was truly a miserable affair. After the war Kreizinger's World of Toys had collapsed. They had imported toys, electric gadgets from America, whimsical novelties that arrived by steamship—hardly essential things, but people loved them. The day came when Herr Kreizinger couldn't even buy a pencil from the Americans, so they sold him some merchandise on credit and hired a lawyer to sue him. The lawyer had taken everything, and Hermann's father had lain down on the railroad tracks. Thomas preferred people who jumped from the tops of towers. A moment of soaring through the air—at least one brief instant of greatness—why not get one last thing out of life?

After his father died, Hermann went hungry. Thomas was generous with him and taught him how you could get all kinds of things in Berlin for free. At least once a week, after school, they would make a circuit of a few upmarket hotels. Thomas would enter the lobby in the guise of an exiled Russian prince, for whom German luxury was a kind of insult, while Hermann, who played his faithful attendant, carried his suitcase. If the doorman asked too many questions, Thomas would put on an arrogant air and dumbfound him with a volley of Russian phrases. Hermann would then translate, in measured tones, a sequence of horrible insults and threats. Usually the doorman would retreat and bow before the young prince.

They would stroll along the corridors, ride the elevators and roam the stairs, with a single aim: to fill the suitcase with food. Sometimes they would come upon baskets of rolls or saucers of jam outside rooms, but usually they scouted for some festive event: a reception in honour of senior executives at Siemens-Schuckert, a family wedding, a party of American movie producers. On such occasions, it was easy to find crisp rolls and smoked sausages, cheeses and—on good days—beef cooked in prunes. Sometimes they dared to sit in the hotel restaurant, and Thomas would charm the waiters with the innocent look of a pampered youngster who never imagined that his father might be late for a meal, just as it never occurred to him that any delicacy might be beyond the reach of his lazy fingers. And there was that summer night, when they drank wine in the lounge of the Adlon, listening to a Mozart divertimento, and, as though they had all the time in the world, calmly stuffed smoked salmon and herring seasoned with allspice into their paper-lined suitcase. Hermann eyed the honoured guests in their smoking jackets, whose cloth changed colour in the bright light, and said to Thomas, half in admiration, half in anger, 'Around you, people learn how to fake it, because it's as easy as breathing for you.'

There was gratitude for you.

In any event, Hermann's gang drank and chattered in the café. Finally the old waiter shuffled over with the bill. He understood exactly what kind of task the proprietor—a coward who stayed behind the counter clutching a loaded pistol—had given him.

'Five million five hundred marks?' one of them shouted. 'Couldn't you at least have rounded it off, you filthy dog?'

The gang stood and cheered while two of them set fire to the bill and forced the waiter to hold the burning paper and chant the new price. The waiter shouted in pain. His veins stood out and seemed to wrap themselves around his neck like a noose. Then Hermann pushed him to the floor. 'Not worth the candle!' he shouted.

Thomas knew that Hermann was taking a risk. Some of his friends would understand that the shove was intended to free the burning paper from the waiter's hands. In short, Hermann had shown pity, and Thomas reckoned that now he would have to display his cruelty in some new way.

Hermann stood on a chair, waved his stick. 'Are you crazy?' he yelled. 'We couldn't even pay the old amount, so now you want more? How can the price jump by forty per cent during the two hours we were sitting here? Can't a person even drink a beer in this damn city anymore?'

He threw his stick at the café's display window. His friends sneered. Did he really believe they would think he had intended to break the window?

'Isn't that your friend from school?' his father said to him.

'Yes, but for years now he's been treating me like a leper, that punk,'

Thomas answered, unable to stop looking at Hermann.

It dawned on Hermann that he had no choice. If you want to be a bully, you have to obey the rules. He stepped down heavily from the chair and looked around. The sun threw yellow light into his eyes. He blinked. His friends were standing erect, as if listening to a speech at an assembly. Their shirts were wrinkled, their peaked caps pushed forwards, their hands thrust into the buckles of their belts. Hermann turned around, picked the chair up in both hands, and looked back into the café. Thomas imagined he saw regret in his eyes. Then he bent his body and, with a mighty swing, hurled his chair at the window. The glass shattered, and the fragments showered down upon two old women who were having an evening coffee. Hermann's friends cheered and pounded him on the shoulder, while the other customers stared. A few of them probably supported his actions or at least identified with his fury.

To Thomas's astonishment, his father approved too. Animated, he started to chat with people at nearby tables. 'They paid my salary weekly. Then I asked to be paid daily. I told them that the money I got at the end of the week wasn't worth much the following day. The foreman sent me to read my contract again. "Herr Heiselberg," that bastard shouted at me, "do you see a clause here about a daily salary? How come workers pick on the factory? Are you a Communist or something? Does your contract say how you should compensate *us* when not a single customer in the world bothers to answer our letters? They laughed at us even in Mozambique when we suggested doing business together. The German people are on the mat being torn apart limb by limb. Our economy is waltzing to hell, and everybody thinks it's party time."'

'The cheek of it,' somebody shouted.

'I'd have belted him one,' hissed a young man in a brown shirt, apparently a member of Hermann's gang.

'The next day they fired me,' Thomas's father complained with gloomy resentment designed to inflame the small crowd even more.

Thomas stared at the floor the whole time and squeezed his father's wrist, trying to calm him down, but his father took no notice.

'Those rich guys have no shame,' a young woman called out, cuddling her little boy.

'No shame,' his father roared.

In the expansive boardroom Thomas sank sweating into his regular chair, which was a bit higher than the others. The white light struck his face. He had asked for the lights to be changed several times, because lighting that imitated daylight was unbearable.

Indeed, it seemed that Frau Stein was cleverer than he had thought. Now he understood why she had turned up on the very day the news broke about Vom Rath's death. The woman was a nuisance who had haunted him since childhood. He would gladly turn her over to the mercies of Hermann and his pals—not that those good-for-nothings would know how to get the job done.

It was almost seven, and Carlson Mailer hadn't reached the office yet. Which was strange, because the meeting with Daimler-Benz had preoccupied Carlson, who was still, at least officially, the director of Milton. In fact, he and Thomas ran the company together, but Carlson, 'the bosses' man', always had the last say. He was Thomas's age, a tall American with short hair and the jawbone of a predator. Enormous boredom lurked in his black eyes and always made Thomas want to interest him in something. More than anything, though, Thomas was outraged by the way people admired Carlson because he made them doubt their right to take up his time. Even the clients were in awe of him. Thomas had long since understood that this human dynamic—which went beyond business connections, contracts, research documents—lacked any rhyme or reason. Carlson Mailer had a special gift for seeing into people's souls and motivating them with the urge to please him, even if it contradicted all business logic. The man was admired simply because he existed, even though he hadn't had a single brilliant idea his whole life.

Unlike Carlson, Thomas was a man who advanced in leaps. About a year after he joined Milton, an exciting period began when he set up the Department of German Consumer Psychology. The department went out and won clients, but within a year his energy had begun to drain away. He started to imagine that nothing new would ever happen again. One day followed the next and he didn't understand where the time had gone.

The summer of 1929 triggered his meteoric ascent in the company. The senior directors of Milton went to the Ibero-American Exhibition in Seville, and he was chosen to join them as the representative of the German office. Frau Tschammer, who had not been invited, was insulted and threatened to resign.

'Frau Tschammer, I don't understand,' Thomas said. 'When I come back, I'll tell you everything. We'll even take pictures for you. It'll be just as if you were there.'

On that fateful trip to Spain the idea that was to change his life took shape in his mind: he was standing between Jack Fiske and Carlson Mailer on the second floor of Plaza de España, the splendid building that had been constructed in honour of the exhibition. As he touched the terracotta tiles on the wall, he looked down to the ground level, where there were benches decorated with maps of Spain and its regions. A hot wave flooded his body. He closed his eyes and saw a similar plaza in his imagination, which would be the centre of the Milton Company, and they, the managers, were standing above it between the arches, while at their feet were the branches of the French, Spanish and English Consumer Departments of Psychology.

Two years passed before the German office once again settled, under the leadership of Carlson Mailer, who had replaced Jack Fiske as the director of Milton Berlin. At the right moment Thomas had laid out his great expansion plan before him, in this very room. Carlson frittered away two months pondering things, but in the end, after Thomas managed to contact Fiske, who had meanwhile returned to head office in New York, his plan got the go-ahead. A magnificent period ensued, the best in his career. Every morning, he would piece the clouds together to redraw the map of Milton Europe, and the changing skies would urge him to conquer Europe. He travelled to

Rome, Warsaw, London and Paris, familiarised himself with different societies and cultures, each of which demanded a different set of assumptions. When Carlson commented at a meeting, 'I see that we've raised a miniature Alexander the Great in our company,' Thomas answered, determined to avoid any personal conflict, 'Don't be afraid of challenges, my friend. We'll set up a pan-European network, which, at first glance, might seem uniform, but which will accommodate local patterns of thought wherever it is implemented.'

He met dozens of people, some of whom inspired him with exciting ideas, and all of these encounters kindled his restless ambition. He planned that by the end of 1940 there would be ten branches of Milton in Europe. At night, in trains, he envisioned a Milton Train reserved for its employees; he dreamed of an American giant who extended his hand to him, and together they soared over the Atlantic, conquering the continent in one splendid move. Then the Far East, the British Empire—Australia, India—wasn't the world grand?

Thomas looked up. A man wearing glasses entered the boardroom. He was not tall, and his thick arms were sheathed in the pressed suit of a government official, and there was a gold pin on his lapel. The man nodded to Thomas and limped lightly to the chair opposite him.

'A ski accident in Cortina.' He pointed at his leg. 'My poor wife broke her collarbone.'

Thomas was not interested. This was one of those petty bureaucrats making between 250 and 1000 Reichsmark a month who had filled the streets in recent years. He had probably been sent to deliver some kind of message to Carlson, who maintained close connections with all sorts of government offices.

The man sat down and looked at Thomas again, pointed at the door and said softly, 'Close it, please.'

Obeying the order, Thomas was disturbed by a number of things: it was 7.15 p.m. Where was Carlson? Where were the Daimler-Benz people? Aside from that, he despised meetings not arranged through the ordinary channels, and for which he wasn't thoroughly prepared.

Mainly he gathered that the man sitting opposite him had no doubts about the seniority of his own position, and probably with good reason.

'The American Milton Company and German Consumer Psychology. An elaborate name,' the man said.

'The gentleman appears to be interested in the subject, otherwise he wouldn't have favoured us with a visit.' Thomas stretched his body, emphasising its flexibility. His anxiety had faded. In moments of uncertainty, he believed, his superiority to others would be apparent. Never give people the feeling you aren't worthy of the position you occupy, or that anything they do might surprise you. 'It would be a privilege if the kind sir would allow me to tell him a little about our company.'

'Georg Weller,' the man said. Thomas had the impression that this casual introduction was calculated.

'My name is Thomas Heiselberg, and I manage the company along with Herr Mailer.'

'Of course, of course,' he said with a hint of mockery. 'I was so overwhelmed by Milton's impressive offices that I forgot my manners. It is my honour to work in the Foreign Office as senior adviser to Dr Karl Schnurre. By chance I was nearby, and remembered that Herr Mailer, whom I was privileged to meet recently, had invited me to visit him here.'

'Dr Schnurre's name arouses admiration in many circles!' Thomas said. 'Just last week, Herr Mailer, my colleague, told me that he had taken part in a meeting to discuss the expected challenges to the Foreign Office, in view of the poisonous diplomatic attacks against us in Europe, especially in Paris, London and Warsaw.'

He didn't have the slightest idea who Karl Schnurre was. He mentioned Warsaw and Paris simply because it was clear to him that Weller's position in the Foreign Office was connected to Europe, and if Schnurre was interested in Milton, he would therefore be curious about the company's offices in France, Italy and Poland.

Weller's forehead creased, and his cheeks bulged. He had apparently expected that his appearance here would arouse greater awe.

'I am acquainted with the company and with the Department of German Consumer Psychology. And I have heard about your offices in Europe: Paris, Rome and somewhere else, right?'

'Our flourishing branch in Warsaw, of course,' Thomas said. Now he was convinced that the man had done his homework, but he hadn't encountered such an amateurish manoeuvre in a long time. One could only hope that the Foreign Office showed more sophistication in its contacts with other countries.

'A truly daring idea these days, to use Jewish ideas to sell merchandise to the Germans—or even to the Poles.' He was speaking like a radio announcer, accentuating every word, and his voice was loud and clear.

'We don't use Jewish ideas.' Thomas gave him a disapproving glance. 'This is an entirely original adaptation of universal principles, developed long before the appearance of psychoanalysis in its present version, of which, by the way, I am also not enamoured. Here we have been developing principles formulated by German philosophy. We at Milton Berlin divert the decadent principles of Jewish psychoanalysis into rational and productive channels that befit the German spirit. I established the department to inject true Germanness into the discussion of the improvement and perfection of human abilities.'

'Sir, you express yourself well.' Georg Weller rose. 'Herr Heiselberg, it was an honour to visit Milton's headquarters. I just happened to be passing by and I won't take any more of your precious time. Would you please convey my cordial greetings to Herr Mailer.' He extended his hand to Thomas across the table. His handshake was soft. 'I expect that an invitation to a formal meeting at the Foreign Office will soon be issued,' he added.

'That will be a great honour for Milton,' Thomas answered, pushing open the heavy wooden door and accompanying the visitor out into the corridor, taking the opportunity to mention the strict qualification examinations for prospective employees that Milton had instituted in cooperation with the SD, the intelligence arm of the SS. Weller nodded and polished his glasses with a handkerchief that bore his initials embroidered in blue thread. They stood in the lobby whose broad windows looked out onto a narrow street decorated with poplar trees. Beneath the windows, around the entrance, stood benches in French Riviera style. Something about the room made Thomas uncomfortable, like his mother's parlour. In every corner was a fountain with a statue topped by an alabaster spear—the work of an American sculptor whom Fiske and Mailer mistook for a great artist. They exchanged a few courtesies and parted with a friendly handshake.

...

The hours passed. Only Thomas and the janitor were still in the office. Should he let Carlson know that the meeting hadn't taken place? Why hadn't the Daimler-Benz people shown up? After Weller left, Thomas questioned the staff. No one knew anything. Carlson had disappeared and it was impossible to reach him. Had he not come to the office because he already knew that the meeting had been cancelled? 'Maybe, maybe, maybe,' Thomas grumbled. But there was no point in being disappointed, and it wasn't all bad: a meeting with a senior official from the Foreign Office was preferable to a meeting with some client, right? He began to work out which clients should be told about the meeting, and which ones didn't need to know. Of course, he wouldn't tell them directly. The information had to be circulated in the form of a strictly controlled rumour. That was a tactic which he had mastered. Still, he would have felt better if the Daimler-Benz people had shown up.

He paced through the dark corridors and stood in the lobby. He shook his jacket slightly, passed a hand through his hair, adopted a pleasant expression and stepped outside. Thomas liked walking out into the street at night. Standing beneath the canopy of poplar trees, he would imagine he was in a thick forest, plunging into the darkness that enveloped him, becoming invisible as he groped his way along until, with a few quick steps, he would be out the other side.

An intense glare burned above him, and light spattered in every direction. Blinded for a moment he shut his eyes. How he loved to emerge into the glowing city lights. The sources of these great lights were big companies, and every new and surprising glow was a sign of an idea that had bloomed in the world, a stirring opportunity. He was always curious about new patents that other people invented, and nothing pleased him more than perfecting someone else's initiative and doing it better.

In the distance the rooflines sparkled like Christmas trees. It was as if the whole city was bathed in gold. He advanced down the street, at the end of which was Schultz, the exclusive men's clothing store. After darkness fell, a delicate light would bathe the fine suits in the display window, and the store looked so inviting that Thomas felt that every passerby would want to stop and buy something. Frau Tschammer used to tease that he was like Narcissus. 'But Thomas falls in love with his reflection only when it appears in the display windows of luxury shops.'

Flames ballooned on the distant horizon. He heard voices. Looking over at the Schultz window he was immediately struck by the feeling of a routine that had been violated: something was missing. Fragments of glass were sparkling on the pavement. A boisterous group of young men in brown uniforms, carrying torches, passed by. Now he could see that the store was bustling with people, masses of them, with bundles of clothes in their arms. He spotted a familiar figure—the doorman from their office. Was his name Beck? He was hurrying out of the store carrying a pile of merchandise and a little girl with golden hair. Her round face was sooty. Her eyes were wide, and the doorman's heavy coughs shook her little body.

Another band of young men with torches approached. One of them stuck his head in the smashed window and shouted, 'Disgusting! Thought you'd get yourselves some kikes' clothes?' He hurled the torch into the middle of the store. It caught on a rack of fine blue woollen coats with delicate collars, and they started to go up in flames. Everybody ran out to escape.

A familiar voice blared from a radio somewhere above. Thomas raised his eyes. People were looking down at him from their windows.

He began to worry: those people would have seen him standing there every evening, charmed by the Schultz display.

There's no need to get carried away, he consoled himself. At times of crisis, people tend to interpret events as if they were being specially persecuted and their souls were visible to the whole world. Besides, Erika Gelber always said that his feverish mind drove him, whether he was awake or asleep, towards terrifying scenarios that had nothing to do with him, and conjured up horrifying visions in which he was cursed and condemned. And, even if they had seen him, he could always claim that he was standing there because of the disgust he felt for those suits. Maybe he was imagining the ruin of those Jewish tailors? What other explanation was there for his attachment to the Schultz display? After all, in Berlin there was no lack of more splendid shop windows, KDW, for example, decorated with paintings by Cesar Klein, or the windows of Hermann Tietz or Wertheim, stores no longer owned by Jews. In a moment, Thomas was prepared to believe that something in him, something unconscious, apparently, had wished for the razing of Schultz. The murmurings of the soul are such a strange thing—here was another fascinating subject to discuss with Erika Gelber.

It occurred to him that the suit he was wearing now had been bought in Schultz. But a lot of stores sold suits like that. More or less. Actually there were no suits like it anywhere—Schultz had its own line. Those little megalomaniacs always boasted that they made everything themselves. To hell with that stupid desire for bespoke tailoring. His fingers flew up to the back of his neck and felt the label. Fear clung to his body like the incriminating suit.

He was filled with fury at that vicious gang of rioters, idlers who had never done a useful thing in their lives and were bent on mayhem and destruction. It was time they contributed something to the German economy. He looked with disgust at a strapping fellow who had a few looted suits draped over his shoulder. How ugly his gaping eyes were, gawking in the middle of his stupid face, the kind of face you could see in every train carriage, and now it radiated this mindless expression of victory.

He crossed Wichmannstrasse and looked up at number 10, where the Berlin Psychoanalytic Society once had its offices, and on the second floor—Erika Gelber's clinic. Where was she now? This wasn't a good night for wandering the streets. For an instant he was worried about her. Though it didn't seem as if this episode was going beyond destruction of property. He was sure they wouldn't hurt women, especially not a respected psychoanalyst like Erika, who had treated senior army officers—not to mention her achievements in rehabilitating soldiers with shell shock. The army was compelled to admit that in such cases psychoanalysis had produced results no other treatment could. In short, Erika didn't need his charity.

A boy and a girl passed by, arm in arm. The girl was saying something about the synagogue that had been burned to the ground, and the firemen who had rushed to the scene, and the crowds who had driven them off. The sky was hidden behind clouds of black smoke that absorbed the redness of the flames, as if a fiery map of the whole city was spiralling above them.

He heard shouts and turned around. A group of men was approaching, most of them SS. There was something frightening about their uniform movements. They glided forwards like a pack of wolves. He restrained the panic that surged through his body. If he turned into another street now, he would look suspicious. He walked towards them, and caught sight of the tanned face of Hermann Kreizinger.

Thomas heard the pounding of his own heart. The distance between them closed to a few metres. He hoped that this time, too, Hermann would ignore him. But Hermann's eyes fixed on him. More than fifteen years had passed since they had looked at one another. Behind Hermann stood the young policeman, Höfgen. Two deep scratches seared his cheeks and twisted down almost to his lips. For the first time Thomas saw him without glasses and in SS uniform.

Thomas moved his head in greeting. Fear flashed in Höfgen's eyes. He looked away. Hermann, unlike his comrades, was decked out in smart clothes: a white shirt with a brightly striped tie fluttering over it. His black shoes gleamed. They were probably new. Thomas remembered how on the first day of fourth grade Hermann appeared in school especially well dressed, and everybody whispered how his clothes had been bought thanks to the good business his father was doing with the Americans. Hermann sat down and took new toys that had been bought in New York out of his schoolbag. The boys stared enviously at them.

Hermann joined the SA, the Brownshirts, a few years after they finished school. His rise began in the early 1930s, when Hitler's friend, Ernst Röhm, who had returned to Germany from Bolivia to lead the SA, took a liking to him. Young Hermann served him faithfully, and won kudos and honours. He would wander the streets in uniform, or hang around beer halls whose owners were sympathetic to the organisation. Thomas remembered seeing him march on that evening at the end of January 1933. He had a wild look in his eyes, as if he were longing to meet those people who had once doubted him, and whom he would now astonish with his rebirth as a victor.

In 1934, rumours spread that Hermann had been in Tegernsee on the night when Röhm was arrested. It was said that Hitler himself had whipped Hermann outside the hotel. No one saw him for a few weeks, and it was clear that he must have been eliminated along with Röhm and the other Brownshirt leaders. But then he reappeared, and, not only that, he had a position and a rank in the SS, thanks to the intervention of Himmler's office. Hearing that he was alive and part of the SS, Thomas surmised that Hermann must have handled himself well during the crisis; maybe he had underestimated him.

'Herr Heiselberg, isn't it a bit late to be wandering the streets?' Hermann said amiably.

'I'm rushing home,' said Thomas. 'A long day at work...'

'A long day at work,' said Hermann. 'How are things going in that American company?'

'The German branch is jointly owned by Germans and Americans,' Thomas answered reasonably. 'We employ only Germans.'

'Only Germans!' Hermann crowed. 'Your American cronies bring their corrupt democracy here, and shamelessly steal from Germany.'

Now he was speaking to his friends more than to Thomas. 'Lucky the Führer has changed a few things in this country—not enough though, there are too many bourgeois whispering in his ear—but things are different, don't you think?'

'The Führer is doing excellent work. No one could dispute that his achievements are enormous,' said Thomas, feeling a tremor in his right leg. It felt like the city had been stripped of its clothing, and had abandoned all restraint; the only things left in it were boiling soil and humans.

'Interesting to think how your father,' said Hermann, straightening his tie in an affected way, 'would take all this: while the whole country is devoted to building a new Germany, his son is busy collecting dollars from American capitalists.'

'Actually, my father died two years after I started working at Milton.'

'You lot don't know,' Hermann said to his friends, who were all staring at him in boredom except for the policeman Höfgen, who was constantly fidgeting. 'You're too young. But during the 1920s Herr Heiselberg's father was a devoted member of the National Socialist Party.'

'Actually, until his death,' Thomas emphasised.

'Until his death. And while we're talking about death, you must know about the horrible murder of poor Vom Rath.' His upper lip, which protruded slightly, like the remnant of a smile that reached the dimples on his cheeks, gave his face a kind of childish impishness. His skin was still smooth, mocking the passing years, and still tanned. The boys at school had thought of the tan as an 'American' touch.

The familiar smile allayed Thomas's fears somewhat. 'We were all shocked to hear the sad news,' he said, nodding once again to Höfgen, who stepped back and stood behind one of the youths.

'The kike coward didn't dare take out the ambassador himself,' Hermann chuckled, 'so he made do with a miserable clerk. It's a good thing he didn't shoot the doorman.'

'Murderers like that are usually cowards,' Thomas said earnestly.

'People who always dreamed of some glorious deed, with a narcissistic desire to be loved by the masses, whom they actually despise. But there is nothing heroic about them at all.'

'Yes. I like that: people who desire heroism, but have none,' Hermann agreed. 'You doubtless understand the reason for our interest in recent events. This is a difficult night for the German people, and we were asked to keep order in the streets. Would you believe that a Jewish criminal scratched Höfgen, our faithful policeman?'

Other memories of Hermann surfaced: had Thomas done him a great injustice? Hermann had suffered as a boy from his failure to behave well, and at a certain stage he began making out that Thomas was some serpent-like, seductive figure, dragging him into sin. But Hermann always acknowledged that Thomas had helped him in hard times. In short, they had had good and bad days. But for years they had had nothing to do with each other...Had he said anything against Hermann that might have reached his ears? It didn't seem so. Thomas seldom spoke ill of people. Gossip was an indulgent weakness. Slander wasn't useful; it was likely to give listeners the residual feeling that you were unworthy of their trust. In the final reckoning, the harm outweighed the benefit.

'A nice place, isn't it?' Hermann pointed at the building where Erika Gelber used to treat Thomas. 'Do you still go there regularly?'

'Much less in the past two years. There's a lot of work in the office.' Thomas looked him in the eye. He didn't intend to show him that he had been surprised.

'Does your friend, the Jewish psychoanalyst, help you?' Hermann asked.

'Much less in the past two years,' Thomas repeated, beginning to wonder whether this might be the right time to tell Hermann that a senior official from the Foreign Office had just visited him.

'Very nice, very nice,' Hermann laughed. 'Baumann told me that his dad went a little crazy after the war, and that the Jews treated him...All kinds of things that you don't understand that you know, or you don't know that you understand. Something like that. Quite a deceptive business, no?'

'Yes, they helped a lot of soldiers,' Thomas said. 'In fact I heard that they got a medal from the War Ministry.'

'All this is very well, but we have a lot more to do,' a tall Brownshirt, behind whom Höfgen was hiding, said to Hermann irritably. 'Maybe you could chat with your bourgeois faker some other day?' He stepped back, and now the policeman was in front of Thomas. Höfgen stared at him as if he were seeing him for the first time and was at his wit's end.

'Speaking of Jews, I'm interested in hearing your opinion about the murder in Paris,' Hermann said calmly, raising his hand and poking his index finger right at the tall man's face. 'Maybe it's time to react against the French, too?'

'It's a terrible thing, a great shame to all the Jews,' Thomas answered. 'And as for the French, those are matters that the Führer knows best how to handle.'

'Believe me, tonight is the great shame of the Jews,' Hermann said quietly. His dimples deepened, but cold mockery flashed in his eyes.

An alarming certainty crept into Thomas's mind: it was no coincidence that Hermann was speaking to him now. He had ignored him for years, but tonight, the very night for which Hermann had been born, he was choosing to devote time to Thomas.

'And maybe for their friends too,' Hermann added. 'There are Germans for whom the laws of the Reich are merely recommendations.' The arrogant smile, ostensibly polite, vanished, and his flaming eyes scrutinised Thomas with hatred. 'Didn't you say you were hurrying home?'

Thomas looked past Hermann and focused on Höfgen, who was in distress. There was no doubt about it. The policeman's gaze roamed over the group, as though trying to explain to Thomas that he had no other choice.

Thomas now knew that Hermann and his gang were planning to harm him, or, even worse, had already harmed him.

Far behind them they heard a powerful explosion. Bluish-orange flames burst out of a row of buildings. A pillar of smoke rose and was swallowed in the darkness. Everyone gaped at it as though hypnotised. Little fires burned in the whites of their eyes.

'Yes, run along now, Thomas,' Hermann said. 'On a night like this, you really shouldn't leave your mother all alone.'

Now he understood.

LENINGRAD
AUTUMN 1938

One by one the guests fell onto the red Turkish sofa, eyeing each other in a way that reflected years of friendship tinged with suspicion. With a thunderous greeting the massively built Vladimir Morozovsky, reputed to be one of the largest men in the city, approached the sofa, upon which the poets Konstantin Varlamov and Emma Feodorovna Rykova had already settled, while between them, hunched over and shrinking into himself, sat the literary critic Brodsky. Varlamov placed his hands over his ears, and Emma waved to Morozovsky to show there was no more room. He retreated, leaned against the faded wallpaper and looked out at the murky evening sky.

Even before greeting each other, they had ticked off the names of those who had been invited but had not come. It was well known that, at such gatherings, the absentees were the most important people—their timidness endowed those who did come with an aura of courage and gave them the right to condemn those absent as disgraceful cowards. Nevertheless, the more absentees there were, the more intrusive the doubts of those present. Do they know something we don't? they asked themselves in panic. What do they know? If someone warned them, why didn't they tell us? But if someone wanted to uncover any plots being hatched at the meeting, then he needed an informer to be here. So those who hadn't come were harmless cowards, while the really dangerous person, the traitor, is actually here among us!

The hidden recesses of the informer's heart cannot be laid bare— better to hope that there was no person in the world so base as to betray his friends. Still, rumours circulated every day about people who turned in those closest to them. 'In 1938 a wise person reveals nothing to anyone,' Brodsky had declared, 'except his name and place of work.'

'Where is Osip Borisovich?' complained Varlamov. 'Ever since they arrested Nadyezhda Petrovna he's vanished.' With his fingers he smoothed the white locks that fell rakishly over his dark, wrinkled brow, while darting looks of satisfaction at the men around him, as though to ask: and you, young fellows, do you have such a splendid head of hair?

Indeed, the absence of Osip Borisovich Levayev made the people sitting in the living room uncomfortable. He was an enthusiastic admirer of Nadyezhda Petrovna, and in the past he had even obtained handwritten permission from Sergei Kirov, when he was the most powerful and admired man in Leningrad, to print a book of her poems. And then there was the scandal when he headbutted the author Alexei Tolstoy, after the latter labelled Nadyezhda Petrovna's first book 'decadent cosmopolitanism'.

'His wife would rather he was dead,' announced Emma Feodorovna. She took off her broad-brimmed hat, fluffed her hair up and lit a cigarette, blowing the smoke straight at Brodsky's spectacles. Her greenish eyes glowed with the argumentative light that tormented the offended faces of her friends, but Alexandra, whom everybody called Sasha, always saw in that light the lovely lament of a dissatisfied soul. 'So long as he isn't arrested,' Emma went on, 'because then she'd have to run around for him instead of lying in bed all day with that stammering sister of hers, slandering the whole world.'

Sasha was standing against the wall in her darkened room. A mocking twitch fluttered over her lips. When she was little, Emma used to pick her up, cover her face with kisses smelling of cigarettes, and tell bad stories about everyone, even about Sasha's own parents. Now Sasha nudged the door so she could see the whole living room, including the eastern side where her parents were. This was the second time in a month that this weary bunch had met to make a plan about Nadyezhda Petrovna's arrest, but in fact to ward off the danger to themselves. Once again they would probably adopt 'urgent action points' that no one would dare implement.

She couldn't restrain herself and poked her head out to peek at her father, Andrei, in the mirror between the bookshelves. He was in his rocking chair, gazing at the fine glass frame that hung on the wall opposite him: a map of 'The Great Factories of the Soviet Union', a gift from the head of the Physical-Technical Institute to the physicist, Comrade Andrei Weissberg. From time to time he looked at her mother, Valeria, who was leaning over the kerosene stove and pouring tea for the guests while asking after their health and that of their families. Sasha despised this ceremony: every time her father looked at his wife, his gaze would cloud with helplessness. In her presence he behaved like a man stunned by the vagaries of the world, who needed Valeria to speak for him.

For example, last summer the head informed Andrei that he would have the honour of representing the institute in Moscow at a meeting of the People's Commissariat for Heavy Industry, where the plans for 1939 would be discussed. It was widely known that anyone who went to Moscow would be arrested as soon as they came back, because they had met too many people, and had been asked too many questions, whose answers aroused someone's suspicion. And, in general, a visit to Moscow attracted unnecessary attention to a person's existence, which was why the head preferred to send a worker whom he hoped would say the right thing when asked about him.

Her father didn't dare reject the unwelcome honour, but as soon as he got home from work he went to bed and refused to get up. The next morning Valeria visited the head and explained that her Andreyusha was prone to nightmares in unfamiliar environments, and would spout nonsense in his sleep that a stranger might misinterpret. The next day the head announced that Weissberg wouldn't be going to Moscow.

Now her mother sat down on the chair next to Andrei and placed his hand on her slim hips. She sat straight, taller than her husband; her chin seemed to hover over her long neck, and her presence bespoke chilly pride. It was clear that she wanted everyone to know that she had no truck with petty personal calculations, and would rise above her husband's weakness.

Sasha scorned her. Only someone abandoned to her own illusions could think that any of the guests might be taken in by this performance. True, unlike Sasha, none of them had seen Valeria sitting on her bed night after night, pretending to be lost in a book, waiting for her husband to come home—but even if someone decided to believe in the impression she was trying so hard to make, the inevitable moment would come when the spell wore off, and only the hard evidence remained. All the strategies of a betrayed woman cannot negate the fact that she is betrayed.

A soft knock on the door.

Brodsky hid his face in his plate, Emma Feodorovna stubbed her cigarette out in the ashtray and stirred the butts in it, Varlamov's head sank back into the sofa. How easily they scared, Sasha raged. A gentle knock like that didn't sound dangerous.

Her mother hurried to the door. 'Osip Borisovich,' her voice rang out from the hall. 'How good to see you.'

'My wife is sick,' Levayev's proud voice bellowed. 'I just popped over for a moment.'

Meanwhile, in the living room, the guests started up again. 'Strange, Nadya's arrest, very strange. If she was involved in something improper…' Varlamov repeated exactly what he had said at the earlier meeting. Had age impaired his memory, Sasha wondered, or does he not want to say anything else?

'If they arrested Nadka, they must have had a good reason,' mumbled Brodsky. Crumbled egg yolk clung to his red beard. He sliced his second egg into thin strips and arranged them on his plate. Nadya once told Sasha that it was enough to see how Brodsky handled an egg to know he had never slept with a woman.

Her mother took the arm of the strapping young man, who was as usual impeccably dressed, and sat him down at her side. Emma Feodorovna lit another cigarette, aimed the smoke at his handsome face and made fun of his new hairdo: short at the back with a wild black curl at the front. 'Osip Borisovich, is that a gesture to your boyhood in the Ukraine, that thing on your head?'

Konstantin Varlamov hid his face in his cup of tea and slurped. He was primed to explain, as usual, why any appeal to his highly placed friends on behalf of Nadyezhda Petrovna would be futile. If they arrested people like Radek and Pyatakov, Rykov and Yezhov, Garniko and Petrovsky, not to mention Bukharin and Zinoviev, how could his friends do anything for an unknown woman poet? Varlamov recited this litany each time he thought he might be asked to help someone who had been arrested. Everyone was impressed: 'The old man's a genius! After the last litany—it went for twenty-seven minutes, including memory lapses—no one will dare to ask for his help ever again.'

Emma rested her elbow on the cover of the black piano. Out of all the men and women who were poets in Leningrad, Emma Feodorovna had chosen Nadyezhda Petrovna to be her satanic double—her close friend and even closer enemy. Nadya always beat Emma to it, making conquests that Emma had merely dreamed about, leaving her only scraps of glory. One of Sasha's clearest childhood memories was a poetry evening at the end of which Emma had emptied a bottle of kerosene on Nadya's red rubber cape after she had declared that Emma's poems put her to sleep standing up, just like the stories of Maximich. The insult of the comparison with Gorky pushed Emma over the edge as, visibly trembling, she stood in front of Nadya, who was leaning on the windowsill.

'Go ahead,' Nadya said, 'light a match if you dare, but only if you dare, my dear.'

Osip Levayev looked at their faces as though wondering at their faintness of heart. He turned to Sasha's father and said, 'Andrei Pavlovich, it's true I missed the previous meeting, but this evening you've invited us to your home again. Perhaps you can explain to us what, in your opinion, we should do? It goes without saying that all of us are asking questions about the arrest. I don't know a thing about it. In the past few months I've hardly seen Nadya at all.'

From her hiding place Sasha surveyed the young man, whose cold expression emphasised the distance that had come between him and Nadya and her close friends. If so, why had he turned up here this evening anyway? Was he the informer? Or maybe he had been going out of his mind with fear at home and wanted to find a way to avoid arrest? This gathering endangered them all, but Nadya's arrest had taken her friends to the brink. Maybe a demonstration of innocence at a meeting that would doubtless be revealed to the NKVD was preferable to staying at home. Osip Borisovich's lips were now dancing in front of Sasha like a pink half-moon. Four years earlier, on her eighteenth birthday, they had kissed at the beach. He had begged her for a whole year not to tell her mother, and took pains to praise all her poems. They weren't especially good, she knew that, and anyway her dream of becoming a poet had recently lost its charm. She might have been enchanted by Nadya's and Emma's poems when she was growing up—but was poetry really how she wanted to spend her life?

Andrei Pavlovich Weissberg, the man now called upon to lead the group, rocked in his chair and gazed out at the sky, over which the early autumn darkness had spread. Cold gusts struck the window-panes, and they all wrapped themselves in their coats. Her father, too, removed his coat from the back of the chair and put it on like a scolded child. His tormented face told of the horrors he had conjured up in his imagination: his beloved Nadka in jail, dragged out of a narrow cell, where she had been forced to stand up, on her own, for many days, unable to tell day from night, into the interrogation room, where they sat her down—though sometimes they punished her by making her stand there too—for eight-hour sessions, and then another hour, demanding again and again that she tell the story of her life, name names, confess.

Sasha understood that her father was already mourning for Nadya. In recent years he had grown weaker, as if he no longer believed in anyone's ability to decide his own fate. If it was up to him, he would have already held a memorial ceremony for her.

He had only dragged her to Nadya's house once. She must have been around twelve. The poet was ill. She had been in bed for weeks, and her father went to her tiny, unheated room every day. Sasha felt as if someone was shoving her nose into a bottle of oil. Tangled in her bedding, Nadya whined that her body was betraying her, that two old women and four children were living with her in the apartment and torturing her, that Emma Feodorovna was smearing her with oil as if she were the axle of a wagon.

Her father pulled the blanket off and wiped away her perspiration. Sasha turned around and stared at the wall. Nadya kept complaining: no one came to visit, a person was ill for a few days and everyone had her in the grave already, her back ached from the treachery of her friends. 'Look at me, girl!' she shouted at Sasha. 'You're the only one who won't betray me!'

Sasha turned around and watched her father kiss her eyes and forehead, purring endearments. He fed her beef soup from the cafeteria at the institute. Sasha could see how he came to life around this woman. When Nadya became drowsy, her father kissed her hand, pressed it to his heart and consoled her with stories about all the influential people whom her poetry had moved. Soon she would receive a special grant, Brodsky was terribly impressed and was going to write a review.

Now Sasha stretched her legs, which had fallen asleep, and paced her room. She stopped at her desk, and in the dim light from the living room sorted the slips of paper on which she'd written her tasks for the coming week. Everything seemed boring, especially the interview her friend Zhenya had arranged for a job taking shorthand. Her mother railed at her for never getting through more than a quarter of her tasks. But her mother didn't understand anything. Naturally if she had an interesting job like Brodsky, who wrote about books in the newspaper, or even like Zhenya, who translated articles into English for the foreign news section of *Leningradskaya Pravda*, she would work day and night.

She went back to the door. Silence reigned in the living room. Her father sat bent over, wearily drumming on his knees. There would be no salvation from Andrei Weissberg. Now everyone turned to Vladimir Morozovsky, who had not said a word. Morozovsky worked in a car repair shop, mainly for high-ranking officials. He loved poetry, and loved talking about poetry with poets even more, no matter if he bored them. 'No, no one said anything. I asked a friend who is a member of certain institutions, and whose circle includes men whose influence is not to be sneezed at—'

'And what did he say?' Emma broke in.

'He said that there are no rumours, and that's usually the worst sign.' Morozovsky shrugged and spread his huge hands. People joked that in a single fist he could hold Weissberg's and Brodsky's heads and all the women who had slept with them.

'There was a reason to arrest Nadya,' Levayev said, adopting a serious expression. 'More and more sabotage networks are being discovered. Loyal citizens must remain vigilant and help the authorities uncover the truth.'

'You, Andreyusha,' Emma said to Sasha's father with a mischievous look, 'were the closest of all to Nadka, even at night. You must have some idea why she was arrested.'

No one dared look at Valeria as she sat by her husband, massaging his hand—except for Emma, of course.

'Emma Feodorovna, Andreyusha already said that he doesn't know anything. He's busy all day at the institute,' Valeria scolded her. 'I suggest that we turn to Comrade Stepan Kristoforovich Merkalov, the new head of the department...'

'No, we need someone in the literary world,' Emma objected.

'Brodsky can write to his beloved teacher, Tolstoy!' She made sure everyone had caught her mocking tone. 'He must appreciate our friend's critical perspective.'

Emma really had a noble soul, Sasha decided, since her life would be easier in a world without Nadya—but she was prepared to take a risk to try to save her.

Brodsky scratched his reddish beard and appraised his friends with his bright, grave eyes. Now Sasha saw her mother glare at Brodsky. Her imagination shaved his beard off and examined his naked face: was he the informer? Maybe all these fears were exaggerated, unnerving them, kindling constant suspicion? Maybe there were no informers here at all?

'It would do no good to speak to Tolstoy,' Brodsky's silky voice crooned. 'He read Nadya's long poem where she says what she thinks about his writing: "Footprints in the snow are better literature." Not long ago we asked him to give her coupons for a sweater and a coat. He authorised the sweater, but refused the coat.'

'Why did she have to ask? Isn't she getting a pension?' inquired Morozovsky.

'They replaced it years ago with old-age benefits,' Brodsky chuckled. 'Barely a hundred rubles. Her father told me they wrote to her: "You are receiving an allowance by virtue of your devoted work on behalf of Russian literature, and because it is not possible to use your services at the present time." And someone from the Writers' Association told her, "It would be better if you stopped writing poetry."'

An image glimmered on the edge of Sasha's consciousness: they were sitting in Varlamov's garden, and the old poet was giving one of his speeches. Nadya hugged her. 'Girl, if you want to be a poet,' she said, 'just remember one thing—true poets resist the enchanting spells of nostalgia.'

She struggled to drive away the memory. Her mother was placing a platter of poppy-seed cookies on the round wicker table. Beneath it she could see the twins' tattered slippers. 'I remembered something,' said Osip Borisovich. 'It would be wrong not to mention it: wasn't there some kind of connection between Nadka and Bliumkin in the twenties? Could that be behind the accusations against her?'

Stillness fell in the living room, interrupted by the clink of Brodsky's fork.

Her father shut his eyes as he always did when he knew he was hearing something because of cruel fate.

'Bliumkin! A despicable human being!' Varlamov shouted at the wall. 'A murderer who betrayed the proletariat, and had the effrontery to start scheming with the Trotskyites. His execution was a happy day for the party!'

Sasha stifled a laugh. This habit of talking to the wall was new. No one doubted that the telephones were tapped, and now people had started asking: were they installing microphones in the walls too? If so, in which ones? Many believed that it couldn't be done, or they were listening to more important targets. Nevertheless, niggling doubts remained: perhaps some things were best said directly to the wall.

'Bliumkin was a filthy dog, an enemy of the people. Death was too good for him,' Brodsky proclaimed to the faded wallpaper.

'They say that the traitor Bliumkin used to give women pleasure until they went mad,' commented Emma Fiodrovna, 'almost like our friend Brodsky.'

Why did Osip bring up Bliumkin? He wouldn't have dared, Sasha concluded, unless he received an order from someone. The NKVD? No, that was too simple and suspicious a move.

'Osip Borisovich, we admire your sincerity, but there's no point throwing rumours around with no evidence to support them,' said Valeria. She brought her hand up to her face and divided it horizontally at eye level, then plucked at the air with her fingers until her hand moved towards the sky, as though giving a sign that her words had evaporated. Sasha was charmed by the perfection of this gesture every time her mother made it. The guests, still traumatised by the very mention of Bliumkin's name, did not take in the way she softened her reprimand. 'You're still young, and you don't know that this isn't our way of behaving.'

Sasha watched: her father now picked up on the caressing tone. He glanced at his wife in surprise. She was looking straight ahead. Her body relaxed, and her chin sank.

Sasha turned away, finding it hard to breathe. It was unbearable to watch this miserable woman not daring to defend her dignity. All of her friends knew about her husband's infidelity. Now she could see the whole evening from her mother's point of view. Valeria had been enlisted in the effort to help her husband's lover, and the sight was so saddening that Sasha knew she had to kill her compassion dead, so it could never emerge again, making her incapable of venting her anger against her father.

'Of course. I hope the whole thing is a misunderstanding,' Levayev sputtered. Valeria poured him a healthy shot of vodka, and he sipped it with a faint gurgle of pleasure. 'But it's impossible to set things right if we don't know the source of the inaccuracy.'

'What a loss the death of Kirov is,' Konstantin Varlamov lamented. 'He had a rare talent for stating things accurately.'

'Perhaps Comrade Varlamov could list his friends for us and ask our advice...' Brodsky chuckled, gaily surveying the shock he caused to everyone who could hardly believe he was crazy enough to invite another litany of names.

'It's really not necessary!' Osip Borisovich blurted.

'No need at all,' Emma Feodorovna groaned, glancing in despair at Varlamov, who looked like a statue come to life. 'A dreadful idea.'

'It's actually very necessary,' Brodsky declared.

'It would be too much, and besides, we've talked enough about sad things,' Valeria called out. 'Emma Feodorovna, how is your new collection of poems coming along?'

'Please let the esteemed poet Varlamov address his friends to help Nadya,' Brodsky repeated like a stubborn child.

A chill ran down Sasha's back. She thought she understood why he was so amused: Brodsky could think in abstractions and he respected power; he always looked for the principles guiding events, and this was because it was mostly impossible to find out who was responsible for a certain act or from what building an order had been issued. He was often tormented by the question of who had empowered something to happen, determined its effects and restricted its outcomes; he was always disturbed when lawless voids opened up in his world, the chaos of visible but faceless power. He had dedicated years to deciphering the logic of arrests and betrayals, and had concluded that they had no chance of being saved. Nadya would name names, and they would all be arrested. All he could do now was deride his unhappy friends, who still clung to the hope that it was possible to escape their fate. Sasha no longer dared to look at his pale face, on which an amused grimace was fixed, as if he had no more strength, and had only one last expression left. She shrank back and sat, panting, on her bed.

'They didn't answer my last letter,' Varlamov said. 'They're preoccupied by important matters.'

'Preoccupied! And how could they not be?' Emma interrupted. 'These days everyone is busy.'

'They arrested Radek and Pyatakov, Rykov and Yezhov,' Varlamov whispered. For a moment there was only the tortured breathing of the defeated people in the room. 'And Tukhachevsky and Yakir, and that fellow Petrovsky, plus Bukharin and Zinoviev, and also the guy from Kiev, what's his name?'

A few years ago Sasha had sat with her father in the garden of Varlamov's house. 'I'm asleep now,' the old poet said, 'and all the things I once believed in are sleeping with me. Poetry and beautiful ideas. Everything I was is asleep now, and if nothing unexpected happens I will sleep until my last day. Maybe death will wake me up.'

...

A body touched her body. Hot air blew on her chest. Something pointed—in the first flash of waking she imagined an arrow, but then realised it was a nose—poked at her neck. Hair tickled her cheek. Her eyes opened to cobwebbed walls, a blue wooden table and a small chair draped with her crumpled clothes. Through the window she saw black sky, swirls of clouds nibbling at the moon. Sasha moved away from the body that clung to her. 'Kolya,' she whispered and pinched his face. 'You're nearly fifteen. You know you mustn't sleep here.'

Nikolai woke up at once. He leaned his head on his arm and focused on her. Sometimes it seemed to her that even when he was deeply asleep he was always on the verge of waking up.

'I can't sleep in the same room with Vlada,' he whined. 'He goes on all the time about how they're going to arrest Dad because he's screwing poets who are spies, and Mum too, because she's married to someone who's screwing spying poets, and you as well because you want to be a poet-spy.'

Sasha sat up and kicked Kolya in the ribs. He yelped with pleasure. The alarm clock went off under the pillow. She rolled over and silenced it.

'Zaichik, where are you off to in the middle of the night?' Nikolai sat up.

'I told you not to call me that,' Sasha chided him. She stood up, and shivered in the cold air.

'So how come Mum's allowed?'

She didn't answer. She put on a white dress, pulled on thick socks and tied a scarf around her head. She wouldn't take off the scarf in his presence, she swore. No living soul should see her hair when it was so messy.

Nikolai curled up on the bed again. 'You know that Vlada is smarter than we are, right?' His voice came through the blankets. 'If you come back here, I'll tell you things that you don't know. He listened to the whole meeting, and said that Mum was a lot less stupid than Dad and the others, but it won't help. We're all going to pay.'

'Shut up. They'll hear you.'

From far away came the soft hum of a vehicle. How harmless it sounded, like a fly. Soon it would grow stronger and recall the first rumbles of thunder. There was no one in the city who didn't recognise the sound of these cars—the black crows were crossing the city at night.

In her parents' room the bed creaked. An urgent whisper from her father; her mother was consoling him: 'Andreyusha, it will be all right.' The scuffle of bare feet, another creak, and he was in his wife's arms. A low gasp. 'Run to Varlamov in the morning. They won't arrest him. Don't say a word to Brodsky or Levayev.'

Her parents probably thought that they were paying the price for the meeting already, that the informer had wasted no time and now the black crow was coming. Sasha took a deep breath to drive away the spasm of forbidden pleasure that made her body shudder. Maybe now, at last, the great physicist Andrei Pavlovich Weissberg would be overwhelmed by the pure dread of his judgment day. He would no longer be able to cheapen himself with excuses. Maybe now he would repent.

The rumble seemed to be moving away now, delivering its grim news to other streets. Silence descended on the house again, except for the symphony of breathing—her father and mother, the twins Kolya and Vlada, who wasn't asleep in any case. Tyres screeched at the end of the street, the paralysing shriek that announced the black crow's destination. There was more frightened muttering in her parents' room. She thought she heard her father give out a little whimper.

Sasha looked in the mirror. How she loved seeing her body in the darkness that emphasised her tall silhouette, and sharpened the line of her hips even more. She had always envied her mother's hips and been angry that she hadn't inherited them.

'The children must stay in their rooms.' Fear scored her father's voice. Sasha smoothed the wrinkles on her dress and leaned towards the mirror to apply lipstick.

In the apartments around them, people were waking in horror, hovering between consciousness and sleep, not yet recognising that the life they had known was ended. Instead they rushed about chaotically in the mazes of their memory: the people they had last met, had they said anything to them, expressed criticism? Had they objected strenuously enough to the criticism of others? In their consciousness the portraits of enemies and friends flickered, and the piercing fear arose:

the men in the black cars know.

People would swear that, when the knock on the door came, they would jump out the window. But the most they did was jump out of bed, get dressed, follow them down the stairs, get into the black crow and submit to their doom. That was all they were good at, all those miserable people—Sasha pursed her lips, brought her face close to the mirror again and used a handkerchief to wipe away some excess lipstick—awaiting their fate.

'Bunny rabbit, where are you actually going?' Kolya asked again.

'I told you it's none of your business, right?' she whispered angrily. 'The moment I leave, you go back to your room. Mum doesn't like you sleeping here.' She didn't allow him to stay in her room in her absence, because he poked around in her old poetry notebooks and wrote comments that he thought were funny.

In the street a freezing wind lashed her, scratching her face like a vine. Strange how in this city a person was exposed to the whipping of several winds at the same time, as if the wind were a multiple thing made up of gusts that struck at you from every direction. The trees swayed wildly. The top of the tree next to their building was thrust against the wall. Even in her childhood she had imagined that the seeds of adversity were planted in that tree, latent malice that would burst out one day, so she was careful to give it a wide berth. With long strides she turned towards Zarubina's alley. Zarubina was the nasty old woman who was in direct correspondence with members of the Politburo and reported in to them about dangerous intrigues. Not long ago Sasha had queued behind her at the theatre. How she would have liked to tighten her fingers around Zarubina's yellow neck! A light shone in the old woman's top-floor apartment; Sasha hugged the wall. When she got to the end of the alley, she couldn't hold back a defiant glance at her big picture window (everybody said it had been enlarged to put more streets under her supervision). For some reason, in spite of the general obligation to be afraid, Sasha had no fear of the old woman with her fleshy shoe-shaped dewlap.

The black car was waiting for her at the corner, exactly as agreed. Her instructions had been carried out meticulously—she was filled with satisfaction. Now the neighbours would go back to bed, the tension would ease. This night would pass safely.

Two men sat in the front seat. 'Hello,' said one of them, waving his hand at the rear seat.

She climbed in. The smell of cigarettes mingled with the odour of their leather coats. The men sat up straight and said nothing.

The car swallowed up street after street. They passed by Varlamov's house. She visualised the garden he was so proud of, and the bright lantern light that brushed the purple leaves of the plum tree, the cherry trees around it, the green benches. Sunday afternoons: she was eight or ten, a spring sun warmed her face. Everyone was devouring fruit and reviling poets and authors, making fun of Varlamov, who, in his old age, had begun writing his 'cherry blossom poems'. He responded generously, declaring that pain was a matter for young people, who were still thrilled by it, but it bored old people like him.

Afterwards the children, having become fidgety around the grown-ups, would run down the long, dark pathway that led to the scruffy neighbouring courtyard, and rush across it, too, and on into the gloomy corridors of the adjoining four-storey building. The moment she was swallowed up by those hallways she felt she had fallen into the unknown, as in a nightmare. Fear rose in her throat as she ran like a blind girl in the shadowy corridor until that bracing leap back into the sun-drenched courtyard. A deep breath. She wanted to linger, but the children were already running down the next dark hallway, and she ran after them. 'Death-birth-death-birth,' they would shout. In the corridors they would be dead, and in the sunlit courtyard they were reborn.

The car passed by the railway station. A group of people was standing outside, the men carrying battered suitcases spotted with travel stickers, and the women holding lumps of wood and crates. These were not city folk but sad nomads who filled the station night and day, and waited—sometimes for months—for permission to travel onwards. They weren't allowed to live in Leningrad, they were required to clear out, but they were unable to leave; meanwhile they had set up encampments next to the station or on the banks of the Neva. Sasha saw them sometimes in the evening next to the canals, digging trenches, lighting campfires, cooking stew for their children. Sometimes they were arrested. Clumps of people from the same village wandered together, intent on clinging to a last bit of their lost world. They were the remnants of the masses of peasants who had been uprooted from their land six or seven years earlier, at the time of collectivisation. Most had died, been exiled or resettled, and those who managed to escape were wandering across vast swathes of the country. Nadya and Emma used to lament the dreadful famine of the kulaks, and Levayev or her father would sometimes make a critical remark, but for the past two years no one had dared to talk about them.

On Nevsky Prospect, their headlights lit up a well-dressed man of about fifty crossing the street. He was apparently drunk, or he would have noticed the approaching car. Now he stood, petrified and astonished, in the middle of the road.

'Out of the way, idiot,' shouted the driver.

The man didn't move. It was clear that he didn't know what to do. His back was bent, his neck was twisted and he didn't dare stand straight.

He must be going home from his mistress's apartment, thought Sasha. These are the hours when adulterers rush home. He was frightened. The black cars aroused fear in people's hearts because of all their sins; even those who were expecting the second coming of Christ believed that the cars would judge them. The black crow was Judgment Day, no matter what your faith.

'I fucked your mother,' the driver cursed. His companion was examining the cleft in his chin in the rear-view mirror, cursing the razor that always missed the bristles there. The adulterer began stepping backwards, making a gesture that simultaneously begged forgiveness and denied his own existence.

As the car swept by him the driver said something and smoothed his leather coat. The other man answered him. Sasha heard them, but they jumbled their words together into a single stream and she couldn't understand. She felt that a mighty force was seething in the car and overflowing like glowing lava, so that throughout the city people were fleeing it to avoid being burned up.

They stopped at a crossroads. One of the agents lit a cigarette and leaned his forearm on the ledge of the open window. Sasha could smell the sweet scent of fresh rye bread. She imagined her fingers crumbling it. It had been too long since she had tasted bread straight out of the oven. People complained that the nomads from the station stood outside the bakeries at night for bread, and afterwards there wasn't enough to go around.

Without turning his head, one of the agents called out, 'Alexandra Andreyevna, you're an attractive woman.'

She didn't answer.

'Comrade Weissberg,' the driver said, 'the scarf is suitable for old women, not for pretty young things. Could you show us your hair? We've heard so much about it.'

With a rapid motion she removed the scarf and her hair slid down to her shoulders. She felt its coarse touch, like a dry scab on her neck. She was sorry she hadn't wet it and combed it. The car slowed, and they both turned around. 'Really pretty, Comrade Weissberg,' said the driver, whose head was brick-shaped and amazingly small, like a child's.

'Very beautiful, truly blue,' his companion said.

She wrapped the scarf around her hair again. Their behaviour amused her. When you saw a black crow, it was hard to believe that two guys like that were sitting in it, jabbering like schoolkids.

They approached the turn to Liteiny Prospect. NKVD headquarters were at the end, near the river. The street would be deserted now. The people of Leningrad avoided this building at night. It was called *bolshoi dom*, the big house, and was an inexhaustible source of horror stories, laments, tall tales and black humour—stories of secret corridors that went as far as Magadan, of so many floors that, if you counted them all, above and below ground, you'd find it was the tallest building in Leningrad. Not long ago, when she passed by, she had the idea that multitudes of thin wires were stretched from it, and every wire was wrapped around someone in the city. In their houses, on the streets, in the parks, she would hear people speculating endlessly, reciting success stories out of the newspapers, and, every time someone approached, changing their tone into a semi-official way of speaking, full of empty pathos, as if they were talking, indirectly, to that building. So much weakness sucked the virtue out of people, diminished them, or, to be precise, the people voluntarily diminished themselves.

She was especially indignant about the wearisome wait for the inevitable: could any of them doubt that Nadyezhda Petrovna would lead them all to their deaths? And yet they did nothing. The smarter ones, like Levayev, were distancing themselves from her, but could not make a clean break. The others dragged along behind, lamenting, complaining. No one did anything. They all preferred to fear, in the hope that the poet might still slip away from inquisitional eyes. But how could she? When there were so many eyes, and Nadya never stopped attracting attention and admiration, scattering poems about her that mocked the achievements of the party—especially of its beloved authors and poets. Hadn't she devoted a whole series of poems to Gorky after his death? All of them—her father Andrei, Varlamov, Emma Rykova, Brodsky and Morozovsky—knew very well that the friends of an arrested person also face elimination or banishment, and they all have wives, children, sisters, husbands, lovers, other friends. Their inaction was endangering everyone…

Somebody had to stop it.

Instead of turning into Liteiny Prospect, the automobile turned south.

'Aren't we going to *bolshoi dom*?' Sasha asked the agents.

'Did you hear that?' the driver's companion chuckled. 'Comrade Weissberg wants to go to *bolshoi dom*.'

'Are we going there or not?' she asked sternly.

'Comrade Weissberg,' the driver intervened in a conciliatory tone, 'your meeting will take place elsewhere. When we get there, they'll explain everything.'

He sped up. She was silent, and the agents also stopped talking. Two planes flew over them. The agent in the passenger seat pointed at them with enthusiasm. The moon pierced the dome of clouds, and silvered the wings of the planes, which looked as though they were flying directly into it. Darkness fell on the road. She wasn't disturbed by the change in plan. It was a foolish thought that he or his men might harm her: he wouldn't allow anything to happen to her. The car slowed, turned into a narrower road, and glided into an unpaved lot where other black vehicles were parked in tight rows. She got out and followed the two men at a distance. They took a sloping path, and when she looked down at the parking lot, perhaps the darkest piece of ground she'd ever seen, she remembered the visions that her mother would conjure up when she wanted to scare her: the black-robed horsemen of the apocalypse, having gathered in their final assembly, would soon storm the world with bows, arrows and swords, but first they would take care of naughty twelve-year-old girls who allowed Maxim Adamovich Podolsky to fondle their breasts.

She trailed after the agents. Her scalp felt hot and itchy. She poked a finger under the scarf, scratched vigorously, and in her heart she cursed the bastards. An annoying eddy of air hovered across the path and buffeted her. Why did the agents look so tall? Her back and calves hurt, but she hurried after them.

'Comrade Weissberg, almost there,' the driver called.

The winds strengthened. Their shriek was piercing. Her panting sounded ugly to her.

He was standing around a sharp bend, hidden from the climber's eye. She almost collided with him. A woollen coat rested on his shoulders like a stylish robe. Behind him loomed a broad and silent building, whose illuminated windows cast pentagons of light onto the courtyard, which the night didn't touch at all.

His proximity surprised her, and she flinched. He placed a hand on her hips, and she pushed it away, but his other arm was already encircling her body, pulling it close to him.

Maxim Adamovich Podolsky winked at her. 'Alexandra Andreyevna,' he laughed, 'be careful not to fall and hurt yourself. Hosts of men will take to the streets to avenge you if we lose you.'

'Hello, Comrade Podolsky,' she said. Here, in the company of his colleagues, she addressed him formally.

'Comrade Weissberg,' he replied in an official tone and brought his lips to her ear. His breath warmed her earlobe. 'I apologise for dragging you out here. This weekend there's going to be an assembly of our people from the whole district. It's a convenient, quiet place, as you see, and there are enough bedrooms for everyone. I gathered from your message that our meeting couldn't be postponed.'

'Correct,' she said.

'Anyway, I'm sorry you had to walk up here. Those weren't my instructions. I intended to meet you down below.'

He was lying, she decided. He had been waiting for her around the bend, and those had been precisely his instructions.

Podolsky reached his hand out to her with the familiar peacock-like gesture that he affected sometimes to amuse himself, copied out of books for foppish noblemen. Had he ever wondered why he chose that particular gesture? Maxim Podolsky was a man whose body was always stiffened with compressed power, confident that his every deed was for the good, rooted in noble motives, in his pure desire to benefit the people around him. He once quoted Mephistopheles from Goethe's *Faust*:

> I am part of that force which would
> Do evil evermore, and yet creates the good.

That was four years earlier, on the first day of their last year of school. Each of the students had been asked to bring a quotation that described who they were. She had chosen lines by Nadyezhda Petrovna:

We studied death
Not that which is not our own
in which we have no interest
We are not philosophers.

'Your mum is a smart woman,' said Podolsky. They stepped back down the path, leaving the circle of white light, and Sasha felt as if she had escaped from a trap.

'I've already heard that tonight.'

'Very smart,' Podolsky repeated. 'To the best of my understanding, she set up the little meeting in your house this evening so that our informer would lead us to the connection between Nadyezhda Petrovna and Bliumkin, and from there to the Trotskyites. An excellent trick. You should have seen the report that was handed to us.'

'Osip Borisovich?' she asked weakly. Sometimes even treachery that you expect can be painful.

He ignored her. 'The agents here were very excited. Reznikov from the second department was shouting like a madman.' Podolsky pulled a face and pranced around her. '"Give me those traitors! Let me get my hands on them!"'

Sasha shuddered. 'So maybe it will help. Bliumkin?'

'It wasn't a bad idea to send us in that direction,' Podolsky mused. 'Bliumkin was eliminated even before Nadyezhda knew your father. The problem is that your father's name already showed up in the Pyatakov affair, and now it's showing up again.'

He linked his arm in hers. The steep path she remembered from her climb up had flattened out. They neared the black cars. In the dark, from slightly above, the parking lot looked like a field of greenish-black trees, like the forests you see stretching away from the train window into another country.

'If you listen, you can hear planes from here,' he said, but she couldn't hear anything. The way that aeroplanes, or, to be more precise, parachuting out of them, excited young men was irritating.

They walked between the cars. Podolsky lit a match and looked into the windows, checking the back seats.

The asphalt in the schoolyard—warm, rough, strewn with trampled leaves. The first autumn of the fourth grade. Podolsky and his mates, a bunch of kids in grey trousers, ignite old rags dipped in turpentine, and the air above them bulges upwards. She and her friends, in their brown dresses, watch the antics from the second-floor windows. Behind the schoolyard gate stands the old man who sells beer. Podolsky collects coins from the other kids. He's taller and stronger than all of them. His eyes shine as if they'd been rubbed with oil. He has a mane of red hair. Sasha takes her friend Zhenya's hand, and they race down the corridor. A nasal welter of shouts and whistles. Children are playing a jousting game, her arm is pushed into Zhenya's face, the principal keeps an eye on things through a crack in his office door, Zhenya shouts, but Sasha drags her outside. They're already in the courtyard, approaching the knot of children.

'We want beer too!' she calls to the ruck of kids.

Maxim Podolsky emerges. His neck is red, and white foam clings to the hair on his upper lip. 'What will you give us for it?'

She snatches the bottle from his hand and drinks, enjoying the knowledge that his lips were there a moment ago. A bitter taste on her tongue. Maxim Podolsky examines her, working out how to react. For a moment she's frightened. Will he hit her? She saw him poke an elbow in a boy's face in the jousting game, and, when his nose began to bleed, Podolsky said, 'Kids make too much fuss about a little blood.' Obviously someone like that, whose father was a Chekist and tortured people, wasn't afraid of blood.

Podolsky looked at her and made a servant-like gesture. 'My dear lady,' he said, 'the bottle is my gift to you.'

Now she wanted to hold him. She repressed the urge. If she showed weakness, he might decide that his job was to protect her, and then he wouldn't tell her the truth.

'Tell me,' she said. 'Was Pyatakov really guilty?'

'You're asking whether Pyatakov, the Assistant People's Commissar for Heavy Industry, really planned to sabotage the ventilation system in the Kemerovo coal mines? Your dad was sitting at home, listening in outrage to the radio broadcast of Vyshinsky's prosecution, and he said that Moralov and Radak and Pyatakov were fools. We know this trick: to describe clever defendants as fools, meaning you think their trial is unjust.'

'My dad didn't say anything like that,' she said, but she was impressed: the account was precise.

'I wasn't referring necessarily to your dad, but to people like him, for example those who admired Pyatakov and worked with him.' Podolsky laughed. 'Really, dear Sasha, I'm a little insulted by your question. You don't understand that I only want what's good for you. And you don't understand that I'm talking to you with the sincerity that you can only show to marked people, the ones no one will believe. So it's possible that Pyatakov didn't sabotage the ventilation in the mines so the workers would die and hatred would be aroused against the government. But Pyatakov had a lot of complaints, and it's quite likely that some criminal thought crossed his mind, and Moralov also talked too much. I have studied history well. Ideologies and fashions come and go, people believe in one thing and then its opposite, and all that stays the same is the startling elasticity of our souls. Sasha, people are contemptible. They always want to change things, to betray others. They dream of a better world, and then recklessly try to make their dreams come true. We're not interested in actions or consequences: people ought to fear their every criminal thought, to suspect everyone, to be secretive and to remember that no place is so dark that we won't find them.'

She leaned wearily against a car. He looked in another rear window, and cursed. When something happened that Podolsky had anticipated he cursed. Then he was inside the car, and when he emerged beside her he was holding a beer bottle. Sasha automatically snatched it away. It was their ritual. Not to perform it would mean the betrayal of everything that was between them.

'All this is too familiar and not our old story,' she grumbled. She drank some of the beer. How many nights like this had they spent together? Climbing garden fences, hiding behind the walls on the banks of the city's canals, wandering the streets, assembling dreams about countries beyond the Baltic Sea. In high school, it was clear to them that nothing would separate them.

Podolsky leaned on the car opposite her. He lit one match after another and watched the flame as it died. His face was illuminated by each little spurt of light. It had become leaner, so the delicate lines of his cheekbones were emphasised. She knew that all his speeches about power and fear were for show. Maxim Podolsky wasn't a man thrilled by power. He had inhaled more than enough of it when his father had been one of the heads of the Cheka in Leningrad and was ferried about in a chauffeur-driven limousine: invitations to a dacha on the coast, the best seats at the theatre, expensive presents for the new year, a spacious four-room apartment. In the Podolsky home the children ate delicacies that others could not even dream about. Drunk on his father's power, little Maxim behaved as if he controlled the fate of everyone he knew, including his friends' parents and his teachers. Then the party was over. Veteran members of the Cheka were discharged and accused of all sorts of crimes. Some were exiled, while others were purged.

Maxim's father lost his job; they were lenient with him. For years he sat at home and waited to be prosecuted or restored to the service, writing letters of complaint to all the institutions. He was not the only one. Millions of letters flooded the country: from the accused, their relatives, the relatives of their relatives, from citizens of good will, and informers. Later they evicted the Podolskys from their apartment. They moved into a shared flat. Maxim's father would sometimes pick his son up from school. He would stand next to the gate in a fine woollen coat, his hair combed elegantly. He kept his head up, but every girl who ran into him immediately noticed that he trembled, his eyes were red, his face lined and his hair flecked with grey.

All that year, the last year of high school, Sasha was trapped in her web of sadness. She couldn't remember a single moment of grace. She and Maxim grew distant and she mourned every day for what they had lost.

They reached the last row of cars. The sky was folded across the horizon. Podolsky told her that an American they had interrogated said that in a city near New York there was a large parking lot where young couples sat in cars and watched movies on an enormous screen. It was cheap entertainment, just a few cents. He liked the idea of watching a movie and being alone at the same time. Even the most corrupt of capitalists can sometimes have bright ideas.

The image cheered her up: couple after couple sitting in their black cars and watching a new film. It was strange how Maxim calmed her down, dulled her senses. More than anything, she wanted to lie down on the hood of one of the cars and look at the clouds. The first sentence that occurred to her was: 'Maxim, if we walk in a straight line, do you think we'd get to the sea?' And at once she heard Nadyezhda's warning voice: 'Resist the charms of nostalgia.'

'Is Nadyezhda Petrovna all right?' she asked.

'She was in solitary for a while. She quoted a line of Khlebnikov to Reznikov, who was interrogating her.'

'The police station—a splendid place! The place for my appointment with the state,' Sasha said under her breath. She always planned to recite that line when she was arrested.

'Yes, despite everything, it amused him. But the next day in her cell she met two young Jewish girls who were accused of leading a counter-revolutionary Zionist organisation, and she explained to them what Zionism was. They recited the lesson she had given them, and when the interrogators discovered where they had heard this, they accused her of everything. Later she even told Reznikov that an upright fellow and investigative magistrate like him ought to understand that those two calves didn't know a thing about Zionism. They had been planning to confess, but they were afraid their answers would be no good and they'd be shouted at, so she helped them out with some ideas. Reznikov screamed that she was insinuating that they were fishing for false confessions, and threw her into the cellar.'

Sasha stopped listening. He was spouting off again. He knew that stories about Nadyezhda didn't concern her now. The hum of an engine could be heard in the distance, and a black car came around the bend. Podolsky gave it a suspicious glance, and a dreadful thought took hold of her: maybe she hadn't understood what his real position was? Maybe he wasn't as influential as he pretended. The car had unnerved them both. An external eye had invaded their rendezvous. Now he became businesslike, severed from the past—from hasty kisses in the school-yard, from looking at the sky from the Republican Bridge in the last hour of the night as the stars disappeared. She hadn't dared ask him directly, expecting that he himself would put an end to the worry that had gnawed at her for so long; it was more than a year since she had concluded that Nadya would be arrested.

She needed answers. There was no more time. 'Can you help my father?'

He exhaled loudly. Sasha imagined that the air he breathed out was permeated with all the things he knew and she didn't. There was a silence. Maybe he was expecting that she wouldn't force him to answer. A second car drove into the lot. Its headlights gleamed on the car roofs.

'It was very smart of you to turn to me,' he said in the end, possibly surprised, possibly accusing. He seemed to have realised how much she expected of him. 'Actually, it was the only thing you could have done.'

A man and a woman emerged from the first car, stood on either side of it, smoked, and spoke softly. Podolsky seemed to recognise them, and grew calmer.

'Your Nadyezhda Petrovna would have been arrested anyway. You figured that out. Her time in Leningrad was over. We just couldn't find the time to tell her. The fact that I was the one who received the information allowed me to take care of the first stage of the investigation. But that woman arouses interest higher up as well. The poems that you copied for us—for example, 'Moustached fuck in Koba's church'—people were shocked by them, but also a bit amused by her courage.* After all, that sentence alone provides three reasons to eliminate her. The NKVD is aware of your contribution to the investigation, and people there know they should consider your request.'

'And my father?'

'He'll be arrested. No doubt about that. I'll do my best to see that he's released.'

'Can you prevent his arrest?'

He looked at her as though saddened by her refusal to admit the obvious. 'No.'

A feeling of weightlessness overwhelmed her. How did people become so small? It happened suddenly. She looked at him. He'd broadened out but he was still of average height: in her imagination he had been tall.

The deal she'd cooked up seemed perfect to her: they could have Nadyezhda, and she wouldn't lose her parents. All the parties would get what they wanted. How could she have fooled herself into thinking she would have any influence at all? Now she was filled with helpless rage: all her actions had been in vain. She could hardly contain the urge to go berserk, to scratch her body until it bled. In her world—what a dumb world, where did it exist except in the imaginations of naive women?—the people at the NKVD saw who she was and paid heed to her requests. But it was all nothing. Instead they saw her as a grain of sand that was flung into the air and then fell to the floor.

'And my mother?' Had she brought this destruction down upon her parents?

'Most likely not up to me. I intended to have Nadyezhda Petrovna sign a confession tomorrow, about the poems and the other poets who were her accomplices, and then send her into exile, so she can read her work to polar bears. But the director of the second department intervened, and now there's the issue of Bliumkin. It's written in the report. Maybe that's good, because it will lead to the links she once had with

---

* Koba was Stalin's nickname when he was young. His old friends continued to call him that.

counter-revolutionary organisations and shift the spotlight away from your parents.'

Podolsky had just admitted it was out of his hands. He had said from the start that giving him the poems was less dangerous than not doing it. And yet, it was dangerous.

Sasha shivered. They were sleeping now, all of them, and catastrophe was overshadowing their house. The final days they would spend together there would be trapped in the slender space between that night and its consequences: they would wake to the morning chill in the living room, to cups of tea and maybe cheesecake sprinkled with sugar, and they would all hurry to school or to work, and there would be some dinners when Dad would sit with them—for he had nowhere else to be now that his Nadya was in prison—and maybe another card game or a logic puzzle that he made up for the twins, who would fall asleep in the living room, and later shuffle up to the attic, and she would follow them, and, in a little while, their parents would follow too.

How quickly her nightmares became facts. She had already wrapped them in a layer of steely acquiescence—she was like someone whose arms have been amputated, who leaves them behind and keeps running.

One final question remained: 'The twins?'

BERLIN
WINTER 1939

'Thomas, the air is full of perfume,' Carlson Mailer called out as he ran his fingers through his hair, which was brushed back against his scalp. Usually he took pride in his pompadour, which the people in the office called an 'American', and without it his forehead jutted over his black eyes, which always looked sombre. 'A great party, isn't it?' His gaze skipped between the ladies in sparkling gowns and furs, and the waitresses in white skirts and silk stockings. He lit his pipe, a habit he had picked up from his new friend, Herr Professor, as he called the man from the Kaiser Wilhelm Institute for Science. In the past few weeks Carlson had prattled volubly about 'that genius': 'He's a fellow you can do business with. During the war he and Professor Haber— that Jew who won the Nobel Prize, you drove him out of here, and he ended up dying like a dog—cooked up some compounds of poisonous gas for your army, and that gas didn't gather dust in warehouses, as you know...' Carlson winked. He was drunk.

He was babbling, and restless, Thomas could see. Something was bothering the man.

They were standing on the broad patio decorated with statues and paintings of ancient creatures: snakes with human faces whose tongues curled out from the walls, a horned beast whose skin was spotted with patches of black fur, and even birds of prey, whose wingtips were shaped like sword blades.

'Look at this.' Carlson's gaze circled the patio. 'It's a European disease, to weave all kinds of historical threads around the present, as if everything has to be a gesture to something old. That's the problem in Berlin: too many clashing styles and periods. A single street looks like a museum and an amusement park.'

How many times could a person say the same thing? Annoyed, Thomas turned away. Through the large windows lampposts were spreading lunar light, milky transparencies melding sky and earth.

'A whole balcony built around a single theme!' Thomas heard the young architect explaining his concept to a group of tall, fair-haired men, diplomats, apparently, from Scandinavia. A pale woman stepped between them. She wore a diamond tiara, and her long body was enveloped in gold cloth. There was a moment of tension as she went past. 'It's a gesture to man's desire to blend with nature. Most of the artists that we've exhibited here are influenced by cave paintings.' His voice was low, and his accent was clipped in an upper-class way. In contrast, Thomas sounded a bit strident. 'Here, for example, is a fascinating version of the carnival scene from the Cave of the Trois-Frères.'

The woman laughed briefly, and Carlson fixed her with a bold look of satisfaction at finding someone who shared his opinion, and such a beautiful woman. 'Wonderful festive spirit!' he shouted and shook Thomas's shoulder. The man really had no shame. Thomas decided to keep his distance for the rest of the evening. Carlson was losing control, and the presence of an undisciplined Yank, protected by the aura of a country no reasonable person would underestimate, could be damaging for a local. Mailer came up close to Thomas and stared at his face. 'Drink something, Thomas! How come you never enjoy anything?'

An SD officer in a black uniform approached them, a strong, straight-backed man who took mincing steps like a girl. His eyes were light, almost transparent, so that for a moment Thomas felt like he was looking in a mirror. He had already met the officer at Milton. For several months Carlson and Jack Fiske, by now the company's president, had been meeting with delegations from the Economic Office, from the SD and from Hermann Göring's office. Someone had told Thomas about rumours connecting Milton with a secret deal, something to do with the Jews.

Thomas wasn't insulted that he had been excluded: one felt insulted only when a clear loss was at stake. All the rest was just mental trickery, reruns of childhood pains, things to be amused by in Erika Gelber's clinic.

'Good evening, Herr Mailer,' said the SD man. He didn't greet Thomas.

'Hello there, Oberleutnant Bauer. Long time no see,' Carlson Mailer responded distractedly, not even looking at him.

'Hauptsturmführer,' the officer corrected him stiffly. 'We met exactly one week ago.'

'These days that's a long time, wouldn't you say?' Carlson called out, and his eyes drilled into the group of tall men who were blocking his view of the woman in the tiara. 'May I order you something to drink?'

'No, thank you, Herr Mailer. I won't be staying long,' he said. There was open contempt in his voice, which was cold in any event. 'The truth is, I was surprised by your decision to hold the party this year.'

'Really?' Carlson raised his glass. 'It's a tradition at Milton. I'm sure you wouldn't deny that tonight we're welcoming in a new year?'

'It's a ten-year-old tradition,' Thomas said to back Carlson up. Had he addressed the officer obsequiously?

'Now that your ambassador has been withdrawn from Germany, the connection between our countries isn't what it was,' the officer declared. He still hadn't even graced Thomas with a glance.

Carlson understood. His eyes narrowed, and a vein pulsed in the middle of his forehead. He leaned towards the officer. 'Hauptmann Bauer, are you speaking on behalf of Germany now? Because this evening I met people who really are entitled to speak on behalf of your homeland, and they believe it's merely a temporary misunderstanding, and maybe we can do without overly zealous young men who are looking for hatred where there is friendship. Tonight, on four continents, fifteen Milton parties are being held, and can you guess which one Jack Fiske, the president of our company, decided to attend?'

Sometimes Carlson was pleasantly surprising. Thomas also despised the pretension of the shoe-shine boys on the street corner who gave speeches in the name of the state. 'Every miserable fool who has nothing at all of which he can be proud adopts, as a last resource, pride in the nation to which he happens to belong'—in his imagination he brandished Schopenhauer like a hammer to smash the shining glass of the officer's eyes.

At least this time Carlson was considerate and did not refer to him as 'our senior colleague, Thomas Heiselberg'. In his first meetings with people close to the regime he used to gush, when introducing Thomas, that he was 'a four-hundred-per-cent Aryan fellow', as though speaking about distilled alcohol. In private Mailer and Fiske used to make fun of all the stupid Aryan gibberish, and their laughter would ring out from behind closed doors, laughter that emphasised for Thomas the foreignness that separated them. Even though he didn't talk about the race issue in the typical style of party members, to the Americans he would always be a German with affected manners, a foreigner who spoke well 'in all those European languages'.

Bauer said nothing and did not shift his gaze from Carlson. Two identical wrinkles creased his nose. Thomas believed that Carlson's defiance was meant to impress the woman with the tiara, who was looking at them now for the first time, with an air of triumph: finally somebody was performing a manoeuvre worthy of her beauty.

'I very much hope it is only a misunderstanding,' the officer fired back. 'Many of the people you invited won't come tonight because of this provocation. Would it occur to you that we should withdraw our ambassador from Washington because some niggers in America complain?'

'Very well. We're not going to solve all the world's problems tonight,' Carlson grumbled and stepped backwards in an effort to get rid of Bauer. His good cheer had evaporated. Unexpected difficulties always made Carlson feel that some personal injustice had been done to him. And who was to blame? Enemies. Friends. Fate. God.

'You must understand,' Bauer said, 'that these recent events may have an adverse effect on our common project. Reichsmarschall Göring's people are not pleased.' He turned and walked away.

Carlson was perplexed. 'Go to hell, you bastard,' he muttered. He stood there for a few minutes, calling the waitresses 'sweetie' and 'doll', knocking off drink after drink. Afterwards he looked around with bloodshot eyes and called out, 'Make sure that man doesn't get near me again!'

Thomas led him to a corner, where Carlson confessed that Bauer was right on target about the mood in America: Fiske had recently received messages from some damn government officials, yes, even senators, asking him to reconsider Milton's connections with Germany. 'And you know what he said, the sly fox? His friends at Lockheed had let him know that their shitty aeroplanes are landing in Japan right now, and technicians from Lockheed are helping the slant-eyes service them. So as long as there is a single Lockheed employee in Japan, he'll do as much business in Germany as he pleases.'

Thomas didn't ask about the secret deal. He was perturbed by the question: what kind of business was Milton doing with the SD and with Göring's Ministry of Aviation? But after witnessing the latest exchange, he decided he would be better off if he didn't know anything about it. He had no wish to work with that officer, and, seeing Mailer's swollen face—he had never seen him so drunk—he realised that his fondness for any deal was even less than his fondness for Bauer.

He left Carlson on the patio and went back into the hall. He noticed that light from the chandelier fell unevenly: near the dais the white shirts and the gold epaulets on the black uniforms glowed, but thick strips of shadow stretched between the bar and the staircase. Perhaps it would be a good idea to direct the attention of the architect, king of the beasts, to this strange effect. Chains of little German and US flags were hung on either side of the stairs, while above them, as though in a different world, a gigantic poster bathed in the light of the chandeliers:

1939—YEAR OF FRIENDSHIP AND BROTHERHOOD
THE MILTON COMPANY

Thomas twisted his cuffs. He felt that the nauseating odour of Carlson's hair tonic had clung to his suit, and he remembered in disgust the way he had shaken his shoulder. An attractive black-haired man in a striped jacket was leaning against one of the sculptures, and several pretty women had gathered around him.

One of them, about thirty, bared a shoulder underneath a pink fur coat with ostrich feathers on the collar. 'Herr Fritzsche,' she wheedled, 'it's so wonderful to hear you on the radio. Your voice simply relieves all my pains.'

'Really, madam, I just broadcast the news and keep the German people informed,' the man with the famous voice said modestly, wiping his brow with a handkerchief exactly on his receding hairline.

'Did I tell you I'm the understudy in a new production of Schiller?' The woman set her head at a coquettish angle. 'You must know about it, *Intrigue and Love*.'

'Of course, wonderful!' Fritzsche said. 'I had the honour of accompanying the Führer and the Minister of Propaganda to the premiere. Afterwards we talked about the marvellous acting in our theatre, which isn't afraid of pathos, or of good old romanticism.'

Thomas studied Fritzsche: he could see how much he was trying to disguise the feeling that he didn't deserve to be loved. Evidence of people's admiration for him must pile up at his feet every day, and he must long to exhibit the light touch of a man used to being loved, but he didn't have it.

'I've been reading alarming reports in the papers,' a woman said.

'There won't be a war, will there? My two sons are in the Wehrmacht.'

A stabbing pain passed through Thomas's body, sharpening in his ribs.

'As you know, I work very closely with the Minister of Propaganda,' Fritzsche boasted, 'and I can guarantee that Germany is doing everything it can to avoid war.'

'Herr Fritzsche.' Thomas approached him and bowed. 'On behalf of Milton allow me to thank you for choosing to celebrate New Year's Eve with us. My name is Thomas Heiselberg. I am a partner in the company.'

A shadow crossed Fritzsche's face. Had Thomas addressed him impolitely? Since when had he doubted his ability to win people over? He hadn't been at his best recently. A wind was blowing that he found hard to read.

Thomas felt the familiar weakness spread through his body. It was as if dark veils were wrapped around his eyes. People became shadows. Everything blurred—the colours of the dresses, the jewellery, the intricacies of the light. With tremendous effort he turned away from Fritzsche and looked around the hall. Like a drowning man, he sought something to grasp, as Erika Gelber had taught him to do at such moments: find something that has the spark of life and concentrate on it until the malaise passes. He couldn't stand the term 'attack', which was how she described these events. But where would he find the spark of life in this hall? Was there anything here that his imagination couldn't annihilate? The party was already over, wrapped up, stuffed into the past. This wasn't a new feeling: even in his childhood his imagination had cast a pall over holidays or birthdays, coating the people around him in a sickly, dying yellow. People like him, seeing death everywhere, would never understand how others could celebrate the passage of time.

Meanwhile he heard his voice speaking to Fritzsche, praising his talent as a broadcaster, hinting at business proposals. How proud he was that his voice remained steady.

'Let's meet soon,' Fritzsche proposed. 'I'd be happy if a senior representative of Milton such as yourself honoured us with a visit to the radio station. I understand that your company and the government have been working together of late.'

Was Fritzsche referring to the secret deal? Actually, that didn't matter now! He had had a victory—to hell with all the heretical thoughts that only weakened him. Miserable souls like Bauer wouldn't like him, but Fritzsche wanted to be close to him. People like Fritzsche would always trust him. Fritzsche said something else, but Thomas didn't understand. He felt his smile become tense. There he was, standing steadily, radiating charm.

He withdrew but not before he heard Fritzsche complete his conquest of the actress with a story about his beloved mother, who had passed away last year. With tentative steps, he headed for the bar. His body gradually began to obey him again.

Thomas glanced at his watch. He had arranged to meet the head of the Paris office along with Fiske and Carlson at the bar at 11.30 p.m. to drink a toast to the New Year. Thomas was sorry that Federico Tofano, who ran the Italian operation, had to stay in Rome. He would have been proud to introduce the warm and confident Federico to the American bosses. The head of the Polish branch, Mieczyslaw Buszkowsky—they called him Bizha in Berlin—had sent a message that 'in consequence of recent events, I will find it very difficult to travel to Germany, and the continued existence of the branch is in doubt'.

Thomas, whose opinion of Bizha and his accomplishments was limited, wired him back: 'The differences between Germany and Poland should not influence Milton, which has kept its distance from politics since its establishment.'

Bizha had not answered. Carlson was sympathetic: 'Bizha knows— just as you do, by the way—that sometimes politics swallows up everything, including business.'

He decided that Carlson had abandoned the Polish branch as a lost cause. But Thomas—who had established the office himself, located it on the corner of Zgoda and Szpitalna in Warsaw, in a building that housed big companies from all over the world, supervised the renovations, and even cut the ribbon at its opening—did not intend to give up.

A group of women sat beneath the painting of an ochre rhinoceros. A stick was glued to its lips. Thomas gaped at its red eyes. 'An ugly rumour has reached my ears that Göring's baby daughter isn't his,' he heard one say, a woman wearing a white blouse buttoned to the top and a grease-stained black tie. He remembered her name was Scholtz-Klink. She had accosted him at an earlier event to ask whether Milton could advise how their organisation, the Nazi Women's League, could increase its influence.

Then he heard, 'And eternal gratitude to the adjutant,' followed by a chorus of soft laughter.

'In my opinion, it's a scandal for us to mention such crude gossip. Hermann Göring is a splendid man,' said a young, innocent voice. 'He's so romantic. No man ever loved a woman the way he loved his first wife.'

'Did you hear that Elena von Brink committed suicide last week?' the lady from the Nazi Women's League said in a stage whisper.

'It's all because her despicable Jewish therapist disappeared,' an angry voice rejoined.

'But she was in love with him,' the sweet young voice trilled, 'and, when true love disappears, we die.'

Thomas wanted to turn around and look at the woman with the pure voice, but he was reluctant to make his eavesdropping obvious.

'I advised her to stop such unnecessary treatment,' complained a voice with a faint tremolo. 'That Jew only made her sink deeper into morbid fantasies!'

How the devil had it not occurred to him? That is to say, from time to time the idea had flashed through his mind, but hadn't solidified into real understanding. Only fear can make clear something so simple: Erika Gelber's time in Berlin was growing shorter.

Immediately after that night in November she had been evicted from her clinic. Apparently the people who had been protecting her and delayed the cancellation of her licence were no longer able to help. A few days later she had received a letter forbidding her to treat Germans, and she was required to pay a tax for the damage done to her office. She didn't tell Thomas about the tax. She never confided in him about her troubles. Even when the Berlin Psychoanalytic Institute underwent Aryanisation, and she had to sever all connections with it, he only learned the facts from his own sources.

That week he called her to find out whether she was safe and to tell her that his mother had died. She expressed condolences, of course, but a week later she told him that to her regret she could no longer treat him. He begged her to take him for a final session, and at that meeting explained to her that she needed money. He offered to double her fee, in cash, and to hold their sessions in his house. 'After all, I just lost my mother,' he added.

He also convinced Paul Blum, a friend who worked at one of the Jewish banks, to try psychoanalysis. The therapist had to be Jewish, of course, and Erika Gelber was the best. 'Things are happening to you that a person can't bear, Blum. It's horrible the way the world you knew has suddenly ceased to exist. You have to analyse the experience, or else you'll go crazy. You know what a tragedy I had. Without Erika, I would have jumped off some tower.'

Blum was pleased, and Thomas looked for other Jews in distress whom he could send to Erika. She needed money. For what? To clear out. At last he understood that a few Jewish patients wouldn't be enough to keep her in Berlin.

Thomas looked around: the manager of the Paris office was nowhere to be seen. Now Rudolf Schumacher was approaching the bar. He had put on more weight. The seams of his white waistcoat were bursting, and a pin in the shape of two horseshoes was inserted between the buttons. How could anyone dare to dress so badly in public? After Thomas's mother died, Schumacher began annoying him with gestures of sympathy. Thomas couldn't recall that he had ever been close to the fat man, even at university, but Schumacher, who worked in the Ministry of Economics, possessed useful information, so Thomas found subtle ways to keep him at bay.

Now he went to look for the toilet to evade Schumacher. He had to wash his face and freshen up. Attendants in dark blue suits, holding white towels, stood in the hallway.

'Thomas!' It was Frau Tschammer. How she loved the moment when he had to stop and turn back to her and obey the imperative of her voice! The light in the corridor was dim, and Frau Tschammer's shadow towered up behind her. She suddenly looked tall. 'Thomas,' she said again and came close. 'Herr Fiske asked if you could join us this week at the meeting in the offices of the Ministry of Aviation.'

'Have we gone into aeroplane manufacture, Frau Tschammer?'

'Helmut Wohlthat will chair the meeting,' said Frau Tschammer, delighted that she'd managed to surprise him. 'Do you know him?'

'You know that we've met.'

'In that case, you know that in his official capacity in the Four Year Plan he is managing the sale of Jewish assets and their removal from the economy.'

'And the point is, Frau Tschammer?' Thomas snorted. Now it was clear that the matter had nothing to do with Göring's post as Minister of Aviation but with one of the many other hats that he wore: administering the Four Year Plan.

'Maybe you haven't noticed, but things are happening in the office. We are now advising the Dresdener Bank in connection with their acquisition of the Jewish Bamberburg Bank,' Frau Tschammer proclaimed brightly. 'The Deutsche Bank also made an offer.'

'Those are serious competitors,' said Thomas. He had always regretted that Milton worked with the Dresdener Bank and not with the Deutsche Bank, the one he admired. 'The people from the Deutsche Bank are good friends. They have connections—'

'The decision will be made by the Bamberburg Bank,' Frau Tschammer interrupted. 'The government requires the immediate transfer of the bank to German ownership. The Dresdener Bank, thanks to us, has an advantage shared by no competitor.'

Thomas understood: thanks to Fiske's connections, we can obtain

US visas for all the Jewish directors of the Bamberburg Bank and their relatives. Now he understood what Mailer had meant when he said that politics devours everything. He was full of anger: how did they— Fiske, Mailer and Frau Tschammer—dare to risk the reputation of Milton in Europe, a name built out of his own hard work, just to satisfy the greed of Dresdener? His eyes drilled into Frau Tschammer's pink forehead: he had a well-founded suspicion that this cherry face was what had got Milton mixed up in the deal.

'Frau Tschammer, despite your limited knowledge of what's going on in the world, you did know that the Dresdener Bank started managing the great bank merger in Austria after the Anschluss, and now it's active in Czechoslovakia, too. So the Jewish bank is small change for them.'

'But I also know firsthand that the deal does interest them,' Tschammer replied. 'At first the Dresdener Bank wanted us to do market research on the Jewish bank and calculate the chances of resurrecting its good name. To our surprise we learned that, despite the restrictions, the bank was profitable this year: possibly because the Bamberburg Bank charged Jewish businesses fat fees to transfer their assets abroad. At the Dresdener Bank they understood that, in order to beat out a serious rival like the Deutsche Bank, it was wise to have access to the techniques of the Milton company.'

'I once knew a director of the Bamberburg,' said Thomas.

'A *Mischling* named Blum.' Frau Tschammer had surprised him again. 'We received that information.'

'And guess what, I was invited to the meeting,' Thomas laughed. 'Take heart, Frau Tschammer, we'll make sure you stay in the picture. There's no one like you for taking care of the little details.'

Frau Tschammer turned away without a word and departed. He listened to the click of her shoes. Once again she had learned that any provocation would end in defeat. With unconcealed amusement Carlson Mailer used to share Frau Tschammer's interpretation of his personality with him: 'Thomas's method is beautiful and simple, as all truly great swindles are.' (Thomas assumed that Carlson had added the last phrase. It was doubtful that Frau Tschammer would quote an American author.) 'Every one of his actions,' she went on, 'is justified by the Heiselbergian Ethics, which are infinitely elastic. Thomas Heiselberg is actually an assembly of traits, gestures, ideas and feelings that he puts together from here and there. He's a master at taking things from other people and making them his own. Even a marble bust that fascinates him is likely to contribute to the various expressions he glues onto his face. In the darkroom of his empty soul, he develops stolen negatives into charming pictures he persuades himself were always his.'

Thomas rinsed his face and combed his hair. The grey hollows under his eyes had grown deeper. Tomorrow he would see a doctor. He looked at his watch. It was after eleven. He made his way back into the hall, swearing to himself that he would shove aside anyone who stood between him and the meeting at the bar. But meanwhile the hall had filled with revellers. Voices rang out, shouted, laughed. Glasses clinked. The music swelled. Arms and bare shoulders touched him, mouths breathed smelly hot air in his face. Drums thundered, and then a voice was heard—Fritzsche's?—announcing a performance, and the throng turned towards the stage. Thomas was swept along with it. It seemed to him that he saw the square face of Christophe, from the Paris office, pressed against Fiske, who was being shoved, apparently for the first time in his life, and was looking around, bemused, at the people besieging him. His usual lordly expression had vanished.

Now Thomas noticed Schumacher elbowing two notables out of the way and approaching Fiske. Two slim women looked at him with disgust and protested. Schumacher stretched his hand towards the president of Milton, and Fiske wrapped it powerfully in both his hands. They stood close together, with a little hill of four hands between them, smiling and shouting polite phrases that no one could hear. When could you truly admire the power of a man like Fiske? When a sign of weakness becomes visible in him, and a struggle takes place in his soul, and you understand how determined he is not to give anything away. Schumacher disappeared. Now Fiske was alone. Carlson hurried over to him, holding the hand of the woman from the patio. She had the diamond tiara in her other hand. Mailer grasped Fiske's shoulder. The three of them looked like frightened passengers on a rocking ship. Thomas took pleasure in their distress. He had worked it out. Under the cover of doing market research for Dresdener—and probably for a fat commission—Milton was messing with one of those deals to buy Jewish property at ridiculous prices.

An elbow struck his arm. Somebody has to put things in order here, and soon, he thought in alarm as he was pushed against the wall. Looking right and left, he saw only more bodies. A trumpet sounded on stage, and the drums beat a military march.

'Somebody important has arrived,' a young woman told her curly-haired daughter, and her voice was full of the curiosity of people who enthuse over the obvious.

'Pick up the girl!' Thomas shouted to her. 'We might all get ourselves killed here.'

...

The first thing he sees when he wakes is the white wall. He smells the fresh paint. Although he took care to ventilate the room every day, with his first waking breath he sucked fumes into his lungs. He learned to plunge his nose between the sheets. Sometimes it seemed to him as if they had been painted, too.

For the past few weeks he'd been waking early, around five, which gave him a lot of free time before going to the office. He roamed the house in his bathrobe and looked out at the street, waiting to see old Wagner, who at exactly six would take a seat outside the café he once owned. They were both letting time pass. As a boy he would buy ice-cream from Wagner on credit, until his father forbade him to buy 'without money', claiming that Jews seduce children into buying ice-cream before shoving the bill under their parents' noses. Last year Wagner had been forced to sell his café to a German who agreed to employ him as the storeroom manager.

Every morning Thomas played the role of the man who lived here, hoping to stamp his ownership of the place onto the walls, but the barrier between the house and him only grew. Even when he did the most ordinary things—brushing his teeth, brewing tea, stretching out on the sofa—he had the overwhelming sense that he was doing something forbidden. Sometimes he crept from room to room in secret, lest he be caught. He had no idea who would convict him, or for what crime—illegal possession, being a trespasser benefiting from other people's misfortune. Every step that he took sounded loud and clumsy, and where was his mother's voice, calling him from the bedroom, 'Thomas, how many times have I asked you to take off your shoes?' His breath blew ugly, petty life into a place that was supposed to contain memories alone.

No evidence of that night remained, except the broken window in her bedroom. The new furniture didn't remind one of the earlier furnishings, except for the replacement sofa in the parlour, which he had bought in the store where she had bought the old red sofa, after its cushions had been slashed with knives and its stuffing had been flung everywhere.

That night he returned home into a white cloud of feathers. He heard glass splinters grinding under his shoes. The windowpanes, china bowls, lamps, mirrors—almost nothing was intact after the visit by Hermann and his friends. Even the door hinges had been jimmied off. Wooden cabinets and dressers were smashed with hammers, the gas and electricity lines ripped out. At least a dozen jars of fruit preserves had been hurled against the bathroom wall, and flour mixed with soap powder and blood was strewn all over the sink and lavatory.

Frau Stein had been stabbed in every part of her body. She lay face down, her head cradled in her folded arm. He leaned down and turned her over. When he saw her face, coated with a layer of blood-soaked flour, he realised that after stabbing her they had smothered her in the sink with a mixture of flour and soap powder. She looked like a sad clown in the circus. They hadn't even let her die with that stern expression of hers, well versed in suffering, that had always aroused people's respect. He gathered some feathers and covered her face with them.

Neighbours went up and down the stairs and stared into the apartment. Not one of them crossed the threshold except Clarissa Engelhardt, a student who lived with her parents on the first floor. She gathered up shards of glass from the floor and put them in a washbasin. A grey-haired, bespectacled man appeared in the doorway, coughed and wiped his nose with a handkerchief. He leaned over Frau Stein. Feathers clung to his clothes and his neck, and from time to time he brushed a dusty feather away from his face, where the wind, swirling through the room, had blown it.

'I'm allergic to feathers,' apologised the doctor, who must have been summoned by the neighbours.

Thomas didn't know him. It was a good thing they hadn't called in Doctor Spengler, that romantic soul who became attached to his patients and mourned for them. Even the dying had to hear about the suffering of the poor souls who had been buried the previous week.

The doctor stepped to the window and shouted something, and soon two men came in, picked up Frau Stein's body and carried it outside. Only her high heels remained. Seeing them, Thomas remembered how she had crossed the city that morning to come here. She had doubtless walked for hours in those fine shoes that his mother had bought her for her fiftieth birthday, and in her best dress. Had she intended to ask for help? Jews were turning to everyone they knew. She had probably remembered that he worked for an American company. Maybe she had planned to coax his mother into asking for his help.

For the next half-hour he took care of Frau Stein's body, surveyed the damage and tried to work out what to do, but he didn't dare approach his mother's room. A voice in his head shouted that he was in danger—he would be asked to explain why a Jewish woman was in his house—and he knew he had to think things through. If he saw his mother now, he would lose any chance of remaining lucid.

Between his encounter with Hermann and his gang and climbing the steps to his house, he understood that his mother was no longer living. Any faint hope was snuffed out as soon as he crossed the threshold. He had never felt anything with so much certainty as the fact of her death. When he came home from school and knocked on the front door, he always knew by the sound of Frau Stein's heavy steps whether or not his mother was at home.

'Where is Frau Heiselberg?' the doctor asked.

Thomas stared at the man who was streaked with feathers and flour. The doctor shook him and slapped him. His hands were damp. Thomas was afraid that the source of the dampness was Frau Stein's blood.

The doctor shook him again. 'Where is Frau Heiselberg?'

He pointed down the dark corridor at the only door that remained in the house.

The doctor disappeared down the corridor, and in a few minutes emerged from the darkness. Thomas reached out and dusted away some feathers that clung to his lapel.

'It's all right, Herr Heiselberg,' the doctor said.

He doesn't remember how he got to her room. Maybe they dragged him there. She lay on her bed in a nightgown, and pallor had already spread on her face. Her head rested on two pillows, her sculpted neck was slightly stretched, but it didn't violate her tranquil expression. She seemed to have gone to sleep. Her arms were crossed on her chest, and her lower body was covered by a sheet. He cautiously approached the corpse, struggling with the fear that he would be called upon to explain why he had invaded her room in the middle of the night. He shouldn't have left her with Frau Stein. His fingers crept along the sheet and touched her arm. They were even colder than her skin. He brought them to his lips and blew on them. Then he touched her arm, and let his fingers rest there. He didn't dare touch her face. The questions that Erika Gelber would ask him were already whirring in his mind: Did you kiss her goodbye? Were you afraid of her dead body?

At last he gave a wild shout, shook off his fear and in one movement he leaned down, kissed her forehead and straightened up. Then he retreated until his hand felt the doorhandle. He went out, shut the door and stood in the dark corridor. There he stood until dawn with his back to the closed door of her room.

In the morning he hired the services of Clarissa Engelhardt, and placed the reorganisation of the house in her hands. Plump Clarissa agreed to his proposal even before asking her parents' permission, 'out of respect for Frau Heiselberg'. He moved into a hotel near the Milton offices. When he returned to the house two weeks later, not even a hint of that night remained, except for the space that yawned in his mother's room where the window had been. He had ordered Clarissa not to repair it, and she reluctantly obeyed.

No official contacted him regarding the events of that night. About a hundred acquaintances and the entire staff of Milton attended the funeral. Some clients also attended, as well as representatives of government offices, the Four Year Plan, the Berlin municipality, and the French and Italian embassies. Georg Weller, the fellow from the Foreign Office, and two SD agents who worked with Carlson Mailer also came. Rudolf Schumacher showed up with a telegram from Walther Funk, the Minister of Economic Affairs. Schumacher had doubtless managed to boast to him about his connections with Milton, Thomas thought irately. The man was an amateur. The way people like that got on was what Thomas's father called 'wriggling through'.

The presence of people from the government alleviated his anxiety. It had apparently been decided to erase any memory of the incident. He heard that savage criticism in the foreign press of the attack on the Jews had irritated the government. Words like 'unnecessary' and 'stupid' were used openly amid claims that people had acted behind the Führer's back and betrayed the trust he had placed in them. Nevertheless, Weller, who called him up a few weeks after the funeral to find out how he was, told him that in December the Foreign Minister von Ribbentrop had been warmly received in Paris, that the French Foreign Minister had made anti-Jewish remarks and that everyone understood that what happened that night was merely a temporary glitch. After all, very few Jews had been killed. Weller, who, to Thomas's surprise, knew all about the event in his house, did not believe any action would be taken against him: the Foreign Office would not allow anyone to harass a protégé of Jack Fiske. How many friends like Fiske did Germany still have in the United States?

The only surprise at the funeral was the absence of Elsa, his ex-wife—if it was possible for anything disgraceful she did to surprise him. But he had expected her to come, if only to part once and for all from the woman she had loathed so much; in his opinion, the years they had all lived under the same roof should have been enough to temper her loathing with some sadness. Her condolence letter reached the office a few weeks later, and it would have been hard to call it heartwarming. Still, they hadn't seen each other for more than ten years, and had scarcely written after she remarried. Now she gave her former husband some advice: 'I hope that apart from your sadness this will be a day of liberation.'

'If Friedrich Nietzsche and a Hollywood starlet sat next to Elsa in a café, she would turn her back on the philosopher,' his mother declared the day she met her. A few years later she boasted to Frau Stein that she and her son had got rid of their spouses at the same time.

None of the mourners mentioned that night. 'What a cursed sickness,' one of the SD men said. Thomas silently agreed with him; his mother had died of her illness. No one had injured her. Of course the invasion of her house would have terrified her and hastened her death, but, to tell the truth, it also shortened her suffering.

He had not seen Hermann since. Sometimes the question gnawed at him: why had he done it? But, instead of letting it get to him, Thomas started planning how he could retaliate. He remembered that when they sold off Hermann's father's possessions or food stolen from hotels, Hermann was embarrassed and would complain about their damned country that forced him to act like a criminal so that his sisters wouldn't starve. Hermann never concealed his distaste for Thomas's practice of 'swindling people' (though he didn't turn up his nose at the fruit of the swindles), and the moment came when their friendship began to leach away. That didn't worry him: lots of boys swore fidelity to one another and got bored after a month. But even if Hermann now saw him as someone who had 'sold his soul to the Americans' and nonsense like that, it was still hard to understand the hatred in his eyes or that he had violated a house where he had played as a boy.

One day Thomas decided there was no point in thinking about the kinks in Hermann's soul. Taking revenge on an SS officer might lead to his own destruction. Perhaps Hermann felt that they were even now and wouldn't see each other again. But Thomas had to keep an eye out: he wouldn't let Hermann take him by surprise again, make him stand in the street, trembling, humiliated and ignorant. Next time he would land the first blow.

He was still groggy after washing. Thomas stood in the bathroom and wiped his chest with a damp towel. He hung it up, dressed and went to light the fire. How unfortunate that the ugly Delft tiles around the fireplace had survived Hermann's visit. He glanced at his watch: in a moment Erika Gelber would ring the doorbell. Since November they had been meeting in the morning at his house. He sat on the new sofa. There was something that he wanted to bring up in their session: since his episode at the New Year's Eve party, he occasionally lost his sense of time. He would wake up and grope for memories of the previous evening. Was that a symptom of the illness that had attacked him? The doctors told him everything was fine, and to anyone who expressed concern at his appearance, he would say, 'No, I'm not sick. I've had a check-up. Everything's okay,' but he was certain that an illness was incubating in his body: dissolving his muscles, trampling on his chest with its heels, tightening the black veils over his eyes.

The doorbell rang at exactly eight thirty. She stood before him with her face reddened by the cold, and, with the demanding casualness typical of her, said she hoped that the fire was lit and that the coffee was steaming the way she liked it.

'Of course, Frau Gelber,' he answered, bowing like a servant and leading her into the parlour. She sat in the armchair. He couldn't lie down here and stare at the ceiling the way he did in her clinic. That would seem affected. So he sprawled on the sofa, leaning on an elbow, and stared at the fire. The shutters were closed, and the flames cast a weak glow. After some small talk, Erika said, 'We devoted the last two sessions to being an orphan. That's something we've spoken about quite a bit. In 1930, after your father's death, you came to me with a complaint about frightening attacks that left you feeling weak. Aside from that, as you told me with earnest amusement, you were curious about certain psychoanalytic ideas that had become fashionable.'

'Let's be precise, Frau Gelber. I said that it was the fashionableness of those ideas that made me curious.'

'I stand corrected,' said Erika, who looked surprised by his petty obstinacy. 'You must remember that after two years of therapy I told you that your refusal to admit grief was nothing more than stubbornness. You answered—and here I am quoting my notes—"Frau Gelber, I didn't come to you for lessons in mourning. I give you my word as a gentleman, my father's death caused me dreadful suffering. But, in all sincerity, right now I'm less bothered by his death than by my own."'

'I can't explain things I don't remember,' he stated drily. 'I also don't understand what you're driving at. Whose death troubles you now? My father's or my mother's?'

Erika was silent. He detested her silences. Recently he had become convinced that she wasn't happy with his answers.

'What kind of woman was your mother?' she finally asked.

As if she didn't know, he thought. They'd been discussing her for years. 'Imagine the proprietor of a superbly furnished and detailed hotel upon which time imposes its decrees. For example: it might be possible to clean the spots on the tablecloths, but you can't restore their whiteness, can you? All over the hotel, time eats away at its former glory, but the proprietor locks the doors, closes the shutters, sits in her empty office in her pretty dress and waits for the wind to blow it down. Imagine a sailor on the seven seas who hears that his city has changed unrecognisably. He decides not to go back, to remain on the high seas with nothing but his nostalgia for the beautiful days he had at home, now lost.' He offered as many images as he could conjure up, and sweet warmth crept into him as they multiplied, as if he were sending bright balloons into a dark sky, performing a flamboyant dance against his petrified awareness of loss.

'Thomas, for several sessions now you've only been talking about your mother in metaphors,' Erika complained. Her voice sounded imploring. 'And they're all amazingly similar.'

Her coy tone struck him. He suddenly understood that Erika didn't say the first thing that came into her head, but replaced it with something different. He felt he could read the shifts in her thinking— a tiny manoeuvre, partially conscious, that might shatter years of trust.

She's trying to appease me, he thought, prevent me from getting angry. And it had been Erika's blunt candour that captured his heart when he started seeing her. She always demanded memories of things that had happened and scolded him every time he used the images he liked so much. For a long time he had sensed her weakness, but he still hoped that in their sessions they could ignore the noise of the outside world and keep things the way they used to be. In the past few months he had glimpsed stirrings of a change even in the way her body moved. Her gestures lacked the poise of a person who knows her place.

He was filled with disgust, apologised and rushed to the bathroom. He rinsed his burning face in cold water and considered whether to bring the matter up in the session. The problem was that, if he spoke about it with her now, she would revert to her earlier style in order to appease him. One thing was clear: it would never again be the way it was. For a long time he had been yearning for the hours they had had together, years ago: for the mournful light of the setting sun, lengthening the shadows of the cacti on the shelf; for her too-colourful dresses, all of them suspended on hangers in his memory; and for her attentive expression with its calm tolerance even of his worst deceptions.

He was a man who respected restraint, but Erika was the only soul for whom he felt a fondness that he couldn't restrain. Around her he became childish, inventing affectionate nicknames for her that he only used to her after pretending they had come to him in his dreams. Damn it, for years he had been passing by shop windows and choosing presents for her.

'Thomas?'

He took a breath and left the bathroom. 'Sometimes it's hot here,' he cheerfully observed.

The session became buried in worthless verbiage. Most of the time he stared at the vase of crocuses that Clarissa had picked in Professor Bernheimer's abandoned garden.

When it was finished Erika smoothed her trousers and passed her fingers over the carnation on her lapel. He wondered whether he should tell her that in the Foreign Office they made fun of the English ambassador, Sir Nevile Henderson, calling him 'the carnation with a man'. In the past few years, inspired by Thomas, she had stopped wearing those old-fashioned, unflattering dresses and decked herself out in a wardrobe that he called 'more up-to-date': straight skirts almost to her ankles, buttoned blouses with sheer fabric and thin mesh, and hip-length jackets.

Erika told him she wanted to talk about something personal, and that of course he should stop her if he felt this would not be proper. He didn't know whether to stand up—he wanted to stand now, as he did in his office—but in the end he remained on the sofa, leaning on the armrest.

Erika repeated that perhaps the matter was inappropriate.

'You've said that already, Frau Gelber.'

Erika added in a low voice—his comment had apparently weakened her resolve—that the times weren't appropriate either. Then she asked him directly if he could help her and her husband and their two children obtain visas to another country. Someone had informed on them to the Gestapo, and they were being constantly harassed.

In his heart he thanked her for not mentioning the children's names; at least she had spared them both that kitsch. She hadn't specifically mentioned the United States: a vain effort not to show that the idea had occurred to her after hearing his stories about the negoti-ations with the Bamberburg Bank and Jack Fiske's connections in the State Department. Maybe he should offer her a job in Italy? A wicked thought poked its head up. If anyone was really capable of making a deal with the German government, it was Federico, the man who had gone to parties with the Italian Foreign Minister, Count Ciano.

'It's strange that you're asking me in particular, Frau Gelber,' he said. 'After all, there are psychoanalytic societies in Europe and the United States, and they're filled with Jews. Can't they help you?'

Erika recounted in detail the tribulations she had undergone: in the early 1930s therapists in the Berlin Psychoanalytic Society wanted to help her emigrate to the United States, but she and her husband chose to remain in Germany. In the past year, when dozens of Jewish analysts from Austria joined the race for visas, she realised that her chances were slipping: the British Psychoanalytic Society refused to sponsor her and she had received no reply from New York. There were rumours that a movement against immigration was spreading among analysts in America, and a handful of friends in other countries, who had made generous efforts on her behalf, had achieved nothing.

'I understand,' he nodded. 'You're putting me in a delicate situation. We're talking about an illegal action.'

'I'm sorry.'

He must have looked like the most sanctimonious person in the world. He was always tempted to make the worst impression possible at the beginning. When he came home from school with a good report, he used to inundate his mother with terrible stories about failures and fights, just so that he could see disappointment crease her forehead and her eyes close as though she wanted to sleep. Then, just as she was about to reproach him, he would pull out his report—indis-putable proof that refuted his own testimony. Erika once asked him why he did it, and he answered that it still happened sometimes, for example, he once told Schumacher that Milton had been hired to consult for a euthanasia project. 'We have to root out the degenerates, don't we?'

It simply amused him, he explained to her, that people, even your mother, would believe whatever you told them, if you made it sound credible, even if it didn't fit in with your personality and everything you'd ever done—the dopes would adjust whatever ideas they had about you to accommodate this new information. We are only silhouettes in the minds of others. 'Don't be sad. Of course I'll help you,' he told Erika, and he rose from the sofa as a sign that the session was over. 'If I succeed, it'll be because there's a law somewhere—or, rather, there is no law, and this fact can be used.'

The next morning he met with Carlson Mailer and Frau Tschammer in the office. They met once a week to discuss their negotiations with the Bamberburg Bank. It was clear that the governmental agencies were committed to the order to remove Jews from the economy. Wohlthat told Thomas that in fact the Bamberburg was the last remaining large Jewish bank not yet transferred to German hands. Before Schacht had been forced to resign as the Minister of Economics, he defended the Jews, but now the office of the Four Year Plan wanted everything resolved.

Frau Tschammer was in daily contact with people at the Dresdener bank. She reported that they were worried, because apparently the Deutsche Bank had already made an offer to the directors of Bamberburg regarding the countries that would take them in. Carlson Mailer, as was his wont recently, stared out into space, and said little.

After the meeting, Thomas went into Carlson's office and told him about a secret plan that he had been working on: he knew the therapist who was treating Blum, from the Bamberburg bank. 'She has considerable influence on him,' he hinted, as though sharing a secret, and it would be a good idea to use her services to coax Blum to move in the right direction. In response Carlson leafed through a colourful magazine. That weak man had lost any desire to do anything, and was now an obstacle, Thomas thought.

'If it's a matter of money,' Carlson rumbled, 'do what you think best.'

'It could be that other considerations are involved.'

'So find some stunt for them, too.'

'I'd like to talk about the essence of the deal,' Thomas insisted.

'We've spoken about it enough.' Carlson lit his pipe and puffed smoke. 'And with you every bar of soap has some essence.'

Thomas decided not to say another word. It was clear that all Mailer cared about negotiating was the price of a villa in Nice, overlooking the Promenade des Anglais.

Was Mailer contemptuous of him for promoting the Bamberburg deal? Maybe he would respect him more if he also sat in his office like a scarecrow, doing nothing? There was no point in behaving like a child learning for the first time that history is filled with bloodshed and war: the spirit of the time weaves deals like these, the Dresdener Bank was Milton's largest client, and that was the only important thing.

It was time for Plan B: he telephoned Jack Fiske in New York, presented his initiative and asked if it was possible to add Erika Gelber and her two children to the Bamberburg list.

'It's no secret that we at Milton don't see eye to eye with the German government about the Jews,' Fiske answered. Thomas was aware of the pause while the man's tongue licked his upper lip, which was always dry. 'Listen to this, but keep it to yourself,' Fiske purred; no one loved revealing secrets more than he did. He regarded it as one of the pleasures of his position, which enabled him to fear no one. 'One of the Milton partners is a friend of Henry Morgenthau, and Morgenthau told him that President Roosevelt once complained about the number of Jews at Harvard. In the end, thanks to him, they decided to limit the number. Cultured people solve problems wisely.'

'And in the matter of the Jewish psychoanalyst?' Thomas focused on the subject.

Fiske, who understood that he might have insulted him, answered cordially. 'My good fellow, a request made by one of Milton's most successful partners is sacred for me. But the State Department is under heavy siege. Yesterday I heard from our people in Berlin that their office has received a hundred and sixty thousand visa applications, and in Vienna there are around a hundred thousand—absolute madness! And I also saw a poll that said that more than fifty per cent of Americans think that Jews are avaricious and that Jewish immigration would damage American values. So tell me honestly—I'm very careful about asking for special favours in immigration matters—will a visa for that woman clinch the deal for us?'

Thomas hesitated. He wanted to say that he still had some doubts, but he immediately understood that that would be an amateurish answer. He should have resolved any doubts before speaking with Fiske. 'In my opinion it could be critical,' he said, keeping his voice steady.

'Okay,' Fiske said, 'if people from Bamberburg ask us for that Jew, I'll act on her behalf.'

'They hinted to me that it would be better if I spoke about this delicate matter on their behalf. Psychoanalysis is a very secret matter,' Thomas chuckled. He knew that this lie might cost him his career.

'Don't worry, my good fellow,' Fiske said cordially. 'It'll be enough if Blum asks me, and I'll take the next step.'

The upshot was clear: Fiske wouldn't do a thing unless Blum spoke to him.

Plan C was pathetic: he met with Schumacher and asked him whether an appeal to the new Office of Jewish Emigration managed by Heidrich could help Erika Gelber.

Schumacher was horrified. 'Apparently everyone but Thomas Heiselberg has heard the Führer's warning to Funk to stop exempting Jews from restrictions. Anyway, as a friend, I tell you that your connection with that Jewish therapist of yours has become suspicious. Soon you'll be identified as a friend of the Jews. Is she really worth that?'

Thomas struggled against the words, 'Yes, she's the last person left to me in this world. Except for her, there are only people like you,' which, for some reason beyond his understanding, he wanted to say aloud.

There was no choice. He would have to manoeuvre Blum so that, first, he asked Erika Gelber to be included in the bank's list, and, second, he made the Bamberburgs choose the Dresdener's offer. Those two conditions had to be fulfilled in tandem.

So here was Plan D, which was a desperate measure. There was no reason why Blum should help Erika in particular. Quite likely he had other obligations. And even if Thomas explained to him that the place was reserved for Erika and for her alone, and that no other Jew could be preferred to her, Blum would probably not believe him. He was suspicious of Thomas. One of his acquaintances once told him that Blum had said, as a kind of joke, that Thomas Heiselberg was a talented person, but he was also the best possible proof for Hölderlin's dictum that there were no people left in Germany, only professions.

Thomas decided that the time had come for a personal gesture towards the Bamberburgs. He convinced Carlson to host a friendly dinner where representatives of all the parties in the deal would sit together. But first he had to explain to Carlson that it was impossible to invite the Jews to one of the restaurants favoured by the Milton people. He felt it was unjust that he was the one who had to explain the country's laws to Carlson: if he read a newspaper now and then, he would understand everything. He teasingly asked Carlson whether he had heard that in France—where Carlson had finally bought a house—a law against foreigners had recently been passed. 'Really? Thanks for informing me,' Carlson answered, but he invited everyone to an 'American dinner' in his luxury apartment on Rankstrasse. He defined the event as a 'gesture of solidarity with the people from the bank who are in trouble'.

Carlson's chef prepared meatballs and other roasted chunks of meat, wrapped in rolls dripping with sauce and embellished with lettuce. There were fine china bowls overflowing with fried potatoes. But, despite the cheer that Thomas tried to inspire in the guests, the atmosphere was gloomy: the Bamberburgs complained the whole time, and Carlson made some venomous remarks to the Dresdener people. Towards the end of the evening, Blum told Thomas that if the Dresdener people promised that, when conditions in Germany improved, the Bamberburgs could buy their bank back, the directors would regard this as a noble gesture and would accept Dresdener's offer.

Thomas thought this was just another of Blum's delusions, and mentioned it to Carlson, who backed Blum up. 'That sounds fair,' he declared.

At a meeting with the directors of the Dresdener bank he suggested they add a clause to this effect, explaining that in any case it was unenforceable, and could do nothing more than warm the hearts of the Bamberburgs a little. The directors refused even to consider the proposal.

He conveyed their answer to Carlson.

'Why are you telling me this?' Carlson muttered. 'Just take care of it.'

These days Carlson was sending everyone away with the response: decide for yourself. Carlson's secretary told Thomas that in a letter to his wife he had cursed Fiske and boasted that he hadn't lifted a finger 'for that stinking Bamberburg Bank deal'. The days passed. Thomas was running out of ideas. Multitudes of Jews were looking desperately for countries that would accept them—one day they were all talking about Switzerland, and the next about Shanghai. New regulations were published every day, amid an aggravating buzz of whispers and plots, gossip and slander. Rumours circulated about agents who had obtained visas in return for the property of the fleeing Jews, about doctors, scientists and businessmen who had escaped Germany, which was shedding Nobel prize winners like someone who straightens a wrinkle in his cuff, and about embassies whose policies were about to change. But one fact remained: the supply of Jews exceeded the demand by thousands of per cent.

Thomas had another session with Erika Gelber. 'I feel that my steps have been clumsy,' he complained to her. 'They lack my characteristic drive.' He could feel the odour of failure wafting from his body. 'You understand, I'm assailed by doubt, I take steps and then regret them, as if I were a foreigner in Berlin. And Frau Tschammer is getting in my way. For ten years I've been striving to get rid of that woman, and she's still there. The trouble is that thousands of people are concentrated on this subject of the Jews: government people, private companies, businessmen, go-betweens, Jewish organisations all over the world. I'm looking for new areas, you understand, where I can act freely, areas that only exist because of me. I'm not one of those mediocre souls who opens another department store or restaurant in a city that already has a hundred like them.'

They would both have to ask Blum directly, he told her. He would host a dinner for them at his house. 'Blum admires you, Erika. He says that therapy helped him to understand a lot of things.'

In the past Thomas had taken pleasure in sorting out tangled situations. He always believed that his most impressive ability was to grasp lots of strings—the source of a certain organisation's power, people's desires (sometimes contradictory), greed and a host of other weaknesses—and to wrap them up in a ball which only he could unravel. But now he was worried: the lack of time was forcing him to make imperfect plans.

…

Clarissa blushed. Too much rouge, he was disappointed to see. This girl—you could give her the most expensive cosmetics in Europe and she'd still look like she was plastered in cheap paint from some discount shop in Wedding. She appeared in the parlour in a blue dress she'd bought with his money especially for the occasion. It was a bit too tight and emphasised the roll of fat on her lower abdomen. Her steps wobbled, and it looked as if she was going to stumble.

'Dear, do you need help?' Erika Gelber asked.

'Thanks, I'm all right,' Clarissa laughed.

Clarissa poured wine into Blum's glass. He leaned back in his chair. He was clearly ill at ease. Thomas studied her: rounded face, tufts of blonde hair, tied in a ribbon, curled around it. An expression of gentle puzzlement, trying to look severe and thoughtful, along with the solid evidence of a decent home, respectable parents and a model education.

Girls like Clarissa were sheltered by a deeply rooted knowledge that in the end the puzzlement would fade away to their satisfaction, and they would find their place in the world.

Thomas waved his wine glass—a cheap purchase, he grumbled to himself. At least she had remembered to remove the labels. He was seized by the urge to explain to the guests that these common articles had entered his house after it was trashed by the savages who had killed Frau Stein, their beloved Jewish housekeeper. But he clung tightly to that card, their shared fate, to be played only if there was no choice. He hadn't told Erika about Frau Stein's death.

'This morning I accompanied Wohlthat to a meeting with some Japanese businessmen,' Thomas said. 'I reported to him that the negotiations for the sale of the Bamberburg Bank were proceeding with great purpose and would soon conclude.'

Blum sipped his wine and nodded. He was a broad man whose body terminated in a huge skull, which was now jutting out of a rough, grey sweater. Carlson once said that Blum 'dressed like a Communist'.

'I believe the decision is close,' Blum said. 'We also spoke with Wohlthat yesterday. Naturally he once again expressed reservations about the role he is required to play.'

'What impression did Dresdener's latest offer make on the bank's board?' Thomas asked. If Blum wanted to flaunt his connections with Wohlthat, let him. 'We worked hard to convince them to raise the price.'

'The offers we are examining are very similar,' Blum answered. 'I watched our colleagues from the Warburg Bank sell their splendid institution for pennies. We're smaller, and we have no illusions. After the tax and all the government's other tricks, we'll be left with less than fifteen per cent of its real value.'

Clearly Thomas was not the person to whom such complaints should be addressed. Blum was stuck in a world where his bank was worth another eighty-five per cent. Some people hovered between this world and another one that once existed or that they imagined, and afterwards they bargained with this world with the logic of their imagination.

'No, that's definitely not enough,' Thomas agreed. Restrained anger grated in his voice. Once again, as in Carlson's office, it was incumbent on him to convey the spirit of the time.

'Some people on the board argue that it would be better not to sell the bank at that price.' Blum's right shoulder leaped up, and he pinched it with the fingers of his left hand. 'If Germany wants it so much—let her confiscate it.'

'Listen, Blum,' said Thomas. It annoyed him that Blum had hissed the word 'Germany' like a curse. 'To be honest, the country is in trouble. And, aside from that, there isn't a single Germany. Germany is this way now, and once it was different, and in a few years maybe it will be something else. The company I work for is taking a heroic stand against the pressure to leave Germany. The economy is moving away from the world, and I believe that this is bad for all of us.'

Now he looked at Erika Gelber for the first time in some minutes. She gave him a puzzled look in return. Blum sipped again and exhaled a gloomy breath.

Clarissa's approach interrupted his thoughts. A plate of cutlets sprinkled with silver grains of salt and breadcrumbs was laid on the table. 'Please, veal cutlets such as are served only in the finest restaurants in Germany...' Her clear voice filled the parlour.

'Fräulein Engelhardt is from the educated bourgeoisie of Hamburg. In my opinion, they produce the most remarkable young women in the country,' said Thomas.

'Young lady, it looks delicious,' said Blum, waiting impatiently for Clarissa to serve him. Blum liked cutlets.

Clarissa minced around the table, returned to Blum, and topped up his glass. Thomas wondered whether she might be laying it on too thick. She had told him that she excelled at every task she took on, and stuck to her agreement to play the role of cook and waitress even after he let her know that the guests would be Jews. But they knew that she wasn't a servant, and hamming it up might give them the impression they were being made fun of. Jews were on the lookout day and night for changes in every glance from a friend or acquaintance. That was completely logical: the shattering of their status as Jews had modified all their human connections. They were forced to scurry about to discover how everyone they knew was responding to the new spirit. Clarissa hummed a tune when she leaned over them, withdrew and straightened up. Now he was reconciled to her little exaggerations—the thick make-up, the clumsy movements, the twisted collar of her dress— the play-acting of a young thing who had disguised herself as a servant and as a woman.

Blum didn't look at or speak to Erika Gelber. Thomas, though he wanted nothing more than to bring the evening to an end, was drawn to Erika. She seemed so lost, with her dishevelled cinnamon hair, her light make-up emphasising her dark eyes: here was Erika Gelber, greeting the night. The same woman but not exactly.

Both of them were looking at him now: Blum was waiting for an explanation of why he had been invited, and Erika for her signal to speak to Blum.

But perhaps they were demanding something more. What were they demanding? That he would take responsibility, curse the homeland, explain to them how it had all happened? Blum coughed, Erika said something to him in such a self-effacing tone that it didn't even sound like German. As if she were trying to curl up in his lap like a little girl.

Clarissa wasn't the only one in disguise tonight.

He decided to address them both together to strengthen the closeness between them: 'Herr Blum, Frau Gelber,' he said, 'I understand that these are difficult times for you. I don't believe that it's really possible to console someone whose world has changed so much for the worse. With all sincerity I'll tell you that even in the hard times that I have endured recently, like the horrible night a few weeks ago when, in this parlour, our devoted and beloved housekeeper, Hannah Stein, was cruelly murdered—even then I clung to the faith that Hegel was right, that in the end history and reason progress, despite the most dreadful events. Naturally, of course, being trapped in the moment, we cannot judge its future purpose, but sometimes what's rational hides its highest qualities inside irrational mischief.'

'That's small consolation, to see our suffering as a tool in the hand of reason.' Erika gave a twisted smile. She showed no surprise at the news of Frau Stein's death, and was entirely concentrated on Blum.

Blum nodded gloomily to show he'd heard her, but he was leaning away from Erika, revealing his reservations about being bound up in the same group as her. Unlike Erika, who was regarded as completely Jewish, Blum was defined by the regime as a *mischling* of the first degree. Blum had never seen himself as Jewish. His father had converted to Christianity after the war, and his mother came from a Protestant family in Heidelberg. Blum hoped to assimilate into the German nation. He was exempt from most restrictions, but he still complained that his senior position in a Jewish-owned bank was driving him into the bosom of Judaism and 'all those Jewish organisations'.

'I'm not a big expert in the irrational!' Blum hissed, and the creases on his forehead deepened and turned red like cuts. 'I've worked in the bank for forty years. We built up an excellent institution from zero, an institution that has garnered nothing but praise, and now they're robbing us of it!'

The smile faded from Erika's face. Thomas gave Blum a warning look. How dumb could the man be, to shout nonsense like that at eight in the evening in a private home, in an apartment that SS people had recently destroyed?

'Herr Blum, a little patience.' He couldn't restrain himself. 'We've all taken a risk to get together here. It would be a shame to allow bitterness to lead us to a dead end.'

Blum fixed his eyes on his plate.

Clarissa appeared again and cleared the table. Now her movements were stiff, and her cheerfulness was gone. If the things she had heard here were not supposed to be said, she might tell her parents about the dinner, or her friends at the university, or the NSP, the National Socialist welfare organisation where she volunteered. But she wasn't the informing type. Thomas had already ascertained that.

'Despite recent events, I expect, indeed I demand, that you regard me as exactly the same friend I have always been to you,' Thomas declared solemnly.

'Don't you like cutlets?' Blum said to Erika Gelber, staring at the meat on her plate.

'If you want it, please.' She returned the cutlet to the platter.

'We'll share it,' Blum concluded.

Before dessert Thomas offered Blum a cigar, and Erika saw her chance. She turned to Blum, and told him that she wanted to talk to him about something. Blum shrank into his chair. Erika told him that her husband had been arrested in November, had been detained in Buchenwald, and now he had been released. He had been ordered to emigrate without delay. Her two children, Max and Eva, had been expelled from school. They were sitting at home now, after some hooligans had forced Max to weed the football pitch with his teeth. They were being evicted from their apartment. They were looking feverishly for a country to take them but there was nowhere. No one was helping them.

Blum nodded from time to time, and puffed smoke. Thomas wondered whether he should leave them; after all, Blum had been in analysis with Erika, and maybe he was keeping his distance from her because there were three people in the room. In any event, Thomas was tired of hearing about their distress.

Blum peered down the hallway, as though expecting dessert. Really, where was Clarissa with the cake?

Erika said something about the United States, that because of the children there was no point waiting until things changed here. Blum nodded again, a sign that significant things had been said, and closed his eyes.

'It's cold…' Thomas rubbed his hands together and hurried over to stoke the fire.

As its heat warmed them, he realised that Blum wouldn't help Erika. He couldn't understand how he hadn't admitted his failure earlier. Maybe Blum couldn't help. He had obligations to many people, his partners would be likely to reject the idea and maybe—a hair-raising suspicion—they had already decided to sell to Deutsche Bank instead. One thing was clear: Blum wasn't going to help Erika.

The statement tormented him, yet he could not stop repeating it to himself, as though wanting to have his punishment at once. His head hurt, and he closed his eyes. A minute or ten passed. The wind howled outside, and he imagined it surrounding the house, ripping down the walls and the ceiling as though they were made of paper. When he shook off these visions, Erika was still talking to Blum in the same caressing tone, and Thomas was horrified: how could she not understand that all was lost? He apologised and announced that he had to check the dessert.

'At such a late hour?' Blum said, looking at the front door.

'We were supposed to have had, as it were, a cake,' Thomas said, babbling.

Where was Clarissa?

Erika gave him a pleading look not to leave her alone with Blum. But he couldn't stay and watch her clinging to a vain hope that he himself had planted in her. He gaped at a blank spot on the wall, announced that they would be serving dessert immediately and hurried out.

As he wandered among the rooms, half-listening to Erika's voice, he realised how fateful this struggle to get her out of Germany was for him: in part he was struggling to erase the things he had said to her about 'losing the magic touch', seeking desperately for proof that Thomas Heiselberg was still a master tactician in the corridors of Berlin. Maybe not like in the past, but he still knew how to arrange deals and astonish people with his ability to cut through the most complicated issues.

Erika was saying something about her driver's licence and a law that forbade her to walk in certain streets. How many damned stories did she have left? All he wanted now was to escape her voice. In the background Blum was cursing the Jews from Eastern Europe. From the moment they had began to show up here, en masse, something bad was going to happen.

Clarissa wasn't in his room or anywhere else. Now he understood where she was. He rushed back to the parlour again, taking care not to look at Blum and Erika, and walked through it and then down the corridor to that room. A freezing wind blew through the broken window. Clarissa lay in her dress and shoes on his mother's bed. A heavy blanket was spread over her lower body. How many times had he spread that blanket over his mother, exactly there? There was the sound of hoarse breathing, and he saw the slow movement of her chest. The dress was pressing on her. Maybe he should undo a button or two. And if she woke up? To his surprise, he was not irritated by her disappearance or her invasion of his mother's bed. He was not the kind of man to build a shrine to a dead woman. Every time he heard women gushing over the rumour that Göring had built a temple for his first wife, he felt shame that a man like that could rise so high in Germany.

Maybe Clarissa's boldness promised a change for the better. If his most alarming capacity, the quality that defined him during an attack, was to snuff the life out of things, perhaps this young woman would lead him in another direction. Even in a room containing only a bed and a shattered window she made a youthful spirit glow in him. He suddenly wanted this sleeping beauty, wanted to have her, to keep her in his possession. It appeared that he had finally met with something that he couldn't dispatch to death with a single gesture.

. . .

The next morning there was a commotion when he got to the office. The receptionist greeted him in tears, and Carlson's young assistant sneaked away, pretending not to see Thomas. He went to Carlson's office, and was astonished to find Frau Tschammer sitting in his chair, shuffling through his papers. It was clear that disaster had struck.

'Thomas!' She stood up. There was a ripple of panic in her voice. 'Mailer has gone to New York. He didn't say when he was coming back.'

She was staring at him. In the end, even Frau Tschammer believed in his talent, in his storied reputation: if the staff at Milton encountered an abyss, before anyone could even think of moving, Thomas would have already have leaped into it and, God knows how, landed on his feet. He would blaze a trail across it, and everyone would follow.

Thomas didn't know what to say. He couldn't summon the strength to trade barbs or make toxic small talk with Frau Tschammer. It was all pointless now. After all, collapse was a simple matter.

'Frau Tschammer,' he said, 'the Milton Company is liquidating its business in Germany. And if we had been brave enough to examine things as they truly were, we would have seen it coming long ago.'

LENINGRAD
WINTER 1939

That night the iron bed creaked in her parents' bedroom. Sasha could hear them still discussing whether or not to sign the protocols of the investigation, even though it misrepresented their answers, and whether or not to write a confession. They ran through the same names over and over: A confessed and only got a short sentence, B confessed and disappeared, C refused to confess and was liquidated, D refused to confess and in the end they decided he was innocent.

Her father had already been interrogated twice, her mother only once, and to their surprise they were allowed home, to reconsider their pleas of not guilty. Meanwhile her father wasted time collecting documents and letters that testified to their good character and their loyalty to the party.

The next day an article appeared in the newspaper about the discovery of a counter-revolutionary cell in the Physical-Technical Institute. Two agents from the West, Germans, had joined forces with the last followers of Pyatakov, and, under the influence of the Unified

Centre, led by the criminals Trotsky and Zinoviev, they had plotted 'to sabotage major industrial facilities'. Monstrous treachery had been discovered in the institute: 'Enemies of the people planned to kill thousands with a single goal: to defile the revolution.'

That day her father was fired. He returned home at 10 a.m., closed the shutters in the bedroom and lay down on the bed. Her mother had been busy with housework since early morning, pickling mushrooms and beans, making wild berry jam, her white apron stained crimson and brown. Sasha was listening to a record on the gramophone. Arthur Rubinstein, whom her father had called 'a pianist for sentimental salons', was playing the first movement of Beethoven's Fourth Piano Concerto. In a moment the Funeral March of Chopin's Second Piano Sonata would be heard, and then the finale would thunder, a piece that her father called 'the greatest musical manipulation of the nineteenth century'. Sasha always listened to music in the same order: Beethoven, Chopin, Liszt, sometimes Mendelssohn, and finally Schumann. She dusted the little shelf on the bookcase that was allotted to her: Schumann's 'Carnival Jest from Vienna', Hanon's piano exercises for beginners, copies of *Le Nouvelliste*, yellowed issues of *Nir* magazine, a book of poems by Balmont with a dedication to her parents.

Mother had not played the piano in a long time. She used to play with the twins and she and Kolya had occasionally performed together. A few years ago, after a few weeks of practice, they even played a short piece from a Borodin symphony, 'In the Steppes of Central Asia', which Kolya renamed 'the evil steps of Asia'.

At 2 p.m. Valeria called her husband. 'Andreyusha,' she shouted. 'Andreyusha, I need you!'

He shuffled into the living room in underpants and a filthy undershirt, as if he'd been fished out of a deep sleep. Thin strands of silver hair dangled on either side of his head. Her mother told him to pick up a heavy jar of cucumbers and place it next to the window. He looked at her incredulously. 'You called me for that?' he whined.

'Yes, exactly for that.'

He hoisted the jar up, pressed it to his chest, carried it to the window and thumped it onto the shelf.

In the afternoon Vladimir and Nikolai returned from school, and hovered at the door to the apartment. Kolya lazily leaned his long, slender body—a beanpole, according to Maxim Podolsky—against the wall. Next to him, Vlada stood erect in his grey coat, with blue and black ribbons on the sleeves and two rows of buttons on the breast, like an old officer's coat. Vlada wasn't tall like Kolya, but his body was broad and muscular, and it seemed as if he always demanded more space for himself. His hair was short, his face flushed with a babyish pink that softened the severity of his know-it-all expression.

Apparently someone at school had read the article. Sasha wondered at the stories that circulated in the schoolyard. Boys were usually obsessed with punishment—guillotines and nooses inflamed their imaginations—and were disappointed to learn that most traitors were shot. Once they had some fun at the expense of a boy whose father had been arrested: they painted their faces white, pounded their chests and roared like bears. Then they extended their index fingers, raised their thumbs and 'shot the traitor'.

Their mother looked at the twins and at the jar of jam, and then she glanced at Sasha. Each was hoping that the other would recover her wits, break the silence and scold the boys: Kolya, Vlada, don't stand at the door like a pair of dolts! Quickly, wash your face and hands and sit up at the table. But all Sasha wanted to do was hug Kolya and stroke his hair—it looked smooth from a distance, but felt like straw when you touched it—and to assure him that he should forget the nonsense Vlada had told him at school and remember that Vlada couldn't cope with his own fears, and that was why he poured them down his brother's throat like medicine.

But she couldn't chastise Vlada now. His expression of terror at a catastrophe he didn't yet understand showed that he had never believed in his own doomsday scenarios. In fact he had prepared Kolya for a nightmare that he didn't think would come true.

Valeria spoke at last, and her voice was so muffled that it seemed to be emerging from the jam jar. 'Children, wash your hands and sit at the table.'

Vlada headed for the stairs and disappeared into the attic. Kolya wandered aimlessly around the house, sliding his fingers along the walls, pressing his face against the window, stroking the books on the wooden shelf, touching the back of the armchair, gaping at their father's charcoal drawing of the moustachioed war hero Chapayev. Andrei was proud that they had met at the front in 1919. The minute they parted he sat on the ground and drew him from memory.

Her mother, still on her feet, looked at the stairs and at Kolya, as though expecting the twins to recover and come to the table. Then she wearily returned to the jars.

Sasha went up to the roof. Rain slashed down, but a warm April breeze lurked in the cold air. The bald black branches of the birches shone silver and above the river the sky was grey up to the horizon. As it darkened in the twilight the horizon was like a gate about to close upon the city.

Some branches at the top of the alder tree knocked against the windows. How many letters of complaint had they sent about that? Kozlov, who worked with her father at the institute, had volunteered to trim them, but her father didn't want to risk it. Suppose someone complained that they were taking liberties with the building, disturbing the neighbours? They would be evicted. 'For two metres of cold floor, a window looking out on a filthy courtyard and a little iron bed, in which a man can lie on me but not next to me, I will marry a horse,' Nadya wrote once, and as a kind of joke she had sent the entire article to the editor of *Izvestia*, Comrade Nikolai Ivanovich Bukharin.

Now Sasha felt exposed on the roof she was so fond of, as if the neighbours' eyes were jabbing her from every side. 'Sometimes,' Emma Rykova had laughed once, 'you have to plan the look you're going to throw at a neighbour who's accused of crimes: the way you look at your neighbour who was a friend can't be the same as the way you look at a neighbour whose face disgusts you, or the look you give a neighbour you slept with behind his wife's back.'

She returned to her room and saw a slip of paper lying on her pillow, with a sentence in Vlada's handwriting: 'Good citizens wear red stockings in the winter.' She was furious: the notes in her sock drawer were a secret between her and Kolya. She went over to the drawer and fossicked for the red stockings. Inside one of them she found a small folded note: 'Hurry up and check whether you can be our mother.'

She silenced the callow impulse to scold Kolya for blabbing. Even with catastrophe in the offing she was still concerned with petty account-keeping. The time had come to leave the world of childhood behind.

At dinner Vlada was lively. He had spoken to the nephew of the head of the Komsomol at the Physical-Technical Institute, a reliable fellow: the party's decision to purge the last remnants of Zinoviev's and Trotsky's Unified Centre was logical. All the sabotage committed by enemies of the people in mines and factories, in industry in general, would soon disappear.

Kolya said that at school someone had told him in secret that, after their parents were arrested, the twins would be expelled and sent to an orphanage.

Vlada snorted and declared that it was nonsense. Comrade Stalin had stated explicitly that children would not be punished for the sins of their parents. Boys weren't guilty if their parents hadn't done what was required of them.

Andrei shook his head as if he didn't believe what he was hearing. Sasha was desperate to see her weakling of a father impose his authority. She imagined him sending Vlada away from the table, caning him, and the boy crumpling beneath his father's rage.

If she got even in her imagination, then her anger would fade: if you surrendered to it, imagination was a perfect god of vengeance. Vlada's black eyes sparkled. She despised his habit of shocking their parents, and understood the remorse that haunted him when he realised that the scars left by his words wouldn't easily heal, his disappointment at learning that there were other people in the world who would read his actions in their own way.

Vlada whispered something in Kolya's ear, looking both conspiratorial and amused. Despite the danger threatening them, Vlada would continue to scare Kolya until that poor boy found it hard to breathe; he would conjure up the dark abyss into which their severed heads would roll before restoring his hopes by describing the crafty moves that would save the day.

The closer Nikolai drew to Sasha, the more bitter Vlada became. His wildness was tinged with cruelty. The previous winter, after he had attacked Kolya one morning and pressed a pillow over his face, pretending to be an NKVD operative, their father had built a plywood barrier between their beds. Each boy was left with a thin strip of space. Vlada had smashed the plywood twice. Once again there was nothing to separate them. Nikolai complained that while he could put up with Vlada's voice at night, he couldn't stand the sight of his face. Their father had brought in Koslov from the institute, who built a barrier out of heavy wood, and screwed it to the wall. He told Vlada that if he broke it he would build a cement wall, like in a prison.

'Vlada, if you don't shut up, I'm going to peel your skin like an onion,' Sasha said, gripping a knife.

'Zaichik, that's completely unnecessary!' Valeria scolded.

Her father smiled at her, but when he realised that her mother had noticed he reverted to looking like some stranger.

'Just try it,' Vlada challenged her and looked at the knife, fascinated. She expected him to answer back again to show that he wasn't easily intimidated and then shut up. Her father dipped a piece of bread in goose fat and offered it to her mother, a trick that sometimes won her heart.

Valeria waited until the performance was over. 'Andreyusha,' she said, 'why don't you play your game with the children?' She was spoiling for a fight, taking pleasure in frustrating Andrei's hope of hearing the usual sentence: 'Andreyusha, you're tired. Why don't you go to sleep?'

Meanwhile Kolya was prattling about the blue sled: every winter they used to decorate it with swirling ornaments like butterflies and trees, but this year they hadn't, and, besides, the cord was almost completely frayed, and they had to get thicker rope.

Suddenly Vlada asked sweetly if she had decided what course she would take at the university. 'This year you and Zhenya are registered together, right?'

Sasha had expected a poisoned arrow of revenge, but the precision of his attack stunned her. No doubt, the boy had a rare talent for identifying other people's weaknesses. Around the table the clink of knives and forks stopped, and Vlada bent over to tie his shoelace. His sharp movements, as if his body were made of something flintier than skin and bone, gave her the creeps. Maybe she was frightened by his perfect control over his body. An image arose in her memory: a father, mother and little girl in front of a building in the university. The father pointed at it. 'Here you will study and study,' he said, 'until you're the smartest woman in the Soviet Union.' And the mother said, 'Like your father.'

You idiot! she wanted to shout at her father. Where was Nadyezhda Petrovna then? At what bend in the road was she waiting for us?

The university hadn't been on her mind in the past few weeks. She knew that no academic institution would accept Weissberg's daughter. There would be no study of history, no physics, perhaps no studies at all. Maybe she could get a job somewhere but that was doubtful. She was desperate to escape the apartment, to see Zhenya, to go to the movies or listen to music. Maybe they'd sit in Café Europa, and then dance in some club full of artists and actors and foreigners, as well as shady fellows who invite you on holiday in the Crimea. This house suddenly seemed rotten to the core; maybe it really did deserve to be obliterated.

Her father said that he had read something interesting in a Jewish history book that day, and before her mother could interrupt him Sasha shouted, 'How silly of me! I made a date for this evening...'

She pushed her chair back defiantly, got up and shook off Kolya's look of betrayal. In her room she changed into her blue dress in a hurry and put on the 'little accessories' that one of Zhenya's boyfriends had bought for them once in Torgsin: a black silk scarf, boots with a tapered heel, decorated with shiny brass buckles, a fur coat. A few minutes later she slipped out the door.

'Mother, I'm meeting with Zhenya. Maybe we'll see some other people. I'll find out whether they're talking about us. I'll be back late.'

Zhenya and Sasha went down the stairs to the basement of what had once been a mansion. The corridor leading to the dance floor was dense and laden with perfume. In one of the rooms leading off it she saw two foreign men with their hair combed back leaning over a billiard table. Zhenya waved at the tall doorman in his grey uniform, and he waved back. She took Sasha's arm, and as they pushed through the crowd she muttered disparaging remarks about the girls who weren't ashamed to be seen here wearing rags. When they reached the doorman, he greeted them, but Zhenya ignored his existence.

Columns topped by arches divided the hall into booths, where large and noisy groups sat. Red wooden stools were scattered next to a stage where a quartet was playing happy dance music.

'Well, you see I wasn't exaggerating,' Zhenya said proudly.

They sat at a table for four. A few young men were sitting in the next booth, and Zhenya boasted that they were from the Ministry of Foreign Trade. Two of them approached and invited the girls for a drink. Zhenya asked for a bottle of Château D'Yquem. The men looked alarmed.

'That sounds really expensive,' Sasha said.

'Don't worry,' Zhenya laughed. 'Kostya has an account here.'

When it arrived, Zhenya kept filling Sasha's glass, chatting away about the delicacy of French wine. 'Drink a lot,' she advised. 'Forget about the bad things.' Then Sasha caught sight of a handsome young man standing by himself against the wall. Zhenya knew him, his name was Alyosha, and he had just come back from a job in the embassy in Japan.

'You want to?' Zhenya suddenly hugged her.

'Now?' Sasha was surprised, but she let Zhenya force her up and drag her over. They stood in front of him, bowed, and together they recited the rhyme they had once written:

A prince with crown
Is needed in town.
Princesses two, with hearts so true,
Let him choose:
One for glory, and for the other: end of story.

Alyosha chose Sasha, and Zhenya withdrew with little steps. 'Eighty-two—seventy-four,' she announced. It was the tenth year of their competition.

The young man led her to the floor. They danced a rumba. He danced nicely, step-slide, step-slide, and they moved together marvellously. In his arms she leaned on his shoulder, her lips floated over his neck and she breathed in the delicate odour of his body. She moistened his skin with the tip of her tongue. 'At the tumultuous ball, I met you by chance,' she said in his ear. Her body leaned into him, and she was already tempted by his slightly pouting lips, when she became aware of a kind of halo of dust around her. Everyone saw it, except for him. He was too close. Her tongue grew dry, her movements grew stiff and heavy, and that lightness of desire, which had bubbled up inside her, vanished. All it would take was for Alyosha to pop into the bathroom, and one of his friends to say, 'That's Alexandra Andreyevna Weissberg. Do you know what her father's been accused of? Don't you read the newspaper?'

Over his shoulder she could see a woman watching them dance.

'That's my wife,' Alyosha said, maybe sadly. She was with two other women, and the three of them whispered to each other. His wife listened and then straightened her body. Her gaze—amused, almost friendly—was fixed on Sasha, translating itself in her imagination: Dance with him, my dear. I'll lend you my husband gladly. But really, just between us, how many dances do you have left?

A strange flame was kindled behind her eyes, as sometimes

happened to her mother. Valeria's behaviour that day now became explicable to her: it was a kind of lament for the dead. As if she had been yearning to shake her husband and shout: Wasn't I worth more?

She realised that she wasn't dancing with Alyosha anymore. She was just hanging on to him, being pulled around. Nearby she saw Grobman from her school, the girl from the theatre who saw to the sets. She heard the nattily dressed fellows from the Ministry of Foreign Trade laughing away—all of them doubtless amazed that she had dared to come here tonight. In desperation she looked for Zhenya among the tunnels of crimson light and found her at last, hiding in the shadows. Zhenya's sympathetic nod was replaced by a tense look. She knew that Sasha needed her, and glanced at Alyosha's wife and her companions as though to find out whether they understood that it was her duty to help her friend. Was she actually asking: Will you permit me to help Weissberg's daughter?

She woke up in her bed with a hangover. She stretched lazily and raised her feet to the wall. A shout of pain came from the twins' room. She listened without moving. Another shout, this time sharper. She wanted to call out: Mother, where are you? Can't you hear them screaming again? But she knew her mother would not answer.

Sasha got out of bed. In the living room she could see her mother was hunched in her father's rocking chair. The shock of the icy floorboards seared her bare feet. She skipped up the stairs and burst into the twins' room. Vlada's small space between the wooden screen and the wall was empty. Kolya was curled up in bed, and Vlada was standing next to him in his school uniform.

'Kolya,' she said.

He didn't answer.

She gave Vlada a threatening look, and he rushed to defend himself. 'He's such a baby. He wants to stay home. I told him we have to go to school today.' A triumphant smile puffed out his pink cheeks. She remembered baby Vlada in her arms as she kissed his cheeks and said,

'Mama, it's unbelievable, they're the colour of peaches.' Later, when he was older and wanted people to think he was grown up, he used to douse his face with cold water to wash away the pinkness.

They both knew he was right. She took a deep breath. Her irritation transferred itself to Kolya, that spoiled little brat who didn't understand the twins had to show up at school today and behave as if nothing had happened.

'Get dressed at once!' she ordered him.

Kolya sat up in bed. She noticed that his face, which his mother used to praise for its 'angelic beauty', was spotted with little pimples.

'Yes, get dressed already, baby! Mama will make you your porridge,' Vlada taunted.

The complacency in his voice sickened her. 'Shut up!' she shouted.

Kolya began to dress. She left the room.

Vlada hurried after her. 'Did you check?' he asked.

'Not yet,' she answered.

Downstairs they could hear footsteps against a background of a sleeper's breathing. They were both silent, horrified by the import of his question.

'We can't talk now,' she told him.

Vlada grabbed her hand. 'In a week or two they won't be here.' She heard the suppressed venom in his voice. 'You have to check whether you can be our mother. Ask your friend from the NKVD. Otherwise we'll end up in an orphanage or in prison.'

She listened to the clink of cups and the running water. Every familiar sound was precious to her now, like her mother's voice, rising and falling. 'Vla-da, Kol-ya, wash your faces and come down. You're late.'

Vlada leaned against the yellowed wallpaper. Sasha gazed at the pattern of crowns on it. She discovered shades of yellow that she hadn't noticed before. 'Do you remember Benoît, the biologist who was Father's friend?' he said. 'He and his wife were exiled to Saratov in 1935, and then sent to a labour camp. Their children were bundled off to an orphanage. There were relatives who wanted to raise them, but they were worried that the children were also under suspicion, and in fact they were.'

He was looking at her. She knew he was beside himself with anxiety. He had always despised her parents' circle, all those 'weakling bourgeois poets, who complain instead of working'. He was convinced that their father hadn't put his soul into the revolution, hadn't appreciated the party's achievements enough, hadn't educated his children in the correct spirit, had thrown his lot in with unhelpful people. Like her, he understood that he and Kolya were in danger because of their father's sins and their mother's habit of turning a blind eye, and he was certain that if they had heeded his warnings none of this would have happened. At last he was being taken seriously, it was a kind of victory, but he might well be sent to an orphanage or a labour camp, and he would have no future in this country.

He was a kind of victor-victim. Sasha trembled and a malicious laugh flickered inside her. She immediately suppressed it, ashamed of her spitefulness. How pitiful she was.

'Children.' Their mother's voice chimed again.

'I'm telling you. You have to find out now!' He loosened his grip on her, as if trying to figure out whether his feckless sister—who had disappeared the past few nights, out partying—understood the extent of her responsibility. 'After all, you love Kolya,' he said and drew away from her.

How humiliating for his fate to depend on his sister, 'the lazy princess of poetry', who was above doing any actual work: she had some job in a library for three months, and had then copied plans in an architect's office, filled in all the application forms—and left. Last year she had decided not to enrol in the university, because she only wanted to study with Zhenya, and had idled away the summer at Varlamov's, earning twenty kopecks a day for supposedly working in the garden.

'Vlada,' their mother called. 'Don't fight in there.'

He turned around and went back into his room.

Sasha's throat tightened. How sorry she was that he had said that last thing. She stood in the kitchen, behind her mother. 'Where's Father?' she asked.

'In bed, imagining that he's a tragic hero lying in Dagestan with a bullet in his chest, like his beloved Lermontov.'

Everything at home was now steeped in sarcasm. She considered getting dressed and hurrying to Podolsky's office, to tell him how they were suffering, but there was no point in that either. In the last few days dear Maxim had gone to ground, and she didn't know how to reach him.

Suddenly she wanted everything to be over, for the punishment to be meted out. They must have been guilty of something, so let the axe fall.

In the afternoon, too, Valeria hounded her husband with chores: she sent him out to line up for bread, then to the seamstress, then to the neighbours to borrow matches. When he came back she mischievously asked him if he wanted to shake out the sheets. He looked exhausted and peeved and mumbled something under his breath. Finally she announced that he could go back to bed.

He took off the old coat with raglan sleeves, padded with thin goatskin, and stroked the lining with his fingers, as if to remember every stain and seam. *Did you tell them?* Sasha wanted to ask. *Did you tell them that the coat was a present from the doctor from the Kikabidze Division? That has to be worth something.* But he left them and lay down on his bed, with his Jewish books around him, which he had secretly obtained, with great difficulty, and whose titles, according to her mother, all sounded exactly the same: *Antiquities of the Jews* (Josephus), *The History of the Jews from Jesus Christ to the Present Time* (Jacques Basnage), *The History of the Israelites from the Maccabees to the Present Day* (Isaak Markus Jost), *The History of the Jews* (Heinrich Graetz).

'Half a year ago he couldn't remember that he was Jewish,' her mother sneered when he reached the bedroom, 'and now he's full of Jewish history, including in French, though he can barely read it, even with a dictionary. Maybe in five years he'll get to the Present Time. Suddenly he's full of the bondage of Egypt, the Babylonian Exile, the expulsion of the Jews from England, France and Spain. He won't let up—Kishinev, the Black Hundreds, Petliura, Dreyfus, Beilis—cowards like him become true believers in God in seconds. Apparently he understands that his stories about the Civil War, where he served on all fronts and met all the heroes at the same time, don't interest the NKVD at all. Now, according to him, he's not guilty of anything. It's his Jewish destiny, always ending in catastrophe, that's the culprit.'

She mercilessly poked fun at her husband, not because she wanted to get even with him, but because she hoped to expunge him from her soul. She was rebelling against his idiosyncrasies as if she was only just now aware of them.

Sasha had more important things to discuss with her, such as how to protect the twins, but her mother just said, 'Not now, Zaichik,' and found another urgent chore to do.

It was one of Valeria's talents: to bury certain subjects, whole periods of her life, in some recessive part of her mind. For years she had hidden her husband and Nadya there, and now, too, she managed to deny the simplest facts. How did she do it? After all, the boys walked past her, spoke and breathed, roamed around the only house they knew, and yet their mother would not broach any discussion of their fate.

Sasha realised that Vlada was the only one she could talk to.

...

The last weekend in March.

Sasha lay in her bed as though in a coffin. She alone remained in the house.

Trains departed from Leningrad, who knew where to, and on them the bodies that once filled this house. Nightmares stalked her sleep, and in her waking hours she was feverish with memories and guilt. Sometimes a single reproach broke through, in Nadya's hoarse voice: *Was it you, you cursed girl, did you bring this disaster down on us?*

Although, when her father returned from the first interrogation and told them that they had asked him less about Nadya than about the Physical-Technical Institute—eight of whose ten directors had been arrested—and about the United Centre, she still believed that if she hadn't given the poems to Podolsky their fate would have been different.

Outside—the noise of the city. There was no choice but to hear it. 'Through bloodstained panes sometimes it is hard to see Europe,' wrote an anonymous author in an article called 'Letter of Complaint to Comrade Pushkin', but she had no expectations that her family would become a landmark on this city's map of grief. After all, there were people more eminent and courageous. But she constantly heard the bustling city and was tormented by the ease with which it had shaken them off. She dreamed she was standing at the foot of a high chair in which Barabash, the owner of the German hair salon, was sitting, dressed in an elegant suit because to her surprise he was now the head of an important institution. *Barabash,* she complained, *didn't Father help them plan the Magnitostroy Steel Plant in the Urals? Didn't he refuse their request to manage the nitrogen plant in Gorlovka? And didn't he also tell us that Leningrad was the only city for us?*

Can't you help us?

She had always been the negotiator: Mother, I'll be back late, not now, Kolya, maybe later, girl, don't get out of the bathtub with only a towel, Zaichik, where were you? Come back by dinnertime.

Now inside the house everything was silent. Enfolded in the sheets, which had absorbed her perspiration and the oil from her hair, she searched for traces of Kolya: the scent of her father's cologne that he used to borrow, the smell of his hair. Her fingers groped around the bed, pursuing him. She discovered the hollow made by his sharp elbow, until she realised it wasn't anything left by his body, but rather traces of her own.

Her imagination tickled his smooth skin. Like touching silk, yes?

Her mother chuckled. She was sitting up straight in the living room, watching them through the walls.

Am I doing something wrong? He isn't really fifteen, is he? It's like

sleeping with a child. If he was eight, it would be fine, wouldn't it, Mother?
All the memories and images came to rest for a moment, and the contact she felt with him faded from her body. There was nothing now between the expanse of skin that still gave itself over to the caress of her fingers and his total absence. The talons of loss dug into her body.

There was no air. She gasped for breath in the darkness. Another breath and another. *Do you really want to get away from here? What life does the future offer you?*

Disgusted with her own cowardice, she threw off the sheet, spread-eagled, and sucked in the cold air. She prayed that her mind would be silent, but it immediately kicked up a din again, creating a chaos of memories. In the archive of her mind their nights were already forming an epoch.

On Monday her parents had been summoned to another interrogation. All week long they had been sifting through their life histories, indeed not so much sifting through them as packing them up. Sasha was in bed again, guessing that it was evening. She, too, was sifting through her life history.

Father and Kolya were busy. They were sitting at the desk, and Andrei was dictating a letter to him addressed to the Supreme Economic Council. Better for it to be written by hand than typed. Father blushed while talking up his loyalty to the party and his own worthy qualities, pouring out information about innovations he had introduced at the institute.

Vlada was standing by the window. He had recommended that Kolya write the letter, because his handwriting was rounded and feminine and touched the heart, and they needed some heart in Moscow to be touched a little bit. But when he noticed Kolya's self-satisfaction and his boastful voice, like the voice of a minor official who has become privy to a secret, his expression darkened.

Near the cupboard Mother was sorting old papers, and she said to

Sasha that the matter was closed, the verdict had been signed. Father ought to have accepted their offer to manage the factories in Gorlovka but now it was too late. Sasha wondered how much sincerity was in this surrender to fate. Maybe Mother could not believe that what had happened to other people would happen to them. For they weren't exactly like the others, were they? Their circumstances were so different; many events that took place here couldn't have happened anywhere else, or to other people, so it wasn't conceivable that soon they wouldn't be here.

At dinner her father cheerfully observed that maybe the letter would still help. In the books of Jewish wisdom it was written: 'There is no weed that doesn't have a star in heaven.'

'So now you've become a believer in God,' Vlada muttered.

As though he'd been waiting for the opportunity, her father hurriedly explained the flaw in Jost's book, how it ignored the Jewish people during the biblical period and jumped directly to the Hasmonean era.

After dinner Sasha slipped out again.

'Don't you dare,' Valeria said, 'your little brother is begging you to stay.'

Vlada looked at her with indifference mingled with a hint of triumph. His suspicions were confirmed: it was futile to expect anything from their frivolous sister.

There is no suffocating person who can't find a party somewhere, she joked to herself. She floated out and fell into the street and the refreshing chill. She slipped on the ice and buried her face in the snow. A fleeting moment of purification.

She and Zhenya passed the time in Kostya's house. Kostya was Zhenya's boyfriend, a guy who had avoided the army and hadn't been arrested, a true magician, Zhenya gushed, a black-market-and-dance-bar type, expensive restaurants, played billiards all day long and made a fortune. He also had good wine. They drank, giggled and danced in the middle of the room. He clung to them from the back, embracing them both. His fingers pinched their hips, they pushed them away, he lectured them: Comrade girls, be less individualistic, more cooperative, learn how to fuck in groups. Sasha kissed him. He invaded the gap between her and Zhenya, slipped under her sweater and undershirt, kissed her navel. His tongue was hot. She stretched, and his tongue slipped down her belly, she stifled a moan, heard her breath.

The heat disappeared. She saw his head moving under Zhenya's sweater. She stood neglected in the middle of the room and felt the place where his saliva was drying on her skin.

Zhenya said to her secretly that in her opinion he had a death wish: they killed his father, maybe he wanted to die. He had foreign currency and bought clothes for the women he liked in Torgsin. He frequented the famous nightclubs in Moscow: Metropol, National, Savoy, with artists and theatre directors and architects.

Then he said, 'Nadyezhda Petrovna? I've never heard of that poet. The only Nadyezhda Petrovna who interests me lives in Moscow, and she sews the best dresses in Russia.'

Sasha was amused. 'It's wonderful that you know such special people,' she said.

Now she lay on the sofa next to Zhenya's boyfriend. She rested her head on his belly. He leaned towards her, lifted her head and brought his tongue to her lips. His hand groped under her skirt. 'How many guys have you been with already?' He blew warm air into her ear.

She ignored his question. She had kissed a few boys, and also Osip Levayev, but she had only slept with Podolsky. Pleasure spread through her when his hand slipped between her legs, and two of his fingers touched her. He moved them delicately, arousing desire in her for full, strong contact. She led him to lie on her, but Zhenya was complaining: she wanted to go home and wouldn't leave her alone with the boy. He got up. At once Sasha was assailed by all the worries that had disappeared for the past few minutes.

At the door the guy hugged her and whispered some lines from Pushkin:

A comrade's broken words on leaving,
His hail of parting at the door:
Your chant of luring, chant of grieving
Will murmur in my ears no more.*

Zhenya said he was too theatrical. Then he gave them parting gifts: pickled herring for Zhenya, smoked bacon for Sasha.

She returned home towards morning. Her father was sifting through letters in a box. 'Did you have a good time?'

'Yes, really lovely.'

Her mother scolded: How dare she go out at night? Where did she bury her shame and her heart? But now her father was being sympathetic. Fondness for him burbled within her. She hadn't thought a lot about what he had lost, maybe because it was all so predictable, and now she remembered how one day, after he was fired, he started waxing lyrical about the new windows in the institute that had expelled him. He had absolute loyalty to whatever touched his soul, whether it was the institute or Nadyezhda Petrovna; they remained as exalted in his eyes as on the day they first enchanted him.

'Pay no attention to Mother's shouting,' he said. 'She's suffering a lot. Envy of the young poisons the blood.'

No doubt he got a cheap thrill from this coward's revenge. She used to think that if disaster ever struck them their loyalty and love would be on show, but now, as the days passed, aside from isolated flashes of compassion, each of them was being devoured by fear and blamed the other.

'Father, why are you up at this hour?'

'I'm thinking about the story of my life.'

She heard a foghorn on the Neva, Vera's children singing, their voices bursting with life. Soot drifted through the shutters. Her nightgown

---

* Alexander Pushkin, 'To the Sea', trans. Babette Deutsch.

was as damp and filthy as a rag. Faint pain swirled in her belly, passed, maybe hunger. She swallowed some bitter saliva and then dampened her dry lips with spit. She was half-awake, and that's when the memories piled up.

She's walking up stairs strewn with cabbage leaves and cucumber peels: Grandfather's roomy parlour is crammed with faded velvet furniture, and four giant mirrors extend almost to the ceiling, hanging at an angle as though bowing to the room. They cast multiple reflections, distorted, upside down, until one day Vlada broke one of them, and after that the parlour lost its charm. Narrow alleys are visible from the window, crammed with little workshops, the smell of tar, tinsmiths and cobblers. Grandfather looks at them and plucks at his beard. Those new arrivals, they've stolen my view. After the Bolsheviks stole power, rats appeared here, disguised as human beings, and they're taking over the street. Lots of Jews, he casts a look at her father, thugs from Voronezh, and from villages of illiterates where no trains stop. I'm telling you: in the streets, right down there, the blood of heroes and saints didn't flow just so that all sorts of Chukhonets could sneak in here and make every last trace of our Saint Petersburg disappear.

Her father says nothing. Grandfather mocks him as the *intelligent* while Andrei calls him the 'murderer from the Okhranka'. Grandfather is actually proud of his twenty years' service in the Czar's secret police. He tells Sasha, 'We took good care of Communist *intelligents* like your father. But to my regret we underestimated them.'

When they leave, Grandfather always rumples Vlada's hair, calls him the enthusiastic Young Pioneer, and explains how gullible the boy is for believing all the Bolshevik tales that his father and schoolteachers and the newspapers tell him. Once, as they were leaving, her father had muttered, 'Your grandfather makes me grow fond of the Chekists.'

Sasha and Maxim Podolsky are strolling down the street. It's a summer night, late, around one o'clock. There's a light breeze, their sleeves are bare. Maxim says that he heard from his father, who had heard from someone high up, that after Kirov's death the people in Moscow had decided to deal with Leningrad—the eternal stronghold of bluster, revolt and opposition—with a firm hand.

Maxim hugs her. 'We have hard days before us, Sasha.'

She shook off the blankets. Dust began to filter into her eyes. She closed them, but the tears came anyway. Neighbours had gathered in her room. One of them was holding a lamp. In its light a layer of dust and soot was visible on her body.

'Impossible to remove it,' they shouted, 'all the dust and soot of Leningrad has stuck to you. You'll have to scrape it off. Sorry, we don't have the right tools.'

'Can't you buy them?' she begged. 'There are stores downstairs. Mother will pay you back.'

The last dinner. Mother drinks coffee and Benedictine liqueur and in a cackling voice imitates Reznikov, the interrogator: 'Look, Comrade Weissberg, it sometimes happens that a person wrongs his friend. There are all sorts of reasons for that…Perhaps you aren't really an enemy of the people. Maybe you were just associated with real enemies who influenced you!' The twins laugh and plunge their forks into the pork chops. 'And if a person confesses, then his friend can forgive him. Their friendship will be rehabilitated, and they will be even better friends than they were. But a complete confession is needed…Stay home for a few days and contemplate the history of your life.'

An hour passes. Father and the twins are playing at riddles: Father asks what temperature all sorts of things melt at, and the twins guess. Sasha is getting dressed in her room. She's listening to their game, which is being played as if nothing is wrong. Fine, she has no time to be sad now. You don't sob after you've put on make-up.

Summer in Varlamov's garden. Nadyezhda is reciting a few sentences from an article she's writing in response to Ostrovsky's book: How was the steel tempered? you ask. I'll tell you: by means of oceans of shitty factory literature, the biggest load of garbage since the journals of Genghis Khan. Monkeys are now more advanced than we are. Russia is full of books, petitions and articles by mosquitoes constantly shrieking: Execute the traitors, liquidate the dogs. And our new history? One huge lie. 'Stalin carried out Lenin's instructions and led the Bolshevik brigades,' they write. Or 'Stalin in the war against the Whites in Tsaritsyn, in Rostov.' Or 'Stalin Defeated Denikin.' It's all Stalin. We'll have to rebuild Russian culture from scratch.

Silence, cherries being savoured, Varlamov coughs. Nadyezhda is aching for a response, yearning for affection. History is so boring, she says, and moves on to discuss insomnia: Everyone here is insomniac— the black cars, the bright nights, the foghorns, the smoke and the soot from the factories. They all join in and offer examples of their own: the summer dust, the autumn winds that pierce your bones, you're always in some damned whirlpool. And Nadyezhda again: When sleep comes at last, you glide in European dreams—Paris, Rome, Berlin— and then lightning whips you awake: your fate is here.

Evening. Vlada is cutting a cucumber, slicing bread; he's found some sausage, too.

Don't expect that Mother and Father will come back soon! he says. They'll get a few years in a gulag. The sabotage at the institute is even worse than what Pyatakov planned, apparently because of the involvement of the fascists. For quite a while I've been saying that the alliance between traitors and fascist infiltrators is going to set us back many years.

No one answers.

It's clear that Father isn't involved in the matter. He just happened to be in the firing line. Some piece of filth apparently told stories about him.

No one answers. It's odd that they still haven't searched the house. He looks at Sasha suspiciously. They always do a search when they arrest you, or right afterwards. Anyway there's nothing here. I checked. Mother and Father had enough time to prepare. They even got rid of the book by Balmont.

Kolya is sitting by her side. She's tired of consoling him. She hugged him all day long.

It's four-six-eight-ten o'clock.

Their parents didn't come back from the interrogation. She clings to the hope that Podolsky can tell her something about their fate, but for two weeks now he hasn't been around. At night, she imagines his severed head rolling on one of the bridges over the Neva.

She is aware of the weight of time, of all those seconds and minutes until supper, until sleep. If Kolya doesn't fall asleep soon, she will lose her mind. She's petrified by the thought that tomorrow a long day will dawn, with so many hours and minutes and seconds.

A door slams, she wakes up, it's late. The fourth night without Father and Mother. She is starting to accept that every time she wakes up she will remember the fact of their absence. To her relief she's alone in bed. A silhouette near the door.

Brodsky's house burned down; Seryozha and I helped them put out the fire. Vlada's tone of voice is light and sweetish.

Was everything burned?

It was a big fire. It probably had something to do with candles. You know how absent-minded he is, all day long with his nose in books.

Is he all right?

Trembling like a rabbit, but all right. I told him that in a little while our house would be vacated, that he should get ready to break in. If we're doomed to lose the house, at least we'd have the consolation of knowing it had fallen into the hands of a loyal friend like him.

The last morning. Vlada tells more stories about the fire in Brodsky's house, about the smoke that hid the stars and the moon. Sasha cooks porridge for Kolya and makes a jam sandwich for Vlada. How could she have been so complacent?

Five in the afternoon. *They haven't come home.* She races to the school. The headmaster receives her in the hallway, makes sure that a few teachers witness the meeting. He says that two NKVD men were waiting for the twins with warrants, and seated them in a car. They didn't say where they were taking them. He assumes that, as in earlier cases, they will be sent to an institution for boys whose parents have been arrested. He has no doubt that the matter will be resolved in the best possible way, because it is impossible to leave boys without a supervising adult.

Perhaps she says, Thank you, Headmaster.

A few hours later she woke up in bed.

How many days had she been there? She stretched her muscles, wondering whether to get up, and her limbs protested: Now you want to move? She stayed in bed. How many days had she been there? Night-morning, night-morning, maybe another two days. She heard steps. She recognised them: they were his steps. A light turned on in the hallway. She wanted to move but couldn't. Now he was standing there. His body filled the doorway, pushed the light back. Her gaze rose, trying to take all of him in, and she couldn't.

His shoulders supported his neck like two bricks, his hair was twined with cobwebs that hung from the ceiling. His movement towards her was enormous, swallowing the small room. You! she wanted to shout, Maxim Adamovich Podolsky, I know you, stop looking so different!

She closed her eyes and opened them, he was standing above her. 'You finally remembered to do a search?' she asked. Her lips stung and her throat was hoarse.

'Do you remember the play we saw at the end of eighth grade?' He sounded excited, as if he'd been waiting for this moment for a long time.

Suddenly she was filled with happiness. If he had come to announce that her parents were dead, he wouldn't have mentioned any plays, and he wouldn't fool around with parables.

She gained strength. I don't remember, she wanted to say. You and I, we're always sweeping up memories and putting them in piles.

He sat on the bed. He was holding a cup in his right hand. He dipped his fingers in the water and moistened her lips. Then he supported her back, and with a delicate movement he helped her drink: a sip, a pause, a sip, a pause.

'Ismene was right,' he said. 'It's foolish to exceed your ability. You aren't powerful enough to oppose the will of the people.'

The city wafted from his body: crisp bread and cooking oil and tar, the saltiness of the wind, the sweat of a street bustling with people, a wet leather coat. Hunger went wild inside her, and she imagined bread with goose fat and her grandmother's meatballs.

'And you, Sasha, have only two choices: Die or become another person.'

PART TWO
THE ARTIFICIAL MAN

LENINGRAD
AUTUMN 1939

The sound of someone breathing: Sasha heard him grunt, exhaling his dreams. She once tried to stay awake the whole night just to throw open a window onto his dreams. In their June nights, when they were sixteen, a dazzling light poured into the city, whitening the stone bridges, stirred in the currents of the river. Midnight, and the strange feeling of a city not sleeping but fainting. They lay in parks or under bridges or even on roofs, exchanging the same secrets, pretending they had never heard them before, guessing at what window a face might appear only to recoil at a cruel blow of light. Sometimes after a few kisses, before they had done anything, he would fall asleep. He was one of those people who went to sleep as soon as they lay down, no matter where. He hid in the mystery of sleep, and she negotiated with his body: pinched his arm, whispered to him, tried to guess his dreams. His imagination flew off to distant realms while his body clung to hers, yearning for her warmth. Are you your body? The question stayed with her.

Now he was sighing. His right hand tunnelled under her back to link up with his left, which lay across her stomach. She never understood how he managed to do it—she resisted and pressed her back against the mattress, and he had to struggle against her. It amused her to see a person show such determination even in sleep.

His manoeuvre ended with victory. His arms tightened around her, his stomach was pressed to her hips, his lips on her neck. Now he'd encircled her. Even in winter he slept half-naked, and his nakedness demanded that her body defend him against the cold. Sometimes she was put off and drew away, and would then run her fingers with pleasure over his goosebumps. Sometimes it got so cold that she imagined there were no walls, only the dark trees that swayed in the wild nights and shook off clumps of snow.

How simple relations were with a sleeping body. You could erase all trace of your actions as if nothing had happened. In childhood she used to dream she was wandering in a world that had gone to sleep and she could do whatever she liked. She turned beggars into kings, and cut noblemen down to size, but she always knew she had to put things back the way they were before everyone woke up. She told Nadya about that dream, and Nadya snapped at her, 'Girl, don't you dare even in your dreams to make a mess?'

The illumination of the room in the dawn light gave her the strange sensation that it was orchestrated against her in particular. She tried to convince herself that she was in charge now, and had arranged the furniture in their new apartment to her satisfaction, but with every glance her eyes sought traces of the house that was lost. At least twice a week she woke in the middle of the night with anguish crouched on her windpipe. She would wander through the apartment, groping for the familiar hallway, the living room, the sofa next to the window until she stopped before the absent mirror. She would realise that it wasn't Kolya lying in her bed, and in the living room, between two bookcases, there was no black piano with paint peeling from its legs. Resist it as she might, she came to the realisation that the only thing left to her now was loss. What kind of person would she be without it?

The minutes passed. Their room brightened. The picture hanging opposite the bed—a reproduction of Surikov's 'Morning of the Execution of the Streltsy'—was the first thing to emerge. Sasha and Maxim had both liked that painting ever since they were in school. Once a week the members of Maxim's class used to act out the execution, piling up old wooden beams to look like the platform in the picture. Podolsky sometimes played the judge and sometimes the hangman. The judge would announce the verdict to a chorus of cheers, and the children would crowd around in tight circles. Girls weren't allowed to squeeze to the front—except for her, of course. Two boys would snatch the trembling little boy whose turn had come, and the hangman would tighten the noose around his neck until the victim coughed.

The reproduction was their first joint purchase. They laughed when they hung it up, and they laughed when, for just one day, they stole a cartoon version of it that Podolsky had found during a search of some provocateur's lair, and stuck it on their bathroom door: Stalin and his entourage taking pleasure in piling up frozen corpses. They enjoyed tired old jokes from the days when Yezhov ran the NKVD:

A breathless elephant turns up at the border checkpoint. 'I have to escape from here,' he begs the guards.

'Why?' they ask in surprise.

'Come on! Didn't you hear the NKVD is purging Russia of sheep?'

'But you're an elephant.'

'Go tell that to Yezhov.'

How did the dawn rise in her window? First in secret, as though lazily climbing the walls, until in one swoop it swallowed the night. Then Maxim awoke. He yawned. His white tongue looped out like a dog's, he stretched his arms, and his chest expanded. She rushed to the silver-plated samovar in the kitchen to boil water, and sat at the wooden table, which was painted a happy orange. At her side was another chair. She heard the water bubbling in the samovar, 'A Wedding Present to the Young Couple', that they received from Stepan Kristoforovich and the comrades from the second department. Soon the whistle would blow, and the four little legs would tremble. Sometimes they scuttled a full six inches before the water boiled. She got up, brewed tea, filled two cups and sat down again. In the bedroom bare feet shuffled, then she could hear running water, and the sound of the razor blade against skin, which always gave her the chills, and in a few minutes the tapping of shoes. She sipped the tea and gazed down the corridor. Now her husband appeared, washed, dressed and perfumed. He sat down next to her, and gave her a fond smile that seemed significant. Sometimes she imagined that his ginger sideburns were shaped like smiling lips.

'Good morning, dear,' he called.

He liked the morning. He always woke up ready to take the world by storm. But then the passing hours wore him out: the new day never met his expectations, and in the evening he crawled home weary and brooding. And she? She hated the morning. It was clear to her that she wouldn't make it through the new day safely. She needed at least an hour to wake up in silent preparation for what was to come. After that her anxiety faded, and she felt stronger, and when evening came she felt like putting on her prettiest dress and strolling arm in arm with Maxim, attracting admiring gazes: a tall, handsome young couple, people always said.

Her husband stuck a cube of sugar in his mouth and sucked on it. Sometimes the first noise that tickled her ears in the morning was the sound of that sucking. In the first week in their new apartment, she used to turn on the radio while he was sucking the sugar. One morning the announcer quoted a speech by Stalin from 1935: 'Life is getting better, comrades, life is getting merrier.' Strange how sad those words made her feel. Afterwards she decided to get used to the sucking.

He looked at her and slurped his tea. It dripped from his stylish moustache—a project now two months old. That was a sign for her to head for the bathroom, to wash in cold water, put on a faded skirt and a yellowish buttoned blouse, and tie her hair in a single braid. She wore no make-up except for a pale strip of red lipstick. 'Comrade Weissberg, you must not look too pretty at work,' Stepan Kristoforovich

Merkalov, the head of the department, had instructed her.

Now it was a quarter past nine. Four short blasts of a car's horn were heard from the street. 'A lot of honking this morning, Stepan Kristoforovich,' Maxim growled. He was the only one in the office who insisted on calling him by his name and patronym. Everyone else called him by his nickname, Styopa. Each morning that honking made Maxim frown, the first sign that today wouldn't be any different from any other day.

'Almost ready,' she said and hurried to the bedroom, stuck her pocketbook and a few files under her arm, and stepped out the door. She rushed down the stairs, waving goodbye to a boy who was sitting there, looking all dressed up and sour. He was holding a package wrapped with colourful ribbons. 'A present for your teacher?' she asked. He didn't answer. A good spanking wouldn't harm that child.

The black car was waiting for her at the end of the tunnel that connected the building to the street. Every morning, when it parked there, other tenants were forced to squeeze between it and the wall to get outside. Of course no one complained. She always wondered whether Styopa even saw those people.

'Good morning to the chief editor of the NKVD publishing house in Leningrad,' her boss called out gaily. This was his constant line. Now it was her turn, as in an orchestra. 'The best life stories that will never see the light of day,' she recited.

Styopa smiled. Even after four months he was still entertained by his fake description of her position.

From the window of their fourth-floor apartment Maxim watched the car. The department head's new custom of picking Sasha up every morning didn't please him. It was better to keep a distance from your superiors. Otherwise you got friendly with them, and friends always quarrelled, and that could lead to unnecessary trouble. But Sasha and Maxim both understood that that wasn't the issue. Maxim Podolsky, the man who restored Sasha from the dead, as he claimed, was forced to accept a new patron, a department head no less, who used to pat Maxim's shoulder with infinite condescension. 'Young Comrade

Podolsky,' he would say, 'they're very pleased with your work up there.'

'Comrade Weissberg, you look tired,' said Styopa. 'Had a hard night?' He winked.

'I'm fine, Comrade Merkalov,' said Sasha.

'Very well.' Styopa stretched in his seat. 'Now listen to a funny story: Reznikov calls me yesterday and says, "Punin? This is the NKVD. Please report to our office tomorrow morning at 11 a.m., room 229, the pass will be ready at the gate." And I say to him, with the pathetic stammer of the poor soul who suddenly understands that we're on his tail, "Sir, Comrade NKVD, I'm a decent and loyal citizen. I've never done anything. Decent and also loyal…Besides, tomorrow my daughter Natalia is getting married." And our darling Reznikov gets furious and shouts, "We'll see how loyal you are. As far as I'm concerned, your mother could get buried twice tomorrow," and he slams down the receiver.

'Then I call Reznikov, and I say to him, "This is the head of the department. First, you have to learn how to speak more politely to citizens." He realises that he called me by mistake, and he starts panting like a dog chasing a train. "Second," I ask him, "does Punin have any daughters?" He's quiet for a moment. "Yes…two," he mumbles. "And what are their names?" "Eva and Yelena." "So there's no Natalia? Not only did you mismanage the matter of the daughters, Comrade Reznikov, but according to the protocols you're supposed to identify yourself by name. We don't want citizens to see us as something inhuman. And to bury Punin's mother twice, even though he hasn't admitted anything yet?"'

He laughed and pounded the seat with his fist. The driver let out a snort of laughter. Sasha looked at Styopa with gratitude, feeling her body warm up at Reznikov's humiliation.

Every morning the department head regaled them with amusing stories inspired by mishaps—letters, minutes, orders and misdirected telephone calls, innocuous errors made by his subordinates. But when a mistake involved senior people, Styopa crawled through the rooms of the department clutching a pile of crumpled papers, cursing under his breath.

Stepan Kristoforovich was a hefty fellow who was light on his feet. But his bloodshot face always made him look sickly. He was a polite, pleasant man to share a joke with or trade gossip, but some people misread him. If, for example, he started to pat his shirt down, or to take an interest in the furniture, this was a sign he had lost interest in you, and you'd better clear out. He held a grudge against people who didn't take the hint, and the grudge might last for months, until he got even with them. In general nothing faded in Stepan Kristoforovich's world, which was why he never saw fit to respond to his subordinates' requests or to sort out their disputes. His greatest talent, so he claimed, was putting time to work, to harness the advantages that could be drawn from its passage, to understand how the curve of its usefulness rose, and then fell—and to act only after its advantages had been entirely exhausted. 'And that, young Comrade Weissberg,' he always said, 'is something that, unfortunately, cannot be learned. It's the holy trinity: intuition; principles that you never abandon; and friends who would inform on you only at the last.' In the office people said he was loyal to his subordinates, and also one of the most accomplished liars in the history of the *bolshoi dom*; he could talk your mother into swearing she was a virgin.

Masses of yellow, red and brown leaves swirled around the car, like swarming bees. She and the twins had loved to stand in the summer gardens at the end of October, Kolya wrapped in layers of clothing and Vlada in his officer's coat, surrounded only by trees, with no people, no houses, no sky, and the cold autumn wind would strengthen, and the three of them would spread their arms and abandon their bodies to the circling flurries of leaves. How lovely it was to hear the world when it was hidden behind clouds of leaves. Sometimes a withered leaf would cling to someone's face, and Kolya would say that leaves like that were frightening, like the fingers of a skeleton. Then they would go wild, running away from the gardens to the bridge. The leaf-skeletons would pursue them, and even the sparrows would be terrified by the onslaught of the leaves. She and Vlada would sprint ahead of Kolya. Vlada would look across as though to say, You see?

We're the same, you and I, he's the one who's different, and he couldn't resist shouting back, 'Run, you crybaby!' And he would look at her again, understanding that the shout had divided them, that he shouldn't have shouted, and she would stop and wait for Kolya, and the sparrows would fly ahead, and the leaves would whirl behind them, and the game would be over.

The car turned onto Liteyny Prospect, and Styopa patted his belly, which had grown rounder in the past months. He blamed the meat his wife served him. The driver said something and pulled up across from a building whose ground floor looked like the wall of a red fortress. The enormous doors between granite pillars no longer impressed Sasha, and now seemed to her like a stage set. They walked through the lobby, past two columns faced with black marble—there was an identical lobby on every floor—and on the wall to the right fluttered leaflets, posters and announcements. Styopa skipped up the stairs, his back straight, his arms held aloft, and she followed him. White light shone from his office: there was a window opposite the door beside a large wooden filing cabinet; in the middle was a wide table covered with a coloured cloth sporting birds and butterflies; and two more cabinets flanked a door in the western wall.

'Reznikov wants to paint the cabinets red,' Styopa said in a dismissive voice. Once again she had missed the opportunity to ask whether he had found out why her fourth letter to the district council had not been answered either. She hadn't forgotten the severe look he gave her the last time she asked him about the twins. It was clear that he would rather she didn't mention the subject again. Not long ago she had heard, actually from Reznikov, that the twins had been transferred to a labour camp in the north. But Maxim claimed there was an orphanage in Moscow that took in all the children from Leningrad whose parents had been punished. She didn't believe either of them.

Styopa examined her, but his eyes lacked that cruel spark of admiration that calmed her every other morning. Had she disappointed him somehow? Her memory surveyed a jumble of recent events—everything seemed the same. She wasn't endowed with the particular talent that men have, Maxim or Reznikov or Styopa, to pilot their memory deftly among hundreds of incidents. If you say D, they immediately answer: Dubnov, 1934, plotted to deceive the public regarding the achievements of collectivisation; Professor Dubrovin, 1936, incited students inspired by the Unified Centre; Dibenko, 1937, plotted with the Japanese to take over the Far East, spied for England, delivered gold to enemy agents. Dibenko was a busy man.

'Styopa, is everything okay?' she couldn't resist asking, even as she retreated.

'Everything is absolutely fine, Weissberg,' he answered in an impersonal tone and sat down. He placed an elbow on the desk while removing a pile of papers from the drawer with his other hand. She looked at the wall behind him: a silver-plated display of a knight's sword shone there, and next to it two rusty sabres and an old helmet that one of his relatives had worn fighting the White Army. Above them were a picture of Stalin and a handsome portrait of Sergei Kirov. She liked the portrait of Kirov. In the parades of Pioneer Girls she had always insisted on carrying it. You stood on your tiptoes, stretched your arms till they hurt and lifted Kirov high.

She went out to the broad corridor where grey walls were covered by wooden panels, and through the window looked at the choppy little waves that licked the banks of the Neva. Far off, between clouds, peeked the narrow, gilded spire of the fortress. As usual, very few people were in the street, and that always seemed strange to her—as if they were scattered over the city, miniature ants among giant bridges, magnificent buildings with their broad facades, rearing statues, banners fluttering from high windows. Grandfather once said that this city was the product of a hallucination imposed on the swamps, on serfs and on wealthy officials who were forced to live in it or at least to buy a house here. 'It wasn't built for the Russians, but as a gesture to their dreams.'

In her office, she looked at her watch. It was ten already, and at least a dozen files were piled on her desk. She had planned to discuss some recent confessions with Styopa towards the end of the day, to impress him with her thoroughness, and to give her the chance to ask if he could speak with his friends in the Obkom. Not to intercede on behalf of the twins, just to find out where they were. She stroked the dossier on top of the pile. Every morning, seeing the pile, she would feel weak, as if her brain couldn't contain so many life stories with their infinite details. A familiar feeling, like standing in her parents' library, terrified by all those books and characters and events that she had to cram into her memory. As she grew older, she had learned how to contain her dread of an endless profusion of things. In her heart she knew that no one could do this work better than she.

The files had been her only reading matter in the past few months. Morning and evening she read the accounts of the investigative magistrates describing the interrogations. The accused always signed the protocols, most of which were horribly confused, full of accusations of different sorts—cosmopolitanism, provocation, membership of a Western spy ring, sabotage of factories. In the NKVD headquarters of Leningrad they loved the accusation of loyalty to the Unified Centre of Trotsky and Zinoviev.

But the accused confessed, and a few pages later denied everything. They gave fantastic descriptions of places where they had never been and of people they had never met, and linked events that were decades apart. Recently Styopa had received a warning letter from Moscow: out of 150 confessions he had conveyed to them, an audit had shown that thirty-two were flawed. The most embarrassing mistake to provoke a reprimand, according to Styopa, concerned the confession of a certain Holtzman, who admitted he met Trotsky's son in 1932 at the Bristol Hotel in Copenhagen, and was ordered to commit acts of sabotage and terror. Not until they were about to include this man in the show trial of Zinoviev's and Kamenev's gang did Vishinksy, the prosecutor, discover that the hotel was destroyed by fire in 1917.

Maxim told her that this had happened while Styopa was working in Moscow, and that in fact Holtzman had testified at the trial, and the terrible error had been revealed by a newspaper in Denmark—a humiliating blow to the USSR in the eyes of the world, which had allowed Trotsky, that rotten bastard, to celebrate a small victory. Maxim also said that you could infer from the letter that certain people remembered Stepan Kristoforovich's failure. 'It's not possible that Holtzman consciously lied to mock us, because we broke him completely,' Styopa had complained at their first meeting, when he explained the job to Sasha. 'Maybe he made a mistake because of the pressure he was under, and the conditions in prison. In general, a person doesn't remember everything. No one remembers which day he drank too much and chattered idly against the party, or even the name of the woman he screwed behind his wife's back. Not everyone has a lover who is also a poet much admired in dubious circles, wouldn't you agree, Alexandra Andreyevna?'

After hearing that sentence, she decided to like him—there was no choice—for his sincerity and humour and desire to provoke.

Styopa had created her job to help deflect criticism. The idea popped into his mind when he read her application to work in the department. In it she reviewed her own history and condemned her parents and the circles of decadent bourgeois intelligentsia in which they moved, whose members, to her regret, 'saw every single subject from their own particular point of view'. Styopa thought it was the most perfect auto-biography he had ever read: sincere, organised, correct, connecting awareness of her errors to 'the reshaping of consciousness' with an artistic touch. He knew that he needed an assistant like her, someone who could edit the protocols to put together a complete, coherent and convincing story, who could then meet with the accused to produce the most precise confession. Because 'imprecise details are liable to do an injustice to the accused who wants to confess with sincerity and submit to rehabilitation'. The job of the investigative magistrate was to identify with the accused's intellect, Styopa explained, but hers was to identify with his tormented soul, to help him purge his story of flaws, evasions and non sequiturs, so that he, too, could see the picture of his life as a whole. 'An accused who writes a confession is a kind of author, and every author needs an editor, Weissberg, don't you agree?'

Should she delay the interrogation until tomorrow? She'd been putting off the meeting for two weeks. The previous evening Maxim said to her, 'You're afraid, because he's the last one.' Indeed, Vladimir Morozovsky was the only one of her parents' friends not yet dispatched to a gulag somewhere. Did she want to prolong this chapter, because while one of them remained she could delude herself that her loss was not absolute? Had Styopa noticed? Was he assessing her motives? But surely he had appreciated her work with the Leningrad Group? Everyone had written fine confessions, everyone: Brodsky, Osip Levayev, Emma Rykova (they didn't touch old Varlamov, who was going to die anyway). They all gave up other names, about fifty people were arrested, and they, too, had written their confessions under her direction.

She especially appreciated Brodsky's dignified conduct. While in prison he had become very thin and from time to time a convulsion shook his body. Without the talcum powder that always disguised the pockmarks in his cheeks, his face looked particularly miserable. But he didn't complain, didn't make requests that would be ignored in any event, didn't swamp the interrogators with too much detail. He understood the rules and didn't expect any privileges. He behaved as if he had never met Sasha before. He wrote his confession, she made comments—he accepted some and rejected others with an explanation—and by the end of the day it was signed. Only then did he give her a chilly look and say, 'It was a fascinating experience to work with you, Comrade Alexandra Andreyevna Weissberg. Apparently you learned something from us.'

'A person who doesn't appreciate Brodsky's irony ought to sit in the monkey enclosure or join the Proletarian Writers' Association.' Was that Nadya or Emma?

Of course, some of them kept recalling their previous acquaintance. Emma, whose ample body, after a month in detention, had become a shrivelled stick with a wrinkled head on top, declared that she would sooner cut off her hand than be interrogated by a stuttering brat whose nappy she had changed. 'May I be permitted to ask for a grown-up executioner?' she shouted.

Sasha saw to it that the following morning Emma received a double portion of bread and pickled cucumbers, and in the evening a whole litre of cabbage soup. At the end of that week the portions reverted to their former size. After a few more days, the accused woman asked to meet with her again.

Why, she asked Sasha, was she doing this? But now her venom was tempered with caution, and even a sincere desire to understand. Sasha was insulted: was she to blame for their glaring irresponsibility? For all of the defiant poems? For the provocations, the self-indulgence, the neurotic devotion to Nadyezhda Petrovna? Hadn't she lost more than any of them? And, after all that, she still helped them write decent confessions and express sincere remorse to minimise their suffering and their sentences.

'Would you do the same for your parents?' inquired Emma, who had never excelled at suppressing her curiosity.

'Certainly,' Sasha replied. 'This is only a procedure. If I had been here while they were being interrogated, I could have helped them confess and perhaps avoid the labour camp or at least obtain a more lenient punishment.'

'I won't write a confession. I'm not guilty of anything,' declared Emma.

'It's reasonable that there will be differences of opinion about the accusation,' she answered in the set formula. 'It is possible that you didn't understand the significance of your acts, but in the broad perspective you are guilty of counter-revolutionary activity. I read the dossier. You do not deny your actions.'

'I don't deny anything, and I didn't do anything.'

'Fine, so let's write down the things that you didn't do. No one wants you to write even one word that isn't true.'

'I won't write a confession! There are lies that I wouldn't tell even to a scheming little snake like you.'

'Emma Feodorovna, perhaps we are just speaking in generalities. Perhaps we will make progress if we concentrate on the details.'

'We can talk about whatever you want,' Emma replied. 'As long as it's clear that I'm not guilty of anything.'

'I identify the point when you deviated from party principles in 1928. You took part in a meeting of the OBERIU at the Institute for the History of Art. Whom did you meet there?'

Emma cracked her knuckles. 'You've read all the protocols. Do we have to bore ourselves by repeating them?'

Sasha didn't answer. She lit a cigarette, and to avoid blowing smoke in Emma's face she turned to the right and looked at the poet's reflection in the mirror on the large cabinet. Sometimes she used that manoeuvre. She had learned from colleagues that it can make someone restless to look at him in a mirror. The accused knows that his reflection is visible, but he can't look at it without turning his head, and he does not want to turn his head to follow the interrogator's gaze, in case he appears alarmed. So he looks straight ahead, but senses that another eye is surveying him from a new angle, and he must keep up his pretence before it as well. Usually, in order to bring the interrogator's gaze back, he simply improves his answers: a bored interrogator is more dangerous than one whose curiosity is satisfied.

'Kharms was there, Vvedensky, Zabolotsky and some others that I don't remember.'

'I am surprised you have left out Malevich.' Sasha turned towards her. 'A man dies, and is forgotten?'

'He was there, too,' said Emma in a muffled voice.

'Would you say that Malevich was loyal to the party line?'

'In my opinion he wanted to be. He suggested visual realism as a correction of socialist realism.'

'Emma Feodorovna, Malevich was a mystic. You have been deeply influenced by his art.'

'To tell the truth, it disgusts me to hear someone like you even pronounce his name, and, as for influence, there were many others.'

'Did you admire him and Kharms?'

'I have a habit of admiring great artists.'

'Was Chagall at the meeting?'

'Obviously he wasn't!' Emma shouted, coming to life. Her cheeks were flushed, and she seemed eager for battle. 'None of us could stand him. He is pure garbage, a nothing who envied Malevich everything he was doing in Vitebsk: it wasn't Malevich's fault if all of Chagall's students went over to him.'

'So, you admire great artists. Did you also admire Nadyezhda Petrovna?'

'But you know the answer. Nadya was never a great poet. Her poetry has nothing special about it. Sometimes it's one thing and sometimes it's something else. She stole a little from everyone. You can say this about her: she was the best mixer of other people's genius.'

'Did you read the poems she wrote condemning the party leaders?'

'I don't remember,' she answered irately. 'She was always reading her scribblings aloud. In the end no one listened to her except for your father and Brodsky, who were in love with her and didn't understand a thing about poetry. She had charisma, no doubt about that.'

'So you were charmed too.'

'Absolutely not,' Emma declared. 'It was a kind of feverish, annoying charm. She was always overflowing with discoveries, plans, opinions, and they all changed every day. Weak men loved her, but Varlamov, for example, couldn't stand her. They were opposite types, like Turgenev and Tolstoy.'

'And you, Emma Feodorovna.'

'She was mainly a burden for me,' Emma sighed. 'She used to sleep in my room and torture me all night with stories about other people's misfortunes.'

'Why did she write the poem about Stalin? Brodsky and a few others admitted that it was in keeping with the atmosphere in the group,' Sasha said, remembering Stepan Kristoforovich's instructions: do what Lenin did, learn how to trade—in people.

'But you know why. She wanted attention. From your father, from Levayev, from Brodsky and from all the other men who admired her. At some point she realised that she would only be a great poet if her scribbles got swallowed up by a horrible event in her own life, if her poems became inseparable from her tragedy.'

'Did she say that to you?'

'I said it to her.'

'So in fact you're arguing that Nadyezhda Petrovna is not an enemy of the people?'

'The bureaucrats might see her as an enemy. But her only ambitions were for herself. All she cared about was for people to admire her and say she was a genius. She dreamed that one day she would have masses of admirers, that she would receive grants and especially that she would have an apartment, like Varlamov. She was always complaining about how we are crammed together like cucumbers, four to a room, eight to an apartment, grandmothers knitting, aunts making borscht, adolescents masturbating, babies howling, while that cherry-tree poet idles in a hammock in his beautiful garden.'

'Are you willing to begin your confession with the story of the meeting in 1928? It's now clear that the people you met there had discarded every idea of responsible art—Malevich, Kharms, Vvedensky, and we know that Narbut was there, too. You were a confused young woman. They made a big impact on you.'

Emma looked at her furiously. 'Listen, you insect, I've already told you I'm not guilty of anything.'

'Look, Emma, for now they're treating you kindly, but your file contains enough to put you on trial. They can make you confess any number of ways, and in the end you'll confess. Everybody writes a confession in the end.'

It was evident that a powerful desire to curse had billowed up inside Emma, but after a short struggle she decided to keep silent. Sasha stifled a laugh. How easy it was to toy with a person's weaknesses, to tease him with the one thing he couldn't bear to lose; strip him of it and he would no longer be the person he was. Styopa was so impressed with this ability of hers that he would invite her to his office every week, and ask her about her recent interrogations. 'Marchkov is a tough guy. How did you persuade him to correct his confession?'

'I made him cry,' she would answer happily. 'We cried together until we came to the conclusion that the party had failed, everything was lost, there was not a shadow of hope left. Our final task was to prevent a bitter civil war, and for that the government needed the public confessions of its opponents.'

He praised her, blushing like a proud father, and the artery in his neck swelled; she liked looking at his artery and imagining she was talking to it. What she had done was so simple, in a world full of marvels and mysteries, that his excitement was hardly justified. Styopa understood and blurted out, 'Your talent is precisely that everything looks elementary to you!'

In the case of Emma it was even simpler. Nibble away at the image she had fabricated for herself—a brave, rebellious poet who would tell the truth at any price—and she would do what you wanted. People like that cling to the image they've invented for themselves. They have nothing else. Have one little exchange that spoils the image—just now, for example, when she wanted to curse and didn't and was ashamed—and maybe one or two more like that and she would be prepared to make a deal.

Sasha sometimes wondered whether the stories she told Styopa helped him to coax her talent out. Perhaps she was teaching her future hangman the spell that would lead to her own ruin.

Maxim Podolsky and other simpletons, men and women, found it hard to understand her dazzling rise in the second department: people said, at least according to Maxim, that she had more influence on the boss than Reznikov, and that was because Styopa had formed a passion for this pretty young girl from the detested 'intelligentsia', which he publicly mocked while being secretly pleased to have one of them working for him. Even if there was some truth in that, he might not have wanted her to do more than her duties as a stenographer. But in fact he promoted her because he respected her talent. Styopa insisted that she at least supervise every confession for which he was responsible, and if Reznikov appeared in his office, waving a confession he had extracted from a stubborn target, he immediately asked him whether Comrade Weissberg had read it.

'So now I'm taking instruction from a girl who has only ever known enemies of the people?' demanded Reznikov.

She stood in her office holding a dossier with the protocol of the interrogation of Morozovsky. She was familiar with the chilly touch of dossiers after they had been stored for a night in the unheated office. Apparently she mustn't expect a more significant sign of appreciation than 'Good work, Comrade Weissberg' at the end of the day. That was the logic of the organisation: no nostalgia for past achievements—all that counted was the last thing you did.

She rushed through the door and hurried to the interrogation room. She had to sweep away all suspicion that she wasn't doing her job properly. Was there really something broken inside her? Perhaps Stepan Kristoforovich was right. 'We all struggle, Weissberg,' he said. 'We all have a degenerate side that tortures us. We haven't been redeemed yet. Do you remember Mayakovsky:

I purify myself to be like Lenin
So that I can float
On the stream of the revolution?'

Sasha remembered Emma and Nadya standing in the living room reciting that poem. Brodsky was laughing. 'It would be interesting,' he chuckled, 'to identify the circus clown who's been passing himself off as Mayakovsky.'

Nadyezhda crowed, 'Do you remember the excellent comment of Poe's Inspector G.? "Not altogether a fool, but then he's a poet, which I take to be only one remove from a fool."'

Her throat was dry. All her memories were polluted. What had Maxim said on her last night in her childhood home? 'Your history belongs to the dark side of the party. In Islam they would call you *mahound*. You have to be reborn. Otherwise you won't finish this year alive.'

Osip Levayev had been the most miserable of all the members of the Leningrad Group. He had sat in the interrogation room, his eyes red, with pale yellow blotches on his cheeks and two creases intersecting on his forehead. The man has a cross on his forehead, she laughed to herself. Can a person like that be innocent?

Meanwhile he was griping that he had an eye infection. He hadn't been allowed to see his wife for more than a month, and he wasn't getting her packages. For ten hours they made him sit, forbidding him to get up, or stand next to the wall. He expected that sitting would be easier than standing, but a standing person could ease his pains and shift his weight. 'Comrade Weissberg, I've already prepared the general outlines of my confession,' he complained, 'and now they also want me to confess that at the university I established a network to incite public opinion against the party.'

'And didn't you?' she asked. She understood that he was testing her: the accused liked to call the interrogator 'Comrade' to flatter him, and were often answered with curses and blows. Osip Levayev had undergone this ritual, and now he was looking for a small proof to reinforce his faith that she was the person to whom he could entrust his fate.

'Perhaps.' He stared at her as though trying to extract the right answer.

'You have to make up your mind. We don't want false testimony.'

He coughed, seeking direction. She found it hard to look at the man who had squeezed those soft looks out of her mother, the man she had kissed on the beach, whose tongue tasted so sweet; now he was nothing more than a limp tangle of limbs.

'I don't believe I did,' he said. 'Damn it, my whole miserable back is paralysed.' He was like an old man, attaching adjectives to his body to emphasise its weakness. 'So tell them I didn't, although if they're asking they may have firm evidence.'

Then he added quickly, 'Maybe it happened and I don't remember. Since my arrest my memory has been swerving off into strange realms. I can only see my future as rotting leaves rustling on the horizon, if you understand me.'

'Naturally, I understand,' she answered. 'A person's future is unknown. But regarding the past there is certainty. Brodsky wrote in his confession that on a trip to Tbilisi in 1936, standing next to Griboyedov's tomb, you told him that the persecution of the lecturers at the University of Leningrad was an embarrassing act.'

'Brodsky said that? I don't remember saying anything like that,' muttered Osip Levayev. He stood up and felt for his trousers, from which the buttons had been removed.

'Brodsky has an excellent memory. Maybe the time has come to exercise yours.'

'Yes, you're right,' said Levayev. 'My meaning was that if I don't remember things exactly, how can I recall exact details?'

'Really, Osip Borisovich,' she said, exasperated, and stood up too. It was clear to her that remaining in the room any longer would reduce her pity for him. 'After all, it's simple. There aren't many poets with your imagination. If you insist that you don't remember, hatch the plot again, think about what you would do, and who you would turn to, and that's probably what happened.'

'A brilliant idea!' Levayev shouted. He sat down and rubbed his eyes with filthy fingers. 'But my body is paralysed. I can't even move my miserable fingers. Could I have a nap? It will be better if I'm fresh when I write the confession.'

'According to the procedures, we can't cooperate about other things until we have a first draft,' said Sasha and walked to the door.

'Will you read my confession after I finish it?' Levayev called to her. 'Because of my condition some mistakes may creep into it.'

'But of course,' she encouraged him. 'We'll work on it together until it's perfect.'

She moved quickly down the crowded corridor. The Monday morning crew. A few stood chatting, others were reading the bulletin board. Natalia Prikova, a secretary in Maxim's department, was picking dog hairs out of her grey scarf. Everyone stared at Sasha. What was the rush?

Reznikov passed with his nose in the air and straightened the sheepskin lapel of his coat, which looked like a duck's bill. 'Good morning, Goncharova,' he whispered. When others could hear he always addressed her as Comrade Weissberg, but she rather liked Goncharova. If it was meant to be an insult, it also acknowledged her influence: better to be a wily seductress like Pushkin's wife than one of those weepy women who crowded around the post office for days to beg for information about their arrested relatives.

She paced down the passageway that connected the office building with the courtroom on its upper floors and with the adjacent building, which served as a detention centre. Whenever she passed between them, excitement gripped her: here she was, stepping through the famous passageway of the *bolshoi dom* as if she owned the place. She went downstairs to the interrogation room. It was cold and damp. She sat across from the barred window and stroked the tablecloth embroidered with butterflies. She lit a cigarette and leafed through Morozovsky's file. He had already confessed to ideological nearsightedness and to cooperation with the Leningrad Group, but he refused to confess to planning sabotage. He did declare that he had participated in meetings where people voiced severe criticism of the government, and that he had been prepared to help publish the poems of Nadyezhda Petrovna and of other poets who mocked the achievements of the party. A list of works, such as 'If I Were a NEPman' (Nadyezhda Petrovna, 1926) and 'Realistic Writers Always Look at the World, Never in the Mirror' (a short article by Emma Feodorovna Rykova, 1934), was included in the file. The works themselves were kept in a safe.

She heard the creaking of a door, and when she looked up Vladimir Morozovsky loomed before her. He passed his fingers over his moustache, and his shoulders seemed to rise and become even broader. His face glowed. It was leaner, and his hair was dusty, but otherwise he was exactly the same as the last time they met. He was even wearing his red sweater and his sailor pants. He was simply a giant, she said to herself.

'*Bonjour*, my dear Sashka,' he called out.

She immediately understood he was plotting something.

'If it wasn't improper, I'd hug you.'

'Vladimir, are they treating you well?' She gestured to the chair. Morozovsky approached it, shook it as if to test whether it would hold his body, and sat down.

'Yes, yes,' he answered. 'I got a small room, two windows, a night table and a bed. It's been years since I slept alone.'

'I'm glad to hear it.'

'I could use some books,' said Morozovsky. 'Seven hours to sleep, they give you, but the light is so bright you barely sleep for four, a walk in the morning and the evening, twenty minutes, bathroom in the morning and the evening, ten minutes, ten minutes to clean the cell. That leaves nineteen hours and twenty minutes. I would be the happiest of men if they allowed me to have books.'

'I'll see whether I can help,' Sasha said.

'No rush, no rush.' He winked at her.

'Listen,' she said in a soft voice. His cheerfulness and vigour astonished her. 'I read the protocol of your investigation. I have to say that you've done some serious things, but I've seen worse. I believe that you were simply influenced by the wrong people.'

'You know me, Sashka.' He affected a gloomy smile. 'After all, we can talk to each other *sans façon*, I've always been easy to influence.'

'I remember that there were people who were actually influenced by you,' said Sasha. Seasoning his words with French—a language not in favour here—also seemed strange to her. 'Maybe you don't know the nature of this organisation. We aren't the prosecutor's office of the Soviet Union. Even if we are informed about a crime, we aren't required to provide information to other agencies—if we see sincere signs of remorse, of course.'

'I understand that very well and that's why I have cooperated.'

Something was bothering her again: Morozovsky was behaving as if he were playing checkers with an old friend. 'So, for example, when you testify that in 1932, at a meeting in Citizen Konstantin Varlamov's home, members of the Leningrad Group claimed that the struggle against the kulaks led to dreadful cruelty, that the corpses of peasants were strewn all over the country, that the party took bread away from their villages when they were dying of hunger, your position remains unclear. You're sitting there like a ghost.'

'You know me, my little Sashka.' Morozovsky stretched as if he had just woken up. 'I was a spear carrier. Nobody listened to me.'

'I was really puzzled by that bit,' Sasha said, ignoring his last remark. 'The main problem in the dossier is that your crimes don't seem to have any history, so that even you don't seem to know when you joined up with the enemies of the people. To write a sincere confession, it's always best to start at the beginning.'

'And where's the beginning?'

'There are all kinds of beginnings. In my opinion, the most precise beginning is 1924. You were involved then in Trotskyite manipulation of the election in the workers' faculty at the university.'

'That's in the protocol, isn't it?'

'It says that you didn't vote with the opposition, and even worked so that the Trotskyites would lose.'

'Yes, yes, I remember those days well.' Morozovsky spread his enormous hands on the table. 'Regrettably the oppositionists won, but that was only because most of the members weren't really workers, but all sorts of petit-bourgeois individualists who infiltrated the cell.'

'You didn't vote with the opposition?'

'Definitely not, Comrade Weissberg.' His voice was jubilant, but strangely different. 'At that time I was subject to the most positive influences: at night I read Lenin's works, and in the daytime I did my best for the victory of the party. I even remember that, after the election results were known, I couldn't sleep for days, weeks maybe.' Morozovsky turned and examined his moustache in the cabinet mirror. 'Maybe I can explain the source of the error,' he confided. 'I made things up to Nadka and your parents and the others to gain their approval. But now we want me to talk sincerely, right?'

'In their testimony your fellow cell members say you worked for the opposition.'

'Then they're lying,' Morozovsky declared. 'And I'm someone who's finished with lies.'

'We, of course, don't want lies, only true confession.'

'*Chère madame*, if you would be so kind, perhaps I could get a cup of tea. My throat has been hurting for the past few days.'

'Of course,' she answered. She went over to the door, knocked and asked the guard for two cups of tea. She turned and looked at him from behind. His back and neck and even his skull seemed impermeable, as if some mighty power were protecting his body even in prison.

'Sasha, we haven't seen each other for a few months, but even before I was arrested I heard that you'd risen to greatness, and are earning praise at the highest levels.'

'I'm just doing my job,' she said, remaining on her feet. Had she blushed? 'I really feel that I've discovered a truth here that had evaded me for a long time.'

The guard knocked and entered and set the tea down.

'Yes, many people hid the truth from us,' Morozovsky agreed and looked at his cup. 'We did things that weren't pretty. *Nous avons trahi notre peuple et ses droits.** He put a sugar cube between his teeth and let it fall, as if by mistake, into the tea, which he stirred with his finger.

She let out a scream. Icy stabs burned in her belly. 'Are you out of your mind?' She stared at the cup with dread, imagining his scalded skin.

He chuckled, withdrew his finger and blew on it lightly. 'Sasha, my darling, that's a little trick I learned from the grand master Capablanca when he was visiting Moscow. Don't you remember that I almost beat him in the international chess tournament?' He held up a red finger.

She closed her eyes and shrank back, and then opened them again. 'Vladimir Vladimirovich,' she shouted. 'Acts like that won't help you. Maybe you don't understand the severity...'

'Apparently not, since I'm absolutely ready to write a confession,' he said, playing innocent. 'All the two of us are doing is looking for

---

* We betrayed our people and their rights.

the starting point.'

'Maybe you should just write it, and I'll read it later,' she said. The document might be ready by the end of the day, and she could brag about it to Styopa—the confession of the last traitor of the Leningrad Group. Maybe then he would talk to the district council about the twins.

'You know I have difficulties with spelling. I'd rather talk, and you write. I can even recite the first lines for you, if you'll allow me a little nod to a great poet:

> In centuries to come I shall be loved by the people
> For having awakened noble thoughts with my lyre,
> For having glorified freedom in my harsh age
> And called for mercy towards the fallen.'*

She looked for a smile of retraction that would diminish the gravity of quoting these lines. Otherwise they would kill him. But his face remained impassive.

She approached the table again. An inauspicious lethargy crept into her movements. She sensed she was making a grave mistake, but still she came closer, as if in defiance of an irrational fear. She paged through the dossier and looked for blank pages, while he kept blowing on his finger that was now encircled by a large white blister.

Suddenly she felt his hand around her left wrist. At first she refused to believe it—it's a daydream, wake up please, they always said she was dreamy—but his grip tightened. His fingernails dug into her skin. She looked at his mouth, which was twisted with rage, and dozens of little cuts opened up around it. Nevertheless, he still seemed for some reason to be looking at her fondly. She felt her arm being pulled and her eyes rested on his cup of tea. Then he poured boiling tea on the back of her hand. A kind of cracking sound burned in her ears and reminded her of frying eggs. Was he making the sound? She didn't know. Maybe it

---

* Alexander Pushkin, 'Exegi Monumentum', trans. Babette Deutsch.

was another trick? She took a deep breath, but the breath pushed her away from the pain-suppressing shock and concentrated her whole being on her burning hand: the pain raced in the depth of her flesh as though to break her bones.

Morozovsky brought his face close. 'Why aren't you screaming now, you little whore? Suddenly you're quiet? You handed over Nadka's poems and buried us all, and then you even dared to interrogate us, one by one? You got your revenge on Nadka: if you write for another two hundred years you won't scratch the surface of her genius. We all read your miserable poems: "Drowsy in the street, buttoned up in snowy white." You've become the mistress of the world here, writing confessions for people whose boots you aren't worthy to lick. Jew whore, they should have buried you all in Malaya Arnautskaya, so you could rob each other.' He breathed in her face, and his breath steamed like the tea. 'Where are your parents?'

A burst of pain, more searing than the earlier ones, lodged in her hand.

'Where are your parents?'

She yearned to faint.

'What gulag did you put them in? Are they even alive? Where are the twins? Where's the boy you were always hugging and stroking, where is he?' Morozovsky roared.

The room filled with people. Hands and fingers held her, and he was still gripping her and shouting, 'You think I care about dying?' She heard shouts and wails, but Morozovsky's scream ruled the room. 'Did you leave me anything in the world?'

Behind him she saw Reznikov's high forehead, flushed and ugly. More hands touched hers, pressed the seared skin and kneaded it. She heard a soprano scream of horror—the amateur opera singer Natalia Prikova. She saw a gaping jaw and yellow, stained teeth moving towards Morozovsky's throat. For a moment she wanted to shout, 'Watch out, Vladimir! Behind you!' The teeth sank into his neck, and when they disappeared from sight she saw the reddened cheek of their owner, Stepan Kristoforovich.

With a horrifying flash of clarity she understood that they hadn't freed her yet; his fingers were still gripping her wrist like handcuffs. He was the strongest man in Russia. Hands held her hips, her belly, and squashed her breasts. In a fog she saw red sideburns jumping behind Morozovsky. Her husband's face was twisted in an expression of madness, his mouth widened into a black pit: she was a little doll, walking on his tongue into that hole. How distorted it was: would it be possible to recompose it? Shouts and whistles and screams. She heard a shot, a horrible howl, more shots, the stifling smell of gunpowder; now people took her and carried her out, laid her on the cold floor. Vaguely she saw Natalia Prikova tear off the grey scarf, which was spotted with blood. They touched her hand, the smooth cloth of the scarf was wrapped around the skin, she screamed and twisted. They pinned her to the floor, and she was silent, looking up at the white electric light, which suddenly became dazzling. Then faces hid it. She murmured that they mustn't block the sun.

BERLIN–WARSAW
SUMMER 1939–WINTER 1940

They sat in a garden restaurant flooded with sun, paved with fine gravel and surrounded by bright green lawns. Dogs and children raced about, and a kite with the letters NSV glided in the flushed summer sky with its streaks of intense blue. The light filtered onto the tables through the locust trees—his mother always saw in them a pure beauty, and in the spring she would pin a white flower to his lapel for luck— and traced squares on the faces of his colleagues. Platters of cake were arranged on the table, along with cups of lemonade and a pitcher of Berliner Weisse. Waiters circulated on the narrow paths in jackets buttoned up to the neck. The sun's effects always aroused strange happiness in him. How do you take pleasure in a fine day? You trace the paths of the light: a halo crowns the foliage, pebbles glitter, the bodies of the children and the dogs turn yellow, gathered up into twisting ribbons of light.

'In my whole life I have never known a Slav who wasn't a liar. A kind of Asiatic deceit is congenital in them. The mixture of races there has created horribly corrupt human rubbish,' Georg Weller declared. For an hour Weller, his assistant who was a thin young man with the face of a precocious boy, and Hauptsturmführer Bauer had been entertaining themselves by denigrating the Slavs. Thomas, a little bored, and surprised by their zeal, decided it would be only polite to contribute something to the conversation, and mentioned an article in *Germania* that discussed the Asiatic influence on the Slavic race. To tell the truth, he didn't even know what the magazine looked like, but at least one such article had probably been published in it. He was wondering how he could hint to these respectable gentlemen that an hour was more than enough time for gossip, for 'scientific' defamation of the Slavic race and for chatting about 'international politics'. True, Weller, from the Foreign Office, believed that politics provided the most worthy life for a man, especially a man like himself, but since he had invited Thomas to meet for a specific reason they should get to work.

Weller straightened his black tie, now crushed like something from a department store. He turned to Thomas and asked what conspicuous characteristics a Polish man had. It was a deft transition, but Thomas heard the ringing of a bell to announce the beginning of the meeting: he had been invited here because Weller regarded him as an expert on Poland.

Weller's assistant offered a lame joke about the connection between Slavs and chimpanzees, and searched the others for a wrinkle of laughter in the corners of their eyes. His face seemed to cry out: Maybe you'll like me after all?

Weller peeled the crust from his cake and heaped a spoonful of cheese into his mouth. Bauer swallowed his Bienenstich, with its topping of honey and almonds. No one laughed.

Thomas wished the young man would shut up. He disliked him and delayed his answer to focus attention on his shame. He wanted to reprimand Weller but in a friendly way: Of course, my good man, but you don't really expect me to pull an answer out of my sleeve. That would be a frivolous response to such a complex subject.

He was no stranger to meetings like this, where people tried to obtain information without offering anything in return. In such cases, the best strategy was to inundate the listener with information, make him understand its fascination but also its extraordinary intricacy, which only experts can fathom.

'The research department that I headed,' he began, 'synthesised various fields, such as, for example, the connection between the historical-mythological memory of the Jagiellonian dynasty and the vast influence of the Polish-Lithuanian union on the Pole's system of beliefs and the depth of his identification with the Constitution—I refer to that of 1791—which was, of course, the first one in Europe, not to mention the constant cultural flow from France to Poland, beginning with the historical enthusiasm for Jacobin ideas, the translation of literature, the adoption of academic methods of study, and extending to popular magazines with a French fragrance, so beloved of the women of Poland. These are small examples,' he warned. 'The subject, as I said, is immensely complex.'

Thomas was not satisfied with his answer. It wasn't fluent enough, and he hadn't managed to embroider its detail into an overarching story. He was like a rusty spring. For months he had talked only with Clarissa.

The young man scraped snakes of dry cream off his lips, and Bauer, making a show of turning away from him, accused Thomas of obfuscation: Milton set up departments of the national, not the racial, soul, he said, and employed all sorts of psychological theories. Thomas dismissed his words while removing the powdered sugar from his apple strudel with his fork. He avoided Bauer's transparent eyes, which were a kind of lure for reflection. Weller gave him an astonished look: How come you're just playing with your strudel? Where's your appetite?

Abashed, Thomas plunged his fork into a piece and brought it to his mouth. The taste of the sweetened apples repulsed him, but he swallowed and sipped from his drink. Weller was thinking of offering him work, and most likely all the men at the table knew that he was unemployed. The term sickened him so much that he didn't dare say it even to himself. His endless hours of idleness had taught him that the day's nightmares were more horrifying than the night's. They horrify you with their simplicity.

Bauer had probably been invited to the meeting because, having worked with Milton, he would know whether Thomas had truthfully described his role in the company. Aside from that, he couldn't stand Thomas and would make every effort to come between him and Weller. For most of his life Thomas had ignored types like Bauer. It was beneath his dignity to devote time to nuisances who didn't understand either irony or good ideas, in fact didn't understand anything but headlines. Now he was forced to answer that ass? He looked at Bauer with compassion, as though he felt truly sorry for his ignorance. 'Gentlemen, Jewish psychoanalysis,' he said, 'is to blame for everything! The Jews copied German ideas—Nietzsche, for example, or all those notions of self-improvement that inform the concept of *Bildung*—and distorted them. Remember, the Minister of Propaganda warned us in 1933 that it was forbidden for Jews to be interpreters of the German spirit. But Milton's German models aroused the envy of marketing companies all over Europe. In fact, Milton offered a kind of *Bildung* for business: acquire a deep knowledge of the belief systems in the states where you are active, and shape your own future by constantly improving your ability!'

The young man objected that the idea seemed fantastic to him. Thomas sipped his cold drink; it was best for them to realise that not everything was worthy of his response. Around him they made their spoons and forks dance between their plates and cups. The young man muttered something in condemnation of the Americans, and they all nodded. Thomas sensed that between the young man and Bauer a united front might be formed against him in contempt of his work in the service of capitalism, even though they needed Milton's know-how. Hence he had to emphasise the Germanness of his work. Anyway, the young man and Bauer were merely phantoms at this meeting.

He stuffed a piece of strudel into his mouth and swallowed it, as if fired by a blazing appetite for those damned apples. A crumb got stuck between his teeth, but at least Weller nodded to him in encouragement. Then he leaned forwards and explained the principles of the model, cordially hinting at an affinity to be found in education and manners, and an elusive, nuanced point of view: 'When we said "soul" we were referring to race and not to psychological prattle. If the Poles thought it was about their soul, so much the better for them. There's a prominent trait of the Pole for you: a catastrophic combination of arrogance and obstinacy. History has taught us that the Poles did indeed take Rousseau's advice "to set at defiance the power and ambition of your neighbours. You may not prevent them from swallowing you up; see to it at least that they will not be able to digest you." No nation in Europe hatched such crazy plots: any four Poles with a bayonet believed they could defeat the Czar's army. And if I may be permitted to sharpen my answer to your question: the project was set up and designed in Germany, and the other branches are reflections of the original. Anyway, the main point is that we developed a system that can predict the behaviour of the Polish national. Contrary to the theories of all sorts of "experts on Eastern matters", who have never actually been to Poland, Milton's system was perfected through the work of the Warsaw branch.'

Weller nodded with satisfaction, and a wave of excitement surged through Thomas. Finally—months after Milton had collapsed in Germany and put him in a tailspin, without work or decent severance pay or the right to royalties from the branch offices that he had created—he had come to the right place.

Stroking the metal frame of his glasses, Weller told him that his superior, Dr Schnurre, was meeting this evening with the acting Soviet ambassador. He added, as though sharing a secret, that Dr Schnurre was working on a new trade agreement that would be worth hundreds of millions of Reichsmarks. Germany would buy raw materials from the Soviet Union, supplies that German industry needed like air to breathe. His boyish assistant excitedly ticked them off: wheat, mineral oil, cotton, cattle fodder, phosphates, timber.

Thomas chuckled to himself at their enthusiasm, and politely endorsed their admiration for the architect of the agreement: it was a stroke of genius that would change the face of Europe forever.

The young man even added that everyone in the Foreign Office knew that Georg Weller was Dr Schnurre's spokesman, and that von Ribbentrop himself championed Schnurre's policies. But Bauer now reprimanded him severely: No one dictated anything to the Foreign Minister except the Führer.

Why, Thomas asked himself, was Bauer so stiff? In his imagination he spoke to the officer in the same tone that Carlson Mailer had used at the New Year's party. But all that this stupid daydream showed was how much control Thomas had lost over the past few months.

Weller was cajoling—Thomas imagined his voice as an upholstered rocking chair, inviting you to curl up in it—and he tensed. This man could be a dangerous rival. It was no coincidence that he was telling him that the world would shortly be astonished by a new trade agreement between Germany and the Soviet Union. This would remove the final obstacle to resolving the Polish question, which the Führer was determined to do soon. It was impossible any longer to tolerate such behaviour towards the German nation. A war with Poland was weeks away, and the Foreign Office believed that insufficient resources had been devoted to studying the Polish man. Reliable information was needed that could be useful after Germany invaded and took control. 'We in the Foreign Office are concerned: each agency has its own experts on Eastern affairs, who may present strange ideas that will damage the Fatherland's good name. We would like to see a well-defined plan outlining the correct means for dealing with the population. Even if everyone reviles the Pole, he's still a person who believes all kinds of things.'

A tremor of enthusiasm struck Thomas. He declared to Weller that he hadn't the shadow of a doubt that his model could help the Foreign Office. But it would need to be expanded for the purposes of governing Poland. A comprehensive model would need supplementary research, a new synthesis of the data. In fact, this would be a new model...The tongue, like any other muscle, regains its flexibility with a little practice.

A waiter approached and began to remove the plates. Apart from most of Thomas's strudel, nothing remained but crumbs, smears of fruit and whipped cream.

'In this restaurant they serve the most marvellous pastries in Berlin.' Weller sighed, and Thomas signalled to the waiter to leave his strudel, which seemed even bigger now than before he had tackled it. While he was playing with his fork, Bauer asked truculently, 'As an expert on Eastern matters, sir, do you speak Polish?'

He answered gladly that he understood Polish, of course, though he didn't speak it fluently, and he listed the languages that he had mastered: English, French, Italian and Russian. Weller seemed satisfied, the young man looked at him with respect, but Bauer's face quivered, and it was clear he was sorry he had raised the question.

Weller boasted about his own knowledge of Russian—his position demanded it—and asked in Russian, in a somewhat gravelly accent, 'When did Herr Heiselberg manage to learn all that?'

'I always loved languages,' said Thomas, taking pleasure in his Muscovite accent. 'In my youth I studied Russian from books, and then my mother hired a tutor from Moscow for me. I absorb the music of a new language, and then, even if I lack words, everything comes more easily.'

'Indeed, you could have chosen your words with more precision, and you could also improve the declensions. If you want, I would be glad to help with small improvements,' Weller offered, his gravity enveloped with good will. 'But your accent is truly enviable.'

At this affinity between Weller and Thomas, Bauer's face darkened. He leaned over and picked up a few pebbles and juggled them. Then he demanded that the table limit itself to German.

'Herr Heiselberg, would it be possible to prepare a new model in such a short time?' Weller asked.

'How much time do we have?' Thomas asked, and at once regretted that he might seem too eager.

'A few weeks at most,' Weller answered. 'Germany's negotiations with the Soviet Union are going to begin very soon.'

This time, Thomas was in no hurry to answer, and he let Bauer boast about the inconclusive connections between the Western powers and the Soviet Union, as if this were his own personal accomplishment. But if the government dillydallied, the French and English would offer Stalin concessions in the east to tempt him into an alliance against Germany.

'Stalin won't come to any agreement with them,' said the young man contemptuously. 'He kicked the Jew Litvinov out of the Ministry of Foreign Affairs in order to improve ties with Germany. There could be no other interpretation.'

The young man had courage. He was absorbing blow after blow, but he didn't give up.

'True,' said Weller, the expert on the Soviet Union, 'but the model we're discussing isn't supposed to draw on shallow information from the press.'

'No, of course not.' Thomas took advantage of the opportunity. 'The model observes strict research principles. It explains the present and suggests the actions necessary to shape the future. Therefore we avoid direct contact with day-to-day politics.' He gave 'day-to-day' the disdain of a professor responding to a student's questions about current events.

'Excellent. That's just what we need.' Weller's cheeks bulged into two fleshy balls.

Bauer juggled his pebbles in irritation, then gripped them in his fist. 'Your brave words about the Jews who distorted German ideas are ringing in my ears,' he said to Thomas. 'Now you're rescuing Germany from the Jews...'

'I described our methods precisely.'

'...instead of saving Jews from Germany,' he concluded, as though he hadn't heard Thomas at all.

'Why waste time on gossip,' Thomas responded, wondering whether Bauer was referring to Frau Stein, Erika Gelber or both. 'You're not the one to judge my contribution to the Reich. During the party's days of struggle, when you were still reciting Latin in school, my father gave it his all.'

'Gentlemen!' Weller waved away a hovering fly, and looked at Bauer impatiently. 'Let's maintain respect.'

'To get back to our business, we will continue to refine the model until it's perfect!' Thomas felt encouraged because Weller had also had his fill of Bauer. 'Look, the kite has come down, but the NSV only rises and rises. There's no organisation in the world more favourable to the welfare of the people!' In a hoarse voice he told them that yesterday he had donated some items from his dear mother's wardrobe to the organisation. She had passed away, but he was pleased to know that those garments would raise the spirits of so many women. He plunged his fork into what was left of the strudel, and finished off the apples and the pastry.

'You, too, Hauptsturmführer,' he spoke to Bauer—a bit of generosity on the victor's part wouldn't hurt here—'certainly make a fine contribution to the poor children of the homeland.'

Thomas returned home buzzing with ideas and plans. He immediately noticed that Clarissa's red-collared coat was gone, as well as her scent: her hair cream and perfumes, the fresh smell of the grass that clung to her when she returned from the university. She had gone to Westphalia that morning with a group of girls from the NSV to distribute goods in towns and villages. In preparation for the trip she had removed superfluous objects from the house—a coat, shoes, notebooks, textbooks—and she had also packed up his mother's wardrobe, Thomas's reluctant contribution to her organisation.

'All well and good, but those clothes have sentimental value,' he complained when she piled everything into a large carton.

'The greater the suspicion, the greater the contribution,' she chided, reminding him of the events of November. A glow of victory smoothed her face. 'Besides, you were the one who taught me that an obsessive focus on "the good old days" is a disease of the German soul. A house isn't a memorial to the dead but a place where people live.' (Not 'a person', he noted, but 'people'.)

'Did you tell Karlchen that you were going away? If you didn't, he'll turn up here every morning,' he said in mock annoyance.

'Don't worry, I told him,' Clarissa chuckled. 'I warned him not to come near you. You scare him a little.'

In the last few weeks she had taken to sleeping in his mother's room, and did the housework for him in lieu of rent. Sometimes she returned late, a little drunk, in a thin summer dress, with a hairdo that changed every week, while he sat in the parlour, read a book or planned all sorts of 'business ventures'—but actually he was waiting for the moment of her return when she would stand in front of him in all her glory, blushing and giggling, leaning against the wall, a high-heeled shoe in each hand. Then the room would swarm with invisible motion, and, though nothing had apparently changed in him, he would be filled with life, and his whole body would awaken. He would pretend to be interested in where she had been, and how she had enjoyed herself, wanting her to stay near him: in those moments he was permeated with pleasure and hope, and once again everything seemed possible. Sometimes she didn't come home, but would sleep at a girlfriend's house, in her parents' apartment or somewhere else. He never dared to ask where, and would fall asleep in the parlour or crawl into his room, the windows already pale with the dawn.

Thomas wasn't the only one who tracked Clarissa's nights: they also preoccupied Karlchen, her seven-year-old brother, who adored her. From the moment he learned that she was sleeping in the neighbour's apartment—Thomas never asked her whether her parents accepted the arrangement or whether it expressed a kind of minor rebellion against them—he would climb the two flights of stairs in the early morning and knock on the door. If his sister was there, she usually sent him home, but sometimes she let him lie in her bed, depending, she said, on the lesson she wanted to teach him, but Thomas suspected she decided on impulse. Sometimes the kid would turn up very early. Thomas would regard him with groggy eyes, and hear himself saying sweetly, 'My dear little boy, I'm also looking for your sister.' He would warm some milk for him, and together they would wait for Clarissa.

'Where do you work?' the boy asked. 'Clarissa says you used to be a big man. She says that now you sit in the house and complain, and she's going to help you be a big man again.'

Thomas laughed. 'Do you think a man can stop being big?'

The boy gave him an annoyed look, blew on the milk and didn't answer: just like Clarissa when something didn't please her.

Thomas wandered through the house before sitting down to concentrate on the opportunities that were now presenting themselves. He poured himself some cognac and took it to his workroom. Recently he had stopped smoking a pipe. It reminded him of the smoke-filled rooms at Milton, and anyway he had decided it was time to exercise regularly and discard harmful habits. He had applied to join a swimming and a rowing club. Meanwhile, he exercised twice a week at home.

A grey bird stood on the windowsill and picked at breadcrumbs that Clarissa had left there. A breeze ruffled the heavy curtain, which swung out and swallowed the bird up in its folds. Thomas sprang over to it. He imagined the bird plummeting to the street, but it had disappeared.

He turned around and inspected the dark workroom, striped with small enclaves of light. The candle flame trembled in the evening breeze. Clarissa's decision to turn the little room where his mother had kept souvenirs and old things into a workroom had been a good one. But Clarissa's absence now struck him with awareness that he would spend his last days here in total solitude. He was overwhelmed with the certainty of death; it trampled over every other thought, destroying the trace elements of memory, as if all of his consciousness were silent. Death was terrifying, but even more terrifying were 'the colonnade years', as his mother called them, which were already part of its domain. In truth, from childhood he had felt that in some aspect of his soul there was no pulse of life, that something inside him, which was steadily eroding, was already given over to death, and there was nothing left for him to do but look upon it, seized with dread and resignation.

With an effort of will he brought his thoughts back to the meeting with Weller. He had two choices: he could write a report and ask an exorbitant price for it, but he would be paid once only, and the document would do the rounds of the departments; if he didn't include the conventional opinions about the Poles, he might be accused of deviation from party principles, of fondness for Slavs or Asiatics. Or he could write a report that did no more than repeat the familiar invective; the people in the Foreign Office would decide he was an idiot and reject him. Could he blend the two approaches? The result would be muddy and useless.

He had to admit that the model prepared in the Warsaw branch of Milton was comprehensive. All he had to do now was rearrange it. It included a chapter about the commercial practices of the Polish Jews, which he could now refresh, calling it, let's say, 'An Outline of the Character of the Polish Jew'. The challenge was to use the existing material to squeeze his way into the Foreign Office—preferably to a position of influence.

This was a golden opportunity, the first job offer in months that suited his abilities (if you forgot about the offer to serve as personal adviser to that tiresome woman, Scholtz-Klink, of the Nazi Women's League), and he needed to avoid any false steps. But to prepare a document for people without understanding their aspirations or power struggles was like cursing people in the street while wearing a blindfold: maybe someone would fall in love with your blunt style, but it was more likely you would get slugged.

At last he decided to prepare a short paper that would outline the general principles of the Polish model and to attach a proposal to hire him as a consultant. Only then would he deliver the whole document. 'The matter will be settled to our satisfaction,' he said, letting the brandy linger in his throat, luxuriating in its warmth. 'It's a classic case of everyone winning.'

...

The document that he presented, 'A Multi-Disciplinary Model: The Ideal Type of the Polish People', contained twelve chapters, and was approved by senior officials in the Foreign Office. It was read at once and hastily circulated among the various agencies of the Reich. In just a week, on the eve of the invasion of Poland, urgent calls were received from the SS and from the Treasury, the Interior, Justice and Propaganda ministries; from Hermann Göring's office; from a man Thomas admired, Dr Todt, who was now supervising most of the technical projects of the Reich; and from officers of the Wehrmacht and from research institutes that dealt with Eastern European affairs. All of them wanted to meet Thomas, praised the report, raised objections, but mainly offered ideas regarding their future roles in Poland. Dozens of questions were showered on him, on myriad matters, like the extent of the Pole's opposition to accepting the local rule of the *Volksdeutsche*, the best way of neutralising the intelligentsia, the treatment of Polish businesses and the views of the Catholic priests.

The chapter that compared the attitude of the Poles to the Reich with their attitude to the Soviet Union, which Thomas regarded as the most brilliant, did indeed arouse great interest. An idea was going round that harmful Polish elements, especially within the intelligentsia, should be encouraged to move into the zone that the Soviets would conquer. Thomas thought this was crazy and he gave it short shrift: the hatred of the Pole for the Russian would sabotage any initiative to encourage emigration. The only practical possibilities were 'the hastening of emigration by severe measures', or expulsion.

The Foreign Office decided to hold a conference focusing on the model, and to invite representatives of the various agencies that would operate in Poland. Ernst von Weizsäcker, the State Secretary at the Foreign Office, announced that he would chair the conference, an event that of course would be kept secret, and all the participants would be forbidden to speak about it to anyone except their superiors. Weller was full of cheer when he told Thomas that von Weizsäcker would be leading the discussion. 'Do you understand? That means that the Foreign Office endorses the document. An outstanding achievement!'

Weller, who had enlisted Thomas, a step that had cost him 'a stubborn struggle with dangerous elements, who don't like the idea and like you even less', regarded the great interest that the model had generated as a personal achievement, and he felt like the author of a great event.

On the morning of the conference Thomas woke up at exactly four o'clock. He lay in bed for a while and polished the first ten sentences of his lecture. When a phrase especially pleased him, he repeated it. Of course, he didn't write anything down: you had to know the crucial speeches of your career by heart. At five he took a cold shower, and rehearsed the final instructions that he would give to Weller before the participants gathered in the Foreign Office. When he came out, Clarissa was already making breakfast.

'Did you think I would sleep in?' She laughed and pointed at the chair. 'Little Clarissa doesn't like to get up early, but today I leaped out of bed as though the sheets were on fire.'

While they were eating she chatted—her skin smelled of soap and lemons—and regaled him with amusing incidents from her last trip with the NSV Women: the poor people of Germany were terribly funny, some of them didn't have anything in the house except bread and milk, but they still insisted on contributing. One woman in Solingen begged the organisation to take back the clothing that had been given to her.

He listened and from time to time he commented, and inwardly he thanked her for her efforts to relieve his tension. When they finished eating Clarissa cleared the table, and he lit his first pipe in months and sat in silence.

At exactly six she sat on the chair opposite him and he stood and gave his lecture to her. Not a muscle moved in her pretty face until he finished. That was at his explicit request: no encouraging smile, no complicit nod, nothing, since people were coming to the conference who regarded the whole idea as contemptible, who would look for flaws in the model, wanting to throw him off balance, and to report back to their masters that the Foreign Office hadn't a clue about the

Poles. After he spoke, Clarissa called his attention to several sentences whose tone sounded too defiant. They disagreed about this: in his opinion, defiance was necessary to promote a new idea.

He was heading to his bedroom to put on his suit, when Clarissa summoned him back. 'Thomas'—her eyes sparkled—'your wonderful speech will inspire everyone. Even the Führer's speeches don't come close to it. And it's not only the speech, you know. I read the model. You're doing something great for Germany.' She blushed, as though she understood that pathos didn't suit her, and she kissed his forehead.

The moment her lips left his forehead he wanted her. He adopted a teasing tone and said, 'Enough, dear, enough, I don't need any more pressure. Tell me that today will be a triumph.'

She didn't answer but on her bare feet with her red toenails she minced over to the sofa, where she liked to sprawl while she was preparing for classes at the university.

Sometimes he succumbed to the urge to indulge her, and concentrated only on what she might want, but her wishes still evaded his understanding. She seldom showed annoyance with him, but his insistence on humouring her made her sad. Even on the matter of repairing the window in his mother's room it seemed that she objected to the ease with which he had given in to her. Once she told him that Charlotte, her married aunt, had told her that she didn't like men who stretched and shrank according to a woman's wishes; he understood that the words were intended for him. When she begged him to behave in a 'natural' way, as if she were a guest, to do as he pleased in his own home, he felt as if he had been relegated to a twilight realm where anything he did would seem a form of artifice. If it sometimes seemed to him that 'natural' was only another word for 'indelicate', he was in fact anxious about the connection between them, which retained an insubstantial element, as though Clarissa had decided to set aside a certain amount of time for him, when she would grace him with her sympathy—and then one day she would disappear.

Sometimes he imagined her waking up on his mother's bed, rising from the pillow with a lonely expression as though seeking something familiar, as every morning she learned anew that there was nothing familiar here. The plausibility of that fear terrified him; usually Thomas enjoyed fears that he didn't believe in. Erika Gelber claimed that he enjoyed them precisely because he didn't believe in them. Maybe he had feelings Erika hadn't plumbed. Very well, he thought, I won't cure all my mental anguish just this second. He was furious because he had failed to halt his distress in time. Standing before the mirror in his suit, he realised again that his future lay in his own hands; the model was an achievement, and the quibbles of his opponents were irrelevant. Onwards: go out and sell it.

During the months when he wasn't working, just sitting at home doing nothing, Clarissa would declare that his great day was to come— Milton was a small station on his journey, and in a few years, when he looked back, he wouldn't understand why he had shut himself away like a leper. Without Clarissa, whose sweetness and inexhaustible faith brightened his afternoon hours, he would have plunged into despair. She told him he had all the virtues of Siegfried, and whatever he did he would succeed. Thomas could be an architect, or an author, or a film producer, possessed of both creative and business acumen. She could see him in Babelsberg, surrounded by actors…

Twenty minutes later he was ready. His mind was entirely given over to the conference room in the Foreign Office on Wilhelmstrasse. He didn't approach Clarissa again but waved to her. She gave him an astonished look that immediately became an enthusiastic smile, as if she understood that this day had a single focus. 'Siegfried,' she called, 'take them by storm!' He imagined that he heard mockery in her voice.

He went downstairs, offered the concierge a spirited greeting and stepped into the street, giving himself over to the warm summer breeze. A car from the Foreign Office was waiting for him, a gesture from von Weizsäcker.

'Herr Heiselberg, good morning,' the driver said.

'Good morning,' he said, and slid into the back seat. From nowhere the memory of his father telling him about a job offer in Russia pounced on him. It was an autumn day in 1922. He had returned from the university and was waiting for his father in Wagner's café. He appeared unshaven in a raincoat with frayed cuffs. Without preliminaries he informed Thomas that he was joining a small group of engineers, technicians and workers from the Junkers plant who were to help set up an aeroplane factory near Moscow. His father had despised Communists all his life, but he was pleased about the coming trip. The idea that, just a few years after the horrible war, in which his best friends were killed, he would build warplanes for the Russians was an abomination to him, but since Germany had signed a treaty with the Bolsheviks he had given up trying to understand his government. The offer he had received meant a promotion and a higher salary; in addition, he would be away for some time, and perhaps, when he returned, he and Marlene could patch up their marriage.

Wagner served them vanilla ice-cream, and said hello. Thomas nodded, and his father said something in a soft voice. Then they drank coffee, and Thomas taught his father a few sentences in Russian: 'I want a bowl of borscht', 'My son will manage big companies in Germany one day', 'They say that Saint Petersburg is the most beautiful city in Europe.' Thomas suddenly saw Frau Stein looking at them shamelessly through the parlour window of their house. When they parted, his father reminded him that he still expected him to join the German University Ring,* and Thomas told him that he wouldn't wander around the campus shouting, 'Wake up, Germany!' like an idiot, and anyway he wasn't a political man.

His father travelled to Russia and wrote only a few letters home to Thomas and his mother. A year passed; it turned out that the factory was making Junkers bleed money, and the company decided to transfer ownership of it to the Soviet government. His father came back to work in the factory in Dessau and a few months later he was fired. He went from one miserably paid job to another, and adamantly refused Thomas's offers of support. He joined the National Socialist Party and spent most

---

* A right-wing student union formed to oppose the forces of internationalism and promote *volkish* principles.

of his time with his new friends. Thomas's mother and Frau Stein said that the man had finally returned to his true home among the riffraff.

At his father's funeral, in 1930, Thomas was surrounded by several dozen Brownshirts, who delivered heartfelt eulogies praising his devotion to the community and his loyalty to his friends (he asked to be buried next to Horst Wessel, his young friend who had been murdered by the Communists). Thomas felt comforted that, contrary to the way he had imagined him, his father had at the end of his life been a vigorous man with lots of friends. He thanked the eulogisers for the affection they had shown his father. At the end of the funeral they all sang a medley of party songs celebrating the life of Johannes Heiselberg.

The participants seated themselves around a mahogany table. Before each lay a folder containing a copy of the pamphlet, a sheaf of fine paper and two sharpened pencils. In von Weizsäcker's short welcoming speech, he emphasised that the event was a kind of conversation, whose purpose was to generate original ideas in the event 'that Germany indeed is forced to fight against Poland' (the man tried to register a note of caution). He then invited Thomas to speak.

Within a few minutes he sensed that those present—including the opponents of the model, whom he identified immediately—were impressed by the scope and style of his lecture. He allowed himself to indulge in amused irony, and cited historical anecdotes. He felt as if nothing would give him more satisfaction than the opportunity to give the lecture again. When he finished, the participants pounded the table to express their appreciation, but the moment the pounding died down the representative of Goebbels, the Minister of Propaganda, asked for the floor.

'With all due respect,' he said emphatically, 'to our honourable master of disciplines and his fascinating speech, the fourth chapter in his document, which deals with the history of the Polish people, is scandalous. Sir, you write as if these people have a past at all. It's as clear as day that these backward Slavs have no dynasty. That's a fiction spread by lying, base propaganda. There's no such thing as a "Polish national".'

'All the Slavs are a single nation,' said another voice from the end of the table.

Rudolf Hess's representative declared that he shared this view and added that the fourth chapter aroused resentment in the party as well; he even recommended reprinting the pamphlet without it. 'We must not destroy the valuable science of history, which was born here in Germany, with meaningless legends. With your permission, I would like to quote what Herr Hess, the party chairman, said to me: "There are true nations with historical roots, and every proper historian will present evidence of the direct connection between the Aryan German and the ancient Nordic race and the Teutonic knights." Whereas, according to the Foreign Office's model, four monkeys can decide tomorrow that they are descendants of Julius Caesar and claim Rome. The Slavs aren't worthy of all this profound research, and there's no need to understand anything about their mentality in order to deal with them with an iron fist.'

'Gentlemen,' Thomas answered, grateful to Weller and to von Weizsäcker for preparing him for this attack, 'your comments are entirely constructive, and I share your opinion. I regret to say, however, that they are not useful. The fourth chapter is a comprehensive study of how the Pole himself constructs his identity and his views of his past, and it makes no difference at all whether historical research shows that the state called Poland is in fact the kind of hokum that has been put about during the past two centuries. Allow me to offer you an analogy: suppose someone wants to buy a company. First, he will examine its balance sheet. Then he will inquire about how confident its owner is in its future. That's because a man who believes that his company is his whole world will negotiate differently from a man who believes that any company is coin of the realm, even if the first man made only a small contribution to the company and the second devoted the best years of his life to it.'

A silence fell on the room, and Thomas heard mainly the breathing

of Weller and Schnurre. A quick glance at Weller's face was sufficient—it revealed his desire to disown Thomas and at the same time
to rescue him. Thomas understood that his analogy had not gone down
well, and it might have strengthened the hand of his opponents who
were aware of his open admiration of capitalism, his connections with
the Americans, his late adhesion to the party and perhaps also the
strange story about the Jewish housekeeper. (Weller had made him
aware of all these recriminations, as well as his own response, in which
he commended the purity of the late Herr Heiselberg's morals and his
loyalty to the party.) Here was his first lesson, Thomas noted to himself:
never use examples from the business world.

'The degree to which a Pole is willing to fight to the death and
aggravate our lives is not connected to historical truth,' Weller finally
intervened, 'but rests on the whole structure of his beliefs. Therefore,
for the purposes of the discussion, there is a Polish national.'

The representative from the Ministry of Justice supported Weller's
remarks. 'History teaches us,' he added smugly, 'that both fools and
wise men fight in the name of their faith, and a fool fights no worse
than a wise man.'

A young doctor from the Department of Eugenic Research in the
Kaiser Wilhelm Institute inquired about the scientific background of
the sixth chapter, which dealt with the Polish race. 'Why didn't you
consult experts on the subject, such as Hans Günther or Robert Ritter?'
he demanded. 'Why is no representative of the Rosenberg Institute
present?'

Weller replied that the writings and advice of all the experts on
Poland were fed into the model, along with extensive research literature, and original material based on interviews with thousands of
Poles. 'The model presented by the Foreign Office is the most comprehensive one in Germany today,' he concluded.

Then it was the turn of Bruno Beger, representing the Department
of Race and Settlement (Weller had in confidence told Thomas
that this department was considering the mass deportation of Poles),
who had been filled with rage when he read about the work of the

archaeological centre in Poland. 'It's bad enough that those idiots are looking for the roots of the Slavic peoples,' he protested, 'and spend whole days in their gloomy churches gaping at altars, but to establish a research centre? To look for the roots of some Slavic nation in our own German regions?'

Thomas liked the look of Bruno Beger. He moved with the ease of a man who expected people to acknowledge his excellence without any effort on his part. It was rumoured that the Ministry of Propaganda wanted to use his picture on posters exhibiting the perfect Nordic man.

'Tomorrow their scientists will decide that they're the true Nordics, and that we're Mongols,' called out the doctor from the Kaiser Wilhelm Institute.

'Hence the model's strong recommendation is that, immediately after taking Warsaw, we will close the National Museum on Aleje Jerozolimskie, as well as the Archaeology Museum in Łazienki Park,' Thomas said. 'I wish to call your attention to the chapter entitled "Excavation Madness, the Strengthening of Nationalism". In the last few decades the Poles have been digging everywhere to collect evidence about their national history. Every week they discover some jewel. Just last October they held a great ceremony in Warsaw and displayed a new part of the old city wall. Therefore our practical proposal is to add every Pole who has ever been engaged in archaeology to the list of the intelligentsia.'

'Gentlemen,' said Weller. 'Please pay attention to the fact that their empire already existed in the Middle Ages. I refer you to the chapter on Polish literature and especially to the pages covering the historical novels of Henryk Sienkiewicz, rather inferior books that every Polish child reads. And what are they about? The victories of their empire, of course, especially over the Teutonic Knights. In general, it is impossible to deny that the Poles have true achievements they can cling to, like the conquest of Moscow, for example. That is to say, in addition to the military campaign we can expect a campaign that we might call "cultural-historical".'

'Moreover, the chapter entitled "Ardent Francophilia" discusses

French influence on the Poles,' Thomas added, noting to himself that Weller was now defending the ideas in the model as if they were the fruit of his own mind. 'This is expressed in the Polish conception of democracy, as well as in little snippets of life: the way Polish women imitate French women in dress, manners and even in sexual behaviour, or in the boarding-school romances so beloved of Polish girls.'

'So what if some young Zosia enjoys reading risqué novels, even though the priest has forbidden it? How is that supposed to influence the Reich's policy in Poland?' asked Bruno Beger, who then looked impatiently at his watch.

'Sir, if you read the chapter to the end, perhaps you will find your answer,' Thomas answered. 'We are concerned about all sorts of scenarios. For example, assuming that we manage to defeat the priests, we must anticipate local identification with the French Republic, through which democratic sentiment and fierce loyalty to a kind of Polish identity might grow stronger. The model analyses Poland as it is today, and its recommendations should be taken into consideration when setting the Reich's policy. If we explain, for example, why it isn't possible to deport hundreds of thousands of Poles to the east, we expect to be heard out. From the moment our policy is set, the flexibility of the model will, however, enable us to propose practical solutions.'

Beger was impressed by this crushing answer.

Does this upstart understand who he's taken on? Thomas said to himself with exhilaration, a man who used to demand soaring prices for partnerships in Milton branches that only existed in his imagination!

At lunch, while the guests gathered around refreshments on KPM plates handpainted with white lilies, Weller sat next to Thomas and whispered to him that he was worried about the fact that Wolfram Sievers, from the Research and Teaching Society of the Ancestral Heritage, had attacked the model in an irate letter to the Foreign Minister, claiming that it was leading the research into the history of the Aryan race as compared with other races; it wasn't possible for some nonentity to come along and declare himself to be an expert on the Poles.

'Scientific insults from the Society of the Ancestral Heritage are a great compliment,' Thomas answered arrogantly. 'Between you and me, Weller, what is a discipline if not the stretching or shrinking of knowledge according to the spirit of the age? To plunder the African continent, English science determined that the Negroes were quarter human, and the French and the Belgians divided the Negroes in the same village into "white people of colour", "black-skinned Europeans", and "inferior Negroes". American science reached the same conclusions, by the way. Tell me what your needs are, and I'll tailor a discipline for you.'

When they gathered again in the conference room, von Weizsäcker apologised that he would have to leave to attend to other matters. The rest of the day passed in a calmer mood. Thomas met every question and objection with fluency and vigour. Late in the afternoon the representative of the Labour Front asked, 'Herr Heiselberg, why do you call the Pole an "ideal type"? What is so ideal about those Poles?'

Everyone broke up with laughter. 'Hey, where's your spade!' someone called out, and a wave of jeering rolled through the room.

The poor fellow, no doubt to fend off more jokes about the Labour Front's custom of regarding spades as weapons, buried his nose in his papers.

Thomas was struck with dizziness. Not now, he prayed, but curved shadows, like bows of dust, thickened before his eyes. Through them flashed a thick chin, perfectly shaved, a neck wounded with red gashes, a blue ribbon, shining golden epaulettes like a river glittering in the sun as if a net spread on its waters would catch gold bars. He gaped. The faces of the men sitting around him rose up and hovered like balloons.

None of the lessons he had learned at Milton would be of use against these people. There he had learned to sort people into categories. But there were too many people here, too many organisations. All he had now was his ability to improvise. He was in despair, like a boy alone in the middle of the autobahn who had been asked to identify the drivers of a hundred passing cars.

The arcs of dust began to disappear, and the space brightened. Thomas exchanged glances with Beger, whose eyes were sparkling with mischief. It would definitely be possible to make friends with a man like that. Then Beger scowled and reprimanded the unfortunate man from the Labour Front, threatening to tell his boss, Robert Ley, not to send junior officials, whose education was an embarrassment both to the Labour Front and to Germany, to such demanding discussions.

'M-a-x W-e-b-er,' Weller also scolded. 'Look that name up in the encyclopedia.'

At the end of the conference, Martin Luther, an associate of von Ribbentrop, put an arm on his shoulder and said, 'Herr Heiselberg, your lecture was inspiring: we need new blood in the Foreign Office!'

Other officials were full of praise, both those loyal to von Ribbentrop and career bureaucrats like Weller, veterans of the ministry, who despised the former. But Thomas knew very well that even those whose noses were out of joint would get used to the new boss.

'Your model has united the whole office behind you,' a young policy adviser commented, 'but don't have any illusions. From tomorrow you'll start accumulating enemies.'

After the Wehrmacht conquered Poland, the flow of requests to 'purchase' the model increased, and it became one of the most widely discussed documents in the Reich, although it had many opponents who called Thomas a charlatan, a vacuous self-promoter, a capitalist pig. Social scientists rejected some of its conclusions, even those that were similar to theirs; members of the North and East German Research Fellowship described the pamphlet as a disgrace to German science. But that was to be expected: it threatened their influence in the Foreign Office. Joseph Goebbels opposed all the scholarly commotion about the Slavs and said that the model expressed cowardice, and Alfred Rosenberg wrote to the Foreign Minister that the natural place of the author of the model was in the Ministry of Propaganda. But most who had attended the conference praised the reach of the document into biology, art, archaeology, history and philosophy, and the force of its conclusions about the Poles and the measures necessary to rule their country.

In the Foreign Office they began to emphasise the seven years of research by dozens of bodies that had informed the model, the thousands of pages of data that were its raw material. This chatter amused Thomas—no one had ever seen the thousands of pages of data supplied by Milton's Warsaw office that had been used in composing the model. Then, towards the end of September, when the first rumours emerged of Soviet atrocities against the Poles, there was growing recognition of the predictive ability of the model. 'Even when someone predicts the obvious,' Karl Schnurre said, 'he deserves respect.'

A request also arrived from Göring's office to attach them to the Four Year Plan as senior advisers. Weller, drunk with success, responded to all these requests to 'buy the model' with lordly disdain. In October, when the district governors and the new institutions in Poland were organising themselves feverishly, and competing for a share of influence, the Foreign Office decided that Weller and Thomas should move to Warsaw to advise organisations wanting to use the model. Von Ribbentrop briefed them in a letter: they were employees of the Foreign Office and their subordination to the governor of Warsaw was merely technical; the model was the property of the Foreign Office; any organisation that addressed them with an inappropriate proposal 'undermines the efforts of the Foreign Office to uphold the status of Germany in the world'.

They were given a floor in a small office building on Marszałkowska Street, and a pair of roomy apartments on Nowy Swiat. The district governor lent them two clerks to deal with requests according to the system that Thomas had used at Milton: starting with 'extremely urgent'—requests from clients whom we want to oblige—and ending with 'urgent to the fourth degree'—requests from clients we aren't interested in. For secretarial work they hired two *Volksdeutsche* women in their late twenties, who studied law at the University of Warsaw.

At least once a week they held work meetings in the parlour of the

Bristol Hotel, where senior Gestapo men were quartered. Thomas had stayed there on his two previous trips to Warsaw and had been excited by the lively hum, brimming with possibility, that filled the air: the sound of many different languages that he longed to master; guests from all over Europe trading ideas, people with whom he enjoyed discussing business initiatives. Now the hotel was swarming with Germans in uniform, the conversations were brusque and official. But he and Weller made it their duty to be there to meet people of high rank, to spin alliances, to hear and spread rumours, to keep track of changes in the organisations they dealt with, or, as Weller used to say, 'To understand where we stand in this commotion.'

...

'Every time you run into a bunch of kids galloping out of a schoolyard, you understand that you've died once.'

Thomas and Georg Weller were walking past a school. The cast-iron gate to the yard had been shoved onto the asphalt. The domed building had crimson windows striped with blue. Its vacant courtyard was surrounded by a brick wall against which dead leaves were heaped up.

Little Thomas skips down the busy street between the shop windows. Father shouts that he mustn't go too far. Lights shine from the windows and their wonders are reflected in the pedestrians' eyes: a model car, a jacket, an ornate sofa, a glass table with carved wooden legs. Between now and the day Thomas will own these things stretch the rituals of his childhood, then marriage and studies and hard work. Little Thomas imagines his future: fame, death or both. In the morning he meets his friends and goes to his Latin and mathematics and history classes. During recess they create clubs, decide fates. Bruno, the Italian, whines that they have left him out. They all admire an athlete who has sprinted a hundred metres in little more than ten seconds. Thomas feels like he doesn't fit in; their interests are irrelevant. He thinks of them with a kind of paternal irony. He doesn't understand how they are happy to confine their lives to stupid amusements when two steps away true life roars in the grand and shining world. Boys, can't you see that we're stuck here? If we cross the yellowing grass with its swings, slide and marble plaque that says 'Exercise Field in Memory of Johann Heinrich Pestalozzi 1746–1828', and leap the fence, we'll be in the centre of the world!

Father is waiting for him outside the school in the outfit of a badly paid worker whose wife has a small and dwindling estate, who buys suits for himself that won't embarrass her. Father peels the fresh putty from the windows of the first floor. The putty spots his hat, and they both know that Mother will grumble in the evening. They hurry off to Friedrichstrasse. Sometimes Father dreams like Thomas, but sometimes he builds fences around his dreams, counting everything that won't happen: dreams about sad Fredericus after whom the street is named, the conqueror with the bold gaze.

Later, America begins to charm Thomas. Hermann's father becomes one of the men he admires. The children and their parents ridicule him, but Thomas doesn't understand how it's possible to disdain a man who has obtained such marvellous merchandise from the Americans.

Thomas's father also despises America and all the countries that vowed to keep Germany weak, greased the palms of corrupt politicians, spread treasonous articles in the newspapers and encouraged the Communists to march against their own country. But most of all he hates the intellectuals, the degenerate artists from the Romanisches Café, who have corrupted German culture. 'Germany didn't lose the war. Always remember that, son. We didn't lose. They sold us out.'

A freezing gust strikes the backs of their necks. Here's Mother. She always invades his memory and keeps her son and husband apart. Mother and Father stand next to him, it is Sunday noon. They stand close, but they can't protect him from the wind. Father says something that the wind whips away. Mother's hat also blows away. Her hair fluffs up, and she tries to hold it down but strands fly across her face. 'What's happening, Dad?' The hat bounces onto the road, is crushed by cars. Father looks at it. Mother looks at Father. Thomas looks at them both. Cars pass. How small they have become. That was their first loss.

'Warsaw is so shabby. No wonder the Slavs still ride horses into battle.'

Thomas came to his senses, and gave Weller a friendly look. Had he managed to banish the gloom from his eyes? You could stifle laughter or tears, change your expression—those were minor matters—but it wasn't easy to control your gaze.

'Listen to this,' Weller added in a dreamy tone. 'Last August, when I was in Moscow with the Foreign Minister and Dr Schnurre, the night sky was clear, clustered everywhere with stars. Their sky aroused feelings of reverence in me. I understood how vast that country is.'

Weller liked to talk about that trip to Moscow when the Foreign Minister had signed the treaty with the Communists. He apparently didn't realise that everyone in the Foreign Office was gossiping about how he had been humiliated there: he wasn't included in the first, restricted meeting, or in the expanded evening meeting, and he had not been invited at all to the second conference at the end of September. 'Most of the time they left him in the embassy to take messages from Berlin,' Martin Luther laughed and told Thomas how the Minister of Foreign Affairs had sworn that Stalin was the most impressive man he had ever met, except the Führer, of course. Weller was too prudent, Thomas thought. A man shackled by caution won't go far, won't be invited to the really interesting meetings. It was not wise to bet on him as his only patron. He should get closer to Karl Schnurre and Martin Luther.

'Oh, if we weren't friends, I would envy you madly,' he said to Weller. 'How many nights like that has the world seen?'

Weller adjusted his spectacles, a familiar gesture that gave him a moment to restrain his rage. He tugged his sleeves and smoothed his trouser creases. 'Ribbentrop is certainly a source of pride to all the wine merchants,' he said softly.

Weller spoke the language of the government, but occasionally couldn't repress his contempt for senior members of the party. His conservative attitudes, his education, his roots, extending deep into the Prussian bureaucracy (his great-grandfather had been a political adviser to the Kaiser), and the feeling of people of his kind that the state belonged to them—all of these things made it hard for him to be reconciled to the fact that a gang of men from remote villages—or, worse, from places like Riga, Rewahl and even Chile—had become the rulers of Germany.

They were walking down Marszałkowska Street. Scraps of newspaper fluttered in the wind. Through smashed doors and windows they could see destroyed apartments that had been abandoned. People were removing stones from some of the ruined buildings. A group of young men, working in a row, levelled out the sand around the broken cobbles. Three Wehrmacht soldiers, idly smoking, were supervising them. Polish children pushed wheelbarrows full of sand, manoeuvring through the passersby. The trucks, the motorcycles, the hammers and wheelbarrows, the broken stones—all of these gave the street the daily life of a city, but as if swallowed up by the soft Polish language, the cautious clearing of throats, the silent children, the suppressed tension and the trembling expectation of a new decree. The brazen chaos of Jerozolimskie had been reduced to a mournful whimper. Warsaw looked feeble and helpless. At the end of their first week in the city Weller dragged Thomas to the bright and cosmopolitan intersection of Zgoda and Szpitalna streets, where on his first visit to Warsaw Thomas had found an office for the Polish branch of Milton. Now the building was abandoned. Large companies and newspaper offices were no longer there. Only the Chevrolet sign still hung beneath the roof. Scenery for a play that had closed.

At once Thomas grasped the opportunity this city offered him: here was a foundation of wet cement waiting for someone to shape it with laws, regulations, logic, all the hollow spaces in the city, where nothing was really comprehensible either to the Poles or to the Germans. And if he strode onto centre stage as the man with the answers and proved to everyone that only his model could allow this city to fulfil its potential—he would be the most influential German in Poland.

Three young woman stepped towards them. They looked extraordinarily alike—were they sisters?—and were all dressed in black woollen coats, silk stockings and high-heeled shoes. The only difference was in their hats. One wore a round hat that covered her hair, another a high blue hat beneath which her curls flounced and the third a green hat like a military beret.

'Weller, look at those elegant women,' said Thomas. 'Those are hats by Paul Poiret, I can recognise his work, always stylish, but never too much. Our branch in Paris worked with him.'

They made way for the young women to pass, who nodded in thanks. Their silvery grey eyes dwelled on Weller and Thomas, before they looked away into the sky.

'Are they thanking us or Göring's aeroplanes?' Thomas laughed. He was always cheerful in the presence of gloomy people. Not because he felt ill will towards them, but because it relieved him to see that unhappiness afflicted everyone. Someone was sad, you were happy and the next day it was the opposite. 'If you told me that all my problems were routine, typical of the age, or even just of Germans, I would thank you and be off, and glorify your holy name forever,' he once said to Erika Gelber, who, even after many years of therapy, didn't always understand when he was being facetious.

The women passed a group of soldiers who were stopping men in the street, putting shovels in their hands and leading them to a ravaged building in which only the outer walls remained, like the wings of a bodiless bird.

They walked by a row of bare trees that reminded Thomas of an honour guard stripped of its colours. Beyond that were stores selling expensive housewares, clothing and jewellery, and a teashop where women sat, bundled up in their coats.

'War is a strange thing,' said Thomas. 'In one place it destroys everything, and two steps away there's no sign of it.'

'Listen, Thomas,' said Weller, sitting on a bench and signalling to him to sit down. Thomas looked sadly at the three black silhouettes disappearing down the street. 'You know I regard you as a friend. You are the only one who can advise me in a delicate matter. I am sure you know what I mean, the gossip about me because of the way I was treated in Moscow…'

'I heard some things,' Thomas admitted, 'but I avoid rumours, especially about friends.'

'For many years I've dealt with the East, mainly with the Soviet Union,' said Weller, who had not heard him, of course. 'I've devoted my life to that country. I should have been there.'

'I understand that very few people were invited to the meetings.'

'They chose Hilger as the interpreter,' Weller huffed. His face was flushed from brandy. He wiped his forehead with a handkerchief, coughed and put his hand on his heart. He looked like a bitter old man whose soul could no longer be disentangled from a lifetime of insults.

'That's not surprising,' said Thomas. 'Clearly Ambassador Schulenburg would prefer one of his own people.'

'No one in the Foreign Office trusts that bald guy,' Weller hissed. 'He's too close to the Soviets.'

'There will be more opportunities.' Thomas tried to soothe him, touching his shoulder in a friendly way and noting that Weller's cheeks dimpled in the same way whether he was laughing or angry.

A flock of crows flew over the trees with loud caws, then fanned out onto the roofs of the charred buildings. The cloudy sky had the yellow hue of early winter.

Weller seemed encouraged. 'I know we're back in the saddle, Thomas, thanks to the model, and lots of fellows who cold-shouldered me are getting in touch again. But I'm never going to meet Stalin now.'

Thomas was perplexed that meeting Stalin mattered so much to Weller. After all, what could you learn about a leader in a brief formal meeting? Was it to stand next to him, to be photographed with him? Was Weller a lightweight who just wanted to touch a movie star?

'You know something, Weller, my friend,' said Thomas. 'We're only passing through, so it's natural to be impressed by the great events of our time, but in the end we'll only experience a narrow slice of history. If you think about it like that then you can take heart.'

'You mean the night when the treaty with the Soviet Union was signed wasn't a great event?' Weller asked.

'More or less.' Thomas was surprised by his own sincerity. 'When we started to put together the models of national character for Poland, France and Italy, the first stage was a simple historical survey of those nations. Naturally we ran into problems from the start. For instance, when exactly does a nation come into being? But I'll tell you a secret: all the surveys were boringly similar. Every period is dominated by some mighty power—that prince, king, empire, conqueror, et cetera—with endless wars and even more treaties. I instructed them to throw it all in the trash, and look at other details. What commerce took place between northern and southern Italians? How sweet and expensive were the grapes grown on the Cinque Terre hills that slope down to the coast at Genoa? How did the French adjust to secular schools? Every period has its own nuances, but the grand sweep of history is always forged from the same principles. The Roman Empire disappeared in the fifth century; it was no more than an episode in history. A long time before it, in the beginning of the twelfth century BC, the Mediterranean basin was destroyed, entire cultures were wiped out, and the region was relegated to darkness for centuries. Then different empires appeared: the Greeks, and the Romans, and the one after that. The Poles and Lithuanians once had an empire, and they defeated our ancestors in battle. And now'—he waved his hand at the horizon of Warsaw—'look at us today.'

Weller had closed his eyes. He opened them. 'Heiselberg, doesn't the thousand-year Reich have any meaning for you?'

'There won't be a thousand-year Reich. That's not a human timespan. In another thousand years perhaps there won't be any snow in the world.' Seeing Weller's astounded face, he wondered whether he had gone too far. 'Clearly my hope is that there will be a great empire in the lifetimes of as many generations as possible.'

'I'd lose my sanity if I thought about the world that way,' Weller protested.

'On the contrary. Think of that night you missed in Moscow as a minor episode, like that tiny cloud. And Stalin, whom you want to meet so much, is, let's say, a slightly bigger cloud, like one of the Hittite kings.'

They sat in silence. The sky turned grey, and a weak glow came from the streetlights that had survived the bombing. A rumble of thunder was heard.

'I'm tired.' Weller rose heavily. 'Let's go home.'

They reached the corner of Marszałkowska and Jerozolimskie, turned left and started walking rapidly towards Nowy Swiat. It started to rain, and there was more thunder. They sheltered under the awning of a café.

'Look.' Thomas pointed at a poster on the facade of a hotel. 'It's an advertisement for soap, see? There's a running deer. But why is there a circle around it? What kind of dream are they selling people? Run fast, and you'll always be trapped in a circle?'

Weller didn't answer. He made a dash for the bakery next door. Through the window Thomas saw him buy a loaf of bread and a jar of mushrooms. When he came out, he smelled the bread and said to Thomas, 'We'll have a fine dinner. You're going to have the best soup in Europe.'

His gloomy exhaustion seemed to have vanished. When they reached their building, Weller said, 'From the way you spoke about the advertisement, I sense that you still think about your life in that American business.'

'It's hard to erase more than a decade invested in one company.'

For a month he hadn't said that word. For years he had said it dozens of times a day: 'Milton', 'the Milton company', 'we at Milton'. Could a man like Weller, who had jostled with bureaucrats of his own kind all his life—even Frau Tschammer had more intelligence than most of them—understand what real action was like? It was hard to be reconciled with the fact that everything you had achieved in one of the most difficult markets in the world had evaporated because of abstract struggles that had nothing to do with you. But the betrayal of the Milton people was worse. They had arranged another position for Carlson Mailer, but cut loose the man who had made the German branch and its sub-branches his lifework. He carried the cartons out of the office himself. And he, innocent as he was—he only understood how innocent when he started job-hunting in the newspaper—had always believed that Milton was also his company.

The old doorman pulled his hands out of his coat pockets and stood to attention. He opened the creaking iron gate, and they walked down the dark tunnel that led to the courtyard. The two upper floors of the right-hand building had been smashed by the bombing of the Luftwaffe. Only the galvanised downpipe remained erect, like a mast. Someone had hung a flag from it. They turned to a white building whose first floor was decorated with frescoes, sgraffiti and a niche sheltering a statue of the Virgin. Lights glowed from the windows. A tango could be faintly heard.

They climbed the steps. Thomas urged Weller to give him his first Russian lesson now.

'Uspokoytyes, vy slishkom uvlekayetyes,'* Weller answered and hummed the first line of the anthem: 'Poland has not yet been lost.' Both of them had a weakness for childish humour that reversed the order of things. Just a week ago they had visited a church as part of their initiative to speak with moderate priests, and when they walked between the wooden pews, they chuckled together. Weller sang, 'Jesus, I live for you,' and Thomas intoned, 'Oh, Mary, save me.'

Outside the doors on the first floor hung grey military shirts caked with mud, dry leaves and thin red streaks.

It wasn't until Weller gripped his sleeve and started to pull him upstairs that Thomas noticed he was frozen to the spot. He was dragged along, dizzy, until Weller relaxed his grip. They climbed the stairs, and he saw the mud stains on the wall. One of the soldiers had probably cleaned his boots there. Dry red flakes dotted the floor.

On the second floor stood a row of four pairs of boots. The boots on

---

* Relax, you're too eager.

the right were brown. The leather at their tips was black-violet. Mud, leaves and pine needles were stuck to the soles. A brown shirt with buttons, spotted with bloodstains, was hanging on the door handle. Thomas had a strange urge to turn the boots over and inspect the soles.

'Are you coming?'

When he raised his eyes, Weller had already disappeared. Thomas raced after him to the third floor. On the landing he encountered two pairs of upside-down boots. Thomas stared at them and stifled a scream. A thick layer of dried blood clung to the soles. He felt a thump in his chest; he took a groaning breath. The black veils descended around his face. For the first time in his life he wanted to wrap himself up in them, in the darkness.

He muttered something and sat down on one of the steps, gripping the rickety banister. In his imagination he saw Clarissa leaning on the door while he was standing in the stairwell, the valise in his hand. With a smile she whispered, 'You're not moving from here.' Her face was flushed, she approached, pressed against him and he—something stuck in his mind like an annoying leaf to a shoe, a sentence that Fiske once quoted out of a book: 'The right proportion for a woman's head? About an eighth of the length of her body.'

The banister swayed, and his hand scraped against the rust encrusted on it. He was filled with shame, as though summoning an image of Clarissa to pull him through his weakness had polluted her.

'Do you want me to call a doctor?' Weller sounded flat. 'I could call Dr von Wirsch on the first floor.'

He looked up at Weller. The idea that one of them might go back down to the first floor produced a ghastly shared laugh-yawn, which begged to be released. Damn it, that was the best joke the man had ever made.

Weller came downstairs and stood between him and the boots, one hand holding the bag of bread, the other reaching out. 'Heiselberg,' he ordered. 'We're going to our apartment.'

He imagined bodies and faces spinning round, drenched in blood, the parade of souls, coughing and panting, that had come down these stairs in the last month. These were the tenants who had been driven out—university lecturers, a former member of parliament, a journalist, clutching coats and blankets, loaves of bread, sausages and cheese, big squares of butter melting into the blankets—and the young German officer making them hurry. Afterwards the officer had joked to the new tenants, 'You only need one sentence in Polish: "He's off to work, he'll be back in the evening."'

Thomas tripped on the steps. Weller pushed him up. When they reached the top floor Weller sat him down on an armchair in the parlour. The room was redolent with the warm smell of meat and bay leaves. Thomas saw him pick up a silver ladle near the wood stove, and stir the big pot.

'Eight hours on a low fire, and you'll see how great it is,' he called out. 'My grandmother made me swear to cook this stew only on a wood fire.'

Thomas watched the goldfish in the aquarium. In the light from the streetlamp the fish looked like an orange serpent, spitting fire. A little red scratch twisted on his palm.

Weller spread a cloth on the table in the dining alcove and put deep soup bowls onto white plates. On either side he arranged silver forks and knives and soup spoons with gold-plated handles, the legacy of the previous owners. Weller surveyed the table with satisfaction and returned to the pot. Now he hurried towards Thomas with the ladle. 'Taste, Heiselberg, you have to taste, it's a delicacy.'

Thomas felt the heat of the stew. He sipped from the spoon. The liquid burned his tongue, and the taste was thick and rich. His breathing settled. Weller came to the table holding the steaming pot, and again he complained that in Germany, in all Europe really, they hadn't yet understood the potential of root vegetables. 'I believe that this time I prepared a wondrous meal, worthy of honourable diplomats like us,' he grunted with pleasure. 'My dear friend, I beg you to learn to enjoy a fine meal at last.'

Thomas remembered that he was hungry.

...

The days passed swiftly. Thomas worked harder than he had ever done at Milton, beginning at 8 a.m. and finishing late. They participated in meetings full of idle chatter, with dozens of people, and whole days were frittered away—a phenomenon that Thomas called 'the Germans' chronic shortage of time'. They provided evaluations of the situation to the Foreign Office; they wrote dozens of letters every week, and they had to keep the model of the Polish national character up to date. Von Ribbbentrop wanted a new edition by March 1940, and this time it would be bound as a book. Von Ribbentrop proposed removing the word 'national' from the title, and his associate Martin Luther announced that this would make the new edition glow with precious light in many people's eyes.

'In 1940 we'll erase "national", in 1941 we'll erase "Polish", and in 1942, the word "man",' Thomas laughed.

Weller did not appreciate humour of that kind. He believed that cultured people should exercise irony rather than cynicism, and that black humour was the province of nihilists.

Before long, at least in the view of some who consulted it, the scientific approach of the model endowed it with the power of prophecy, and they began to ask questions that implicitly required the delegates of the Foreign Office in Warsaw to predict the future. Thomas and Weller resisted such inquiries, but a predictive tone nonetheless sometimes crept into their answers. They took care to offer these forecasts with a bundle of reservations, of course: while certain events were likely to occur, so were others.

Inquiries were received from every conceivable quarter, ranging from the highest levels of the Reich to a minor intelligence officer from Lublin. One question that gave Thomas particular satisfaction was received in early 1940 from the office of Carl Krauch, chairman of the board of I. G. Farben; the company, in cooperation with the government, intended to build gigantic factories at a cost of 800 million Reichsmark in Upper Silesia, near the city of Oświęcim. Would the honourable representative of the Foreign Office analyse the composition of the population in the region and recommend a strategy to enlist the Poles in support of the project? Thomas devoted a week to a report that would impress Krauch, and attached a personal letter in which he implored Krauch to consult his office on any matter.

Someone from the Gestapo asked whether the Poles, as a group that had been oppressed for many generations by foreign conquerors, had developed manipulative techniques to arouse empathy. Their men complained that they found it hard to behave with sufficient severity towards the Poles. Weller claimed that the model could not answer such a cruel question, and Thomas accepted his opinion. Weller was also the one who insisted on responding to the inquiry of the Foreign Office in Berlin about the lies being circulated by the Poles regarding atrocities committed by the occupying Germans: were there precedents for this 'Polish tendency to exaggerate'? Surely these accusations had been directed against other occupiers—the Russians, or the Austro-Hungarians. From a historical perspective, was it possible to characterise the Poles, like the Jews, as chronic exaggerators?

Many officials—including Goebbels, Rosenberg, the gauleiters of Reichsgau Wartheland, Danzig and West Prussia—completely ignored the model and forbade their subordinates to send questions to them. Krüger, the commander of the SS and the police in the Generalgouvernement, was contemptuous, but the district governor admired it. Hans Frank, the governor-general of Poland, had limited respect for it. Heydrich regarded it as 'a harmless project of the Foreign Office, which is begging for a bit of involvement in Poland', and therefore SS men were permitted to address questions to them.

The speed with which their office became a well-known agency of the Third Reich didn't surprise Thomas: any new organisation, whether a regime of soft-brained bullies or a company that sold the inner organs of corpses, would gradually adopt jargon, ceremonies, departments and nicknames testifying to its acceptance, though it had at first glance seemed totally monstrous.

As expected, Weller rejected opinions of that kind and called those who held them 'degenerate and pathological'. In his opinion, the rise of the model was a tribute to devoted work, clever strategy, to the disorder that prevailed in Poland, which forced confused government agencies to seek advice.

Despite the accelerated pace of work, Weller did not change his habits. He read all the newspapers, and took an hour and a half for lunch. Sometimes, out of personal interest and a sincere desire to help his country, he devoted himself to tasks that had nothing to do with his duties. In response to the venomous criticism by Britain—the object of Weller's deep hatred—of the German bombing of Poland, he spent two weeks making a list of all the places where the Royal Air Force had bombed and killed civilians from the end of the Great War until the present. He roamed around the office as though possessed: 'In India—endless, of course. And in Yemen, Palestine and Iraq. And in Africa—in Uganda and Kenya, and nowhere did they face a threat like Poland's threat to us, so how do they dare?' To clinch his point he would quote Tacitus. *'Solitudinem faciunt pacem appellant.'** The way officials from the Foreign Office could waste precious hours chattering about things beyond their control amused Thomas.

Weller, though wasting time was a matter of principle for him, constantly complained about how much he had to do. Thomas preferred days when he was in the grip of work fever, when he had no time to think, to yearn, to confront the knowledge that another lonely day had passed. Only when he lay in bed at night, hearing music and laughter in the apartments of young officers, did he imagine a blank sheet of paper, and on it, a letter to Clarissa.

'In my childhood, I hoped, just like U, to become a great man. He was enchanted by the natural sciences and modern engineering, and I, who belonged to the next generation, was drawn to the world of merchandise and sales. From my youth I was attracted to it, and that was the world I knew and studied. Until recently I had no reason to see that choice as a mistake. On the contrary, it seemed that the spirit of the age tended in that direction; even Lenin, the great Communist,

---

* They create a wasteland and call it peace.

instructed his people to learn to trade. U was disappointed when he understood that he wouldn't find answers in the paths of knowledge he had pursued, and I was parted from my calling by fate. In a way both U and I were confronted with a moment when the certainties of our lives collapsed. We were forced to start from scratch. To acquire new qualities...'

There was something amusing about it: he wrote to her only in his head, not leaving a single incriminating page behind, but he disguised Ulrich, Musil's hero, as U. He had taught even his imagination a lesson or two in caution, and remembered not to mention the hero of a banned novel.

One night he wrote again in his head: 'The inability to act on love is a curse that has been cast upon me. Recently I realised that she was right, the woman who told me that I would always be alone if I didn't do something about it. Perhaps these nights in Warsaw, in which I lie in a strange bed in an apartment that isn't mine, sharpen the dread of loneliness I have always known. Feelings of longing, possibly exaggerated, rage in my soul, and I think of you, my dear, on the day when you removed from the mantelpiece the brass-plated rifle shells that my father had collected on the battlefield, along with his Iron Cross, and the picture of nine young men in uniform, and reserve officer Werner Heiselberg in the Forest of Argonne at sunrise. Seven of them were killed, another lost an arm and a leg, and the ninth lost his brother, his young wife and his money, and committed suicide. Only my father survived. Even my mother, who casually kicked him out of the house, didn't dare remove those items from the mantel. And you? You didn't say a thing, and two days later they had disappeared.

'Allow me to remind you of at least two sun-drenched mornings in Grünewald and the laughter in your eyes after you had bargained down the cost of the ticket on the Stadtbahn, and how, after you scolded the conductor, he reduced the fare because you were a member of the NSV. And I insist on adding several other Sundays in the ice-cream parlour in Olivaer Platz, where the counter staff took such a liking to you that they prepared a special platter of mixed flavours so that you could decide which was strongest. I think of those days, and how wonderful you were; remember Rilke's lines: *Liebender, euch, ihr in einander Genügten, / frag ich nach uns. Ihr greift euch. Habt ihr Beweise?'**

One night, when they were drunk, he confided in Weller, who asked: Why don't you write to her?

He was silent, then explained that, when they parted, they decided Clarissa could live in his apartment if she wished, but since there was no knowing how long he would be gone, maybe a year or more, there would be no obligations between them, and she could see other men, with one reservation: she could not bring any men back to the apartment. The separation wasn't coincidental. He didn't want to make things difficult for her, especially if she had already given her heart to another man, and in fact he expected her to write to him about her feelings. Weller scoffed at this. How could Thomas display such faintness of heart in love?

'The first letter must come from you. You're the one who left Berlin, and your honour requires you to write to her. If you don't want to know about other men, don't ask. From my acquaintance with women, she will tell you.'

All that weekend Weller urged him to sit down and write, and told Thomas stories about how he courted his wife. He seemed to be intoxicated with their new intimacy and began to give Thomas advice about becoming more aware of the little pleasures of life. He would like to find Thomas's office empty once in a while, to hear that his friend had gone for a stroll along the river, to a fine restaurant, to spend time with a woman. Encouraged by Thomas's nods, he peppered him with other questions. Why hadn't he told him that he had been married? He never mentioned his wife's name. Even more than that, Weller was interested in his mother: there was some little thing that wouldn't let him rest, and he hoped he wasn't going too far by raising the subject. He understood, of course, the tragedy that had struck

---

* Rilke, 'Second Duino Elegy': You lovers, so sufficient to one another/ I ask you about us. You hold each other. Do you have proof?

Thomas with Frau Heiselberg's death, but the few times he had mentioned his mother he had not said at all that she was no longer living. Thomas was sure, he said, that he had mentioned the terrible illness that had led to her death, and in any event Weller had attended her funeral. So it wasn't as if he were concealing anything.

'I wasn't suggesting that you were hiding her death,' Weller said, apparently taken aback by Thomas's answer. He wanted only to remind Thomas that he regarded him as a close friend, and hoped that Thomas also trusted him, since true friends can help one another in situations like this. Silence fell, before Thomas announced that he had decided to write to Clarissa. 'I wish to thank you, Weller, my friend, for your good advice and heartfelt generosity.'

For two days he shut himself up in his room and wrote. He tried to be witty and imaginative and not too wordy. He polished the style and chose the most beautiful quotations.

Clarissa's answer arrived two weeks later. The letter wasn't short, about six pages of dense handwriting, but the main point was in the last two pages:

> Thomas, dear, I think you are clinging to me because now, in horrible Warsaw, far from here, I'm a safe haven. (Father is shouting at Karlchen. He swore at the history teacher again. Father says that Karlchen is probably deranged. I'm getting out of here right away and going up to your apartment.) And to hold on to me, you're taking a leap, maybe a leap of faith, like the one that some of the German people made in recent years, but yours is in the personal sense. It's fine to leap, but some people fall, don't they?
>
> I read your letter and didn't understand it. Does it sound strange that things aren't clear to the object of all the love you poured into your letter? They're clear to you, and that's exactly the point. I think you had a rush of blood, that your heart suddenly filled up. You love me so much now (Mother is shouting to Father to leave Karlchen alone.

If Father doesn't give in, I'll have to intervene. Recently he's been afraid of little Clarissa, no longer the girl they wouldn't allow to read any novel that Mother hadn't read first), but it's a love that's shut up inside itself. Maybe I'm the hollow one who doesn't understand and can't join in your leap of faith, but in my opinion, I'm right: your love is hollow. Maybe your Bildung will eventually lead you to love, truly, not in polished words from Warsaw.

Only cowards love from a distance.

I'm prepared for this journey. I'll stand by your side. You are so dear to me. Sometimes at night I feel faint with longing for you, and all the men who run after me seem like children, remind me of Karlchen. I told one of them, 'I'm talking to you, but it's like you haven't even been born yet.' He called me a Hamburg peacock, and I answered that I'm proud of my pride. You know me, I can't let anyone else have the last word.

But I've strayed from the point: there's something that comes before fulfilment. (Father told Mother that the teacher declared that Karlchen is backward, and in the end they'll transfer him to an institution for children like that. Mother, the coward, is trembling: the same as they did to the Somers' boy? They sterilised him. Father says that they wouldn't dare touch his son, but in any case he has already spoken with a lawyer and a doctor who would represent Karlchen in court if something bad happens. But it would be better if Karlchen watched his behaviour.) You quoted Rilke to impress me, and that's fine. Everyone here is quoting things all the time. But I didn't understand that choice either. Those lines are beautiful, but according to you, we have evidence of our love: days flooded with sun, brass-plated bullets that disappeared, nights that we slept in the same house, and we shouldn't ignore the splendid bouquet of crocuses you bought for my birthday. But what question are you actually asking? Are you asking me or yourself? Or maybe you're asking the clever love that tricked you during all those marvellous, sun-drenched days in Berlin, when you were unemployed and we had plenty of free time—and which suddenly swept over you in faraway Warsaw (in my opinion Father is exaggerating to frighten Mother and encourage her to be strict with Karlchen).

Thomas, my dear, maybe you should be strict with me?

And at the end she wrote:

On Wednesday a schoolmate of yours visited the apartment, Hermann Kreizinger. With his suntan and thrilling black uniform he looks like an American movie star. He's funny. He imitates your laugh very well. He claims that it's never exactly a laugh. I told him that you're in Poland. He seemed pleased and said that it was quite a coincidence, since he had come to say goodbye. He's been stationed in Poland. I told him that I wanted you two to meet, because you're alone there, and he promised to make an effort to see you. That's not enough, I scolded him. The man most dear to me in the world is feeling lonely in that horrible Warsaw. Give me your word of honour as an SS officer that you'll spend some time with him. And he gave it!

I couldn't resist. I hope you won't hate me. I asked him what kind of boy you were. Handsome? Sad? Popular with girls? He said you were good-looking, sometimes sad, and that you weren't interested in your studies, you only cared about money and languages. How come you never told me you're talented at languages? Since when have you been so modest? Hermann told me that your ability to imitate a foreign language is truly rare. In fact, he called it 'a rare talent for imitation'. But I scolded him again: it isn't nice to envy a friend. He apologised and admitted that maybe his way of putting it had soured his admiration. Then he boasted that you had trouble with the humanities, and that he helped you prepare for examinations. Is it true that in history and literature he was one of the three best students in the class? When we drank tea he told me how you used to sneak into hotels, you would be a Russian prince and he would be your personal servant. My dear! Where did you hide your playful side? When you come back to Berlin, we'll do it together. I'll be Princess Yeketrina! He told me that Frau Heiselberg objected to your friendship with him and accused him of corrupting her dear son, and he was very insulted. At first he seemed like someone who keeps a grudge just from habit, but afterwards I felt that the insult must have been really severe. Poor fellow.

LENINGRAD–SOCHI
WINTER 1939–1940

Glowing trails of the city's last lights swirled in orange and gold on the train windows. Why was she pressing her face to the cold glass like a peasant woman whose world ended where the potato fields end? Perhaps because she hadn't left the city in more than two years. Throughout her childhood she had sworn that by her twenty-first birthday she would be skipping through the streets of Paris and Berlin. At least Paris. Sasha looked up at the surprisingly starry sky, where gigantic columns of smoke and dust rose between her and the city. Far off in the fields she could just see a wagon driver, with two flaming torches fastened to the sides of his wagon. He was whipping a pair of black oxen. Next to him sat a boy, or perhaps a sack of potatoes.

While her eyes groped in the darkness, her mind cast a light over the snowy shores of those tiny islands whose names she had loved to roll on her tongue: Aptekarsky, Krestovsky. Her grandfather had owned a dacha on Krestovsky. 'It wasn't luxurious,' her mother admitted, 'but very useful.' That dacha was stolen from them in 1912, when her grandfather quit the Okhranka. 'We were lucky that when the Bolsheviks took Petrograd we didn't own anything except our house,' her grandfather explained.

Her hair tickled her nape. She gathered it in her right hand and in the same movement fastened it into a bun. Now her neck felt strange, naked. Her husband's fingers, still greasy from the *pirozhki* he had gobbled down before falling asleep, touched the tips of hers. A whisper fled from his dream. He touched the white bandage. Every time he came near that bandage, she was stricken with a rage he couldn't comprehend. He liked to find little things to be stubborn about, where he could refuse to compromise—possibly to show his strength and possibly, as in this instance, because he was convinced that the bandage was like a sacred thing for her. Once she had even hit him with her right hand and shouted that he must never dare to touch that bandage again.

It was odd to have to do everything more or less one-handed, and even the simplest thing had to pass the test: getting dressed or undressed, picking something up, writing, leafing through a book, any action involving water. When she first came out of hospital, she refused to go near water, and it did no good to implore or explain. Helpless, Maxim swallowed his pride and invited Stepan Kristoforovich to their apartment to speak heart to heart with her, and remind her how anxious the department was for her to return to work. After that he amused her with stories about the new orders from the Kremlin regarding morning exercises. Concern for the workers' bodies was now official, and even comrades on the verge of retirement were required to keep fit; he, for example, had been signed up for a course in jujitsu. The new boss of the NKVD, Lavrentiy Pavlovich Beria, liked it. After Styopa's visit, she allowed Maxim to wash her in cold water, having wrapped her hand in several layers of cloth. She wouldn't go near the samovar, and every time she saw steam rising, even someone drinking tea, her mind seethed with images of the water bubbling furiously onto her body. There were days when she imagined that the rain was boiling.

His fingers were stroking the bandage, that was clear. She removed her hand and pressed it against her belly. The train slowed; the smell of makhorka tobacco and heavy cigarette smoke descended on her. She got up and stepped over the sleeping passengers wrapped in their furs, looking for fresh air. Two girls sat at the back of the coach and chatted. Their legs, in tight white stockings, rested on the seats in front of them. They whispered, laughed and gave her a cheeky glance. She was tempted to sit and chat with them, to bridge, if only for a moment, the chasm that had formed with bewildering speed between girls like them and herself, a married woman employed by the NKVD. Just a year ago she had sat with Zhenya in a tram, wearing her thin beaded dress, as happy as those girls were and even more insolent.

Two soldiers complained that the toilet was locked. They offered her a cigarette and asked where she worked. She refused the cigarette and asked where they were stationed. They were both army doctors. One of them had fought in Khalkhin Gol during the summer, on the Japanese front, and his arm had been wounded.

'He was hit two hours into the war,' his friend laughed. 'Then he lay in the hospital for a month, sitting in a sauna and having the time of his life.'

She congratulated them on the brilliant victory and stood near the window, which was covered in frost. Cold air blew on her face through the unsealed edges.

All that day images of her first trip to Moscow raced through her memory, shattering into fragments, gathering together again, then scattering into atoms and striking her like a sandstorm. How many times a day could the same memory assail her?

She is sixteen, it's late at night, she walks hand in hand with Father. They approach the platform. She has goosebumps in anticipation of the great moment—her first trip on the *Red Arrow*, the greatest train in the world. In school they had devoted an entire lesson to the achievements of the engineers and planners, followed by stupid mathematical riddles: Sasha rides on the *Red Arrow*. Ulla Kleiss travels on a new German train, the *Flying Hamburger*. Because of friction on the tracks, the German train decreases speed by four per cent, while the Russian train slows down by two per cent, and there are all sorts of other variables too. (In the end she plays the smart aleck and submits a calculation that has the German kid arriving first, and at recess the boys threaten to beat her up. The truth is that her father told her that the *Flying Hamburger* leaves us far behind.)

Father places the suitcase on the platform and wiggles his fingers, which have turned red from the effort of carrying it. She looks at his hand, amazed at how small it is. His fingers and hers are the same size. Her mind is still wearing itself out with dreadful scenarios in which something goes wrong at the last moment—her mother gets sick, there's a crisis at the institute, she vomits on the platform. Meanwhile Father is impressed by the train: seventy kilometres per hour, one of the fastest on the continent! It looks gigantic and splendid to her. You could fit the entire city into its coaches. Father boasts again about Soviet industry, which is catching up to the West at an astonishing pace: 'We've paid a high price, no doubt, but the achievements are enormous.'

Soldiers in tunics, with raspberry-coloured squares on their lapels, ask for their travel documents, and Father shows them. Now it's happening, Sasha is panicked. They'll send us back home. But the soldiers are actually nice and wish them a pleasant journey.

When they start checking other people, Sasha says to her father, 'I want a beer,' expecting he will be shocked, get angry and lecture her: little girls don't drink beer. But he'll have to acknowledge that she has drunk beer in the past, and she's still here, and everything is fine. She's not such a little girl anymore.

'Beer?' he answers distractedly. 'There's no time for that now.'

She gets annoyed, and as if by accident she digs her fingernails into his hand. He loosens his grip. An aggressive thought provokes her: Okay, Father, that doesn't seem to have been enough for you, maybe beer is a trivial thing, and she's almost tempted to tell him about that morning, or actually about the day before, when she and Maxim Podolsky lay naked in his parents' bedroom. A warm breeze blew through the window, and the sun gilded his muscular body. And she would immediately explain, listen, Father, we didn't mean to cause a scandal, we just wanted to feel the breeze, and you can't see the bed from the neighbouring apartments, Maxim checked. Aside from that, true, we were naked, but I only let him lick the upper part of my body, and I only kissed him on the lips. Mother taught me to be careful with boys: you have to refuse as soon as they ask, otherwise you're swept along. It was so nice when Maxim licked my belly and my hips and my back. You always said those Chekists were thorough guys, so look, their sons are too.

But she doesn't have the courage to speak up, and says something under her breath about being in Maxim's parents' bed, until he scolds her, 'Stop mumbling!'

'Okay, Father, I didn't mean to,' she says softly, and they board the train.

She went back to her seat. One of the girls had fallen asleep, and the other was playing with a piece of string, looking bored. That was what being young was like: after high spirits comes tedium, and all the mood swings make you dizzy. You can't get off the roller-coaster, and the only thing that ever changes is how much you doubt your sadness and joy. She didn't envy their youthful lack of self-consciousness. How much time was left for them? She sat down next to Podolsky, who was snoring lightly. He buried his cheek in the hollow between her shoulder and her neck. He smelled her body in his sleep.

She pushed him a little. He breathed hot air onto her neck, woke up, rubbed his eyes and complained that the coach wasn't heated. 'Stepan Kristoforovich should have reserved seats for us in the international coach. There you sit four to a compartment, the seats are upholstered in plush, and waiters serve you wine and cake.' She didn't answer, and he fell asleep again. Saliva dripped from the corner of his mouth.

On the right, the platforms of Novgorod station shone, and their light fell into the coach. It disturbed some of the dozing passengers: arms were stretched, there was coughing and nose-blowing, faces numb with sleep turned to the right and left, people groped in valises. Her husband slept on.

The train stopped. The two girls got off without any bags, and the soldiers followed them. From the platform passengers bundled up in coats stormed the train, carrying heavy suitcases, pursued by whistling gusts of wind. A short man in stained overalls held the hands of two young girls wearing hats whose ribbed edges hid their eyes. Tattered wool blankets were wrapped tightly around their bodies. They tried to push through the dozens of people mobbing the train and were shoved back again and again. What scrawny girls! She was alarmed for them, wanted to shelter them from the wind, sit them down at a table in a warm room and fill their plates. Maxim! She remembered him greedily eating that *pirozhki* while tens of thousands of children went hungry in this country. The cold pierced her; she knew the deceptively drowsy pace of the cold cruising through you, from toe to temple, till suddenly you couldn't move.

The girls in blankets disappeared, and she decided to look for them in the rear coaches after dawn. She wrapped herself in Vlada's old grey officer's coat, balled up her pullover, placed it against the window and leaned her head on it.

Waiting for sleep to dissolve her vexations, she remembered that Maxim had asked her to wake him at Kalinin. It hadn't even occurred to her that she might sleep. Since their marriage, in fact since the day they met, he had hardly ever been awake while she slept. Only in the hospital—while she was stunned with sedatives he sat next to her bed at night and read the newspaper. When she woke up, he would read her articles he found interesting, until she asked him to stop, just to read her the science stories. One night he told her that Stepan Kristoforovich and Reznikov had spoken to a reporter for *Leningradskaya Pravda* and urged him to publish a story about the brave young investigator who had turned her back on the Leningrad Group, including her parents, who had joined up with the enemies of the people, and was attacked cruelly by one of the traitors. The reporter loved the idea. 'We have found the twin sister of young Pavlik Morozov,' he shouted, 'and she was wounded in the struggle!'

'I've never heard such an idiotic comparison,' she grumbled, trying to look amused to hide her horror. 'Even the name Pavlik Morozov nauseates me: I would never have testified in court against my parents, or say that my father wasn't my father.'

Maxim withdrew. 'Of course, of course,' he soothed. 'I told them that the comparison was out of place.'

'Maxim,' she said. 'Never mention that name to me, do you understand?'

'Of course, of course, dear.' He leaned over to kiss her shoulder.

The smoothness of his tongue aroused her. In her imagination her fingernails scratched his plump and perfumed flesh, plucked his copper moustache, which grew redder every day.

Once she heard Father tell Mother, after another dinner when Vlada had talked like a madman, 'That boy is our misfortune. He's made from the same stuff as that filthy Pavlik Morozov.' Mother shushed him at once; Vlada did talk wildly sometimes, but in his heart he truly believed in the party, just like his friends. He might say harsh things at home, but he would always be loyal to his parents. 'He's disappointed with us and with our friends, and he has to express his opinion, don't you agree?'

Sasha also remembered Nadyezhda pulling a face at Brodsky, brandishing a newspaper story in which it was reported that Gorky had called Pavlik Morozov a 'shining example' and proposed building a monument in his honour. Nadyezhda had screamed, 'And you praise Gorky, that piece of filth?'

Why had Maxim mentioned that dreadful name? Since his first visit to the hospital—dressed to the nines, brow furrowed, bearing roses and chocolates—she suspected he was pleased about what had happened to her, even if her punishment had been too severe. He was satisfied like a teacher who had warned a disobedient student. The next day, when he told her that he had taken care of the matter of the newspaper interview, her body shook with rage. How he loved to be patronising, her husband!

The two girls returned to the coach, and one of them was holding a little teapot full of boiling water. When they passed by her, she couldn't help flinching, and dug in behind Maxim's body. The train emitted a loud whistle and started moving with rhythmic clicking on the rails. She seemed to hear the girls tapping the teapot with their nails and giggling again. The two doctors came back and sat behind her, where they peeled hard-boiled eggs, and cursed their antiquated army equipment. One of them said that maybe the time had come to write a letter to 'the doctors' best friend'.

His companion reprimanded him. 'Comrade Stalin is busy with the war in Europe now. We're expected to solve these problems for ourselves.'

The first doctor coughed. 'Perhaps you're right.'

She turned around to them. 'Maybe you'd better shut up.'

They stared at her. Perhaps they guessed where Maxim worked, or her tone indicated her status. People learned to identify NKVD in all sorts of ways, some of which, like a certain distance between the lips and the eyes, were entirely imaginary. Her temples throbbed; too many troubles were crammed into the train: the hungry girls, the faulty medical equipment, flakes of the *pirozhki* on Maxim's moustache. She closed her eyes and pressed her ear to the pullover, and Brodsky's caressing voice cradled her together with the rocking coach: 'In times of distress, innocent people turn to their friends for help, but smart people, who understand a thing or two about life in this country, turn to the kingdom of sleep, where their secrets are safe.'

...

Every morning her husband rose early, thrust the axe into his belt and joined the men from the dachas on the hillside; they planted lemon trees, chopped wood for heating and weeded the gardens.

'In this season, there aren't too many high-profile people on holiday in Sochi. It's a bit cold,' Styopa said with a wink when he told her about the vacation. 'So I could get one of the best dachas for you. You don't want to know who lives in them during the summer, names everyone knows.'

'Styopa, I just want to get back to work,' she had replied. 'I need you to make me laugh.'

'When you come back, I'll make you laugh as much as you like,' Styopa had answered. 'Would you rather go to the healing waters of Borjomi? Anything is possible. Just say the word.'

'Dear Styopa, your concern truly warms my heart.' She had practised the line. 'But I need the routine of work. I believe that's what's best for me.'

'You'll come back, my dear. After all, without you we're done for.'

He had been adamant about the need for a holiday. He was as cheerful as ever but he looked at her forensically, doubtless seeking evidence for the rumour Reznikov had circulated, that she had gone mad after the incident with Morozovsky. 'But first of all, you have to get your strength back. Your husband will join you. We decided long ago that he needs a vacation. We must take very good care of such a dedicated man.'

After Maxim went off with his axe, she would lie in bed for a little while, picking at the tray of little treats he prepared for her every morning, and then she would dress and sit on the balcony that surrounded the wooden building. The house was at the top of a steep hill overlooking the sea; a few smaller dachas were scattered below it. She would sit at a round wicker table with her chin thrust into the fur lapel of her coat (when they reached Sochi she discovered that Maxim hadn't packed a single one of her scarves, but he had somehow squeezed her spring wedding dress into the suitcase) and look across the slope which gave way to a dark green fringe. It was a panorama of enchanting movement: horses and their straight-backed riders galloped on the shore; in the west, bands of hunters with shining rifles belted to their backs strode towards the forest. Small boats bobbed on the waves that turned grey as the hours passed, and on the distant horizon clouds swirled around the jagged, snowy peaks of Krasnaya Polyana, which looked like small human heads. Sometimes, in the afternoon, the sun would shoot against it and a white gleam, as silver as mercury, would quiver up there. She called it 'a burning angel dancing on the mountain', and a swift glance was enough to bring a tear.

After lunch she would walk in the garden and sometimes, with her unbandaged hand, she would prune the raspberry bushes alongside the path. Those were the hours when old men dressed in rags and Circassian women in colourful capes could be seen—Podolsky told her that the villagers looked for odds and ends of food here, because in the summer the vacationers lit bonfires and roasted meat, and sometimes scraps were left over.

'It's not enough that those fools haven't figured out that there are no barbecues in winter and always beg for food,' he said in annoyance, 'they also whine about all the injustices done to them. It's a good thing that there isn't a political party for every complaint.'

In the evening the world darkened. It was too quiet, aside from the whistling of the wind, as if something terrible was about to happen. Of the two of them, only she understood that quietness, because Maxim was yet to suffer: his father died in bed from heart disease, he visited his mother and sister once a week; he didn't realise that these were luxuries. The previous evening, when sadness and silence overwhelmed them, he suggested that they visit the neighbouring dacha of Semyon Emilyevich to play roulette and cards. In the schoolyard Maxim had been the king of card sharks, and he loved to invent games. With the help of his shining eyes and the odd curse, he would force his friends to play, although they all knew that he would be the only winner. But in recent years he had abandoned his boyhood fondness for gambling.

She declined the invitation, and sternly ignored his expectation that she would let him go without her. She knew he wouldn't dare ask, and swore she wouldn't give her consent. There's no choice, Maxim, she chuckled to herself, that's married life, you wanted to get married, didn't you?

And even more than refusing him, she enjoyed seeing him stifle his request, or, on the other hand, resist his impulse to shake off the woman who had taken over his hours of leisure by saying to her, 'I'm playing roulette tonight, and you can do what you want.' Sometimes she thought she was abusing him for no reason: he was devoted to her, bringing a tray to her bed every morning with bread, a hard-boiled egg, jam and tea, quick to respond to her requests, coming up with ideas that might give her pleasure, and yet if every reason for annoying him were a skein of thread, it would be possible to knit pullovers from it for all the Circassians roaming the area.

One evening they were sitting on the balcony, and a ballad by Verstovsky, warbled by a soprano voice, came from Semyon's dacha. Maxim gave an irritable smile and recited gloomily:

> How I caressed him at night,
> In the silence and darkness!
> How we both laughed together
> At your hideous greyness!*

Then he delivered a querulous sermon about the Circassians, who blocked the traffic with their lazy wagons, and yesterday annoyed a group of holiday-makers. He talked and talked, just throwing down words, bored, while the enthusiastic shouts of the gamblers in Semyon's dacha grew louder. After they had gone to bed, and were barely asleep, a muffled, sad ballad crawled into their room:

> Oh, did you ever hear
> The longing, yearning sound
> In the heart of the silent fields
> Mourning love that is gone?

In the morning she told him, 'Maxim, even if I wanted to join you, I don't have a nice evening dress.'

He looked at her as though wondering whether she wanted him to bring up the idea that would infuriate her. Finally he said, 'Maybe

---

* Alexander Pushkin, 'The Gypsies', trans. G. R. Ledger.

you could wear the wedding dress? I packed it.'

She couldn't help admiring her husband, who had clearly identified the unconcealed trap and yet still limped into it. 'I'll never wear that dress again!' she shouted, but her sympathy for his courage softened her anger.

Then it occurred to her that he hadn't actually sacrificed anything, since he knew that was what was needed to calm her down. She got even angrier: it's all a mess. It's impossible to blame him for something and its opposite! But why was everything her husband did so annoying?

'Tomorrow I'll go into town and buy you a new dress,' he said.

'Fine, Maxim.'

At night he desired her but didn't address her body openly; he approached her with childish stratagems. Usually he produced some twisting motion or stretch that pulled her against him, as though by chance, and then he acted as if desire had overcome him, and he was forced to submit to it.

Sasha saw Maxim as the general outline of a body in the dark wooden house. Sometimes a high wall clock emerged from the gloom, with bluish numbers from one to twenty-four in the centre, the kind of clock that Sergei Kirov used to give to outstanding workers: her father had received one of the first models from his hands. The clock became her favourite landmark in the room, and she kept her eyes on it while Maxim positioned her body, which, to her surprise, responded to him. Now she was lying on her belly, rolling onto her back, sitting on his knees, whose bones were so sharp, touching his skin with the fingers of one hand.

In those nights she discovered that her body still craved him.

They would lie zipped together, and her eyes would wander between the clock and the ceiling, from which pointy hooks protruded like sharp blades; she struggled against her imagination, which pictured the hooks coming down and skewering them. He murmured words of love, reminisced about their youth, and a week later she was astonished to realise that he had built a bridge from their school days to their marriage, delicately knitting together the huge rifts. For him their marriage was the inevitable consummation of youthful love. In their story, at least the one they discussed, no trace remained of that dreadful night when he had stood in her room and told her to be someone else or die. He had taken her from the bed, and, when he understood that she hadn't breathed fresh air for days, he pushed her head out of the window. While she was taking in the night breeze, he told her straight: they had to marry now to pre-empt the NKVD investigation. She listened, torn between knowing she had to stay in Leningrad for the twins and wanting to chase after them, to be swallowed up by some camp and die. She asked whether he believed that their marriage would make any difference; if she was lost there was no reason for him to be lost too.

He had answered sincerely that it was possible; such matters were sometimes decided arbitrarily, but it was the most correct action. In recent years they had arrested husbands and wives, and even the wives of high-ranking people, as in the case of Budyonny, but sometimes they left the little people alone. 'And in our case,' he said, looking around as if the severity of the punishment that had been inflicted on the occupants of the house had only now become clear, 'no one is left but you, and maybe they'll be satisfied with that and pardon my wife.'

The next day he told his superior that he intended to get married; now, after the saboteur parents had received their punishment, there was no longer any obstacle to their connection; and Alexandra Andreyevna was prepared to help root out the entire Leningrad Group. In the evening he reported with satisfaction that his superior sounded favourable, but he made it clear that he had to consult with Stepan Kristoforovich Merkalov, the head of the department responsible for investigating the group.

Maxim drank some wine and seemed fortified, and suspicion flashed through Sasha's mind that the question she had asked the day before had been too innocent: he had certainly spoken with his superior before coming to her house, and if he had felt that he couldn't help her he wouldn't have come at all, just as he had disappeared for the last few weeks. She weighed that suspicion against the possibility that she was doing him an injustice, and decided that she would probably never know the truth.

'If we marry, will they return the twins to us?'

He had anticipated that question. 'In 1937 the NKVD issued a secret directive following a decision of the Politburo, that the children of traitors who were not yet fifteen years old would be placed under the authority of the state, and older children would be judged according to the particulars of each case.'

'But Vlada and Kolya are almost sixteen. They aren't supposed to be placed automatically under the authority of the state.'

'A few months here or there—in their view, if you're not sixteen, you're fifteen,' he joked. 'Look,' he added, when he understood the rage that his little witticism had provoked, 'I'll do whatever I can. You know I always was fond of the skinny one, but the chances are poor. Even the son of a marshal with so much to his credit like Yakir was thrown into jail. I can't remember his name.'

'Pyotr, maybe.' During her parents' last days at home, she and Vlada had researched all the precedents for their case.

'Yes, perhaps. A lot of people intervened on his behalf, but nothing helped. It's possible to prevent a decision, but it's very hard to reverse one.'

Colleagues from his department and other senior people had attended their wedding. Maxim assumed that this was evidence that she was safe, at least for the time being. She wore a pink dress with a lace collar, her mother's wedding dress, and her skin crawled the whole time with fear that she would be caught in a hot and blinding spotlight and the whole picture would be revealed to the guests: a little traitor in the dress of a big traitor who had been sentenced to ten years in Kolyma without the right to send or receive letters. Her memory of the wedding was of an endless swirl of movement, where she was continually avoiding guests, picking up snatches of conversation—maybe she'd overhear that final accusation.

Was that her hope? Was she disappointed not to be exposed? It was stupid of her to burrow into the past to locate the moment when the desire to die had overcome the desire to survive. If she was still here, it was clear which urge had won.

After the wedding, when they were lying in bed drunk, she asked about the twins, and he recited resentfully, 'Sashinka, people at the highest levels are making inquiries, and I'll let you know as soon as there's any information.'

She lay beside him, and the memory of the twins stung her throat. The clock said 4 a.m.; the commotion in Semyon's dacha had subsided; through the window their yard was already sprinkled with the silver gleam of dew. How had Maxim manoeuvred her into this sweaty lovers' tangle?

Since their wedding, they had exchanged only a few broken sentences about the twins. After she began working in Styopa's department, she learned that Maxim was less senior than he had hinted—but still he could have done more for them. For too long they had pretended everything was normal as if, as the weeks and months went by, she would have to accept the separation from Kolya and Vlada, and become used to guessing every morning whether they were dead or alive. Until finally she would kill them in her imagination, and they would fade in her memory, like other people who had passed away.

She choked. Was she putting a different blame on him now, a crueller blame—her own?

'Tell me, Maxim,' she said, detaching herself from his sleeping body. As their skins separated, a peeling sound was heard. 'You never said: did you shoot Morozovsky in the head, or was it Styopa?'

When she got up, the clock said eight-thirty, and she felt an annoying itch beneath the bandage. The urge to scratch had been irritating her for several days. Maxim asked her gently when she would get rid of the bandage, and she didn't tell him that, when the doctor said that she would have scars there, she decided she would never take it off. She'd learn to live with one hand.

The sweetish scent of his cologne filtered into her nostrils. 'Good morning, sleepyhead,' she heard him say as he placed the breakfast tray on the bedside table. She opened her eyes. He was sitting on the bed. 'Maybe you don't remember. But last night you asked me a very strange question.'

She remembered how impressed she had been with his shrewdness, and she understood that he expected her to admit that she didn't remember.

'I don't remember,' she said at last.

'You asked me whether I shot Morozovsky.'

'Really?' she said. 'I must have been having nightmares.'

'Of course,' he crowed, full of happiness because she had conceded to him. 'It's no wonder, after the terrible thing that happened to you. No matter what, I don't want it to come between us: I didn't shoot him, it was Stepan Kristoforovich.' He looked down, as though embarrassed. 'I would have shot him! But I didn't have a pistol in my hand—believe me, it would have been a pleasure to dip my hand in that reptile's filthy blood,' he shouted. 'But I remembered how fond your parents were of him, and how close he was to you, and I was afraid that, even though he had attacked you like an animal, you wouldn't forgive me if his blood was on my hands.'

'I understand. It really doesn't matter,' she said.

'My love, let's not remember that cursed event anymore. I'm going to buy you a beautiful dress, and this evening we'll visit Semyon Emilyevich's dacha, okay?'

She didn't answer. He chose to interpret her silence as agreement and went off on his business.

She spent the whole day resting. In the evening, when Maxim returned, he lit a fire in the living room. There were stones of all sizes and colours on the mantelpiece: sharp-edged and round, rough rocks and trimmed stone, black and white, ochre and gold. With great ceremony, he handed her a box with a new dress in it, and went to set the table. He arranged delicacies on it that he had bought in a 'disgustingly expensive, bourgeois shop' in the town centre, and produced a bottle of good wine he had received from Semyon Emilyevich.

Sasha sat at the table in the blue dress, which was cut from fine cloth to a design she liked. She complimented him on his taste. He ate fast, hardly bothering to chew; fatty grains of barley clung to his ginger moustache. She was hungry too, and helped herself to fish liver pâté and onion, and slices of bread slathered with butter and cheese. She covered a slice with a thick layer of barley, placed pickled cucumber on it, and cheerfully called out, 'I've invented a new Russian dish. Register it now in the patent office. Does that still exist?'

Maxim seemed encouraged by the improvement in her mood. He poured more wine and then he remembered that he hadn't yet told her how, on the morning of their departure, he had gone to the office to make some final arrangements, and Stepan Kristoforovich had buttonholed him in the hallway—Maxim had the feeling that he was lying in wait for him—and invited him to his room. He served Maxim tea, and behaved with exaggerated courtesy, chatting about the New Year celebrations. 'How about that—1940,' Maxim imitated him, 'a new decade is cause for a big party!' He announced that he had chosen Podolsky to play him, the head of the department, in a skit that one of the imprisoned writers had written for the celebration. 'And believe me, that poor guy sharpened his arrows and skewered me with no mercy.'

Then Stepan Kristoforovich added that he tried to intervene as little as possible in the private affairs of his workers; while marriage was a holy covenant in his view, love like that between Maxim and Sasha wasn't common around here. He lamented that young couples these days delayed having children, a grave error in his opinion because there was nothing more wonderful for a couple than a child who will always embody and rekindle the purity of their love.

'A philosopher is sitting on the second floor, not a department head,' Sasha grumbled—she couldn't believe that Styopa would be so sentimental. She looked around. The stones on the mantel looked like babies' faces. Once, Nadyezhda Petrovna had said to her that with a little imagination anything in the world could resemble part of the human body, and that made it a lot more interesting. It was possible, for example, to fall in love with a chimney. It was also possible to become a poet of the changing seasons, like Varlamov.

'But there's some truth in what he says,' Maxim whispered. 'How long have we loved each other? I've never loved another woman. If you're worried that a baby will interfere with your future, remove that concern from your heart. Stepan Kristoforovich promised me that he would put you back in your former position whenever you want, and in the morning, when you're working, my mother could—'

'Let's talk about this later,' she interrupted him.

They went out to Semyon's dacha, plunging down the hill into the cold night winds. Their boots left tracks in the damp, slippery earth. Sasha bent down and ran her finger across it. Like touching clay. Maxim looked thoughtful, gripping the white trousers that hung off his hips, whose cuffs were stuffed into his boots. Once again she probed something that rarely surfaced in their daily routine in Leningrad: the webs of imagination that Maxim wove around their marriage, at first perhaps self-consciously, but afterwards without effort. Now a pattern had taken shape, and all his memories were stuffed into it. A child was only a matter of time, especially now that Stepan Kristoforovich was involved. The strange thing was that, as soon as he raised the question of a baby, the slight revulsion she had for him was crushed by a heavier feeling: she envied him his faith in their marriage. He was thrilled by the baby that would be born; this holiday was only a belated honeymoon for him while she was tormented by the events that led to their marriage. There was no one around her now who was truly engraved in her soul.

She imagined him repeating those inanities to their child, and felt disgusted. She remembered what he had said to her in the parking lot on the evening of the NKVD assembly: the only consistent thing in history is the terrifying elasticity of the human soul. Then she believed he was referring to human cowardice and the citizens' willingness to be reconciled with any lie, to praise someone and a week later to demand his death. Now she understood that he was describing something else: the flexibility that allowed people to lie in bed at night and imagine or dream about the most horrible crimes, but wake up the next morning feeling that everything was fine; the flexibility that allowed Maxim to filter out every memory that would endanger the story he believed in. That elasticity was the hidden hand that smoothed out every wrinkle in the flag of truth. Sometimes blasphemous thoughts arose in people, doubts vexed them, they were bowed down by memory, but then they stood up straight and rushed at their story again and clung to it by force of a supreme command of the soul.

The walls of Semyon's dacha were covered with crimson satin, and the wooden floor was coated with burgundy lacquer. It reminded Sasha of the red room in *Jane Eyre*—hell for sinful girls is what her mother would have called it. Cigarette smoke gathered above the roulette table like a many-branched tree, in which people and their arms were moving, pushing and intertwining. Chips in a welter of colours were thrown down on the green cloth and shoved about.

Maxim was swallowed up in the smoke. She heard him call out, 'Here he is, here's the bastard who's going to rob you all,' and she followed him as he patted people on the shoulder and sent joyful barks into the air. He disappeared, and reappeared. Apparently he had won his first bet. 'Twenty-seven red, twenty-seven red,' he called out. Then he shouted, 'Yes, comrade, my sister, yes, God!' Sometimes he called out things like that when they were lying together, and she surprised him with an unexpected movement.

He raked in a pile of chips and turned towards her, glowing with a sweet smile. He expected her to be happy with him, and when she didn't react, he showed surprise: Really, can't you be content, at least this evening?

A petite woman of about forty in a tight black lace dress turned away from the table and approached her. 'Are you feeling better, dear?' she asked.

'Feeling better?'

'Yes,' she said brightly. 'Your husband said you weren't feeling well, and that's why you stayed inside the dacha.'

'Yes, much better, the air here is invigorating.'

'Indeed, invigorating,' the woman echoed with forced gaiety. 'And you, my dear, are you betting?'

'I don't like gambling so much.'

'Sometimes it can really be a soul-restoring pleasure. It might look like a volcano, definitely not recommended for people with weak hearts, but for me it's a place of wonderful tranquillity. You can concentrate on the ball for hours and all the world's troubles disappear, everything falls silent.'

'Truly? Does roulette do that for you?' Sasha asked.

'Truly. I always tell Semyon Emilyevich that a bet brings on the greatest calmness apart from death. Look, that's my husband.' She pointed at a small head and an amazingly long neck that rose out of a lemon-coloured sweater stretched over a pudgy body. 'I'm Evelina Sergeyevna.' Her eyes were fixed on the bandage. 'My dear, I have to say: you still look a little ill.'

She showered Sasha with advice about the remedial effect of elderberries, and went back to the roulette table.

Maxim approached her, a bit sweaty. 'Luck is on my side tonight,' he panted. He seemed to have pardoned her already. That was how he was: his anger was short, and he didn't bear grudges. 'All the time, red and red. I won't bet on black…that Evelina Sergeyevna is a fine woman,' he added. 'She told me—apparently she didn't want to embarrass you—your bandage is unravelling, and the wound can get infected. She has bandages and antiseptic.'

Sasha looked at the bandage: the woman was right. 'Tomorrow morning I'll take care of it.'

'Great.' He gave her a hug. 'It's not as if I haven't changed a few bandages in my life, but in these matters women prefer other women.' He hurried back to the roulette.

'I met a wrinkled Circassian man,' Evelina Sergeyevna said in a clamorous, drunken voice. 'He begged me to lend him money. His little boy was at his side. I asked: When will you return it? And he drew a picture of a house, and the boy, who can't have been more than eight, shouted: Give me your address and the money. We swear we'll send it back.'

'Those Circassians really are a nuisance,' called out Semyon, who was now standing next to his wife and coughing heavily. 'They do nothing all day long, and they bequeath their laziness to their children.'

'Yes,' exclaimed the woman, almost shouting, 'I did want to help them, and bought a few bracelets that were supposedly made of copper, but they broke the same day.'

'They're made of copper the way the mountains here are made of gold. They just saw a generous, good-hearted citizen and decided to exploit her,' responded a handsome man in a stylish dinner jacket. He had an arrogant, embittered look (with types like him—she had already interrogated a few—the bitterness was always connected to money).

'It's impossible to talk with them. They live in a stagnant world!' Semyon shouted. 'They don't want to integrate into society, and they have no interest in any of our values.'

'Exactly,' Maxim trumpeted. His hair was unkempt, and his sideburns looked thick and scraggly. 'I say: we have to teach them a lesson once and for all.'

The old, wild tone was back. How many times had she heard Podolsky as a boy, shouting, 'We have to teach them a lesson!' His new, respectable look hid the violence in him, but apparently everything you are is always sizzling somewhere in your soul. Was she speculating about his personality again? He was constantly revealing contradictory character traits, and it was hard to put all the particles together into a consistent structure, a single person. She compared him to a Ferris wheel: at any moment some feature of his character shone high on top, and you thought, here at last is the essential Podolsky, but that man disappeared at once, and from up there a different person was waving to you.

'I say, let's wake them up with a little lead over their huts, and then maybe they'll understand that it's time for a change,' shouted the man in the dinner jacket, urbane and aggressive.

'Their village is too far away for rifles,' said Podolsky.

'Even better, we'll fire in their direction. Semyon Emilyevich, are you with me?' It was clear that he intended to stir his friends up; actually he was making fun of them.

'Yes,' Semyon grunted. 'We'll send some bullets their way. It's been two days since we did any shooting. We were told there were partridges here, but there aren't. Let's wake up those fakirs.'

The men headed in a group towards the gun rack near the door. Sasha tried to catch Maxim's eye, but he avoided her. Suddenly they were grasping their rifles. Sasha sat down, withdrawn. She heard their footsteps on the stairs and then the pounding of boots on the floor above. The boards creaked, and dust filtered into the room through the cracks.

'You're lucky. Your husband is the kind of man you read about in books,' said Evelina Sergeyevna. 'Do you like Marian Anderson? I was a little sorry they stopped broadcasting her on the radio. What about Skomorovsky's jazz? Does he still have fans in Leningrad? He's a genius, I know that.' She leaned an elbow on the table, turned the roulette wheel and complained about the men's impulsiveness. 'You know that Stalin called him.' She pointed at the roof, which was raining shouts and whistles down on them, and the metallic click of rifles being cocked. 'Stalin had got a letter from one of the workers in the factory, who said there was no hot water in the showers. Semyon Emilyevich had everything repaired. It was just that no one had complained before, but I'm afraid they won't understand how devoted he is to his work.' Trust glowed in her face.

A mighty clap of thunder was heard from the second floor, followed by another one. The roulette table shook, the chips danced, a cup and a pitcher shattered. Evelina Sergeyevna shrieked and looked wide-eyed at her palm, which had begun to bleed. It's lucky, my dear, you have excellent bandages and antiseptics, Sasha silently mocked.

Why did this Evelina Sergeyevna tell her about her husband? Did she hope that Maxim Podolsky, the man out of books, would help, if she channelled the request through Sasha? Perhaps Evelina Sergeyevna had actually asked for her help? Even outside of the building, where she edited confessions, people regarded her as one of *them*.

'Take that!' shouted the man she called her husband. 'Ready, aim, fire…' More shooting thundered above them, and whistles. She felt as if gunpowder had been thrust directly into her nostrils. The whistles melded into a strong, monotonous buzz. Evelina Sergeyevna said something, but Sasha didn't hear her. She looked at the window. She expected to see flashes of fire on the horizon but, except for one weak flare that died far away in the mountains, there was nothing.

…

*'Before us dread, and dread behind us. Sit with me a while, for God's sake, sit with me,'** Styopa recited, chuckling, and with the familiar, masterly sweep of his arm he invited her to sit. It required a great effort to approach him, because those lines were enough to make her understand that great trouble had befallen the head of the department. 'Look how shiny the floor is,' he grumbled, 'we worked like dogs all morning to wax it.'

'You did well,' she said, and impishly patted the seat next to him.

Styopa turned his back to the auditorium, which was filling up. A sheet was hung from a side wall:

1940

HUGE ACHIEVEMENTS

HARD WORK

SPLENDID FUTURE

He glanced at her bandage. The message was clear: Do you have to keep on reminding us? She sensed his doubt: maybe he overestimated her; maybe he hadn't understood that she was just a spoiled little girl? And maybe she had come back from holidays as a different person.

'Did you have a good time?'

'It was wonderful. We're both grateful. Towards the end I had a

---

*   Line from a poem by Sergey Klichkov.

slight infection, and a pesky woman doctor dressed it,' she said, raising her bandaged hand in a light, graceful way that she immediately remembered was inherited: every time her mother wanted to hint that something important had happened and was over and done with, she languidly raised her hand towards her shoulder, while her fingers plucked do-re-mi in the air.

He looked at her fondly. Her answer satisfied him. 'Hundreds of unedited confessions have piled up here: prisoners swore they murdered people who are well and truly alive, conspired with people who are totally dead, in places that were wiped off the face of the earth in the eighteenth century! All enemy agents owe you a debt of gratitude, Weissberg; thanks to you, we haven't arrested anyone in the last month.'

'Stepan Kristoforovich, from tomorrow morning on, I'm at your disposal.'

'You know, Alexandra Andreyevna, guilt is an emotion people like us have to expect. It's a cunning, malicious demon we have to struggle against and expunge from our bodies.'

She didn't understand what he was driving at, and was alarmed. 'I don't feel guilty. In the past few months I've done everything I could for...'

'Of course, of course,' he soothed, his thin eyebrows arched, astonished that she hadn't caught his meaning. 'You did excellent work. Just the opposite, perhaps guilt troubles you because you've saved your people from this group of traitors that conspired against all of us. Sometimes a person is struck by guilt precisely because he did what was required, especially if people who were close to him are involved.'

'But I did save them,' she said hoarsely. 'Without me, they would have confessed to worse crimes, and their punishment would have been more severe. You yourself said that, if it weren't for me, Emma Rykova would have been executed, and others, too.'

'No doubt, Alexandra Andreyevna, you did them a big favour, even if some of those *intelligents* didn't understand that.' He gave her cheek a fatherly pat. 'But guilt isn't rational, it's a cunning, ugly demon, I say. Sometimes I'm attacked by guilt because after the murder of

Kirov some of my closest friends, including Medved, my commander, were criminally negligent in dealing with the enemy, and I was forced to oppose them. Could I have done anything else? Of course not. Yet in my dreams, they still complain.'

The band started playing jolly music, and the head of the first department came over the loudspeakers. 'Dear comrades, you are all invited to the dance floor.'

'My health has improved a lot, and I look forward to getting back to work. But soon I'm going to want to speak with you.' She was surprised by her defiant tone.

Did he understand the equation that had come clear to her on the train? Enough time has passed. Without progress in the matter of the twins, I can't go on working here, and, for my part, you can execute me. She was stricken with anguish: maybe she had wasted too much time, maybe Styopa couldn't help her anymore.

He excused himself and ran after two men with bony necks in mustard-brown suits. The colour reminded her of a sick man's skin. He caught up with them and started chatting, gesturing to the waiters to bring a tray of vodka. Two old women, secretaries from the third department, approached her. She didn't remember their names, but they always treated her with kindness and called her *sirota*, 'orphan'. One of them once told her in secret that her sister, a former worker in the Kirov factory, admired 'the great physicist Andrei Pavlovich Weissberg'. They took her hands in theirs. '*Sirota*, we're so pleased that they shot the villain who tried to burn you.' They glanced across at Styopa. 'Look at him, the head of the largest department,' one of them whispered. 'It's interesting they didn't choose a man for that job who knows how to read. He sits in the projection room every day, a hundred times he's seen *Chapaev*, two hundred times *Alexander Nevsky*, and he already knows how to sing "If War Comes Tomorrow".'

'He even asks his prisoners, the poets, to write love letters in his name to the actress Smirnova,' said her friend.

'Dear comrades,' Sasha reprimanded them fondly, 'I suggest you stop drinking.'

They exchanged glances.

Styopa came back. The old ladies didn't move. 'Comrade Weissberg.' He bowed slightly, and made a theatrical gesture. 'Since your husband is backstage getting ready to play me in the first skit, permit me to play the lucky bastard.'

As she and Styopa turned to leave, she saw that the women were looking at her as though to understand whether their message had got through. They had tried to gossip with her. Had Styopa sent them so she would be seduced into badmouthing him? She linked her fingers with his. Did he suspect her?

They stood on the dance floor. Familiar faces surrounded them: Natalia Prikova in a pretty dress, a bouquet in her hair, blew her a kiss, acquaintances waved, called her name and complimented her, hands stroked her shoulders. Styopa spread out his arms as though to emphasise that she was returning to work under his protective wing.

He wrapped an arm around her waist. The contact was loose and cautious, and hope burned in his eyes. They stood, breathed and didn't move. It seemed to her that he was about to retract his invitation to dance, but at the same time he was urging his body to behave naturally. For the first time she wondered whether the rumour that he was in love with her was groundless. From the start she knew that he delighted in her personality—in particular her scheming side—but tonight his attentions were delicate, even awestruck, and she suspected it was contact he had desired for a long time.

She laughed. 'Styopa,' she scolded, 'a dance is a dance.' And with her left hand she tightened his grip.

He woke up, and his familiar pride straightened his back. With a sudden motion he brought her close to him. He was a skilful dancer, even a bit arrogant, and he led her with surprising speed. She felt that he was filling her body with lithe power—the twins always complained, screaming and scratching, that they couldn't move when she wound her legs around their bellies. She acknowledged to herself that Styopa was one of the best dancers she knew. He glided fast, but without haste, which gave his dancing a kind of spin that made everything else fade, and concentrated you inside your own movement. Nor did he exaggerate like those fops who pulled you around so much that you were afraid of falling over, and he was good at finding a moment to pause, not so long that you were helplessly flung out of the dance, but a pause in which the movement still whirled. No question, Styopa's body was strong. She hoped that her intimations of disaster were wrong.

The music stopped, and everyone clapped.

Outside the windows snowflakes fell onto the Neva and gathered up the city's lights. Snow always sneaks up; you don't look for a moment, and there it is. The high roofs and the spear-towers were already covered with white, to which the light of the streetlamps gave a lacy smoothness.

She returned her gaze to Styopa. He was breathing heavily and sweating; tufts of his thinning hair stuck to his forehead. He kept looking at the row of notables, the functionaries whose faces she recognised from the newspaper, and another dozen or so middle-aged men dressed in faded jackets. They were concentrating on plates laden with quiches, barley and cooked vegetables. Podolsky had told her that for budgetary reasons it had been decided not to serve meat. Behind the men hung a giant picture of Stalin, and on either side of it were smaller pictures, draped in black ribbons, of the two beloved departed ones, Sergei Kirov and Sergo Ordzhonikidze.

'Comrade Zhidnov won't be coming,' Styopa announced drily. The two old secretaries passed by them again. He greeted them in a cajoling tone that suited him less than his usual teasing. 'Grumpy geese,' he muttered to Sasha. She looked at the stage, where the orchestra was tuning up. 'Start playing,' she prayed.

Styopa waved to one of the functionaries, and she stared at him, seeking another hint of weakness. The orchestra began to play again, and Sasha drew close to him.

'My old age is shaming my youth, Sashinka. One more dance and I'll die. How about a drink?'

'Good idea, my ageing commander.'

They walked over to the bar. How could she have been so stupid, after her first certainty, to be seduced into some illusory hope—the hope, by the way, that always throbbed in all the weak people she investigated—that everything was all right? Even when it was clear that the game was up, and there was no chance of evading punishment, their miserable souls groped for some sign of redemption. At first these quests were heartwrenching, but after witnessing so many she only felt demoralised. Why would they in particular be saved? Because everyone believed he was special somehow, that the story of his life was different? Almost everyone, whether guilty or not, clung to this illusion: whoever understood every aspect of their lives would also understand how deep their tragedy was. Most people believed there was an eye somewhere, expert in the hidden recesses of the human heart, that peered into the caverns of their soul and made them, in particular, gleam among the dusty masses. Those in lofty positions knew they still had plans, were loved, could be useful. None of them, not even Brodsky, understood how insignificant he was, fluttering in the wind. His degree of guilt or remorse made no difference at all, and they wouldn't even discuss his case, because his face had already blended in with the multitude; how could he be found now?

The room was darkened, and then the stage was spotlit. Maxim Podolsky stood there with a red face, lightly made up, wearing a black wig and a tight suit, upholstered with a pillow. He staggered like a drunk.

'Dear comrades, good evening. As head of the second department, I am forced to admit that I find nothing more disgusting than books and art. People write and paint and take on all sorts of spiritual endeavours, aspire to greatness, dream about Pushkin and Lermontov, and meantime lots of work piles up on my desk. Friends, we must beat our breasts!' He had begun to shout. 'Graphomania is a dreadful Russian disease! Is it easy to obtain pencil and paper? Certainly. Is it easy to be an author? A cinch. A poet? A breeze. A man writes:

It's cold in Moscow
in Kiev it's dark

And in Leningrad? Brrrr!*

And then he complains that he's being deprived, that jealous poets are plotting to get rid of him, and he demands money and a holiday house for the whole summer.'

Two women and two men in prison uniform, shackled, crawled to centre stage.

'Accused!' shouted Styopa-Podolsky. 'Are you poets, too?'

'Citizen Investigative Magistrate, aren't you embarrassed to ask?' one of the prisoners shouted back. 'Can't you see that here at your feet crawls the eminent poetess Yekatrina Mikhailovna Ulitskaya? And she wants to read one of her masterpieces to you: "Stars in the Windows of the NKVD"?'

'A counter-revolutionary poem of the first order!' shouted Styopa-Podolsky.

'Precisely the opposite. Have you read it?'

'Of course, it's by Boris Lapin.'

'Shame!' shouted the woman. 'Lapin wrote "Stars in the Windows of the Cheka", which is an entirely different poem! And you still call yourself the head of the department responsible for literary matters?'

Suddenly Sasha realised that she hadn't seen Reznikov all evening. 'Styopa,' she said and turned to him in the dark.

He gripped her arm, and dragged her after him. It was plain that something terrible had happened. They walked around the bar. Styopa pushed a wooden door with no handle, painted white like the wall, and they slipped through it. She remembered he had once said to her: 'Every clever investigator has to have his own Kerkoporta.' They stepped down a tortuous corridor. They could hear the actors clearly, and she understood that they were behind the stage.

'We won't have another opportunity to speak freely,' whispered Styopa. 'Maybe I'm being followed. In another seven minutes the first

---

* Podolsky is making fun of 'Ariosto', a poem by Osip Mandelstam: 'It's cold in Europe. In Italy, darkness.'

act will be finished, the lights will come up, and you and I will already be back in the hall, in exactly the same place.'

'Reznikov?' she said.

'He and none other,' he said with a bitter laugh.

'We love Comrade Stalin!' an actor shouted. 'Did he give us glorious industry or not? He gave us a prize—the union took what we got. He gave us a flat—the neighbour and his sister came to squat. Our poems he read—people said, "Print them when he's dead." He lowered prices—didn't give out ration books. He repaired the roads...'

'Too bad he sent us to the boondocks,' chorused the other actors.

The small windows in the corridor were broken. It was cold, but her body was burning.

'They wrote a charming skit, those saboteur authors,' Styopa said.

'I don't understand,' shouted Styopa-Podolsky from the stage. 'You're not being straight with me. Write a proper confession, and maybe I'll arrange minus twelve for you instead of Kolyma. Are those poems bourgeois or not? Subversive or not?'*

'Do you remember Agranov?' Styopa said quietly. He was standing against her. His lips clung to her ear, and his breath warmed it. 'He was one of my closest friends. He was tried for treason and shot in 1938. I was very sorry. He was a man I admired. When they arrested him and Molchanov, it was clear to me that I would be arrested too. Nothing happened. But apparently my name still came up in their investigations, and Reznikov, our old friend, heard about it, saw an opportunity, and exploited it. He went to Moscow and "revealed my true face". These days, Sashinka, that's how to get ahead. He accused me of continuing on with the plots of Agranov and his band. I don't know whether Agranov was guilty—maybe he wasn't particularly clever, but meticulous and loyal, and in any event we were only colleagues. Okay, we also shared a few women. But it wasn't just Agranov: Reznikov invented some more accusations. In short, I'm in

---

* Minus twelve was a punishment denying the accused the right to live in one of the twelve largest cities in the country.

a life-and-death struggle with him, and for the moment he has the upper hand.'

'No one will believe a contemptible man like Reznikov,' she said in despair. 'Your friends surely know he's a liar.'

'I've already heard that I'm going to be investigated. Most of my friends don't know yet. When they do, they'll turn their backs on me the way we have on everyone who got into trouble. I'm innocent,' he said sadly. 'From my youth I've tied my fate to the revolution, have wholeheartedly done everything asked of me, but sometimes misunderstandings arise…No matter, time is short. By the end of February you'll be transferred to western Belorussia. I'm taking care of it so that the transfer will seem orderly. We mustn't give the impression that you're sneaking away in the dead of the night. We're kicking you upstairs. They need sophisticated investigators there—in the past few months, after we liberated western Belorussia from the Polish dogs, we've discovered how many enemy groups are there. Don't say anything now. You understand that there's no alternative. If I fall, Reznikov will bring you down. He goes hard and fast, one of those shock workers who always outperforms. He's an *Udranik*, he'll have all the right arguments. The very fact that I employed you here, even if I was given permission—that will be enough for him. In Belorussia you'll be far away. You know how to stand out, Sasha, and how to find strong patrons who can repel an attack if it comes. I know what is tormenting you. Believe me, for a long time, secretly, being very careful, I've been making inquiries. I'll tell you this: one of them is serving in the Fourth Army, which is stationed in western Belorussia, and you can meet him there.'

'Styopa,' she whispered and leaned her cheek on his shoulder.

'Don't worry.' His voice sounded muffled. 'In the interrogation I won't say your name. I give you my word of honour.'

What kind of a person did he think she was, if he thought that was disturbing her now? Her temples pounded. She heard them and felt burning in the place Styopa had breathed on.

Maybe he was right? How could she know? Recently some of her gestures seemed to have been made by themselves, and she found it hard to determine whether there was truth in them or whether they were entirely false, if they were hers, or if she had copied them from someone else whose behaviour seemed flawless. All these things whirled through her mind while she raced down the corridor after him.

Styopa-Podolsky screeched from the stage, 'You fools! Compete with me in real poetry!

> Love of the proletariat burns in my heart
> I grip its malicious enemies in my fist
> I shall crush the poisonous snake
> But, comrades, please: my sister's pension...'

Just a few scraps of memory remain, hinting that once, long ago, we believed there was a kernel of truth inside us, something that we wouldn't buy or sell. We imagine we are putting on a show for the world, but in the bedroom we still retain that old truth, as sweet as the taste of childhood. But in the soul there are no partitions like in Vlada and Kolya's room; everything slips into everything else. We think we can keep juggling, pretending, until one day, with unexpected sobriety, we understand what perhaps we already knew: our habits are us.

Only when they were standing in the hall again and clapping for her husband, and Styopa enthusiastically stuck two fingers between his lips and produced a deafening whistle, did the meaning of his words become clear to her: Vlada or Kolya.

WARSAW
SUMMER 1940

I've become a sentimental person, Thomas thought.

Just now he had sat down to breakfast in the Bristol Hotel with respectable men. A friendly spirit enveloped the table, and all the participants, especially Albert Kresling, who had recently been named to a senior position in the *Haupttreuhandstelle Ost** and was regarded as Göring's man in Poland, were keenly interested in his work. And while everyone was praising the model, where had he been? He was composing a few passages to Clarissa in his mind: 'Darling, your last letter upset me, and since then a month has gone by. Are you hinting that I'm not making an effort to see you? There's nothing I desire more. I have already explained to you why the idea that you should visit me in Warsaw doesn't please me: my workload won't leave us time to be together. But in September I swear we'll travel to wherever you want. I'm putting the whole world at your disposal.'

---

* Main Trusteeship Office East, in charge of confiscating property belonging to Polish citizens, including Jews.

Thomas now stood in the plaza outside the Bristol Hotel, which was bathed in sun. He felt drunk with the light. He looked at two trees that appeared to be leaning on each other. While they were sitting on the second floor balcony, Weller had pointed at them: 'See, Thomas, they're just like us.'

That remark was of course meant to mollify him. All week long tension had raged between them about building the wall around the Jews. Thomas opposed it, especially in the centre of the city, arguing that such a large ghetto would consume more than it produced and seriously damage the economy. It would clog the traffic and basically strangle Warsaw. Besides, 'It was liable to cause despair and desperate acts,' as he had written in answer to a question from the district governor. Weller disagreed: 'The economic calculations are incorrect. Herr Heiselberg calculates the needs of the Jews as if they were Aryans, but the idea of a ghetto surrounded by a wall is not new and has proven effective in the past. In the fifteenth century, when it was decided to build a wall around the Jewish houses in Frankfurt, doubtful voices were raised. But Friedrich III's decision was firm, the wall was built, the Jews had their *Judengasse*, and that arrangement remained in force for nearly three hundred years.' Weller could have mentioned the ghetto that had already been established in Lodz, but it was typical of him to embellish his argument with a pointless historical example.

Thomas replied to Weller with a stiff memorandum: 'In Frankfurt at that time there were about two hundred Jews, and one or two streets were enough for them. How many Jews live in Warsaw? Nearly four hundred thousand. The planned wall will surround extensive parts of the city. The comparison is an insult to one's intelligence.' Thomas suspected that Weller didn't really disagree with him—he also felt, like his colleagues in the Foreign Office, that the persecution of the Jews harmed Germany's international image—but he was taking the opportunity to demonstrate independence and extend his influence. Maybe he sensed weakness in his colleague. Thomas identified the challenge and declared that the idea was opposed to the spirit of the Model of the Polish People. Weller retorted that he understood the model just as well as Thomas. In the end, Thomas accepted Weller's opinion and was satisfied with the stipulation that his nuanced reservations should be presented in their official response.

After the dispute was settled, more or less, they resumed discussion of their work. Weller kept insisting that their friendship was dearer to him than any controversy, but tension seethed under this veil of cooperation. Even their Russian lessons were postponed on various pretexts. Thomas suspected that his rapid progress was putting Weller off. He already had a fine accent, and if Weller were to lose his advantage in grammar and vocabulary, the student might outdo his teacher.

Now Thomas looked closely at the trees and saw that one was standing straight, while the other was leaning on it. He hoped that Weller had noticed too. He lazily crossed the bright plaza, and tried to skirt the facades to stay out of the sun. At that late morning hour on Nowy Swiat the only shade was a thin strip on the corner. Thomas loved these weekend mornings, especially on clear days, when the horizon seemed endless behind the roofs and the tall streetlights—but lately it had taken an effort to be enthusiastic about the beauty of the day. He had to admit that the sky, for all its splendour, no longer stirred him as it had. The world was observing the Wehrmacht with astonishment, as it won impressive victories in Western Europe, where new and thrilling opportunities lay at the feet of the Germans, but he was stuck in Warsaw, juggling expert reports and sparring with Weller. Even the compliments that Kresling passed on—telling him that the Reichsmarschall, while spending a weekend at Carinhall, had leafed through the model and admitted that indeed there were a few people with common sense in that useless von Ribbentrop's ministry—were somehow dissatisfying.

Two SS officers were walking some distance in front of him. One of them, tall and broad-shouldered, with light hair and a suntanned face, looked like Hermann Kreizinger. Thomas was afraid it really was Hermann, though he knew it couldn't be. Perhaps this certainty even preceded the fear that it might be him. Since Clarissa's letter, when she had told him about that bastard's visit, Thomas had abandoned any hope that Hermann would leave him alone. No doubt the fact that Thomas was thriving fanned Hermann's hatred, but he would have to get used to it: Thomas had no intention of fading away. And so, even though he suspected Hermann was plotting against him, his sting grew duller as the months passed, and Hermann was relegated to the margins of his consciousness. Perhaps boredom also softened his fear. Sometimes an inner voice grumbled: If that thug wants to invest all his energy in me, let him. When he acts, we'll deal with it; that's life, even my enemies deserve a place in the world. In any event it was hard to prepare for an attack by Hermann, who had become a kind of ghost; none of Thomas's acquaintances knew where he was stationed.

The two officers passed him. The tanned Standartenführer nodded.

'Have a fine morning,' Thomas said.

Soldiers with narrow eyes under helmets gleaming in the sun stood motionless at the gates of the compound where the university had once been. Whenever he passed those poor soldiers he remembered the time that he and Weller had volunteered for military duty at the Wehrmacht headquarters on Bendlerstrasse. That was the day the Western powers declared war against Germany. They made an appointment with Generaloberst Fromm, and Thomas said, 'With respect to my conscience, it is very hard for us to continue with our work in the Foreign Office, crucial as it may be, while our friends risk their lives for the Fatherland.'

'Herr Heiselberg does suffer from pains in his ribs,' Weller added, 'and as for me, by the time I finish telling your doctor about all my aches, the war will be over. Nevertheless we place ourselves at the disposal of the Fatherland.'

Weller put on a steadfast look. They received certificates of exemption and praise from Fromm, who called them 'role models for all those degenerates in the Foreign Office'. That was the end of the matter.

By now Thomas was approaching their residential compound. On weekends the tenants would take chairs and tables out to the courtyard and amuse themselves with cards and ballgames. They smoked pipes, read newspapers and played quoits. Several tables were always littered with warm bottles of beer. The previous Saturday they had held a wrestling contest. Weller surprised Thomas by winning several matches. 'Wrestling is an old hobby of our clan,' he announced while stretching his limbs, and boasted to Thomas that a beloved cousin of his had received the Reich Sport Medal for wrestling.

Dwelling on the heritage of his ancestors was an easy escape for Weller from the troubles of the present. Every time he uttered the words 'our clan' he swelled up like a turkey, as if declaring its achievements: we served Wilhelm and Bismarck, we formed alliances that made Europe dizzy, and, having no other choice, we smashed them. We waved armies off to war and brought prosperity and peace to Germany. We were drunk on splendid victories, and mournfully heard about battlefields that reeked with our friends' corpses—and you, which suburb of shopkeepers do you come from?

At those moments Thomas was proud of the Führer, the way he had abolished the privileges of those Prussians, who had eroded the foundations of society for generations. Jack Fiske had understood that better than most Germans: at their meeting after the New Year's Eve party, Fiske had said, 'My father was a man who worked hard and never achieved anything, just like your Führer's father. In my estimation, a new Germany that dilutes the privileges of the nobility will do well for you. Because, Thomas, and I've already told you this, you're the most talented German I've met!' Despite himself the memory flooded him with warmth, exactly as if he were standing in the Milton offices now, and his spirits rose so high that he was almost tempted to sing a love song to his former employer. That was the last time he had spoken to Fiske; he'd done well not to say more than 'Heartfelt thanks'.

One of the buildings cast a shadow, and with enchanting movements, as though hovering, the three sisters emerged from it. Every time he wandered through the city he hoped to get a glimpse of them. They were always hurrying away somewhere. He recognised them by their tight black dresses, their silk stockings and their fashionable hats. When they drew near, he lowered his gaze, but he couldn't resist watching them move away. Two walked with a rocking gait, typical of young women who just had begun to wear high heels, like Clarissa. Now they walked into the sunlight, and their white napes gleamed. Shimmering light fluttered on their stockings like butterflies. They grew distant, and Thomas felt a sadness that surprised him with its force, an eye-blink of orphanhood.

He had inquired about them. Their names were Wanda and Maria, but the third one had a strange name that flew out of his memory. When he saw them approaching, he amused himself by guessing: was the one in the feathered hat Wanda? Once, when he was drunk, he wanted to call out 'Maria' to see who turned around. At night, in bed, when his imagination made the shout louder, all three turned around. They were friendly with officials and officers, and Weller grumbled that they slept with all sorts of high-up men, who, in return, protected their father—who ought to have been driven out of Warsaw long ago, 'if not worse'. Thomas didn't like Weller's cruel tone. The scion of a good family wasn't supposed to lose his manners upon seeing such pretty and delicate women. But he had long observed the effort Weller had to make to maintain his restraint. A kind of belligerence seethed within him, and it would flash out from time to time only to disappear immediately.

Thomas passed through the dark passageway and listened with a smile to the cheerful echoes from the courtyard. That tunnel always gave an extra muffled buzz to the voices. The commotion heartened him. Recently he had taken to spending time in groups: being alone with Weller oppressed him.

There he was again, standing in the centre of the courtyard with his back to Thomas, negotiating about some stupid matter with the men in charge of grilling the meat. Thomas couldn't help focusing on Weller's thick neck.

'Herr Weller, there isn't enough for your Slavs,' a short man protested and stabbed the roasting meat with a fork.

'Obersturmführer, we have a simple rule: once a week they get meat,' Weller replied.

'Rules, rules. With meat you have to show some flexibility!' laughed one of Weller's friends. He was apparently drunk, sunning himself on a sheet, wearing only a pair of shorts.

Thomas inspected the stairs leading down to the basement doors, which were nailed up with heavy beams. The deathly silence of those little rooms—he had never even heard a cough from them—bothered him. Fifteen Polish workers, whom Weller had obtained with great effort, were forced to lodge in their cellar, because Weller was afraid someone would steal them from him. Every morning at seven they were sent out to work: removing rubble from buildings that had been bombed in the previous year, pulling weeds from between paving stones, planting all sorts of seedlings that, according to Weller, would give beautiful spring flowers. Towards evening, at five, those doors were locked, and the key was deposited with the officer on duty in the compound.

Weller had managed to get work permits for them. 'I sweated blood for them,' he told Thomas. 'They should thank me to their dying day. If it weren't for me, they would be in labour camps now.'

'That cellar isn't exactly the Bristol Hotel,' Thomas spat out. 'The ceilings are barely a metre-eighty, and they don't even have a window.'

'We drilled air holes in the walls,' Weller insisted, 'and they only work ten hours a day and get a good food ration.'

Thomas hadn't raised the matter again, but every time he saw those steps, he cursed Weller. The Polish workers were the source of trouble: the week before, an officer had left them locked in the basement. The following morning Weller discovered that they had been down there for thirty-six hours in a row. They could hardly breathe, a few had fainted and one young man had died.

Weller's preoccupation with trifling details had begun to bother Thomas. Intending to avoid him, Thomas clung to the wall, planning to join the happy group at the end of the courtyard. But Weller noticed him, his sunburnt nose shone and he beckoned him with a finger.

'I saw that blond, bronzed Standartenführer in the street,' Weller said to him. 'Maybe we should invite him over for a drink. He's influential, and people say he has a weakness for attractive men.'

'Good idea,' Thomas nodded.

Maybe Weller wasn't so bad after all. Even when he was immersed in trivia he didn't miss the heart of the matter—there was no need to judge him harshly. In his diplomatic dynasty, everyone was probably like that: formal, polite, fastidious about appearances.

'I see that you've taken a liking to Kresling,' Weller added in a malicious tone that didn't suit his clown's face with its beet-red nose.

'A worthy man,' said Thomas, 'and very knowledgeable about art.'

'How could that not be the case?' Weller tutted in disdain. 'After all, his main job is to increase Germany's national culture by means of robbery and plunder! The representative of the greatest robber of the Reich certainly ought to understand something about art.'

'Kresling is an excellent man,' Thomas retorted.

Look around you, my dear friend, he wanted to tell Weller. You're no longer the proprietor; Bismarck wouldn't have stuck your grandfather in an embassy to read telegrams; it's Ribbentrop, the Henkell champagne salesman, who put you there. A man of value is supposed to eschew honours derived from his high social status and to strive for respect by virtue of his abilities and achievements. In this new age, we all start at the same point, and maybe you didn't notice, my friend, but I've already left you behind.

The officers spoke to Weller with more drunken resentment, and he listened to their nonsense patiently. Thomas took the opportunity to rush over to the happy table, where bare-chested officers sprawled on sheets, smoking pipes, their shoulders reddening. Their debauched slovenliness and laziness angered him, but he also envied them. They were so free and natural; compared to them he was decked out like some old attendant in an amusement park. He and Weller were the only ones in the courtyard dressed in their best clothes. He removed his tie and stuffed it into his pocket, rolled up his shirtsleeves and undid his top two buttons.

His new friend Wolfgang Stalker, a young Sturmbannführer who had recently been transferred to the *Haupttreuhandstelle Ost*, stood on the table. 'Interim conclusion,' he announced. 'Fischer from the Gestapo bet two hundred and fifty on 10 June to 12 June. If the Wehrmacht conquers Paris at one minute past midnight, his money's gone. Our friend Moltke, representing the Wehrmacht, is more optimistic: nine-fifty on 9 June. I, gentlemen, have more faith in the Frogs: two-fifty on 17 June to 19 June. Is anyone buying 14 June to 16 June?'

Excitement about the Wehrmacht's campaign in the West had swelled in the compound. Every night they toasted the most recent victories, and around ten they would thrust their drunken heads out of the windows and shout together, usually conducted by Wolfgang:

> May God be with the Führer
> May God bless his hand
> May God protect Germany
> The beloved Fatherland.

They also sang love songs with fawning melodies. He would listen and wonder why he wasn't also elated by victory. He already foresaw defeat—not for political reasons and perhaps not for another fifty years—because defeat awaits every victor. Though he had learned to fool his colleagues with gestures that would please them, their relentless ardour, and Clarissa's too in her letters, seemed to have been forged in a world inhabited by different people—believers. If he were young like Clarissa, perhaps he, too, would fall under the same magic spell she described in her last letter:

> They gave us an article to read, and one sentence in it
> thrilled me: 'Few races like us are battered by the storm
> winds of a great historical period. We are penetrated with
> awareness that with the decisions of today we shall
> determine the future of our nation for generations to come.'
> Really, my dear Thomas, we are working very hard: we've
> received lots of useful things from the houses of the Jews
> who left, and we're distributing them to the poor as fast as
> we can. Yesterday evening Mother insinuated that it wasn't
> nice to use the property they left behind, and Father

scolded her and said that the property was simply being restored to our hands. In my opinion, if the things were left here anyway, it's better to give them to people who need them, don't you agree? How wonderful and satisfying it is to devote yourself to people less privileged than you. The NSV is the most sublime thing in the world. We've all become like one woman. Sometimes in the evening we take the tram and shout together for happiness, and I, I've been alone for so many years.

But it wasn't just the young. Older people walked around Warsaw giddy with pride. Whereas he, who had striven for success as much as anyone, was not visited by even a single elevated moment; instead he was curious about the measures the German government would take in occupied France. Why? Where was Erika Gelber when he needed her? He hoped she had succeeded in leaving Germany or hiding somehow. He hadn't been able to inquire about her fate without risking the loss of his job. He was here, and she was there, or elsewhere.

'I repeat: two-fifty on 16 June!' Wolfgang called out and scratched the boyish fluff on his chest.

Thomas roused himself. 'Here's two-fifty marks.'

'Thomas, my dear!' Wolfgang crowed. 'Did you miss me? I had some business in Cracow.' He stuffed the money in his pocket, swayed with theatrical grace and sat down next to Thomas. 'It was dreadful.'

'Did your business go well?'

'I hope so. Every moment I was there I thanked Herr Kresling in my heart for transferring me to his office here. Those bores in Cracow sat me down for a discussion with the moron who replaced me.' Wolfgang's laughing dimples turned into a puzzled expression. 'I realised he had no interest in hearing what I was doing now. Do you see? The great goal has fallen apart. Every organisation is in its own little box. On the train I remembered Schiller. Those people in Cracow only listen to the monotonous noise of the wheel they're turning.'

Thomas nodded in encouragement: it was the same tedious rhetoric about government efficiency. Besides, a tormented expression didn't suit Wolfgang, a young, handsome and privileged officer from Hanover who had honey-coloured hair and blue eyes. Putting on serious airs, he behaved frivolously, and made jejune pronouncements about things whose complexities he could barely understand. Thomas was fond of him because of his good nature, his infectious cheer and the fact that he seemed to have been born for others to manipulate.

'Just now I had a meal at the Bristol with your Herr Kresling and a few friends,' said Thomas offhandedly. He could do an offhand tone better than anyone. 'He said that you're the most devoted adjutant he's ever had.'

'Kresling has a great future.' Wolfgang's eyes sparkled. He rolled his undershirt across his belly and wiped the sweat from his face. 'He's praised your model several times already. And Kresling knows how to give compliments, if you grasp what I mean.'

'I propose a toast,' Thomas chuckled. He didn't grasp it at all, but he didn't intend to ask. 'To Kresling's compliments!'

And then Thomas understood. He looked at Weller, who was holding his glasses. Without them he looked weak and lost. He was saying something measured, as if he were presenting a speech to the heads of the Foreign Office, appealing to the reason and decency of the two red-chested officers, and they were responding with drunken shouts. The equation solved itself: Weller was the portrait of the past. The future was Kresling.

...

At last Thomas had a plan.

The principle was simple: everyone reached a point where he had to do something. Either he took a great leap forwards, or he sank into torpor, and when he woke up he would be appalled by the opportunities he had lost. Most regrettably, in the midst of his great leap at Milton, while he was busy creating branches throughout Europe, events beyond his control destroyed the company's business in Germany. A few months later, at the meeting with Weller, he understood that the kernel of the idea he had developed in Milton wasn't going to die, but its creator had to nurture it anew for the present masters. After he invented the Model of the Polish People (or of the Asiatic Slav, depending on where he presented it), his happiness and satisfaction were restored as he advanced, made new connections and adapted to a bureaucratic system with a thousand doors. But now his work was going nowhere while his routine remained exhausting. They had established an agency to advise for governmental bodies, but they weren't initiating events or partners in policy planning. They evaluated other people's plans and often didn't know whether their clients made use of their advice. Thomas had the familiar feeling of walking on a plain without mountains or valleys or rivers. A barren landscape where you marched, actually you were dragged forwards without understanding: but if that was all, why keep marching?

On Monday morning he hurried to work early. In March, after taking on ten more workers, their office had moved to Chmielna, a side street that was lit sparingly. On hot days you could feel the flutter of the wind, and on rainy days the trees and the tight spaces between the houses sheltered you. He imagined himself and Clarissa strolling there in the twilight. He knew exactly where they would stop for ice-cream and a celebratory dinner, and then for a last coffee: in Café Blikle.

He sat down, called Wolfgang and asked for a meeting with his superior. Today he would write a memorandum that would make a strong impression on Kresling, and he would add a few comments about Himmler's most recent memorandum describing events in Poland—he had secretly received a copy from Martin Luther.

He wrote:

> The endeavour to dissolve Poland into small ethnic groups
> and to obscure Polish national identity is justified
> historically. It is not, however, consistent with Polish
> sentiment. The model warned that a limited transfer of

population and the removal of the intelligentsia from positions of influence are both necessary steps, but the Poles, as a national entity, cannot be eliminated as was possible with the Kashubians, the Ukrainians or the Lemkos. Polish national faith is strong and deeply rooted.

We have already learned from the events in Volhynia that there was an enormous gap between the number of Polish subjects we intended to deport and the number of Poles who were actually deported. The district governors cannot meet the fantastic numbers they are required to expel. This failure, too, was predicted by the model, which warned against irresponsible plans, figments of the imaginations of charlatans who pass themselves off as experts, and who will reduce this region to chaos. Similarly, we have seen that these deportations arouse international disapproval. Just this March the Foreign Office had to fend off complaints from the United States regarding the deportations in general and those of the Jews in particular, and the personal intervention of Reichsmarschall Göring was needed. In any case it is very doubtful whether these deportations will achieve their goal. No less decisive is the statement by the Reichsmarschall that our victory in war is more important than the implementation of our racial policy—and this must be the point of departure for any decision on this subject.

We have recently heard that Reichsführer Himmler rejected the 'Bolshevik method of mass extermination, from inner conviction that this is a non-German and impossible act'. These are impressive conclusions, but an applicable plan must stand behind it in the spirit of the model.

As he was finishing the memorandum, Weller knocked on his door, greeted him with a 'good evening' and departed. When Weller discovered his plan to transfer the model to Göring's aegis, he would fight him with all his strength. Thomas was appalled by the thought that the man would stop at nothing to protect his status and the power he had attained.

For a moment he vacillated—should he delay his leap?—but when doubts began to buzz inside him, he rushed over to the mirror, looking for signs of ageing. Otherwise, how was it possible to explain his surrender to the whisper of fear? And fear of a sad mediocrity like Weller! Hadn't he overcome men far cleverer? So what if the entire Foreign Office struggled against him! Mid-leap, you hovered over the abyss, and you might fall; he had no illusions on that score. But if you believed your destiny lay on the other side, you jumped!

In any event, he consoled himself, if Kresling supported the idea and directed the power of Göring's influence his way, the battle would be decided with ease. And if Göring understood that subordinating the model to his office would give him an advantage in his struggle against Himmler for control of Poland, he would pester the Führer until he got what he wanted. The Foreign Office would raise a fuss, but after all, how could you compare Ribbentrop's status with that of Göring?

Thomas needed Göring's backing because he was thinking beyond Poland. With Göring's help the office responsible for the model would become one of the most influential in Poland; at the same time he would set up model branches in the countries that had just been conquered in the West. And all those branches—in Holland, Belgium, France—would be under Thomas's supervision. So what if he was selling the same idea as at Milton? There was no law against adapting a good thought to new circumstances. Besides, if a man resuscitated an idea and made a few changes in it, didn't the idea become new?

And there was a bonus: if Göring were his patron, Thomas could use the Reichmarschall's power to retaliate against Hermann. The idea gave him great pleasure: for an hour he sat in his office and embroidered plots that ended with Hermann being expelled from the

SS, and sent back to Berlin in miserable unemployment, understanding once and for all that Thomas was beyond his grasp.

...

Kresling's office was in the Reich headquarters on Aleje Jerozolimskie, a ten-minute walk from their office. Kresling received him warmly and immediately began to complain about the interminable struggles between Göring and Himmler.

Model aeroplanes hung from strings on the wall behind him, beginning with old examples from the Great War—two-engine Boeing planes, the Hawk II, a big Stuka and others. Wolfgang had told Thomas that Kresling came from a Catholic family, and during the Great War his elder brother, who was in Göring's squad, had crashed over the Somme. He had heard from Schumacher that Kresling had worked on the Four Year Plan along with Wohlthat, and, like him, was regarded as being close to the Americans. He had served as Göring's representative in negotiations to purchase aircraft from the American manufacturer Curtiss-Wright. Schumacher said that 'we bought two Hawks, because in the industry they thought it was a good idea to build warplanes based on American models'.

Thomas stopped examining the model aeroplanes when his host's chilly gaze made it clear that his guest's interest in his hobbies did not give him pleasure. Kresling cursed Himmler again and looked at Thomas, a sign for him to outline his ideas. Thomas kept his memorandum in his briefcase; after consulting Wolfgang, he had decided it would be better to present his ideas to Kresling without leaving behind any written evidence. Kresling could exploit the memorandum, Wolfgang had warned. 'He's that kind of man, an enthusiast who knows how to use people to get what he wants.'

'A document of some kind, even if it's not official, could be very helpful,' said Kresling, who seemed satisfied with Thomas's lecture.

'At the moment such a document might prove damaging,' Thomas answered, 'because I can only answer questions in my role as an employee of the Foreign Office, and only questions connected to the activities of your office. The model's mandate is to supply local solutions but not to intervene in matters related to general policy.'

Kresling didn't answer. He leaned back in his chair until his little paunch bulged out under the buttons of his white shirt.

Thomas tried not to look at it. 'Herr Kresling, I am offering my assistance,' he said. He was determined not to let the meeting deteriorate into a drowsy exchange of ideas. 'The model predicted all of the failures and successes in Poland. But we are not as smart as people think, only systematic and professional. The fact is that people ask our opinion so they can use it as a shield against errors made despite our warnings.'

'Look, your model has gained respect that one couldn't have expected; perhaps its natural home is not the Foreign Office,' said Kresling.

Thomas swore he would kiss Wolfgang that evening for his help. 'We have earned respect, and everyone enjoys praising us; that's much easier than taking our advice seriously,' Thomas complained.

'The question is whether the Foreign Office will fight to keep such an impressive agency in its own hands,' Kresling commented.

Thomas felt that this compliment was delivered in a prickly tone. 'In the final analysis, only one man has the authority to determine where it is possible to exploit the full potential of the model,' he said, studying Kresling for any further sign of the contempt he had heard in his voice. He was relieved to find not even a hint of it.

Kresling leaned over the desk. There were files on it, an ashtray, a coffee cup and framed photographs of a woman and small children on horseback. The pictures were all turned to face the chairs opposite Kresling. Didn't he like to look at his loved ones? On the wall, to the left of the desk, slightly obscured, hung a framed copy of a copper etching by Dürer. A tremor passed through his body. Sunlight appeared to slide over the grey print, leaving it in gloom. In his youth, Hermann had been drawn to Dürer, and had especially loved that etching, 'Knight, Death and the Devil', which he thought the perfect German work of art. 'Death and the Devil are beneath and behind you, the city far above, the high point of the manly journey—inspired by heroism, in the midst of terror—to fame.'

'You know Helmut Wohlthat, right?' Kresling asked.

'I have participated in some meetings that he led.'

'He took care of the Jewish businesses in Germany very well.'

'On the subject of Jewish property in Poland, maybe I can be of assistance to you,' said Thomas, looking away from the etching. 'In Berlin I helped with the confiscation of Bamberburg, the Jewish bank, and I bought—'

'The problem,' Kresling interrupted, 'is that, instead of dealing with the matter of Jewish property, I have to deal every day with strange requests that the Americans make to Wohlthat, and that he throws onto me. The latest one touches on all sorts of friends of theirs who are listed with us as disturbers of the peace.'

'That's certainly an unnecessary inconvenience,' Thomas said, not understanding.

'And they don't ask, they demand! The American masters,' Kresling snarled. 'I have seen a lot of hypocrisy, but the Americans… forget about the Évian Conference, and forget about that ship, the *St Louis*. Now they have a new man in charge of immigration, Breckinridge Long, who likes Jews about as much as the Führer. He's increasing the restrictions on their visas, and demanding that relatives of the Polish Jews deposit five thousand dollars in their names. If you don't have money, as far as the Americans are concerned, you can be buried. They shout and protest, but they don't even want the Jews who are on their lists. They just want us to make sure nothing happens to them.'

'Not long ago we held a discussion about the American question,' said Thomas. He was disturbed by the allusion to his former job. Since he couldn't determine whether it was useful or damaging to him, he decided to shift the discussion to other areas. 'I'll say this with caution, although the data were incomplete, most of the participants believed that, if you compared anti-Jewish sentiment in England, France, Germany and the United States, the United States was closer to

Germany and France. The surveys of the Gallup company show that more than fifty per cent of Americans believe the Jews bear some of the blame for the events in Germany.'

'That's entirely logical'—Kresling tapped the desk and leaned towards Thomas—'but you still see how International Jewry manages to manipulate the President.' Angry creases formed around his eyes. 'Where does that damn pressure come from? Even the Poles are suddenly complaining about our treatment of their Jews, and the Red Cross is bothering me about the supply of milk to Jewish children. Where were they after the war, when children in Silesia didn't even dare to dream about milk?'

'There's no limit to hypocrisy,' Thomas said, determined to make it clear to Kresling that he was a man after his own heart. 'You remember that the model described the efforts the Poles made to get rid of their Jews.' Kresling nodded gloomily, and Thomas realised he must have only skimmed the pamphlet. 'The plan to transfer millions of Jews to Madagascar, which Franz Rademacher, the head of the Jewish Department in the Foreign Office, is working on right now,' he explained, 'is actually a Polish idea! It was clear to everyone in Poland that their country had too many unproductive Jews.'

'There's no more shame in the world,' Kresling muttered. 'The Norwegians are also giving us trouble. I told them: please examine the section on Jews in your constitution of 1814.'

He stood up, holding a file, and walked across the room, where two sofas were arranged with a fine table between them. He sank down on one of them and gestured towards the other. His body smelled of talcum powder, his trousers were hitched up. Thomas took a look at the carefully folded socks—three folds—visible beneath the cuffs. He had never understood why people wore trousers that were too short. It was self-evident that trousers should reach your shoes even when you're sitting down. Kresling sat him down opposite the Dürer. The sky turned overcast again, and a grey veil was spread over the etching.

'In the most recent list that we got from the Americans,' said

Kresling, putting on tiny reading glasses and looking at some papers, 'there's one Mieczyslaw Buszkowsky. They say he's an employee of Milton. You worked there for many years. In the American office they claim that he still works for them.' Kresling seemed distracted, annoyed at having to deal with such a minor matter.

'And how do you intend to act on this matter?' Thomas asked. Obviously he mustn't express personal interest in Bizha's fate.

'Have you met with that man since you arrived in Warsaw?'

'No,' Thomas answered. 'Our relations were strictly commercial, and they were severed early last year when the company closed its offices in Germany.'

'I understand,' Kresling grunted and asked abruptly, 'Do you like Dürer? That was a present from an old and faithful friend.'

'An artist of the greatest importance.' His voice sounded false to him. He focused on a small point below the horse until the whole etching went cloudy. 'Personally I prefer his portraits.'

'Yes, they're also lovely,' Kresling stated dully. 'To get back to the subject...' He coughed.

Exactly what subject, Thomas wondered.

'It's a big problem even to locate those people. They could be in any hole, maybe they're dead, and now Himmler's men are causing difficulties. We want to make a few little gestures, show a bit of generosity.' Kresling smiled. 'Do the Americans in Milton have a lot of influence?'

'Absolutely,' Thomas answered.

'Maybe I didn't make myself clear.' Kresling's black eyes surveyed Thomas as though seeking some giveaway expression, and at that moment Thomas knew that Kresling had had him investigated and heard unfavourable things. 'We invest effort in helping refugees only if their patrons in America can be valuable friends to Germany.'

'The people at Milton will never be our friends, no matter what gestures we make,' Thomas said.

'Professional to the end, without any sentiments for your previous employer,' Kresling observed. 'Look, Reichsmarschall Göring and his men, including me, are fostering opportunities with American companies in the framework of the Four Year Plan, and I'm pleased to say that the economic connections are good. Big American companies like ITT, Standard Oil, General Motors have all invested tens of millions in Germany, and they want to defend their investments. Last week we received messages from big American banks, Rockefeller Chase and J. P. Morgan, concerning their business in Paris. They're asking us to act fairly with them. We told them that Germany always acts fairly.' An oily tone of satisfaction sounded in Kresling's voice. The man liked to deal with broad topics. 'It's just too bad that their government doesn't act with the same fairness.'

Thomas was stricken with doubt: was Kresling the right man to help him take the leap? Was the gamble correct, or was he taking a risk in vain? Just now he looked like the kind of provincial who makes you yawn, hardly a man of action.

Kresling spread his arms as a sign that everything was controlled by more powerful forces—Göring, and maybe the beneficent deity. 'As for our grand plan, I respect your loyalty to the Foreign Office. Loyal men like yourself have become scarce. But we might need to consider a change in your status. You wouldn't be hugely opposed, I hope?'

'I'll do my best for Germany.' Thomas sat up. Now he understood what Wolfgang meant about Kresling's compliments: the more effusive they were, the less he meant them.

...

No one knew where Hermann was, but Thomas could feel his breath: the feeling that someone was observing you, noting what you did, waiting for your first error.

He was reconciled to the fact that at least for now Hermann had the advantage. On top of his old fear, as soon as he left Kresling's office a terrifying drone began buzzing in his ears that the plan to transfer the model would prove to be a trap. He had never in his whole life been superstitious and was contemptuous of those who were—so that drone confused him. Horrible fantasies split open in his imagination— a cursed piling up of death, violence and pestilence—and filled him with shame. Nevertheless, as days passed, one single thing became clear: every time he set about transferring the model to Kresling he failed to act because of some mysterious gravitational force—he had no other name for it—that opposed him.

Meanwhile, in the compound they were organising a party to celebrate the conquest of Paris. The Polish workers scrubbed the courtyard again and again, built a wide wooden stage, and started to put up a gigantic tent. Every day trucks unloaded loudspeakers, wooden beams, lighting stands, chairs and tables. Wolfgang, who was chosen by secret ballot to run the festivities (ahead of Weller), announced that the artistic program would be extraordinary. Then he confessed to Thomas his braggadocio had got him into trouble again. He hadn't the faintest idea how to carry out his brilliant program.

That morning Thomas woke up despondent: for days he hadn't done a thing to advance his plan. Perhaps his inactivity was a hint that he should give up on the idea of transferring the model to Kresling. Since he had always believed that his actions were strengthened by his rare creative talents, by his ambitions and his dreams, by his deep understanding of people's motivations and the dynamics of power, he regarded submission to some abstract fear as a betrayal of Thomas Heiselberg and everything he had done in his life.

He resolved to act, to take a risk: he shut himself up in his office, and composed a letter with a precise explanation why the model should be removed from the Foreign Office: the Foreign Office was now pushing the Madagascar plan, intervening in matters out of its jurisdiction, irking Heydrich and the SS and everyone who knew anything at all about Poland. Transfer of the model would be useful to Reichsmarschall Göring and the *Haupttreuhandstelle Ost*, and would enhance its reliability, since it would no longer be subject to the half-baked plans of Franz Rademacher and the Foreign Office. He didn't bother to re-read the letter; in the afternoon he walked to

Kresling's office and put it on his desk. Back in his office, he sat in his armchair and his heart pounded. Voices within him shrieked impending disaster. But he was relieved too: he could not have acted differently.

Too tense to concentrate, haunted by the image of Kresling reading his memorandum beneath the Dürer etching, he cancelled his meetings, locked the door, and wrote to Clarissa:

> My beloved, I expect huge changes in my status soon, but of
> course I can't tell you about them now. Our plan to meet at
> the end of the summer can be confirmed. Apparently I am
> to receive a whole month of holidays. In general, if my
> plans go through, we can see each other regularly in the
> coming year.

He imagined her skimming over his letter at her desk, her fingers playing with her hair, and now she was choosing a new sheet of paper; she always liked to write more than to read, and sometimes ignored his questions when she replied to him. Every time he wrote to her, he imagined the dust of battle swirling around him, as factions were briefly formed and shattered, while she dwelled in a white bubble—to touch her would be like touching a freshly painted wall with a sooty finger.

In the evening, upon leaving the office, he was astonished to find it was empty. The air outside had cooled. On his right rose the lower part of the Jewish wall. It always seemed to pop up in front of him, wherever he turned. Even when he walked away from it, its red bricks seemed to stab his eyes from behind buildings or trees. He focused on the street corner where he would turn left and get away from the wall, but the streetlights dimmed his vision, and he no longer knew whether he was looking at the thing itself or at its reflection. He imagined that a wall quivered before him as well; he walked towards it but it receded. Rain began to fall. He was wearing a summer suit. The wind whistled into his body through a cold hole it drilled in the back of his neck.

Soldiers stopped passers-by and examined their documents. He length-ened his stride, but that sight had deepened his sorrow. He remembered a phrase that Frau Stein used to say when she was asked how she was: 'One and no other.' As a boy he thought she was talking about God, and he even asked his mother which god Frau Stein believed in. His mother answered that she was referring to loneliness, not to God. In his teens that phrase would sometimes ring in his head: 'One and no other'. Again he quickened his pace and almost ran down Jerozolimskie towards Nowy Swiat. Their compound towered up in his imagination; there would be no walls there.

A soldier wrapped in a raincoat appeared before him.

'I'm German,' he said.

'Documents, German!' shouted the soldier.

He fumbled in his jacket, pulled out his identification and waved it in the soldier's face. 'I'm German, understand? I'm not going to stand in the rain like a slave!'

'You call this rain?' the soldier grumbled. And retreated to the shadows.

At the corner Thomas stopped and looked to his right down Nowy Swiat. There, dominating the horizon, shining above the roofs, was the wall. He stared helplessly at it.

He recovered and lengthened his stride once more. Here was his building. Now, as if on their own, his steps resumed a familiar pace. He buttoned his jacket, and pushed sticky clumps of hair from his forehead. Someone could recognise him here. A small crowd was gathered around the gate, and he remembered: Wolfgang's Paris Party…He couldn't turn up in a sodden suit with his hair dripping with sweat. A quick glance at him would arouse revulsion in any cultured person. Could this be Heiselberg from the Foreign Office?

He pushed through the crowd, relieved that none of his acquain-tances was there, and passed rapidly through the entrance, planning to slip up to his apartment and put on a dinner jacket. (In honour of the event Wolfgang had confiscated a few dozen tuxedos from a depart-ment store and distributed them to tenants.) Thomas walked over to the white tent that was decorated with colourful ribbons and flags of the Reich.

'Thomas!' Wolfgang was standing at the entrance to the tent, a brilliant figure in a white tuxedo. He was holding a small tray of brimming flutes, 'Straight from Champagne,' he boasted. 'All the wines and cheeses at the party are from France! My friends there made a big effort for us.'

Thomas sipped the sparkling drink. 'Bless you, my brilliant friend,' he intoned.

Astonishment flickered in Wolfgang's eyes, and, as always when he was hesitant, the tip of his tongue curled over his front teeth. 'You're the man I was waiting for. Tonight is your big night.'

'Really?' Thomas stuttered. The bright light whipped his face and he felt that his flaws were visible to everyone.

'Of course,' answered Wolfgang magnanimously. 'You thought we wouldn't pay up? That we'd run away with the money? We're honourable men.' He withdrew an envelope from his breast pocket and handed it to Thomas. 'Exactly one thousand Reichsmark, between 14 and 16 June, what an extraordinary nose for history! You beat us all.'

Thomas gripped the envelope. 'Thanks,' he said. Out of the corner of his eye he noticed a group of officers playing quoits. About five metres away a short man in a broad-brimmed hat was playing a Polish folk song on the accordion. One of the officers twirled a quoit in his hand, measured the distance to the musician and threw it—to the laughter of his friends—at the accordion player's neck.

'Is that part of the artistic program?' Thomas asked Wolfgang.

'Not at all,' Wolfgang answered nervously. 'I don't know them. They just showed up here. The news about my Paris party seems to have spread like wildfire.' A few figures enveloped in smoke passed by. 'My friend, I'm a bit insulted by your lack of trust. The artistic program tonight is in the finest German tradition. They wanted me to perform crass songs like "The Watch on the Rhine", but I told Kresling and the rest we wouldn't stoop so low.'

Wolfgang apparently expected him to ask which songs would be played, but Thomas said nothing, waiting for his chance to sneak into his apartment. Maybe he wouldn't come back to the party at all. Finally Wolfgang turned away, somewhat disappointed, and Thomas walked through the courtyard among the white dress shirts, the black ties and the black dress uniforms. He raised a hand and touched his own shirt—like touching plaster. He was disgusted.

Too late he noticed that he was walking right towards Weller, who was with a baby-faced man wearing glasses, and whose shoulders were so broad that his shirt seemed to be suspended from a hanger.

'Heiselberg!' Weller called. 'I want you to meet Raul von Thadden, a friend from my student days in Heidelberg. Unfortunately I could only dream about his grades.'

The man extended his hand to Thomas, 'It's a great honour to meet you, sir.'

His pleasant baritone reminded Thomas of the broadcaster Fritzsche, and he was constrained to look straight into the man's eyes. His stylish appearance—hair coated with brilliantine, stiff tie, dinner jacket hanging off him with casual elegance—aroused resentment in Thomas. If they would just let him get out of here at last, he would look like him, and even better.

'You look tired, Heiselberg,' Weller declared. 'A hard day?'

He wanted to excuse himself, but von Thadden started talking. 'In the past I supported the Social Democratic Party, and when my cousin Eberhard von Thadden—I'm sure you've heard about him in the Foreign Office—joined the National Socialist Party, I refused to speak with him.' He held forth like someone used to imposing authority, as though his right to pontificate and your obligation to listen were ceremonial rules, as though you were an uncouth idiot if you didn't know his tribe. Weller, von Thadden and their ilk thought that what they had to say was original, but in fact they were masters of the obvious. 'I spent the day with Georg here in the courtyard. We helped prepare for the party, and when we spoke with the Slav workers I understood how true National Socialism is. Among them were someone from a rich family of leather dealers, the son of a professor, as well as a trolley driver and a fishmonger—and they all received the same pay. The Social Democrats spoke eloquently about equality, but here is the living evidence! My son has been writing the same things to me about his unit in the Wehrmacht.'

'Shattering social classes isn't a universally good idea,' cautioned Weller.

This time Thomas agreed: von Thadden's socialist prattle sounded childish to him.

'Georg always leans towards conservative positions,' von Thadden declared. 'I am interested in Herr Heiselberg's opinion.' He turned to Thomas. 'I read the model with some interest, but didn't manage to infer its author's world view.'

'The model is me,' answered Thomas, 'and what isn't lucid in it isn't lucid in me.'

A faint chortle came out of von Thadden's mouth. Thomas concluded the man had that kind of tiresome arrogance that comes across as sincerity. A vague memory connected with Eberhard von Thadden disturbed him.

'When in fact did you join the Party, sir?' von Thadden asked him.

'Father joined in the mid-twenties,' Thomas answered, trying to recall the von Thadden cousin. 'He was very active in the Berlin branch. In those years I was immersed in my studies and later in work. From 1929 on I voted for the Nazi Party out of respect for my father, and I got my membership card in 1936.'

A smile crawled across Weller's face, and his cheeks puffed out again. They had composed that speech together while writing the model, and even though he had never asked, he didn't believe that Thomas had voted for the Party. But as for his father, there were solid facts, Party veterans full of respect, letters of recognition.

The activity around them increased, the buzz of the lights, the sizzle of the roasting meat. He had given them more than enough time. 'Now, gentlemen, I must attend to some arrangements.'

Weller's eyes penetrated Thomas from behind his spectacles, as if he had found a previously invisible weakness in him. Thomas met his gaze with a cavalier defiance, but Weller remained calm and unblinking.

Thomas suddenly understood. Weller had heard about the meeting with Kresling.

'Your friend Kresling is here, too,' said Weller coldly. He took von Thadden's sleeve and they were swallowed up in the crowd. Had he already reported to the Foreign Office that Thomas wanted to transfer the model, of which they were so proud, to another agency? Thomas was appalled, but then he calmed down: if Weller had done that, he could always deny everything. Kresling wouldn't take Weller's side, and even if he did he hadn't told Kresling explicitly that he wanted to transfer the model to the *Haupttreuhandstelle Ost*.

His body prickled with anxiety: his letter was already in Kresling's hands. His manoeuvre had been dangerous and unnecessary. After all, his situation wasn't bad; why had he taken such a risk? Apparently intrigue was something that dwelled independently in his body and directed his actions. He was heading for the abyss. Perhaps he was already there.

The wooden stage in the centre of the courtyard was surrounded by a crowd. A black grand piano stood on it. Wolfgang leaped onto the stage and tapped the square microphone. 'Gentlemen, I'd like some quiet,' he called out merrily. He named a few notables who were present, read out a message from the district governor and praised the achievements of the Wehrmacht in Western Europe as if describing a charming prank.

Meanwhile Thomas was trying to push through the crowd to the stairway, on which masses of people were standing and sitting—not even a pin could slip through.

'The National Socialist League of Jurists has been so kind as to lend us their best singer of Lieder,' Wolfgang shouted. 'It is my honour to invite Raul von Thadden to the stage. Likewise I wish to thank Dr Georg Weller from the Foreign Office for his musical advice. At the piano is our comrade Lang from the SD.'

He heard cries of joy. Von Thadden took to the stage with graceful steps, removed his grey jacket and placed it on a chair. Thomas watched Wolfgang as he stepped down and stood next to Weller. The two exchanged smiling whispers, and Wolfgang put his arm around Weller. He had never seen them together, and while they were vying to organise the Paris party he had the impression they despised each other. Now he recognised the catastrophe he had brought down upon himself.

To his surprise, even though he understood that he was caught in the trap they had set for him, he felt relieved: what he had feared so strangely had come to pass. At least he had proof that he wasn't delusional; now he could emerge from the whispering forest where he had been wandering. He was back in the world of action. He could plan how to outflank Weller and his friends. He was already going over his strategies. Weller couldn't defeat him.

But was he seeing the situation correctly? Weller had laid the trap, predicted his actions precisely, brilliantly orchestrated events. He remembered their first meeting and his impression—it had faded as Weller's weaknesses were revealed—that the man could be a dangerous rival. Was it still possible to conciliate him? Weller had already tightened the noose; nothing would shake it loose. Not clever explanations, requests for a second chance, reminiscences about their collective endeavours.

Von Thadden had begun with Schubert and was already at the end of the first song.

> *Es ruft noch manche Schlacht.*
> *Bald ruh' ich wohl und schlafe fest,*
> *Herzliebste, gute Nacht!**

He bowed and glared at the audience, as if to ask: Did you understand that brilliant, subtle performance?

Wolfgang returned to the stage, thanked Dr von Thadden and

---

* from 'The Warrior's Foreboding' by Ludwig Rellstab: 'Many battles still call./ Soon I will rest well and sleep fast,/ Beloved of my heart, good night!'

took a sheet of paper out of his pocket. 'In order to appreciate the present day,' he read, 'we must remember our past, the cradle of our greatness. There were times when the French conquered our land, and we knew distress, shame and weakness. But even then voices arose out of the German spirit claiming a glorious future. Germany shall forever treasure the words of Fichte, the clearest voice from those days. While the people moaned, Johann Fichte taught our fathers to believe in their greatness, and I would like to read from his Addresses to the German People.'

Thomas tried in vain to steady his trembling hand. He gaped at Weller. With peacock pride he had straightened his shoulders when his name was mentioned. Weller always believed that Germany owed him a great debt, and only malice stood between the nation and the truth. Wolfgang was still prattling away on stage. There was a kind of crazed avarice in his eyes. He and his chatter seemed filthy to Thomas—that naked desire for greatness, exposed to everyone. How could he have ever been fond of Wolfgang?

The crowd headed for the bar and for the tables, laid with trays of cheese, vegetables, fish and bread. A slight drizzle began to drip on the tent. Thomas yearned for high winds, a downpour that would scatter the tent and its notables in every direction. He tried again to move towards the stairs but had no idea how he would get through.

Two of the three Polish girls passed by. They were as pretty as ever, but he had imagined their appearance at the party as a more splendid spectacle: silk dresses, fox-fur coats, tiaras and diamond necklaces. In fact, aside from their fluffy hairdos, which reminded him of Pola Negri in *Hotel Imperial*, almost nothing in them had changed. Up close their black dresses proved to be made of simple cotton, little runs could be seen in their sheer stockings, and the pointy tips of their shoes were scuffed. From the cut of the necklines and the line of the hips, he concluded that a seamstress had copied patterns from French magazines. The white glare of the lights had dried the rouge on their cheeks as if grains of sand had stuck to them.

'Young ladies, where is your sister? Without her you can't be

Gorgons!' called out a short, solid officer, to the laughter of his friends.

They turned to him in a single motion. 'Be careful,' one said in good German, with a heavy accent, 'if you look at us too much, you'll turn into a Nazi officer.'

Silence fell, and Thomas looked with admiration at her grey eyes. The officers were surprised by her boldness. If they dared to punish the sisters, he would intervene. If he was going to fall, better heroically.

The officers looked at one another. 'Wonderful idea!' one called. 'The Gorgon will make us into good Nazis.'

They all laughed and pounded the wooden banister.

'Tomorrow they're deporting her. Today she's getting married,' said the sister.

'And they aren't deporting you?' asked the friendly officer.

'Tomorrow they're deporting her,' she repeated.

'Young lady, we won't allow that to happen,' called out the officer.

'Will you help our sister?' the first one intervened. 'Tomorrow they're deporting her, they're treating her like a miserable Jew, she didn't do anything.'

'Drop in on my office tomorrow morning,' said the officer. 'Meanwhile have a good time. Soon there will be dancing. I'm already asking for a dance.'

'But tomorrow they're deporting our sister,' said the second sister, and an expression of childish amazement overwhelmed her. She was twenty at most.

'So the day after tomorrow,' laughed the officer, and his friends laughed again.

The two women gave the officer another look, as though to discover whether he had really withdrawn his offer to help. Then they moved away.

A young couple sat on a bench beside the damp steps leading down to the cellar doors. The man was tickling the woman, and she was laughing. The steps had been whitewashed for the party, and the barricade had been removed. Was he standing on their ceiling now? There was no way of knowing. He had never been down there.

'Everything that I haven't personally seen,' Weller once said, 'is just a rumour, and only the ignorant masses believe rumours.'

Wolfgang now announced a song contest to celebrate the conquest of Paris. 'Friends, we have the approval of the Minister of Propaganda, Dr Goebbels, that the best song will be presented at the great exhibition of German art.' After the applause, Wolfgang listed the judges—himself, of course, Albert Kresling, Stefan Kruger, who had a doctorate in poetry, Georg Weller, as a representative of the district governor, and another representative of the Ministry of Propaganda.

'Say it.' Thomas could now see the whole picture.

'Hermann Kreizinger from the SS delegation to the Generalgouvernement.'

I won't stay here any longer to put up with their displays and surprises. His entire body felt split open, as if the stitches had come out in the middle of the courtyard and people everywhere were staring at him. Hermann and Kresling, von Thadden, Weller and Wolfgang—they had all disappeared now, but he knew they could see him. The noise of the crowd disintegrated into particles: shouts, calls, whispers, throats being cleared, plots, the SD report from Stuttgart, a pregnant woman, the economic worries of the individual, perfidious Albion! I would strip her naked right here, neutralise their ability to do damage, we showed them in Bydgoszcz, we showed them about Bromberg, how many children? And as for the English? *Si vis pacem, para bellum.** We have a satanic task, the Führer ordered, she excelled at university, soon I'll be a grandfather, in March he told me in secret, I wrote to your honour and asked for a transfer, go to the grave with that, just yesterday we shouted, 'Fucks for the ugly, too!' in the Vienna Opera and it's already 1940?

In his imagination Thomas was ripping Weller to pieces. Frightened by its savagery, he struggled to get rid of the picture, but he only managed to replace Weller with Wolfgang, Kresling, the damn singer,

---

* A Latin proverb: 'If you want peace, prepare for war.'

but not with Hermann. Even in his imagination he didn't dare fight Hermann.

Perhaps he was falling victim to visions of persecution, believing again—as Erika Gelber used to tease him—that the world was plotting against him. Maybe he needed a touch of humour: there was no reason for a little intrigue among colleagues to become a duel to the death.

He reached the staircase. 'Gentlemen, excuse me,' he called out, putting on a friendly smile as he climbed the steps amid cries of indignation. Some of the partygoers leaned to the side, others rose and dusted off their uniforms, he pushed at the bodies, hot breath mingled with the smell of brilliantine, alcohol vapours, lemon perfume, radishes from Weller's garden.

'Gentlemen, when is the dancing?' he called out with a clownish look at his watch. He had no idea where that gesture had popped up from. 'Gentlemen, please let me pass, some items from my apartment are needed for the last performance.'

'Gentlemen, thank you very much, thank you,' he said again.

He was stricken with dizziness, took a deep breath. If he fell, he would never get up. In one rapid movement he gained the head of the stairs. An officer whose uniform buttons gleamed thrust his elbow into Thomas's ribs. 'Oh, I apologise, thank you, thank you very much,' the officer said and his friends cheered.

'Thanks a lot,' Thomas whispered in response, pushed the blue wooden door open, entered and closed it. He took a breath and raced up the empty staircase like a child skipping home, believing he had left all the horrors of school behind. Had they searched his apartment? He pushed open the apartment door, stormed into the parlour and his gaze whirled: a thick strip of light crossed the floor, trailed over his body and kept advancing until it flowed onto the statue next to the wall. His nervousness increased: the parlour looked like a dusky replica of the illuminated courtyard. His desire to return home seemed contemptible. What home? There wasn't a single thing in his life that linked him to this Polish apartment—he had not even taken down the picture of Polish soldiers mourning the failure of the revolt of 1830.

He began to check the apartment. Everything was still in place, both in his room and in his drawers. He took off his clothes and lay on the bed, covered himself with a blanket and pressed his cheek against the soft wool. From below came the vague cheerful playing of a piano, and von Thadden's baritone trilled:

> Ade! du muntre, du fröhliche Stadt, ade!
> Schon scharret mein Rößlein mit lustigen Fuß;
> Jetzt nimm doch den letzten, den scheidenden Gruß.
> Du hast mich wohl niemals noch traurig gesehn,
> So kann es auch jetzt nicht beim Abschied geschehn.*

It was a song he happened to know, 'Abschied', from Schubert's 'Swan Song'. A choice that must have amused his enemies.

…

Four knocks on the door, growing louder. He wakened from his troubled sleep and pulled the blanket off his face. When he was a child, his mother had instructed him, 'Tell your friend that two knocks are perfectly sufficient.' He had never told him. Had his mother said something to Hermann? Not likely. His mother always greeted his friends cordially, even Hermann.

He felt like curling up between the smooth sheets until he went away, but he knew he had to face him. There was no choice. He took a black sweater out of the closet, washed his face in cold water and straightened his hair. Four more knocks.

Before him stood Hermann, in a pressed dress uniform, with a second-class Iron Cross pinned to it. When did the bastard manage to become a hero? Hermann looked tired; above his upper lip bristled a silvery moustache, wet from the rain. It seems we've both aged. His

---

* 'Departure', text by Ludwig Rellstab: 'Adieu! You brave, happy city, adieu!/ My steed with joyous foot already canters/ Now take the final, parting greeting./ You have really never seen me sad,/ So let it be, too, now with departure.'

weariness aroused hope in Thomas that perhaps he hadn't come to cheer at his downfall; perhaps the recent events were only figments of his imagination?

He was ashamed of himself for grasping at a straw. That was the malady of the weak.

'You aren't celebrating?' asked Hermann. 'We conquered Paris.'

'I've celebrated enough.'

'You look tired. They say you're working hard,' said Hermann.

'Please,' Thomas pointed at the parlour.

'Unfortunately, I have to reject your generous invitation. I'm in a rush to get back to Cracow,' said Hermann. 'And about that guy you've been looking for, the one from the American company.'

'I haven't been looking for anyone.'

'Not looking for anyone,' Hermann said under his breath, 'Buszkowsky, the manager of your Polish office? Anyway, he hasn't been among the living since May—eliminated along with lots of others.'

'I understand,' said Thomas. 'Anyway we came to the conclusion that he wasn't very valuable.'

'The special plan to impose order: Krieger and Streckenbach's people took about four thousand members of the Polish intelligentsia on a hike in the forests around Warsaw.'

'I didn't hear anything about that,' Thomas answered. He remembered the bloodied boots, and imagined them stretching to the sky, like the skyscrapers of New York, while he, a small pin-man, hopped around them. He swallowed his saliva, determined to conceal his nausea. He could not afford to show Hermann any indication of weakness. 'You know that here in Warsaw I am mainly concerned with advising agencies of the Reich.'

'He was on the list of the intelligentsia, didn't you know?' Hermann said, as if he hadn't heard. 'His father and uncle were archaeologists. Maybe you'd be pleased to hear that their expertise in digging stood them in good stead. Unlike their comrades, they weren't buried folded up.'

'No doubt, the German spirit will heal the world.'

'I understand that you didn't know they were lovers of archaeology,' Hermann continued with pleasure. 'In your model I read about the great danger of Polish archaeologists. Quite convincing, I have to say.'

'Thanks a lot. I'm glad you found time to read it.' Thomas tried to sound calm. Knowledge of Bizha's death was already a distant memory. In an instant he had managed to digest his death, to become accustomed to it, to see it as another death that had snatched away one of his acquaintances.

His fingers itched. He remembered something his father had told him when he was a boy, a revelation from the battlefield: there isn't any single thing—any one thing that you learned or believe in or inherited—that you won't discard on the spot in order to survive. Later, at home, the whole thing will seem like a bad dream.

Thomas felt that he was soaring over the familiar terrain of his soul. His self-control, which had always been his pride and glory, had been surrendered to this survival reflex; he was in the midst of a tiger-leap into the unknown. If he were forced to fight Hermann to the death, he would do it.

He wanted to shout *This fear is marvellous!*

'Well, maybe not every word.' Hermann laughed. 'Sometimes it was boring and obscure, a little like that book by Rosenberg.* The true myth of the twentieth century is that it's possible to read this thing.'

'Reading demands discipline. While I was working on the model, I read the whole book and enjoyed it.'

'Sure you read it,' said Hermann, 'like the books you read at school, or was I the one who actually read them?'

'Maybe one book, whose simplistic message matched your intellect,' Thomas retorted. 'If you came here to reminisce, I also have some memories.'

Hermann leaned across. 'I've heard that you've made enemies here too.'

---

* *The Myth of the Twentieth Century* by the Nazi ideologue Alfred Rosenberg.

'There's no success without enemies,' Thomas answered. 'You know that.'

'How unfortunate that you can't consult your Jewish therapist. I heard she's in the labour camp at Ravensbrück. Finally she's doing some real work.'

'I never spoke about work with her anyway.'

'Maybe a smart man like you should wonder why decent men like my old friend Kresling and your colleague Georg Weller have become your enemies?' Hermann suggested with feigned courtesy.

'I assume that, with respect to Kresling, I have you to thank for it.'

'Naturally it was my duty to tell him with whom he was dealing.' Hermann rubbed his hands together and pretended to be thoughtful. 'But I'll tell you something: he would never have trusted a man who was willing to betray his place of work and his partner Georg Weller, who gave you an opportunity when no one in Germany even remembered that you were alive.'

'Nonsense,' Thomas hissed. 'Weller was a marginal figure in the Foreign Office, and thanks to my model he rose to greatness.'

'You really believe that, eh?' Hermann cleared his throat. 'First, don't exaggerate the prestige of your model. Most of the agencies of the Reich regard it as pitiful gibberish from our incompetent Foreign Office. Second, as to our little matter, I have to inform you that even if there were no Hermann Kreizinger in the world, your treacherous intrigues would still be doomed to failure. Weller is very close to Eberhard von Thadden. You remember there was a suspicion he was Jewish? Maybe you also remember the old family friend who invented the dubious story that Eberhard is the great-grandson of a Russian aristocrat, and, presto, extricated him from the quagmire.'

Now he recalled. 'Of course,' he answered, and there was a catch in his voice. 'Reichsmarschall Göring.'

'The great patron to whom you longed to deliver the model,' Hermann said drily. His high spirits had faded. It seemed that ridiculing Thomas had given him less pleasure than he anticipated. 'Weller is very close to him, through von Thadden. Your arrogance set you against a network of forces which had already withstood every test while you were still selling umbrellas in your American company. But even without me and von Thadden, everyone would have come out against you!'

'Well, if you say so.' Thomas smiled. Hermann really did want him to understand why he had become his enemy.

'You can do magic tricks, and juggle too. I have to confess, after your company cleared out of Germany, I believed you were finished. When I heard you had a job in the Foreign Office and that you'd impressed some agencies with your model, I applauded you. And as for what you tell everybody, how you voted for the Party from 1929 on, out of respect for your father—that's a true work of art. No one can deny it, except those who know that your mother threw your father out of the house while you were at university—but even then you can claim that you remained close, and respectful of him, and that can't be contradicted either. The problem is that in your whole life you've never believed in anything except your own ability. You have no national feeling and no loyalty to your nation, and frankly you never had any sense of obligation towards your parents. And, worst of all, you've never devoted even a minute to thinking why you're like this, or how you might improve as a person; you never understood that every act of the individual should serve as a general rule for the behaviour of the entire race. You have devoted all your talents and energy to nothing but your own benefit. You perfected yourself alone, and you can disguise yourself as whatever you want, even a National Socialist. But there's a moment when people figure it out, do you understand? No, you don't; you never understood. That's just what I was talking about with Kresling. You believe that everyone is like you. But I believe there's such a thing as truth, and ultimately it will come out. That's the difference between us.'

'Maybe I'm like that, and maybe not,' Thomas said coldly. 'A person like you couldn't judge. As for my father, don't you dare mention him to me. If you had honoured your father the way I did mine, or at least if you'd helped him get out of his financial troubles, maybe he wouldn't have sat down on the railway tracks.'

Awareness that he had told an outright lie, and that Hermann had loved his father more than any child he knew, only heightened his ferocity. Had he intended to drive Hermann mad? He was impelled by a single flaming image: his teeth gnawing at Hermann's mind.

'Luckily for you, I know this is the prattle of a man who's done for,' Hermann said. 'You're finished in the Foreign Office, and there are no more rabbits in your hat.'

'We'll see about that.' The distortion of a hoarse cough filtered into his voice. 'Remember your surprise when you heard about the model? Get ready for another one.' He had defied Hermann as much as he could. He felt euphoria—mingled with fear, of course, but actually fear wasn't such a bad ruler. Hermann expected him to be stunned and defeated, like that night in the street. That would never happen again.

'So we can only wait.' Hermann hissed his familiar threatening whistle.

'We'll wait. Patience was never your strong point,' replied Thomas. 'There's an unsettled account between us, and it will only be closed when you're lying where my mother is lying now.'

Liberating lightness swept through his body. Suddenly he understood his thirst for revenge, which had worked itself up beneath thickening layers of thought. Now his thirst raged wildly, and his body ached for it: any desire that throbbed with such intensity must be real.

'You should have said that earlier,' said Hermann. 'If you really wanted revenge, I would have seen it in your eyes. But we both know that if I had extended my hand to you and promised to help you out of your trouble, you would have taken it.'

'It's fascinating to see a beer-hall thug struggle to figure out a man like me,' Thomas said. 'I'll settle the account between us according to law, as cultured people do. Long ago I hired a lawyer in Berlin to sue for the damage you did to my house and for your part in my mother's death. You know how harshly the SS deals with robbers who shame the uniform they're wearing.'

'One minute you want to kill me, the next minute you're suing me,' Hermann mocked. 'We didn't steal so much as a napkin from your house.'

'We disagree on that. According to my reckoning, you stole a lot,' Thomas said. 'So maybe you'll extend your hand to me now?'

'I'd sooner commit suicide.' Hermman rose to his full height, a head taller than Thomas. 'Germany, the whore of the 1920s, suited people like you, but now there's a new Germany, and you're like an infection in her body. The problem is that there are too many people of your type in the system.'

'The world is made up of people like me. Look, even the government needs me, and that's what really terrifies you: behind your government and your Party, the parades and the victories, it's my face that pops out in the end.' For the first time in his life he felt that he was chasing his words, but nevertheless everything he said pleased him.

'That's just your weak spot, Thomas,' said Hermann triumphantly, his eyes glowing. 'Ever since I've known you, you've believed, truly believed, that you're two steps ahead of everyone else, that you are the ideal German. And everyone who isn't like you is either lying to himself or a coward and a fool.'

'With your permission, I'm going back to sleep,' said Thomas.

'It's really a pity that you tend to miss the important things: for example, your American company never left Germany. They kicked you out after they used you, exactly the way—and this has already been decided—the Foreign Office will kick you out tomorrow, but you ought to know that the company is still advising clients in Berlin, and it keeps an account with the Dresdener Bank. Now the managers in New York have asked us to be friendly to their office in Paris, something to do with the French soul, sounds like the kind of waffle you used to invent.'

'Why do you always insist on saying "the American company"?' asked Thomas with an anger that sounded childish to him. 'If you acquired all that information, you'd remember its name.'

'Actually I don't remember.' Hermann winked. 'Today when I was watching you run around at the party like a panicked rat, I understood the root of your tragedy: organisations apparently need people of your kind. You're the great spinner of plans, the virtuoso speaker, the tireless booster of your own interests. I've never doubted your abilities. But because of the person you are, you'll never really be part of anything. You're just a flash in the pan. In the end you're always left with nothing.'

'And you? Will you be here forever?' Thomas swallowed his bitter saliva. Hermann's words had wounded him. 'I appreciate the time and trouble you've invested. But if I wanted psychological analysis from thugs, believe me, I would have looked for you in one of your holes.'

'Twice now you've called an SS officer with a second-class Iron Cross a thug,' Hermann said, clicking his heels and heading for the stairs, his arm lifted in feigned despair. 'I can't sleep in this city. The beds in the Bristol are only for dwarfs.'

'Remember!' Thomas shouted after him. If only he dared push Hermann down the stairs. 'Our story has only one ending.'

'Now you're the thug,' Hermann taunted over his shoulder. 'Doesn't a cultured man like you despise us?'

'I've always been one,' Thomas shouted. 'Every man has a limit, you know, and once you go past it, we're all thugs.'

PART THREE
THE WORLD
IS A RUMOUR

BREST
OCTOBER 1940

The rust-coloured spires of the fortress disappeared behind the grove of trees. Cold breezes stirred the reeds and grasses on the riverbank, where birds and butterflies hovered, and the entire landscape was tranquil. Her boots sank into the moist earth and withered leaves crackled. Sasha breathed in the fragrance of the grass and the moss with pleasure. The trunks that leaned over the river were reflected in it like huge railway sleepers. Yellow leaves fell, and she reached out to catch and crumble them into tiny flakes that clung to her skin. She walked to the edge of the grove, where the vista opened up to reveal scraps of the plain, dotted with black tree skeletons, visible everywhere during the winter.

It began to drizzle, the plain widened and the canopy of clouds curved over it like a grey dome. The gloom that had departed while she was walking in the grove pressed down on her once again. She remembered her dreams of the past few days. In each of them something of Vlada and Kolya appeared—the twins were using a knife and a hoe to split the thigh of a large bird that looked like Stepan Kristoforovich, and Mother scolded them: You're supposed to hold a thigh in your hand; Podolsky and Reznikov were gnawing the wooden screen in the twins' room; Circassians were dressed in officers' coats like Vlada's, punctured with bullet holes.

Ahead of her, black smoke rose behind barbed-wire fences. She rubbed her face with her gloved hands; her feet were mired in the claggy soil. 'The bog is cruel, sucking down terrified people first...' her grandfather used to say of his ancestors who had disappeared in the swamps of Saint Petersburg. She stopped, listened to her own heavy breathing and tried to restrain her imagination. It was just mud. It came in a multitude of forms: as black muck, as puddles from which mounds of moss or disintegrating leaves poked out and as grey heaps that looked soft and smooth like fur hats, but concealed a swampy layer. As she stepped, the gluey droppings clung to her feet.

She was assailed by her memories of the past few weeks: Belorussian villages slipping past the train window—Baranovichi, Kobryn and perhaps Molodechno too—huge expanses of earth, galloping horses, mules with their heads down and tails dragging being whipped by wagon drivers, massed prisoners digging a canal with gloved hands. 'This is a mighty national project,' shouted zealous officers still in their teens, 'joining the Dnieper Basin to the Bug, and we will finish it at any cost!' They stood on the banks, and all around them was a motley crowd of shrivelled bodies wallowing in mud, the horizon dotted with wagons and scattered brown specks of humanity. Now Grandfather's stories became real: endless swamps, people crammed together in them like potatoes in a field. That was how Saint Petersburg was built. Were Mother and Father digging a canal in the mud now? For a moment she lost her balance, glanced around, but the grass and the reeds and the birds had already disappeared.

A young officer leaned on a barrel, smoking. When she drew near he threw his cigarette away and stood up. 'Comrade Weissberg. I am Lieutenant Grigorian,' he said in broken Russian.

'Hello, Lieutenant.'

They walked over a wobbly wooden bridge. A truck was bogged ten metres below them. They stepped off the bridge and back into the mud. She could feel its weight clinging to her boots. They passed by piles of garbage with its stench of rotten food, torn leggings, burnt tyre rubber, machine parts wrapped in canvas. On the side were latrines full of sludge. Motor oil fumes rose from two flimsy wooden barracks that were certain to collapse on the first day of winter.

Muddy silhouettes leaned over nearby, shovels in their hands. Around them were red cannon barrels, the only patches of colour on the plain—a group of soldiers in woollen coats. Soup spoons were thrust in their coat belts next to their bayonets. They shouted, pounded on their comrades' backs, trampled the mud, spattered more mud. Why was it that every time she saw a bunch of boys or young men she looked for Maxim Podolsky?

Some of them were cursing two soldiers who were running after a pair of rabbits trapped in a small yard enclosed by a tangle of barbed wire. The two swayed in the mud like drunks, plunging their bayonets into the ground, trying to pull them out to the shouts of their comrades. At last one of them stabbed his bayonet into the belly of one of the rabbits. He stood up and with a lazy, flamboyant gesture twirled the bayonet with the speared rabbit on it above his head, dwarfing the soldiers around him, a statue rising from the plain. Dark red stained his fair hair, dribbled down onto his muddy forehead and then darkened his face to his lips.

Applause, whistles and curses filled the air. The other soldier stabbed the second rabbit in the head and stood next to his friend. The bodies of the rabbits twitched. There was blood everywhere. The soldiers bowed to the cheering crowd. The bayonets and rabbits bowed with them. Soldiers in the vicinity stopped digging and walked across. Their faces were the colour of the plain, and only the white circles of their eyes suggested there was a man behind the mud.

The rabbits would provide each soldier with a piece of meat the size of a matchbox, Sasha calculated.

'They're very hungry,' said Grigorian.

'That's no reason to behave like savages,' said Sasha.

Grigorian seemed to be in two minds about how to respond, but then said nothing. In Belorussia, in its miserable cities, tiny villages and army camps, everybody—aside from other NKVD—kept quiet when she spoke to them.

'Lieutenant Grigorian, is there something you want to tell me?'

'Sometimes the soldiers work for weeks without any meat.'

'I'll make sure the relevant authorities know.'

'The soldiers will appreciate your help.'

'I very much hope that the office of Comrade Lev Mekhlis will view it with the same appreciation,' she said and realised her tone of light friendliness conveyed a threat, the legacy of Stepan Kristoforovich.

Grigorian did not reply. The young Caucasian officer, who had been transferred to Brest from the Twelfth Army (in the NKVD they now sarcastically called it the 'Army of the Caucasus'), had probably never heard of Lev Mekhlis. They walked over to a cluster of soldiers who were casually heading for the wooden huts. Grigorian stopped, thrust his fingers into his belt, and hummed a melody. She was tempted to rebuke him: You know why I'm here. Take me to Nikolai. But his surprised look, as if something obvious had escaped her eyes, stopped her. In her work she had learned that, if you're groping in the dark, unable to apply any logic to your feeling, you keep a courteous silence. Grigorian was following the same principle. She almost laughed.

The image of the soldier waving the rabbit flashed in her mind. She removed the backdrop, the other soldiers, the rifles and the uniforms from the picture, and just when she seemed to understand she heard Grigorian call out the name of Private Nikolai Weissberg. Out of the cluster slipped one of the soldiers. The end of his bayonet oozed with a tiny rabbit eye. A patch of muddy blood bloomed on his pale cheek.

She said to herself: When I saw you before, you weren't exactly Nikolai.

Grigorian walked over to him and took the rifle from his hands. Nikolai's gaze followed the bayonet as it moved away. She came up to him, stripping off her gloves, and when he turned around to her she breathed in the odour of grease that clung to his uniform, the smell of the sweat that she once knew, but which now reminded her of the sweat of the men who gathered in front of the bulletin board on the second floor of the offices. The surprise left his face, his jaws locked and there was a chill in his eyes, as though he was defying her: Look at the time that has passed and now lies between us; forget about gestures that belong to another time.

She was determined to ignore his silent demand, and felt a flicker of contempt: did he think there was any other way? Her cold fingers fluttered on his face. He didn't move. In his childhood he used to hum a tune to the rhythm of her fingers. For two years she had been picturing how she would caress his face, and sometimes he appeared in her nightmares as one of several skeletons, all of which she was caressing with a do-re-mi. The fresh blood on his cheek warmed her frozen fingers. Her eyes stopped there. Strands of rabbit fur, which looked like unravelled stitches, clung to his skin. Without a word, or changing the movement of her fingers, she removed them: her smile concealed the disgust.

He hadn't changed so much after all. He'd grown a little taller, his shoulders were broader, his stance was balanced, his shaven head emphasised his black eyes that now looked too large. His tiny wisps of beard looked artificial, like make-up. She could draw something similar on her own chin.

'How did you injure your hand?' he asked. The childish tone, yearning for her affection, was absent from his voice.

'An accident in the office,' she answered.

'Vlada died in Finland.'

'I know.'

'He fought there.'

'I heard he fought well.' She hadn't intended to lie. It was a ready-made sentence that flew out of her mouth without her intervention.

'I met someone who was there for a few weeks. He said that all his comrades were buried in the snow, their tongues and eyes were gouged out. The dogs preyed on the rest.'

She said nothing.

'Did you know that he and Seryozha torched Brodsky's apartment then?' Nikolai said.

'I suspected it was them.'

'Did he deserve it?'

'No more than them all, and no less.'

'And Mother and Father?' he asked.

'They're in Siberia.'

'Alive?'

'As of July, yes,' she said.

'Did you get any letters from them?'

'They aren't allowed to send letters. I heard from other sources.'

'It's interesting that you're NKVD now.' There was no tone of defiance, just stiff resignation to the facts.

Every fluid memory of the past two years froze at the sight of him standing there. He stroked his soup spoon, as if he only wanted her to clear out—maybe they would save a cube of rabbit for him. Everything that was once between them seemed to have happened in another life—the nights when they had lain side by side in her bed, sorting the shadows on the ceiling and mocking Vlada and Father (never Mother), and imagining the handsome engineer from Paris who would marry her and adopt Kolya—all those luminous pictures now seemed like such a wonder that she could only doubt them. Strange how things that were happening now gripped you and attached you to them, and not only you but everything you once were. Every sentence she wanted to say was emptied of meaning, because this soldier wasn't the object of her longings.

Are you your body? she wanted to ask.

And are you *your* body, his defiant eyes answered.

'You're very close to the border,' she said.

'The headquarters of their Panzer division is about eight kilometres from here,' he answered. 'Just across the river, where those groves are, there.' He pointed at the darkening horizon where abundant copper treetops swayed. 'That's the front line of the Wehrmacht.'

'Really very close,' she whispered, repeating the sentence that Maxim had murmured when he visited her in Brest. They had stood, hugging each other, and looked at the Bug River. Maxim talked obsessively of all kinds of rumours circulating in the Foreign Office—the discussions in Bucharest about the Danube had failed, and, even worse, Molotov's visit to Berlin had ended in fiasco. He knew this from an authoritative source. 'Oh, you move in such enviably informed circles, Maxim Adamovich,' she said, and pinched his nose.

'It's hard to be well liked,' he agreed, and they both laughed.

His friends in army intelligence said that the Germans had already transferred around eighty infantry divisions to the border area, as well as mechanised and armoured divisions. They were paving roads, building railway lines, preparing airstrips. 'My dear,' he said. 'It deeply disturbs me that you're in the city closest to the border. They're right across the river.'

He looked at his watch and called out distances, the time needed to build bridgeheads, to cross the river, and wrote down in his notebook the speed of the German Panzers on various surfaces. At last he announced that if there were an attack they would reach Brest within forty-five minutes.

'Exactly,' Nikolai now hissed. 'We're one of the forts closest to the border. On a clear day, I could show you their foxholes and the cannons and Panzers. Our intelligence doesn't believe that those Panzers are their heaviest tanks. They might be hiding the really heavy model.'

The subject preoccupied him, and there were doubtless other details he wanted to mention. He had always been studious, flaunting facts and figures. She was tempted to say: Kolya, tell me about the Panzers. We have all the time in the world. She scrambled to find the right tone but the words all sounded disproportionate, like furnishing a huge room with one little table.

Kolya wrapped himself in silence and stared at the woods across the river. His gloom saddened her: once there was at least one person who would listen, no matter the hour, to any of his stories, however improbable. A chill passed over her: the chasm of his orphanhood opened up before her.

She sat on a stump. A soldier with air force insignia passed between them and pointed at the mess shed with his chin.

'They've saved your portion for you,' she said to Kolya, surprised by her joy that he was treated with respect. She began to move her feet, which had thawed out a little.

'They drafted him in Belaya Tserkov,' Nikolai stated.

'Are there a lot of Ukrainians?'

'Two.'

'Do you get along?'

'Very well,' he said. 'The Caucasians, especially Grigorian, are sometimes annoying.'

'Well, they're not exactly like us.'

'But not so different.'

'Is there anyone from Leningrad?'

'Nobody. There are Chechens and one spoiled guy from Moscow, who still hasn't figured out that mummy isn't serving him tea in bed.'

'Where do you sleep?'

'There.' He pointed at the sheds that were enveloped in the stench of grease.

'Aren't you cold?'

'Sometimes.'

'You've run out of rabbits.'

'Tomorrow we'll raid some village around here.'

'There's no meat supply?'

'We manage. If we were hungry, could you help?'

'Maybe it's possible to speak to certain people.'

'Please. If we had more than forty grams of meat per week, maybe we wouldn't insist on remembering things.'

'What things?'

'Maybe we'd learn to forgive, Zaitchik.'

He was mocking her but above all his voice sounded strange: every word was a reproach.

'When did you get to the area, Zaitchik?'

Mother stood next to the primus stove and called out, 'Zaitchik, where's the water? Zaitchik, where are the boys?' She was stunned—in the last two years her nickname had vanished from her memory.

'A few days ago.'

'Really?'

'Before that I had other missions.'

'What kind of missions?' Once more she could hear his defiance, as if he was anticipating the usual rebuke: Don't call me that.

'Routine things, nothing interesting. I'm a small wheel.'

'When did you get here?' he asked again.

'About two weeks ago.' Did malice flash in his eyes, celebrating her lie? Could someone have told him in the past few months that she was stationed in Brest? That wasn't possible.

She looked at the lined hands that had thrust the bayonet into the rabbit's eye. His arrogant look, like an interrogator playing with the accused, distressed her. She struggled with the apprehension that his right hand, which was close to her, was about to hit her. She stood up and stretched her limbs, moved away slightly and wondered whether she should tell him the truth. But what good would it do to Kolya to know that she had been in Brest for six months? Sometimes she had been sent on missions to other places in western Belorussia, she hadn't lied about that, but the reason she hadn't wanted to meet him till now was simple: she was afraid that something of Styopa's guilt had clung to her. Only after it was clear that Styopa was regarded as a separate case, which wouldn't trigger other arrests, and was sentenced—she was amused by the charge against him, 'fabrication of evidence and preventing a just trial'—did she decide that her visit would not endanger Kolya. Sometimes she remembered Styopa fondly: an unlucky man, succumbing just when the number of arrests was falling and stories were circulating about citizens whose sentences had been commuted. After years in gulags they were reappearing in cities and villages like ghosts.

He stared at her. 'They say that recently you rose to great heights in Leningrad.'

'The smaller a person is,' she said, 'the more he needs wild rumours.'

He cracked his knuckles, enjoying her answer. Hope blazed up in her that the memory of their nights would grow warmer.

'Last week,' he said, 'when you were still in Leningrad, did you by chance read *Leningradskaya Pravda*?'

He knew something. 'It's been two years since I read that paper.'

'So you didn't read the long poem, 'See, Soldier Dmitry'?'

'No.' She felt like slapping him, peeling off that insolent expression. Everything between them was spoiled.

'Too bad. You would have enjoyed it. It's been years since Nadyezhda Petrovna published a new poem.'

'They let Nadya go?' she asked.

'They don't publish poets in the gulag.'

'She returned to Leningrad?'

'She came back.'

'When?'

'Not long ago.'

Now she understood. The plain began to whirl before her eyes, along with the brass trees to the north—are those Germans, or is it us?—dancing and rejoicing in her downfall. Nadyezhda, with a throng of admirers, recounting amazing tales about the gulag in her raucous voice. She had been dead for a long time, and that was fine. The disappointment at hearing that Nadyezhda was alive weakened. When had Sasha become someone who regarded death as a worthy revenge? There was Morozovsky lying with his head shattered. Lots of questions buzzed: did they know about that evening? Had anyone else been freed? Why hadn't her husband told her anything?

On his nose and moustache there were still blood-soaked hairs.

'You have rabbit on your face.'

He didn't answer. After causing such an upheaval in her soul, maybe he didn't have anything else to say. She was filled with black despair: he would never understand that she had sacrificed everything for him. 'Do you understand that it would have been easier for me to die?'

'Me, too, and we're both still here, maybe the only ones.' He took a dry plug of tobacco from his pocket, cut slivers of it with his knife, rolled it in newspaper, and lit it.

'Don't say that. They're alive.'

'I mean that we always played with talk about death, and envied people who loved life, and now most of them are dead or as good as dead, and we're here.'

'You're saying that we liked being alive?'

'More than we thought.'

'I haven't liked being alive since you disappeared,' she said.

'Maybe you have, more than you thought.'

He handed her the cigarette. She puffed the smoke. The taste was nauseating, like sticking your head in a chimney. Styopa-Podolsky was shouting from the stage, 'The Revolution needs you, body and soul, everything.'

'When did you start smoking?'

'At school.' He chuckled. 'I was afraid to tell you.'

The tumult in her head died down a little: it wasn't clear how much he knew, maybe not much. 'Nadya contacted you?'

'Yes. She sent me a long poem and a letter.'

'What did she say?'

'Not much. She told me that the NKVD made a wunderkind out of you, that you hadn't been in Leningrad for a long time, that Brodsky died in Kolyma.'

'When did he die?'

'Last month.'

'I thought he'd make it.'

'You were wrong.'

'Is the poem good?' she asked.

'Very interesting.'

'Nadka wrote a poem about the heroism of soldiers? Now she's a Party poet?'

'Dmitry isn't a soldier. He's a seven-year-old boy dressed in his dead father's uniform.' He said the last words without any triumph, even with sadness. Most likely he understood that as soon as she returned to the office, she would find the poem. Where was *Boris Godunov* in the bookshelf?* On top. All six volumes of Pushkin were on top.

Now only one thing remained. A film veiled his eyes. Apparently he no longer wished to hurt her. She decided to be generous and say it for him. Anyway, the moment she realised what accusation had been fabricated against her, she swore to escape from this stinking plain: Nadyezhda had dedicated the poem to the dead soldier Vlada.

---

* Boris Godunov became the Czar after the crown prince, Dmitry, the seven-year-old son of Ivan the Terrible, was cruelly murdered. No direct evidence was ever discovered linking Boris Godunov to the crime, but it is commonly believed that, since he was the main beneficiary of the murder, he had a hand in it.

LUBLIN
JANUARY 1941

Keeping to the shadows, avoiding the streetlamps, hugging the buildings, Thomas walked along the main street, then turned left down an alley that opened into Adolf Hitler Square. He felt his way around the small craters made by the Luftwaffe's bombs. Beyond the corner he was dazzled by the light blazing from the second-floor windows of the SS headquarters. How imposing the building was. There was a cold, sharp burning in his throat, and his tongue licked icy teeth. He pressed against the wall, passed his hand over the bricks, looked away from the building: he would always remember the humiliation he had suffered here in the SS headquarters of the Lublin District.

From the windows tongues of fire assailed him, contorting his features into a grimace of fearful malice. Perhaps he still offered an ingratiating smile, but his eyes revealed his acceptance of fate. His was the face of an acrobat who had fallen from the trapeze. Erika Gelber's techniques had long since stopped helping him: there was no spark of life to concentrate on, either around him or in his memory. Maybe he would write to her, in the labour camp at Ravensbrück: Dear Frau Gelber, I hope you are enjoying your work in the service of the Third Reich. Because of a certain deterioration in my situation, I would like to ask you to refresh my memory regarding the Four Stage System for dealing with attacks.

He climbed steps blocked by piles of snow and wandered into a small grove of trees: the branches leaned over the red tiles, from whose edges pointed icicles hung, while smoke curled from chimneys like tree limbs. In the background a frozen city dozed, its sounds muted, its barren streets wrapped in fog; from here it was possible to imagine it as a huge void. The trees restored his strength of spirit—the courage of cowards. Only from another continent do you fire arrows at the god Wotan and his wild army.

At night, among the small stone houses that had become an entertainment district with beer halls, a casino and a brothel, they didn't ask who he was. He would sit on a leather armchair leaning against the wall, drink schnapps, Okocim beer and cognac on the weekends, and listen to the music that was played all night. Cigarette smoke rose, young women dashed back and forth with trays of sausage and cabbage, bread and beer, or sat in men's laps and let them press their lips against their necks. It was as if they were in uniform: a blue-black line around their eyes, shiny cheeks, off-the-shoulder dresses, small bones, black silk stockings.

At the far end of the hall was a small wooden stage, lit with a few coloured lanterns and the bluish-orange flame of a kerosene stove. Sometimes short performances were presented there—choruses of drunken officers, a young soprano who sang arias from *Don Giovanni*, voices humming *'Der Sennerin Abschied von der Alm'** and mournful songs of childhood. A bespectacled officer in a dress uniform with starched cuffs, decked out with medals, read parts of a speech by von Alvensleben from the SS that pierced the heart: 'Nothing has ever been constructed out of delicacy and weakness. New worlds are cast

---

* The milkmaid's farewell to alpine pastures.

in stone, in lead, in blood and in men as tough as Krupp steel.' Then the officer added words of his own: 'In a democracy the government needs the people's love, and we too need it, but we can also manage without it. Sometimes the people will love us, then they won't, and then they will fall in love with us again. We will retain power.' His fiery expression annoyed Thomas. He would have gladly thrust a spear down his throat.

A proud voice rose from a smoke-filled table. 'Have you heard what they call Globocnik at the SS-Führer Headquarters?'

'Globus,' Thomas muttered. That was one of Himmler's old jokes that Wolfgang had told him. Sometimes he hoped that Wolfgang would be sitting among the officers: he was the only one Thomas liked among those who had laid a trap for him in Warsaw. He had made great plans for both of them. He forgave Wolfgang because, from the moment the young officer encountered the Kresling-Hermann-Weller triumvirate, his only choice was to do their bidding with good cheer and fighting spirit. Truly loyal men, who would have acted differently, had never crossed his path. There were too many characters, Thomas felt, in religion, folklore, art and even in public discourse—the inventions of popular morality—who were merely theoretical, who behaved irrationally in unrealistic scenarios; and under the influence of these stories, poor children were filled with guilt because they couldn't live up to such exalted ideas.

A stocky man, one of the district governor's assistants, stepped up to the stage. He closed his eyes and swayed to the tune of the piano:

> My beloved in Nuremberg has fallen in love with a count.
> He showers her with lavish presents.
> I write to her: Flowers from the front
> Are stopped at the border.

The song was greeted with cheers and a jumble of drunken shouting: 'Hans-Hans-Hans.' No doubt, stocky Hans, who had studied acting in Reinhardt's theatre, was everyone's beloved romantic tenor.

Late at night Thomas watched the couples dancing to melancholy French love songs. Was Clarissa dancing now? Every evening he imagined a different suitor for her, the two of them dancing all over Berlin. Once she confided to him that some of her friends secretly listened to swing, and now he imagined her dancing like in American movies.

He hadn't written to her since he was sent away from Warsaw. What news did he have for her now? That his career had been blocked again? That the Foreign Office had stolen his model and handed it to his enemy, while he had become a miserable warehouse worker in Lublin? She had seen him defeated once, and that was enough.

For weeks he sat in the beer hall pretending that no one here could know him until one day, during a poker game, a Gestapo officer asked whether he was Thomas Heiselberg of the 'Model of the Polish People'. He nodded, and said nothing, but the officer, who had annoyed Thomas earlier by shuffling the cards with excessive skill, went on, 'There was great interest in your model when we arrived in Lublin. We had rather shitty intelligence lists then. Okay, the President of the Regional Court and the Vice-President for Appeals were simple cases: a bullet in the head, and no more appeals. But there were school principals, Catholic professors, music lovers...And then the order came down to pay attention to archaeologists. We liquidated people because they had pottery bowls at home.'

As they were leaving, the officer grabbed his arm, breathed beer fumes in his ear and said, 'Sometimes we wonder, Mr Model—you know, even the little guys with their fingers on the trigger have a few thoughts—whether everything that we did was so necessary.' The ghost-fingers of the officer pinched his flesh for a long time afterwards.

At night Lublin was as dark as a small village. The warm lights of Berlin, for which he was partly responsible—'Burners of the Night' was his name for the advertising people who understood the potential of an illuminated aerial display—seemed like a figment of memory. The dark city made him ill at ease, an uneasiness that was muffled in other people's company, but which burst out in a deafening scream when he was alone. That's why he used to wander the city in the wee hours. He would walk along the dimly lit main street, approach the twisting wall of the old town—he became used to showing his documents to policemen, who dubbed him 'the sleepwalking officer'— and would descend into the Jewish area, which stank of sewage and fish, a kind of valley of densely packed wooden houses. Above them, as though in a different kingdom, rose the castle; the Jews' houses below it looked like the talons of a monster from a fairytale. He didn't understand why all the governors of the city—Russian, Polish and now German, too—wasted such a fine castle on criminals.

The buildings, headquarters and labour camps that he saw in his wanderings in Lublin breathed life into the various inquiries that used to reach the offices of the model in Warsaw. An SS doctor, for example, who took care of prisoners in the castle, complained that Gestapo headquarters in the 'house under the clock' were sending sacks of corpses to him and asking him to state ridiculous causes of death such as heart failure, throat infection and influenza. 'My question: is there a group of diseases typical of the Poles that we can indicate in the forms without further details?' Naturally they had not answered that ignominious question, and joked that an alarming number of madmen now wanted help from the model.

Lublin was so small—it was ten minutes from the 'house under the clock' to the castle, and along the way you passed by most of the Reich institutions in the city. Here, the elaborate recommendations that he had formulated in Warsaw and sent off into the unknown took on simple forms: stone, house, roof, wall. There he was, walking along the path taken by the sacks of corpses.

About an hour before dawn he would wander back to his house. He was fond of the darkness in the stairwell, would grip the loose banister, the wooden steps would creak under his boots and sometimes the moonlight would coat the rusty mailboxes. Climbing the stairs, he couldn't help remembering his apartment on Nowy Swiat and the fine buildings on Krakowskie Przedmiescie. During his first week here, disconcerted by his isolation, he had sneaked into a party in a splendid apartment with a fine balcony, a large parlour and a high ceiling. The new landlord made a proud display of a silver Hanukkah Menorah, decorated with a handsome relief of two lions.

Many apartments on that street had become vacant after the Jews were evicted. He submitted several fruitless requests to be given one, and was at last allocated this mouldy apartment on the top floor of an antiquated building on Lindenstrasse, formerly Lipowa Street. He wondered whether instructions had been sent from Warsaw and Berlin to annoy him in little matters as well.

Two weeks passed after his arrival in Lublin before he was summoned to SS headquarters. In those idle days he submitted a request to meet Odilo Globocnik, commander of the SS and the police, mentioning their cordial exchange of letters while he was the director of the office of the model in Warsaw. He received a negative answer, which implied surprise at his very request. When he asked to meet the district governor Ernst Zerner he also alluded to his 'correspondence with my former office' and was answered with a polite letter stating that the governor, being very busy, might find some free time in April.

One morning an officer had appeared at his apartment and announced that he must report immediately to SS headquarters. He pushed open the heavy wooden doors, took in the marble columns, the small light fixtures, and stepped down the broad corridor. The stairs reminded him of the Four Seasons Hotel. He hoped that here, on the second floor, he would be given an office, and perhaps he might still rise again. After all, Lublin could be a place to recover, out of sight, to reflect on things before beginning to struggle once more for his position.

But his hopes were dashed: the two minor officials whom he met lorded it over him and explained that they knew all about 'his tricky manoeuvres in Warsaw'. They told him straight out that the Foreign Office did not like him. He asked whether he was still employed by the Foreign Office and was told that he had not been discharged. Apparently somebody there must still believe he could be useful. But here in Lublin, since all the agencies tried to keep the Foreign Office out of their business, he would be under SS supervision.

'But in Warsaw I was under the district governor's authority,' Thomas protested. 'Why will I be subordinate to the SS in Lublin?'

'Because the district governor doesn't want anything to do with you,' they told him.

The powers that had joined together to bring him down in Warsaw and exile him to Lublin, as if it were a kind of penal colony, were still conniving to direct his life. He was asked in a dismissive tone to draft a report about the Belorussian man, in accordance with instructions he would receive from Dr Georg Weller, the director of the offices of the model. He was stunned by the contempt shown for him by these two little bugs, but remained businesslike and asked what resources for research would be at his disposal. When writing the Model of the Polish People, he had made use of ten years of comprehensive research, but he didn't know Belorussia at all.

'You can write to institutes in Germany. Not far from here, in Cracow, you'll find the new Institute for the Study of the East, and there's also a library in the city,' the officer answered.

'With those scanty means I can't write something equivalent in detail to the Polish model,' Thomas protested.

'You aren't expected to come up with such a brilliant achievement.' The officers exchanged looks. 'Just do the best you can.'

Thomas asked no more questions. After a few cold parting words, he left the room. The instructions from Warsaw never came, of course, but a week later he was summoned to SS headquarters again, and ordered to begin work, and since for the time being there was no office for him, he could surely write at home, and submit a progress report every week. 'Dr Weller,' they said, 'expects you to do the best possible work. Remember that the time allocated for completion of the project is not unlimited.' As he expected, the reports he submitted received no response.

August Frenzel, one of the officers who had mocked him at the first meeting, apparently felt sorry for him and after one of his weekly visits saw him to the door and said that no one enjoyed harassing him here. But explicit instructions had been conveyed to Globocnik. 'You acquired some very powerful enemies,' Frenzel clucked in appreciation. Other clerks and officers, who had heard of the glorious reputation of the model, also treated him like a leper who carried with him lessons that were worth learning. 'If you fell so hard, you must have been very high. Perhaps you could tell us your story one day.'

'Of course,' Thomas answered amicably. 'We could meet one evening for a drink at the Deutsches Haus, and I'll tell you everything. Such a long and complicated story might take a few evenings, but we have all the time in the world.'

The panic that gripped Frenzel at the very idea that he might be seen in his company amused him.

During the first months no one approached him. Not until December did he receive a letter from the German Munitions Company, which had recently been made responsible for the workshops on his street. The writer asked his advice about training Jewish workers who 'until now were mainly employed as shoemakers and tailors', and whom the company was interested in teaching how to use the most advanced equipment in Germany. The man had written to him because someone in the office of Walter Salpeter in Berlin had praised the training program at Milton, which Thomas had once directed.

Thomas had some earlier acquaintance with the workshops in the Lindenstrasse camp. One night, during the first snow, he came home and stood at the window to watch the snowflakes falling on the city. Suddenly, about twenty metres from his window, a knot of naked bodies coalesced in the darkness. At first the sight was so strange that he supposed the whiteness of the snow must be deluding him, but then he understood that naked people really were standing in the snowed court, and the little hillocks around them were prostrate naked bodies. Dogs began to bark. Beams of light crisscrossed the snow, picking up a white foot, a withered buttock, a shaven scalp, a boyish chest, the nape of a man buried facedown in the snow. Some of the limbs quivered in the spotlight, others remained frozen. He realised that he was counting the dead and the living and the ones he couldn't classify. In a few minutes the lights went off, the shapes of dogs moved among the bodies, their barking mingled with the whistling of the wind.

After that night he no longer pushed aside that curtain. He regarded it as part of the wall. There was another window.

That was why, when the man from the German Munitions Company offered to arrange a visit to the workshops in the camp, Thomas refused, saying he had heard stories about inappropriate treatment of the workers, treatment that was of no utility, especially because some of them were prisoners of war. The man admitted that such complaints had also reached him—apparently they referred to initiation ceremonies held by the guards for new groups. He would see to it that these contemptible practices stopped. Thomas replied courteously that it was clear to him that the intentions of his company were pure, but he himself had no relevant expertise and, by the way, conditions were decent at Milton, including professional training, social benefits and even the idea of profit sharing with workers who excelled. 'To my great regret, nothing that I know from Milton can be applied to your Jewish slaves.' He didn't even try to conceal his disgust.

'Your answer surprises me, Herr Heiselberg,' the man exclaimed. 'The expert opinion that the directorate of the Model of the Polish People submitted to us, signed by you, states that the initiative to employ Jewish prisoners from the Polish army in our munitions factory was welcome and useful.'

'I don't remember writing anything like that,' Thomas grumbled. 'And in any event I wasn't referring to a camp like this.'

He would get up in the late morning with no idea how he would pass the time. All the days of the week were fused into a single day: holidays or his birthday he remembered only weeks later. During the day he didn't leave the house. Even after he planned his tasks in the evening for the next day, he put them off as the morning light spread out. In the afternoon he laid the table with a pale turquoise dinner set, a legacy from the evicted owners, and took supper in the small parlour, but went out at night to eat sausages in a beer hall or cabbage rolls in the restaurant near his house, where his custom of folding his napkin at the end of the meal and slipping it into a silver ring always aroused embarrassed smiles.

Once a week he submitted a short progress report to SS headquarters, bought groceries, went to the barber, and that was as far as his contact with daylight went. At SS headquarters they always asked him whether he felt well. Frenzel, who was somewhat closer to him than the others, decided he was sick and urged him to consult a doctor. Even the women who sold meat and vegetables pointed at his pasty colour and volunteered advice. These small acts of kindness caused a strange paralysis in him; the impression he wanted to give, that Thomas Heiselberg was an energetic person with tricks up his sleeve, was wearing thin. He was an amiable pest who still didn't grasp that his life's work had collapsed.

He noticed that his movements were becoming sluggish, as if his body understood that it was best to stretch out time so he wouldn't sink into complete lethargy. He would sit on the sofa with the charcoal stove at his feet—when he moved away from it and got cold his only desire was to warm himself up again there. Sometimes for a whole week he would sleep in the morning and doze off in the afternoon, or keep turning over a single idea which contained the solution to all his troubles: he would walk around the apartment, lie on his bed, lean forwards on the sofa, scrape the red lacquer from the desk, mutter instructions to his memory, trying to grasp all the unravelling threads, and in the evening he would give up, realising that he had succumbed to a new kind of attack. If he felt calmer, he would sit at the peeling desk and type page after page about the Model of the Belorussian People—but his ideas were just abstract thoughts and were not founded on evidence. In fact he was drawing conclusions from the Polish, French and Italian models, and jumbling them together with snippets and theories from books. Dozens of pages piled up on his desk. He had always loved models. There was no distress that didn't have a model, and now he was enjoying the tangle of his sentences:

The Belorussian yearns for the past glory of the Polish-Lithuanian Union, influenced by Soviet Communism to the east and, from the west of Belorussia, by the ideas of French democracy. A reactionary tendency is also interwoven in his essence, the source of which is in forced religious conversion, as well as the shells of religion and morality. Materialism as a form of oppression can ignite in him the aspiration for freedom, given that new structures…

Indeed, ideas from the French model, slightly modified, would fit in here. Grind the formative experiences of the Polish national type and stir them into the history of Belorussia: didn't everyone's desires ultimately conform with a few simple trends? Sometimes, in flashes of clarity, he suspected that his handiwork was a kind of secret code comprehensible to him alone, and that he should be worried about the consequences when Weller read the report. But worrying about Weller and his gang only made his mind cloud over.

This unrelenting shriek of panic, waking and in dreams, proclaimed to him that from now on his life would always be like this. Whatever had gone wrong in his soul could not be repaired. He should bury his old dreams and hopes and be content with his grey future in which he sat day after day in his good clothing by the charcoal stove piling up mountains of pointless words.

He had never imagined how murderous defeat could be. And now something in his soul sought it, rushed upon it with ferocious power, and used it to obliterate his contact with the world. He had always flourished in the company of others, and now any human connection demanded a huge effort. Even remembering people in Berlin allowed him only to imagine the look they would give him when they saw him again, a look of simple recognition: this man was lost.

'We've done wonderful work here,' exclaimed Nikita Mikhailovich Kropotkin before adjourning the morning meeting. Sasha's report about new schools in the city had encouraged him. 'Seventeen schools and professional colleges, excellent education. When the Poles ruled here, most of the schools were private. Every day I receive letters of gratitude from people who couldn't afford tuition.'

'Nikita Mikhailovich, there are no more social divisions here. Now every child in western Belorussia can get free education,' she said.

'Exactly!' someone agreed.

'The people here are smart. They understood from the beginning that it was a good thing for them to be part of the Soviet Socialist Republic of Belorussia,' declared Nikita Mikhailovich, signalling to all of them to leave the room. As usual, she remained.

He removed a thread or two from his Charleston jacket, which clung to his hips and restricted his movement. Today was the first time he had dressed up in his suit, a fiftieth-birthday present from his wife, made by 'Zhurkievitz, the finest tailor in Moscow'. He claimed it was too bourgeois for his taste, and only wore it because his wife begged him.

'Last December I spent a few days with the Fourth Army, a small supervisory job. We got to the Pruzhany region. You won't believe how we were greeted: they threw flowers and sugar at us, the whole city was red flags, dancing night and day. After they drank all the vodka, they brought out the cologne that the Polish police had left. We drank everything and danced on the tanks. With my own eyes I saw how it was possible to do good in the world.'

'Happy days, without doubt,' she replied and moved to the door. Nikita Mikhailovich could blather for hours about those beautiful days, about books that dealt with education and morality, educational methods from sixteenth-century Amsterdam, Alfonso the Wise of Toledo, Baghdad in the tenth century, or, even worse, his great project: 'Education of the Future: Diminishing Units of Time'.

'Alexandra Andreyevna, one more thing,' Nikita called out. 'We're receiving complaints about the NKVD's soft treatment of Jewish parasites in the flea market. They say the place is full of peddlers and cheats. If those people don't want to work here, we'll teach them what work is in the forests of Arkhangelsk.'

'They're mainly refugees from Germany,' she answered. 'We've heard nothing about any complaints.'

'By the end of the month we're going to deport at least two hundred parasites, and the rest will learn their lesson.' His bored tone indicated that the matter was closed. 'I'm only telling you because the Jews are close to your heart.'

She didn't answer. All week long he had been scattering obscure hints about imminent changes. But when she asked delicately whether she should prepare for new initiatives, he played innocent and claimed that nothing was afoot, at least for the moment. At first she suspected that some plot had been hatched against him, as with Styopa, but his energy dispelled her suspicion that he was in trouble.

Every morning she sat next to the office window that looked out on the Mukhavetz River, and she waited for the sun to rise. While she strode to the office, except for weak lights from house windows, the city was enveloped in darkness. But now a tiny spark of fire began to burn above the river—there you are, her heart sang. In a little while the spark would form an orange-grey ball. In Leningrad it was hard to see the sunrise—smoke, bridges, gilded steeples and factory chimneys—but Brest was the clearest city she had ever seen.

The ball of fire rose from the river, still gripped by it, and ascended to the height of the bare trees along the banks. Sasha looked at it through the thin curtain: four golden arms were stretched from the sun like a cross. Sasha played with the curtain: she pushed it aside, pulled it back. A strange light poured onto the river, hiding the water behind a glowing fog, and the small ball swelled, its boundaries burst, the eastern part of the city brightened, it was dawn.

Two hours remained before the meeting of the senior NKVD officials of the district. At these meetings the representatives of the various district committees presented cases requiring special discussion: subversive talk in the wood cooperative in Pruzhany, eighty candidates for expulsion, eight workers to prison, seventy-two children to Siberia; a Pole, an agent of the Suchard chocolate company, made negative comments about the alliance with the Nazis and claimed that it was a betrayal of Stalin's firm positions.

They had a procedure for the boring parts: she would write a private note to Nikita Mikhailovich, and he would rework the comment until it was vague enough to be said aloud. 'We have to remember,' she wrote to him now, 'that the strength to change a strong decision is a rare display of strength.'

Nikita Mikhailovich called out with pleasure: 'Please state your opinion about this proposition: a person transfers his strength from one position to another. The position may change, but his strength remains.'

She perused the papers on the table: Nikita Mikhailovich had put her in charge of the agenda so they wouldn't waste hours on nonsense: the investigation of the chairmen of the collective farm and village councils; lists of those arrested in Pinsk in 1940; expediting the treatment of residents of Brest who had not paid the culture tax. Nothing new. Here was a case that might wake the meeting up: four citizens had caught a man who had worked in their police force under Polish rule. First they chopped off his arms with swords, leaving him standing. Then they peeled off his skin from the shoulder to the waist, on both sides. It sounded like a Cossack legend.

The first time she received the lists of those to be expelled, it took her twenty minutes to mark the main subjects. She realised that the hundreds of people whose names appeared there would be banished with no further discussion, and that some young woman in Leningrad, exactly like her, had moved a piece of paper across her desk, and that's how they exiled her parents to a gulag and sent Kolya and Vlada to an orphanage. In any case, Sasha's work changed nothing; tens of thousands of people had been expelled from the district before her arrival, and now the stream had slowed. At her request, Nikita Mikhailovich had made her responsible for supervising the establishment of schools; she helped with the new archive that had been set up in the city to obtain secret documents of the Polish regime, and she persuaded Nikita Mikhailovich to declare war against workers at the cooperatives who gave service only to wealthy people.

She no longer traded in the souls of the accused.

Sometimes a week would go by and only at the end of it would she realise that the meeting with Kolya on the plain had left no trace in her consciousness, not even when she thought about him. Tricks were apparently being played in her heart to separate her from her despair at understanding that he had determined her fate during the years they hadn't seen each other. The memory of Kolya in his uniform came back, along with the accusations he had made. She had wanted to hit him, to grab his neck and to shout, How could you believe that horrible woman? But even then her imagination insisted on placing them in her childhood room. She was horrified by the possibility that he might dim the clarity of the love that bound them together; without it, there was no point in anything she did, no point in surviving.

Strangely, after that encounter, she began to forget whole areas of Leningrad. In her mind's eye she could see Nadyezhda wandering among mouldy apartments, reading her long poem, 'See, Soldier Dmitry', and everybody understood who the heroine of the poem was and condemned her. Then the buildings and streets and the people she had known began to blur, and apart from her childhood home there was no longer any Leningrad.

Soon she would be called upon to provide a reckoning for her actions. Everyone, the dead and the living who spoke in their name, would demand an explanation: How is it that you worked for the NKVD? How did you survive, flourish even? She imagined the defiant answers she would toss back at them: Apparently I was better than you, apparently I refused to accept the fate you intended for me. Do you hear, Mother? I'm washing my hands before you and saying: I am innocent of those saints' blood. You accuse me of Vlada's death? You're calling me Boris Godunov? Nadyezhda didn't understand anything about history—you all said that her historical allusions were like a blind man leafing through the thousands of pages of *The History of Russia*. And admirers like Brodsky, who edited her poems and rescued her from humiliation, are now sitting in prison or dead. It would be more logical to call me Shuysky, who cleared Boris Godunov and determined that the crown prince fell on his sword by mistake. We both understood that our masters demand the truth. We both worked hard to survive. And if you had a bit of magnanimity, you would praise the survivors: it took an effort to survive.

She sat two seats away from Nikita Mikhailovich, already tired of amusing him, but he still passed notes to her with jokes and gossip, and she answered with as much wit as she could muster. But it was all becoming tiresome. She didn't like Nikita Mikhailovich, nor did she hate him: he was another patron whom she had managed to please. For a long time she had been bestowing affection on and even seducing men whose deaths wouldn't have aroused a thing in her except the question, 'Who will replace him?' But sometimes all she wanted were simple gestures: to caress a dear face, to link eyes with a beloved person.

Moving her arms like a conductor, she invited someone to raise a certain subject, gave the floor to someone else, allotted time with her fingers and silenced them—all for Nikita Mikhailovich. Occasionally her memory would retain a detail: Vasili Abgostinovich, a pig breeder, was sent to prison, a woman and eight children were exiled to Siberia. In the break they complimented the way she ran the discussion, usually flattering Nikita Mikhailovich through her, because the man found it hard to remember names and faces, and even officials with whom he had shared an intimate secret got a blank look a week later. They all tried to coax her to join them for lunch. She fobbed them off, showering them with promises of visits instead, and adding sexual innuendos: things the women of Brest would do for bread and lard. When the meeting was adjourned and the group rose, Nikita Mikhailovich remained in his place and glowered at her. She responded with an irritating smile: Aren't you pleased, Nikita Mikhailovich? So what will you do to me?

He ordered her to come and see him at the end of the day and was answered insolently: 'I didn't imagine otherwise.'

Sasha walked to her office. Now the scowl he had given her made her laugh. The man who had sent tens of thousands of people to prison, Siberia and death, was actually an absent-minded creature, slightly built and bespectacled, playing a role too big for him. In his defence he knew it. On his fiftieth birthday they had got drunk in his office, and he had blurted out, 'Permit me to introduce myself before your highness. I am Nikita Mikhailovich Kropotkin—I regret to say there's no connection with Pyotr—a Bolshevik heart and soul, studied medicine for two years, the author of the educational theory of "Diminishing Units of Time", and mass murderer.'

She locked the door, felt that she was sweating, but when she undid her blouse she discovered that her skin was cool and dry. She sat on her armchair, enjoying the cool air on the back of her neck, and read the letter from Maxim, delivered to her that morning by his close friend, who worked in the finance department. In the last few years he had started to write with his left hand so as to appear to be a balanced and fair person, and his ornate spirals annoyed her:

> My dear, since Stepan Kristoforovich no longer troubles
> even his wife, it's time for you to return to Leningrad. Give
> your consent, and I'll make the necessary arrangements.
> My position has grown a lot stronger, and the atmosphere
> in the city has improved. Let's admit the truth: we've made
> it through the hard times, we did what was required of us,
> and when we had no choice we weren't deterred even by
> cruelty. If so many people were removed, while we survived
> and were promoted, apparently we acted wisely. A reason
> for pride, no?
>
> My dear, I've been speaking quite a bit with Reznikov.
> As you know, he replaced Stepan Kristoforovich. He isn't as
> evil as you thought. If he used to be hostile to you (and
> anyway I'm not convinced about that—perhaps your Styopa
> incited you against each other), he's now changed his mind.
> You might object that no one would dare denigrate my wife
> in front of me, or they'd get it in the face, but his praise for
> the confessions that you edited—how you guided the
> accused to true sincerity instead of the stinking fictions of
> Stepan Kristoforovich—sounded absolutely authentic.
>
> Sasha, upon your request I checked on the matter, and
> you'll be pleased to hear that the poet Nadyezhda Petrovna,
> your parents' close friend, has indeed returned from the
> gulag. Her health is good, and she has already announced
> that she intends to write a new series of poems in which
> she'll lay bare her self-scrutiny of the past few years.
>
> My dear, more than anything, I want us to have a child,
> and I'm worried by your stay in that distant and dangerous
> place. I understand that you're worried about your skinny
> brother. I've pulled some strings regarding the supply of
> meat to the soldiers in the Fourth Army in western
> Belorussia. Difficulties in food supply are common on all

the new fronts: in western Ukraine, in Estonia and in Latvia, in all the republics that have joined our ranks, the supply lines are cumbersome and a long time will pass before they catch up with our achievements. In any event, your presence there won't help your brother. I believe that if you were here by my side (Reznikov is willing to offer you a position that suits your abilities), we could help your brother by other means.

That sentence amused her. Once again he was offering her deals: Come back, get pregnant to me at last and I'll help Nikolai. All their letters were actually endless negotiations, full of strategy.

She skimmed the rest of the letter—everything was so predictable—and then stretched out on the armchair and closed her eyes. Every day she looked forward to the noon break so she could stretch out on her chair and give herself over to her dreams, in which she was another person, and Leningrad was different, and she had exquisitely witty ripostes to the pack of mourners and accusers. In her dreams she could die, and it wasn't so frightening: one turn of the steering wheel, and she plunged into a chasm; pressing a pistol to her neck; standing naked before the charging tanks of the Red Army; on the tracks in front of the *Red Arrow* when it was going seventy kilometres per hour. Only in her sleep could she strip away all her orchestrated actions—her gestures, responses, expressions—in which everything was done according to set procedures, even behaviour that seemed improvised. But living a rehearsed life also allowed her, no matter how busy she was, to think, to withstand a toxic attack of memory, to talk to the dead and hear them—like the chess machine she had read about in a French newspaper when she was a girl, an automaton that appeared in the court of Maria Theresa and defeated the best players. (When she finally learned that the whole thing was a hoax, she was very sorry.) And there were terrifying moments, when, without warning, the machine stopped. Just like an hour ago, standing before Nikita Mikhailovich. Then she was at a loss, furious, as two desires struggled within her: to destroy everything and pay the price, or to deliver herself once more to the machine and remain alive.

A knock on the door woke her. The streetlights were already shining. She had slept for at least two hours. She scrambled to put on her puff-sleeved blouse, scattered some papers on her desk, sipped some water, turned on the light and, while she hurried to the door, patted her hair and smoothed her shirt.

'Good evening, Comrade Weissberg.' Nikita Mikhailovich was leaning against the wall. She tried not to blink. She was already used to the transition from darkness to light.

'Good evening, Comrade Kropotkin.' She emphasised the official tone and gestured to the armchair he liked.

He followed her. The scent of pine wafted from his clothes. He closed the door behind him and turned off the light. 'Please don't ask again whether it's necessary,' he said. He didn't like the lighting in her office. The streetlamps were sufficient in his opinion. He passed her, removed his jacket and sat on her chair.

'In this light your hair is blue.'

'You always say that.'

Nikita Mikhailovich also had a weakness for her, but unlike Styopa he was cautious, and whenever he felt he was succumbing to her charms, he took care to keep a distance for a few days. Of course he desired her, but he acknowledged the hopelessness of it. Unlike other men who allowed her to seduce them, he remained faithful to his principles: she was married to Maxim Podolsky, he was married and a father of two, and that was that.

'You don't have to apologise for falling asleep. This week someone called my attention to your habit of taking an afternoon nap, and I made a ruling: let the girl sleep.'

'Someone called your attention,' she repeated, amused by his custom of blaming other people for providing information that it was beneath his dignity to deal with.

He poured a vodka for them both, and they clinked glasses over the table. She glanced at his hands—he was drunk, that was all. When he was very drunk his fingers trembled and turned crimson.

'Do you remember the last day of your first week in Brest?' he asked.

'Certainly.'

'Where were we standing?'

'On the roof of Building Number Eight.'

Early morning, May, people flooded the small street, men in summer suits, women in flowered spring dresses, straw hats, sunglasses, girls holding colourful parasols, dozens of children clutching toys and dolls. Folding tables, sacks of flour, loaves of bread wrapped in towels.

'Where are the trucks?' she had asked Nikita Mikhailovich.

'There's no need for them. The railroad station is fifteen minutes away on foot.'

'Who are those people?'

'Mainly merchants,' he had said, 'representatives of Polish companies, agents in the wood trade, some of them speculative investors in American companies. All sorts of shareholders in banks, including Jews, and those bastards had the nerve to name one of them the People's Bank. Some are connected to the bank that diverted money to Zionists. Look at them now: they might deserve our pity, and their deeds seem minor compared to their punishment. But remember that for many years the bourgeoisie concealed everything from us. We recommended that the parents tell the children they're going on a long trip.' He sighed. 'Brest is so small, and the world is huge.'

Nikita Mikhailovich tapped the cup of vodka with the finger adorned by his wedding band, as though seeking her attention. 'Of course we knew the history of the Weissbergs, but we still didn't know exactly how your parents and brothers were exiled. Maybe it was like that, maybe at night, maybe they were summoned for interrogation and never returned. I wanted you to see this part of our work here: purifying the district of destructive factors. All of them.

'I knew that in your work in Leningrad you were able to manipulate the accused in interrogation rooms, but I was pretty sure that you'd never seen people crowded together in the morning outside their house on a busy street with the two valuable possessions that they've managed to gather up, a few pennies in their socks, before the caravan marches off, one-two-three, and then, silence. I reckoned this picture might remind you of events that happened to you, and cause you some distress. But you inundated me with technical questions about procedures, making suggestions about efficiency, and I realised that all the praise poor Styopa heaped on you—and I doubted its truth, because I knew about his dopey attraction to young women—all that praise was justified.'

He poured more vodka for her, and she drank. His tactics were obvious: there were people who reacted to a small shock with big gestures, and others were just the opposite. She remembered the conclusion she had drawn when she stood next to him on the roof—above them the blue sky, and beneath them the procession in fancy dresses, scarves and parasols, embroidered kerchiefs. Stepan Kristoforovich was a department head, Nikita Mikhailovich was a movie director.

'The only thing that I didn't understand then,' he said, 'was that it would be a mistake to judge you according to your reactions. You're an artist of reactions.'

'So it seems to you.' She was annoyed. 'Maybe it's because you judge women according to different standards. Even advanced Communists like you are still stuck in the pages of the *domostroy*.* We'll always conform to a type in your eyes: the Great Mother, the Helpmate, the Faithful Servant, Madonna or Whore—and now I'm the Ice Woman.'

'Why don't you assume the man sitting before you also has a many-layered soul? I wasn't born NKVD. Maybe it will surprise you, but until the age of twenty my great dream was to live in Oblomovka.'**

'Nikita Mikhailovich, I tell you what's on my mind. We've even discussed my marriage several times. Maybe you assume that I have

---

* A sixteenth-century book of household rules, usually referred to as an example of backwards, patriarchal views that have become obsolete.

** The country estate where Oblomov was born, the hero of the novel by Ivan Goncharov, a character who became the symbol of the indolent life of the nineteenth-century Russian aristocracy.

thoughts that I don't?'

'I'd like to know what they are,' he sighed, and put his feet up on the desk. 'If I forced you to drink this whole bottle, would we finally hear one true thing?'

His drunken aggressiveness frightened her a little. 'Once I read in a book: if you want to conceal information from an enemy, don't reveal it to a friend.' The laughter cost her an effort.

'As usual, very clever,' he said apathetically. 'We are starting to think—and you'll deny it, of course—that you're no longer able to do the things that we do here.'

'Nikita Mikhailovich, we all suffer sometimes because of what we're exposed to, but we remain focused on the goal we believe in.'

'Well, our feeling is that you've believed enough.'

'Are you firing me?' She was teasing him. She guessed that he bore good tidings.

'Alexandra Andreyevna, maybe you misunderstand me. My intentions towards you have always been pure. I admire you, and feel sadness about the things you've had to endure at your young age.'

'I don't need pity.'

'We have a nice little project that I'd like you to devote yourself to.' He ignored her angry tone, as if he had foreseen the panic that would grip her the moment he doubted her tenacity. He had apparently spent weeks and months observing her.

'You know that some differences have emerged between us and the Germans in our recent discussions with them. We're trying to ease the tension, warm things up. The Italian invasion of Greece is a new focus of interest for the Germans, and this is a golden opportunity to spread some good will. The commissariat for Foreign Affairs has put together an initiative for a joint activity in Brest, as a symbol of peace and cooperation. You remember that in September last year the Wehrmacht and the Red Army met here in Brest. The Germans evacuated the city just as they had promised, but before that, on this very street, our Semyon Krivoshein and the German general Guderian reviewed a parade of the Red Army and the Wehrmacht.'

'Obviously I remember.'

'Actually that parade was organised in a hurry because time was short. But since Brest is on the border between us and the Germans, it's a good place for joint initiatives.'

'That sounds interesting.'

'Under my personal supervision and in cooperation with German elements, you will administer the initiative to spread…'

'…good will,' she intoned.

'Exactly,' he growled. 'And since that good will isn't official, and it derives from operatives on both sides who want to ease the tension, we'll describe this undertaking as "meetings at the lowest levels", so low that in fact they aren't taking place. Your job will be to present creative ideas without committing anyone to them. After all, the major issues between Germany and the Soviet Union are managed in Moscow and Berlin.'

'It sounds like entirely meaningless work.'

'On the contrary, Alexandra Andreyevna. It could be very useful. We expect original thinking and high-flying ideas.'

'Why me?' Her thoughts skipped over all the rituals she would soon be exempt from—discussions, letters, reports—all that bloody muck. She was already reconciled to knowing that, as long as she breathed, this is what her days would be filled with, unless she gave in to Maxim and got pregnant.

'Why you? For all the reasons I just mentioned before, and because I read in your profile that you speak French. The Germans will also be sending representatives who speak the language of that miserable country. One of my close acquaintances, who met their representatives at a conference of the Gestapo and the NKVD last February, formed a good impression of them. In his opinion the Germans are professionals and can be surprisingly flexible.'

'In Leningrad I wore out interrogators as well as the accused.'

'There's no doubt you were born for this,' Nikita Mikhailovich laughed. 'And you're never going to repeat what you just heard. I was only told about these meetings because I was required to authorise the transfer of certain prisoners to the Gestapo.'

'You didn't have to say that,' she said. 'And this will be the main part of my work?'

'This will be your job, nothing else. But there's one condition,' he added. 'I'm tired of deceit. I want us to say true things to each other. I always tried to be faithful to Marcus Aurelius's dictum: "Those who fail to attend to the motions of their own souls are necessarily unhappy."'

His words sounded to her like another amusing note passed between them at a meeting. It always made them laugh when one of them wrote, 'Let's tell the truth.'

'I don't tell lies now either,' she said cautiously.

'You understand exactly what I mean.'

'I'll do everything I can to keep my end of the bargain.' She stretched, and drank her vodka. There was no choice. Assuming that a strange madness had attacked him, she would supply him with a few 'true things', and he would believe he held her soul in his hand. He had revealed that it wasn't a good idea to underestimate him, but there was no need to exaggerate his virtues either.

'So it's all settled,' he said and swung his legs off the desk. 'Your new job starts in a week.'

'It sounds very nice,' she said sweetly. Could she call the warmth that bubbled inside her happiness?

One day Frenzel informed him that he was required to report to Party headquarters on Horst Wessel Street, the building that seemed to be hidden from sight but always rose up before him when he returned home at the end of the night: its iron gate was sunk in darkness, and the first glimmer of dawn emphasised the high pillars of the facade and tricked passers-by into thinking the pillars stood far in front of the building.

'Do you know what it's about?'

'Absolutely not,' Frenzel answered, but the teasing expression in his eyes betrayed that he did.

'Do I have to prepare some of the Belorussian material I've gathered?'

'If you want.'

'What kind of material?'

'The most select, of course.'

Thomas gave a mournful smile. Here was Frenzel—who not long

ago would have been putty in his hands—treating him like an amateur.

But Frenzel was right by his own lights: Thomas had always tried not to let others get the feeling they had information he needed or that he was worried by its absence, but he'd become careless. Lacking an audience to present a character to, he'd let things go. With the excuse that he was tired, he sank onto the chair in Frenzel's room. The glue that had stiffened him had started to disintegrate. The contours of his personality, by which he defined himself—pride, charm, his ability to identify the heart of the matter, the faith that his execution of his plans was correct and would bring about the desired result—had turned out to depend on circumstance. They were traits that had only sojourned in his body and now had subsided into memory. The voice of the consciousness that directed his actions had become a murmur. His weakness and inactivity threatened to drive him mad. Sometimes he wanted to transport himself from SS headquarters to the office of the district governor, to the house under the clock, and from there to Deutsches Haus, so he could hypnotise them all with a spark of his old charm, to plant in their minds the awareness that on the top floor of a building on Lindenstrasse was a man who would be an asset to anyone who pulled him out of his prison.

There were also new thoughts that were strange to him. For example: hadn't Georg Weller given him an opportunity at a difficult time? And how had Thomas rewarded him? With treachery. But that was perverse thinking; he reprimanded himself and excused it as part of his general weakness. After all, Thomas was the one who had written the model, and by virtue of it Weller had become the master and manager of his agency. If Weller hadn't proven to be a nitpicking amateur who jeopardised the future of the model, Thomas would never have thought of transferring it to Kresling. These answers more or less set his mind at ease, but he had to admit that of late he had repeatedly rehearsed his enemies' claims, whereas in the past he would simply have dismissed them.

At Party headquarters they received him cordially and directed him to a room where four men had already gathered: two in uniform and two in suits. One of them, from the Foreign Office, announced that, as a representative of Martin Luther, the head of the New Germany Department, he wished to convey to Herr Heiselberg his heartfelt good wishes. 'A new personality is necessary in the Foreign Office,' Luther had said to him in better days. Weller despised Luther and called him one of Ribbentrop's 'weak-minded, backwards men'. Luther had even been suspected of embezzlement.

After they took pains to make him feel comfortable and to praise his achievements, it turned out they were assigning him to a task so pathetic that for a moment he thought it was a practical joke. They told him a tale about a vague plan, devoid of resources, without clear aims, just discussions with representatives of the Soviet Union about some 'joint military parade'. They told him that it was a Communist initiative, that they had proposed holding a splendid parade, one that would improve on the small and hasty parade that was held at Brest-Litovsk in September 1939. That parade had symbolised the good spirit in which Poland had been divided between Germany and the Soviet Union, while the new parade would demonstrate the eternal, strong friendship between the two countries. For geographical convenience, the plan would be implemented in the Lublin district.

The German government had decided, for various reasons, not to refuse the offer, at least while the Communists were selling us the raw materials our industry desperately needed. In fact, the Foreign Office man added, because of the tightening British naval blockade, German industry was mainly dependent on raw materials from the East. 'The data is hair-raising,' he said. 'Last year the Soviets supplied us with seventy-four per cent of the phosphates we needed, more than sixty per cent of the asbestos and chromium, more than forty per cent of the imported nickel and thirty-four per cent of our oils. Gentlemen, these facts are depriving many of us of sleep: how did Germany get into a situation in which her industry is sustained by Stalin's good will?'

Thomas agreed that the figures were indeed worrisome, but he wasn't the right man for the job, since his understanding of military matters was slender.

In response they explained to him that he would be able to consult various experts from the Wehrmacht, but the Foreign Office preferred to conduct negotiations with its own people, and the word was that he had been an expert negotiator. Thomas answered that a mission of this kind demanded a combination of various branches and they answered that for the moment there was no operation, just discussions whose purpose was to put together the most embryonic, symbolic plans, which would determine the character and essential principles of the parade.

'What principles? What essence?' Thomas was close to losing his equanimity. 'A parade simply parades!'

The man from the Foreign Office corrected him. 'There are aesthetic, historical, geographical and other principles. After all, you're an advertising man. Cobble some principles together, invent some essence. And, by the way, there's no rush. You have all the time in the world.'

The man from military intelligence, in a grey field uniform, added that no one expected immediate results.

The more kindly they addressed him—emphasising that the discussions had to remain on low levels, that this was an initiative the German government didn't recognise, and these were meant to be just productive exchanges of ideas between former enemies to spread some good will in the East—the deeper was his humiliation. He felt as if he was shrinking even further. At this rate soon they would be talking to an empty chair.

'You'll be a kind of *Kapellmeister* for one man,' the intelligence officer added, and they all laughed. Thomas also stretched his mouth into a little smile.

The Foreign Office man said to him, '*Kapellmeister* is what they call the head of a spy ring.'

Thomas wondered whether the other men had noticed that he laughed even though he hadn't understood. Get a grip, a voice thundered in his consciousness. This isn't a game. You know these men are capable of anything.

The representative of the *Fremde Heere Ost** commented that the fact that Thomas wasn't familiar with the Wehrmacht was actually an advantage, because there was no danger that he might inadvertently provide information to Soviet intelligence. 'In fact'—he smiled—'you're the perfect candidate: you have the reputation of being able to produce a document full of brilliant phrases in any area, making everyone happy.'

'With all due respect, I believe you're doing an injustice to the model,' Thomas protested. He pressed his trembling hands to the table. The shabbiness with which they cheapened his achievements offended him.

The Foreign Office man quickly assured him that this was just joshing among friends. 'Our meaning, Herr Heiselberg, is that you are expert at presenting things in a persuasive manner. Of course everyone here respects your accomplishments, which is why you were chosen for this delicate mission.'

Thomas objected that the mission didn't suit his abilities. His current goal was to complete the Model of the Belorussian People.

The Foreign Office man seemed not to hear him: 'In Berlin, too, they're enthusiastic about this initiative, because for a long time you haven't been effective enough, and in fact they were considering the possibility of discharging you, but now a golden opportunity has fallen into your lap to demonstrate your abilities which—unlike your character—even your adversaries don't doubt. And your former partner, Dr Weller, recommended you warmly.'

Thomas stared at the polished buttons on the man's jacket. He knew he should reject the miserable offer, escape from wretched Poland, get rid of the sense that his model, stripped of its style, was an octopus over Lublin, sending out tentacles to strangle the city. He saw the tentacles twisting through its lanes and streets, a monstrous imitation of his hopes and plans in those exaltant early days in Warsaw. He could resign and return to Berlin, and in a few years Lublin would be

---

*   The Wehrmacht intelligence agency that concentrated on the Soviet Union.

flattened under the steamroller of memory and fade into the foggy realm of dreams. He was reaching for the venomous phrases with which he'd tell them to go to hell, but already knew that any plan to resign was no more than the fantasy of a child who makes decisions while sheltering in the confidence that somebody else will mitigate the consequences. Clarissa once wrote to him: 'The moment you acknowledge a single limitation, admit there's even one thing you can't do, the infinite range of childhood possibilities has narrowed, and your youth is over.'

Thomas knew that if he returned to Berlin as an unemployed man who had been discharged in shame from the Foreign Office, his chances of finding a new job were slim. He would probably spend the rest of his days disguised as chocolate like his father.

From their silence he understood that they had anticipated his response. But did they merely want to humble him, or was there something else? He decided to leap into the trap in the most honourable way. He had learned one lesson from Weller: *Humana dignitas servanda est*. A person who has lost his status or rank retains his dignity when he acts as if he still possessed them, like the exiled Russian prince he pretended to be in his youth. If he wanted to survive, he had to behave like someone holding a high position, to sit in an office, to make appointments, to seek allies. From this angle—and he would do well to remember this—Martin Luther had kicked him upstairs.

He gave the men a chilly look: 'Please convey my gratitude to Dr Weller for the trust he has shown me. One day I will return the favour of his extreme generosity. In a week I'll inform you as to where I wish to locate the offices of the Germano-Soviet parade.' It had a pleasant sound. 'And of course I will gladly consider any ideas you may have,' he added, making an airy gesture of invitation. 'It's interesting that you mentioned the historical context of the parade. You must know that the city of Brest-Litovsk was part of the Union of Lublin that was declared in 1569. Thus we must carefully consider which chapter in history we are interested in bringing out. As for the personal letter from the State Secretary of the Foreign Office…' He expected the

Foreign Office man to protest. 'Don't worry,' Thomas went on amiably. 'I'm not going to ask for a letter of appointment. I understand the need for secrecy. My modest request is for a letter from Ernst von Weizsäcker expressing appreciation for my devoted service. From the generous remarks I have heard today, I understand that the ministry, to which I am attached with all the bonds of my soul, values my loyalty.'

BREST
FEBRUARY 1941

Sasha stood in the square in front of the citadel, the heart of the fortress. The snow glowed on trees, whose branches seemed to have frozen in strange positions, it glazed the roofs of the old houses and the turrets of the walls, piled up on windowsills and thresholds. White walls seemed to tower over the space, so that the entire citadel appeared to be a deep crater of ice.

Around her was silence. There was no wind, while within her, from the moment she had woken up, a great tumult surged, harbinger of a mighty event.

He stepped towards her, with a retinue of two behind him. From a distance they looked like snowmen. As they approached she noticed that the man wasn't looking around him. No doubt this was his first visit to Brest Fortress. Nevertheless his eyes didn't wander even once towards the walls, the gates and the buildings. His two escorts sprayed snow to the side like bulls pawing the earth, but he slipped lightly over the snow, erect, trailing a thin plume of foam.

The last few days, when she secluded herself down below, on the bottom of the crater, and prepared for the first meeting of the Committee for the Germano-Soviet Military Parade, had been the best for a long time. If only she could remain here for years, to stroll every morning to the dark tunnel of the Kholmsk Gate and be swallowed beneath the canopy of fog over the Bug River, and to wander afterwards among the arches of the church of Saint Nicholas, and to watch the children of the officers of the Fourth Army race about in the citadel, sharpening sticks, gathering for secret meetings next to the Terespol Gate.

She liked to climb up the white slope at noon and lean her cheek against the icy stones of the wall, to look west at the river winding like a snake. The barrels of the cannon camouflaged in weeds and straw, and the tents, the smoke curling up from the German army camp— all disappeared behind a white curtain. Everything sank into drowsy tranquillity, and almost the only sounds were the tramping of boots in the snow, the shouts of the officers during drill exercises and dogs barking.

Now Kolya was waking for the morning line-up, they were probably getting some bread and tea. Did they pass their days in idleness? When there was snow, they didn't dig foxholes. Even though he refused to see her and didn't answer her letters either, she felt, when she was looking down from the citadel onto the plain, that nothing bad could happen to him as long as she was standing guard there. Not long ago she had made certain that a crate of vodka and bread got to his unit, along with canned fish and beans. She was careful not to tell her colleagues that Kolya was stationed so close, because it might be useful to her enemies. Every morning she was struck with anxiety that Nikita Mikhailovich would ask why she hadn't told him that her brother was stationed near the fortress, and then casually suggest, 'Why shouldn't your Kolya be our mole in the Fourth Army? We're always looking for good informers in the ranks.'

It took her several days in the citadel to understand how constricting everyone's embrace had been—from her colleagues to her husband.

Here, among soldiers who didn't know her, no one asked for a reckoning. No one said, 'Comrade Weissberg, when will you take off your bandage?' She wasn't expected to observe their plans, didn't feel cold at her back every time someone gave her a strange look or asked her an unexpected question.

The small group was already close. She stood up straight, and now, when she saw his face, she thought it would be hard to describe it accurately or to point to any conspicuous characteristic. His hair, greying at the temples, was combed back. Above the green eyes stretched thin eyebrows. His skin was red and taut, but at the edge of his jaw there was a weary tremor, as if the spark of his youth had been dimmed. Average height, a well-preserved body wrapped in an elegant coat with a fur collar, whose sleeves were too short, with a gold watch peeking out of one of them. His address expressed neither eagerness nor curiosity. His expression was restrained and polite, but his courtesy seemed external to the face, a shell carelessly applied to it.

When he drew closer, and their eyes met, he adopted a businesslike and dignified look. Then, as though he had read her thoughts, he gazed around at the fortress and nodded to acknowledge that the sight was making a great impression on him. Less than a minute later his demeanour took on such a natural lordliness that the German representative to the committee might have been born in the fortress, its history and intrigues flowing in his blood.

His ability to play the owner in a place that wasn't his, by virtue of his presence, amazed her. Who had the Germans sent here? He was artifice personified. Even before they had said a word to one another, she passed judgment on him: a perfect impostor. She cursed the fascists for choosing such a man for the committee. She took a deep breath. Perhaps she had judged him prematurely. At the same time, it discomfited her to know that she would have to shake his hand.

He stood close to her and bowed. He smiled warmly, and his eyes sparkled. Suddenly he looked helpless with his desire to please.

'*Monsieur Thomas Heiselberg, au nom du commissariat populaire des affaires étrangères, je vous accueille en espérant que vous avez fait un bon voyage.'* She had practised that sentence over and over until she could deliver it with a light accent, without pretension.

They exchanged further courtesies, scripted of course, and a few words about the good will of both states, the purity of their intentions and their mutual good wishes to the German and Soviet people. They set off on a short tour of the fortress. The two NKVD agents trailed behind. Even before she managed to say a word, he said, 'This morning, after a nap on the train, I reached a very interesting conclusion. The pace of events in our dreams is so accelerated that human consciousness cannot process them. We dream and then analyse the dream with entirely different concepts of time.' While he was chatting away in excellent French, flaunting concepts whose meaning he took care to explain to her, the Russian peasant, she began to doubt her first impression; he seemed indifferent to the question of whether or not she liked him.

He prattled on, lecturing and explaining, as though courtesy did not require him to listen to his host. Did he believe that, as in his country, women here were also minor officials called upon to escort notables from one place to another? That wasn't possible: in their exchange of letters they had both signed with their full names, and he didn't come across as a man who would miss such details. When she told him that the peace treaty between Russia and Germany had been signed here in the Brest Fortress in 1918, bringing the war to an end, he gave a low whistle. 'You chose a symbolic place for our first meeting, Mademoiselle Weissberg, if I may.'

'Certainly, Monsieur.'

'I remember the pictures in the papers: white walls, a small table and behind it a row of men in uniforms or in white shirts and black bowties, as in a chorus. Next to the walls the faces were all blurred. As a boy, those people grabbed my attention. In their old age, they would sit with their grandchildren and say, That's us there, the blurred faces at the Treaty of Brest-Litovsk. *C'est terrible!* And my father scolded me for my tendency to take an interest in the scenery.'

'My father encouraged us to stay away from politics,' she said. 'My younger brother Vlada used to cackle all day long with his boring opinions, so that our dinners became a nightmare.'

The German appeared satisfied: each of them had given the meeting a personal tone to the proper extent. He nodded to signal that these remarks were sufficient.

An amused chuckle tickled her throat: did he think that she didn't know the rules?

He studied the architecture. 'From the outside the structure isn't particularly impressive. I imagined it entirely differently. Wasn't it Trotsky who formulated the fine print of the treaty?'

'As you see,' she said, ignoring his provocative question, 'part of the roof was smashed, and the damage to the facade was caused by the bombardment of the German army in September 1939.'

'Well, the Poles barricaded themselves in here and caused trouble,' he answered.

When she told him about the change of regime in the fortress—how it passed from Russia to Germany to Russia to Poland, and now to the Soviet Union—he suggested that in Europe they should label the streets with numbers, as they did in New York, because conquerors kept changing the names of the streets and squares, and you felt as though you were wandering about in a maze, where the same streets were in different places at the same time. Numbers were the solution: for the benefit of both victors and vanquished.

At first the comment sounded amusing, but seeing his face relax with complacency she understood that he was making oblique fun of her work: Nikita Mikhailovich had asked her to sit on the committee that recommended new street names in Brest. Moscow Avenue had been her idea, and she was particularly proud of the streets that bore the names of two people her father admired, Mikhail Lermontov and Sergo Ordzhonikidze.

But how could the German know that? Her letters had been official, and the representatives of seven different institutions had read them before they were sent to Lublin; nowhere had she mentioned the matter of the streets. Very well, perhaps German intelligence had prepared a report about her. Now she understood that nothing she had said about the history of the fortress was new to him—and it was almost certain he knew she wasn't Mademoiselle Weissberg but rather Madame Podolsky—and perhaps his comment about the street names was a response to the insult of the tourist's survey of history she had recited to him.

Here was something familiar, being pushed into the shadow realm where she looked at the world through another person's consciousness, wallowing in his intrigues and fears. Who was he really? Was he as obstinate as he looked? As eager to satisfy his ambition? Someone who would stop at nothing to get back at his enemies? Would a little sympathy mixed with implicit threats be enough to make him write a confession? Or shouting and a week without sleep? Every day in interrogation she had stripped back dozens of people—suspects, colleagues—and now him.

She refrained with all her power from staring at the grey sacks of skin beneath his eyes. His glance was cushioned with friendliness, and now and then he let it rest on a certain part of her body. When she spoke he nodded generously. She decided that not looking around at the fortress had cost him an effort, because the agitation in his eyes revealed his sensitivity to impressions. Well, she could teach him a thing or two; Styopa always said that her gaze didn't waste any time. The German clearly believed his mask was impermeable, his real face safely concealed. A lot of people laboured under that delusion until they met the NKVD.

They climbed the stairs to the meeting room, where a light meal awaited them, and she described her admiration for the actions of the Luftwaffe in Coventry, an action that history would fondly remember! He responded that he was no less impressed by the achievements of the 'Red Army of workers and peasants' in their battle against the great power of Finland. They began to swoop across the expanses of history, showering compliments: the wonderful work of the Red Army in the battle on the Vistula, the military genius of Kaiser Wilhelm II, the great achievements of Russia in the war against Japan in the first decade of the century ('You really covered the Japanese in your hats'), Bismarck the benefactor, the firm way that Germany repelled Napoleon, and Fichte's *Addresses to the German Nation* ('Never did the eminent conqueror encounter an enemy more lethal'). They were so amused by this game that they couldn't stop interrupting each other, but as soon as they sat at the table their joy disappeared.

'As for Coventry,' he said, 'you know the British bombed our cities. Mönchengladbach was the first, and they killed hundreds of Germans before our planes came close to Britain. To be precise, they attacked our cities for months while the German government was making peace proposals.'

Too bad he had shaken himself out of their amusing game and rushed to defend Germany like a stern propagandist. Perhaps his zeal for his country's honour was stronger than it appeared. He played with a pencil, leaned over the table and sipped his tea. His face and neck had turned red.

'Do you feel well?' she asked. 'Do you need to rest?'

'No,' he answered and straightened up.

They didn't touch the food. She exploited her chance and presented the first position paper, which had been translated into German, on the Germano-Soviet parade, and suggested that they set the date for the spring, because a military parade was a popular festival, and it was fitting to hold it on a sunny day. Then she asked how they could also include German citizens in the parade. It could be divided between Brest and Lublin, and perhaps it would be good to hold two small solidarity parades: the Pioneer Youth would march in Berlin, and the Hitler Youth in Moscow. He instantly responded that the idea would not be accepted by either government, and in any event the people of Berlin and Moscow wouldn't identify with strange youths wearing uniforms they still considered revolting. He surveyed the position paper with a bored face, as if the matter didn't concern him at all, and he had no desire to have anything to do with it.

'Our task,' she said, 'is to present creative ideas, not to decide whether they are practical. We don't have representatives of all the branches of the army here. The committee is just the two of us, and our assistants. Therefore I suggest that we free our imaginations to put together ideas for a parade that will astonish the world and be remembered as one of the most impressive events of the twentieth century.'

He stroked the tabletop with dry-skinned fingers. The prominent veins on his hands betrayed early signs of ageing. 'Look,' he said. 'All my life I've been a practical man. I directed one of the largest market research companies in the world. I dealt with projects that demanded vision, but I always made sure to have a clear plan for implementing my ideas.'

He was so used to polishing his sentences with conceit that he didn't notice he was mourning the memory of his achievements, rather than glorying in them.

'Even though you have a capitalist world view'—she had to move him from implementation to the realm of planning and theory—'you're not working in the private sector now. Other forces govern our task. Maybe we should adopt a different point of view: our job is to write a story about a grand military parade in the Brest region in the spring of 1941. If we believe in it, maybe others will too. Even if they don't— can anyone deprive us of the act of creation?' She had said it to steer him onto the right course, but the idea actually pleased her; a few days in the fortress had convinced her that planning a great potential event was one of the best activities these times had to offer.

'They can take the creation away, but not the time we believed in it,' he said.

So she hadn't fired his imagination but, as their discussion went on, he gave her precise and rich answers, and the occasional brilliant idea: the parade had to avoid making artificial gestures or depending on the good will of the masses, or spreading over large areas. It wasn't a national holiday. The spectacle had to be concentrated in one place, making an emphatic impression. These principles were self-evident, like saying 'amen' in church.

His decisive tone suggested he had devoted time to thinking about the parade, but it was clear to her that these ideas had occurred to him just now. His initial intention had been to oppose some of her suggestions so as to pretend to be involved in the project.

She glanced at the trays, and he looked at her as though he didn't understand. Then she reached out towards the golden pie crust. She stopped; her hand slid down to her hips. If he wouldn't approach the food, she wouldn't either. Instead she told him about Star, the owner of one of the largest estates in the region, who used to eat a roasted, stuffed turkey at the end of each meal. In a military exercise, Star broke the back of the horse he was riding, and the czar, also a large man, patted him on the shoulder. 'Bravo,' he said, 'you beat me.'

Did she tell him that story to stimulate his appetite? She didn't know.

The rumble of motors could be heard. Her limbs, crammed between the table and the wall, had stiffened. However she tried to extricate them would seem clumsy. Of course he was the reason, but how could his influence on her have been so great?

They had already been sitting there for hours. Monsieur Heiselberg? He tore through the position paper, stripping paragraph after paragraph of meaning—not because he opposed them but because his monotonous voice, with all the good will in the world, was enough to nullify them.

Sometimes she imagined that several versions of his face were talking to her together. The version of despair that scolded her: Girl, can't you see all this is futile? The cold, clinical version that mocked the entire situation, her devotion to it, her miserable ideas, her very existence. The condescending, compliant version that cried out: Very well, my dear, I'll volunteer my talents to fulfil your little dream.

Every sentence that escaped her lips sounded like a quotation of an idea they had already discussed. A strange feeling gripped her: she couldn't stay in the same room as him any longer; a spell had been somehow cast on her. Her buttocks had risen slightly, and she pressed them down to the chair. The desire to get rid of him was greater than any professional duty, no matter how practised she was at stifling her will.

She looked at his gold watch. It was twelve-forty. She gave a fluttering smile. That couldn't be. His watch was wrong.

'You look amused,' he said, perplexed, and his face came to life.

'I remembered a story my parents used to tell me.'

'Would you like to share it?'

'No. It's too personal.'

'My mother died not long ago,' he offered, 'in very sad circumstances. She was at home with our Jewish housekeeper, Madame Stein.'

'Your Judaism didn't prevent me from choosing you,' Nikolai Mikhailovich said to her. 'On the contrary. Let those fascists know that we'll never be like them.'

'I'm sorry to hear that.'

'Yes,' he answered and stretched his arms behind him. 'Madame Stein was a Jew but different from the other Jews that I knew. She didn't have the talents that characterise Jews.'

He was like an actor practising sincerity. Or was he really speaking from his heart, and her suspicion was distorting her vision? She told herself that he had noticed her disgust and wanted to win a little Jewish sympathy.

The room was getting stuffy. The cheese and fish on the trays gave off a sharp odour, but he, who sat closer to the refreshments, didn't seem disturbed by it at all.

'I think we need some air,' she stammered.

Never in her life had she met a person who responded so quickly. From the first word he knew what she wanted, was already standing up and buttoning his coat.

'Now you're the one who looks a little tired, Mademoiselle Weissberg,' he said, making it clear that he remembered how she had earlier provoked him.

This man was one of the most horrible and odd people she had ever met. All morning long he had behaved like a man in despair, and in the last hour, when he noticed that his tactics—some of which had been devised spontaneously—were wearing her down, and that, as tiny as it might be, a victory was in sight, he was like a man reborn.

LUBLIN
FEBRUARY 1941

Her eyes were reflected in every window of the railroad car, a gaze without a face, which had disintegrated long ago. He remembered the delicate rounding of her cheeks, lips that up close surprised him with their fullness, but all these impressions were as meaningless as newspaper clippings: she was a disembodied gaze, accusing him.

Suddenly the gaze began to fly from face to face: Clarissa, Weller, Frenzel, the young Hermann Kreizinger, his history class, they all passed judgment on him in the form of Fraülein Weissberg's gaze. Gooseflesh wrinkled his skin. While he struggled to get rid of the boys from the history class, he heard them shouting: 'Doctor, you made a mistake in the lesson! Didn't you hear that the archaeologists are dead? Here is the production line of the future!'

At a certain point, in the conference room in the citadel, he wanted to protest: Mademoiselle Weissberg, Madame Podolsky, Comrade Weissberg, Jew W., whatever they call you. With all due respect, your gaze gives me the shivers. Gradually he understood that he wasn't petrified by the horror that her gaze stirred in him but by the revulsion he created in her. During the hours that they sat there he struggled against that look: he refurnished the room with items from the parlour in Berlin, he calculated the height of the snow between the spires of the citadel, he counted the slices of bread, and suddenly he stared at her, like a predator surprising its prey—but her gaze was steadfast, stubborn and condemning. From what darkness did this woman emerge? Why was she doing this to him? 'Tell me, what do you see?' he silently mouthed.

Dread seized him. He was watching Thomas Heiselberg, composed of scraps of paper and pasted together with old glue, come apart beneath her gaze. From a distance the picture seemed intact, but close up his nakedness was exposed, or was it scraps of another picture?

Comrade Weissberg's eyes shone, asking Thomas: My dear friend, do you really want to defend yourself? What did you sow with your tricks? It's true that people change disguises, but underneath a solid foundation, a home port in their soul makes them aware of the masquerade. And you? Every morning, when you open your eyes, you are flooded with the terror of rebirth. There's no prepared matrix. You slap at the scraps and paste them onto yourself, adopting a disguise that suits the tasks at hand. And you don't even know the man you were yesterday, who did all sorts of things to prepare this day for you. And now? More disguises and lies? I've already seen them all. The gaze kept whispering. Thomas shouted at it to shut up. He hollered childhood songs into the empty railroad car. Mother used to invent them:

> My beloved child lies half-asleep
> My heart is devoted his soul to keep.
> To join the army Father did depart
> If we lose the war, home he'll come
> Bringing a present for his precious son.

When he sang, the gaze stopped whispering.

Hoopah, hoopah, rider
When he falls—he shouts.
If he falls into the ditch
The crows will eat him alive.

Afterwards fatigue descended, and he fell into a troubled sleep. He woke up with a shout. Outside the train: rusted branches of trees. He dozed off and woke up again. His lips burned, drenched in the waterfalls of his dreams. The trip went on and on. He was surrounded by snowy expanses that the night painted blue, and they swallowed the small peasant houses.

His line of sight plunged to the rutted earth. He imagined leaping into the foam of the snow. 'Jump, Manfred, jump!' A shout rings out in the university corridor, the new slogan for a tedious lecture. While the professor was droning on about Byron's Manfred, standing on a mountaintop and not daring to choose death, a girl stood up and shouted, 'Jump, Manfred, jump. We're dying of boredom.' What was her name? Elsa. He fell in love with her on the spot. A year later they were married.

'Actually, you fell in love with the shout.' Wolfgang laughed when he told him the story. They were drunk and amusing themselves with ideas for seducing the Negri sisters in Warsaw.

The train braked, and he slipped onto the floor of the car. He didn't want to move. His head was thrown onto the edge of the seat. He heard whispers again. An attack. Let it be. There was no reason to fear attacks. Fear of disguise was the most real thing in him. Embrace the attack, be a man in attack.

If people saw him, he wasn't bothered. Let them either help or choke on their criticism. He lay on the floor until Lublin station. Good people brought him home. Strong hands held him when he tripped on the stairs. The burning in his body made him laugh. He took some pills and lay on his bed.

He slept for two days, plagued with nightmares. Once he woke to the shouts of guards from the camp, lights that struck the thick curtain, the cracking sound of exactly four shots.

In his dreams children stood on the sides of the road, waved flags and drummed on cardboard boxes. Tens of thousands of soldiers, arranged in little rectangles, flowed in one huge motion from the fortress to the centre of Brest-Litovsk. He woke up. The heat of the sun in his dream remained on the back of his neck. He stumbled to the desk and started to sketch, reconstructing the picture from his dream. Then he slept again.

In the morning he realised that he had drawn more pictures of the parade: a swarm of soldiers splitting to the right and left, surrounding a city that he was seeing for the first time, a small city, but the size didn't matter, what mattered was the brilliant planning of the parade.

How would the Wehrmacht soldiers cross the border? On the bridges, of course. There were still bridges over the Bug River. Would the Soviets allow German planes in their air space for a joint flyover? These were matters for military people. The more questions arose, the clearer the burden of the task became. They didn't give such responsibility to nobodies. The way the Wehrmacht was portrayed in the parade would project onto the entire image of Germany. In fact, he had to decide which Germany to represent in the parade.

Every minute he luxuriated in bed was a shameful waste of time. To hell with that Jew woman Weissberg and her gaze. The days of weakness would not return. For the sake of the parade he would treat her like the dearest person in the world to him, and in time he'd force her to like him. In the past he had specialised in such strategies. People who wanted no connection with him became his fans. He had to show everybody that Thomas Heiselberg was worthy of heading the committee for the Germano-Soviet parade.

He leaped out of bed. His moist shirt and underpants smelled of old sweat. He tottered over to the desk again. The room spun around him: he slipped a blank sheet of paper into the typewriter:

Beloved Clarissa,
　　For a long time now I haven't given you any sign of life.
　　I behaved coarsely and didn't answer your letters. That was

because of certain difficulties I found myself in, which led me to keep a distance even from the people most dear to me, so that I wouldn't entangle them in my affairs. Recently, however, my work has received the respect it deserves, and I have accepted an appointment that represents a huge challenge. Clarissa, from the moment I first knew myself, I have worked for Thomas Heiselberg, I admit it; to increase his power in the world, to extend his wingspan. Now I feel responsibility of a different sort in my bones, responsibility for people in general, and I'm talking about the masses, whose lives are connected to the project that has been entrusted to me. I have to do everything I can so that these people won't be a small spot in the blood-soaked history of Europe. I can't say any more, but, please, believe me, this is work on behalf of the good name of Germany.

You might say: You're a megalomaniac. This task is not within your abilities. You might say, Once again you're cleverly making Thomas Heiselberg the hero. Maybe you're right, dear Clarissa. All that, however, is of no importance. My motivations—visible and hidden—can't change the fact that this is the time to act. Even if my ability to make a difference is minuscule, I am obliged to exploit it to the hilt. On this matter I'm sure you'll agree with me.

Good Clarissa, from now on everything will change. People are swept to their deaths while they are reading the newspaper or polishing their silverware, but I am very attentive to passing time, and my conclusion is that we must act now to fulfil our dreams. One decision in particular has taken shape in my heart: the day that all of Germany sees my work succeed, you will stand at my side, for your words of faith have remained with me in my darkest hours, and we will part no more.

He kept writing. An image flickered in his imagination: he was standing on a mountaintop in a white suit, wearing the striped fedora he had bought in Paris. Beside him stood Clarissa in a bright red dress, a ribbon in her hair, holding a parasol. The parade was spread out below them, all the way to the river, and Clarissa was astonished by the movement of the soldiers, who, instead of lining this earth with their bodies, were marching across it with impressive ceremony. White trails of celebratory cannon fire swirled in the blue sky. Clarissa pointed at them, and there was a golden halo around her finger. The sky became a gigantic mirror reflecting their faces: his had a purity it had never possessed before, that of a man who serves an exalted purpose. He said to Clarissa, You see, now they're cheering for me. A few months ago they wanted to bury me alive. She brought her lips close to his ear, her tongue brushed it lightly, she whispered, How could you have imagined such a silly thing? Think about Siegfried, and the ups and downs in his career. History, remember, clings to greatness like iron to a magnet. The moment I first saw you, Thomas Heiselberg, it was clear to me you were destined to be a great man.

...

Thomas sat in a new suit—a wine-coloured jacket and a striped silk tie—in Frenzel's office, and told him his impressions of the first meeting of the parade committee. Their friendship had grown closer: Frenzel needed his help with questions connected with the deportation of the Jews. In fact Frenzel was amazed at his good fortune—here was the man who had devised the Model of the Polish People. Questions to the offices of the model in Warsaw might take a month or more to be answered, but he could enjoy the services of the inventor as often as he liked.

Naturally he helped Frenzel as much as he could. Both of them kept the matter secret, because Dr Weller, over there in Warsaw, wouldn't look favourably upon such use of the model. After Frenzel had read several excellent memorandums, not a day passed when he didn't sit with Thomas for at least an hour in his office. He accepted most of the advice Thomas gave him.

Frenzel was smoking a pipe. His polished boots rested casually on the desk. He perused the papers and listened without interest as Thomas went on in praise of the parade and the international reverberations it would have: 'It's exactly the type of idea that you have to pounce on when only a few people understand its potential, but when the fog is dispersed—and the German people cheer for those who steered Germany into peace rather than war—our seal on the parade will be an established fact.'

Frenzel wasn't impressed. Thomas was surprised, since Frenzel wasn't someone lacking in imagination. Maybe he was one of those men eager for war with the Soviet Union, or maybe he was too busy to be interested in the parade. In March thousands of Jews would be driven out of Lublin under the auspices of the *freiwillige Umsiedlung,* the voluntary transfer program, and by mid-April the ghetto was supposed to be closed, with just a few Jews remaining in it. This was one of the largest undertakings ever planned in the Lublin district. Frenzel complained about its complexity. In France, for example, they had solved the Jewish problem more simply. Anyway, he had a lot of work now. Globocnik believed in young Frenzel and had presented him to Himmler as one of his chosen young men.

'Listen, friend.' Thomas moved on to stage two, replacing the chatty tone that had driven their rise to greatness with one of sincere concern. 'I'm giving you valuable information now. The Soviet representative for the parade is Jewish.'

Frenzel took his feet off the desk and stuffed the documents into a folder. He passed his hand through his hair and gave Thomas a blank look: the last thing he needed now was a new task. Thomas had no choice but to frighten his young friend a little: 'You understand that this would be useful to our enemies. Rumours can run an unlikely course.'

'You do know a thing or two about getting mixed up in things,' Frenzel growled, as though trying to figure out Thomas's true intention. 'I hope you learned something from your antics in Warsaw. Such things aren't going to happen here.'

'You're right,' Thomas reassured him. 'The main thing that I learned is to respect the chain of command. The matter of the Jewess Weissberg apparently escaped the notice of the Foreign Office, and my suggestion is that we inform them. That's all. In the past, when the Communists wanted to approach us, they replaced that Jew in their Foreign Office with Molotov. And, believe me, replacing this Jewess will advance our goal. Regrettably she's a little girl who should be skipping rope and not getting mixed up in historical events.'

'It sounds like the Jewess didn't please you,' Frenzel grumbled.

'It's not a personal matter,' Thomas emphasised. A kind of screeching hiss entered his voice. 'Believe me, I've managed complex projects with people more sophisticated than she is. The question is: in what light will the incident present Germany?'

Frenzel looked at his papers again. 'Maybe despite everything you did learn your lesson. Very well, do it. But don't do anything else without keeping me up to date.'

Thomas was encouraged. Frenzel appeared to run his life like an organised and efficient man, but in fact he acted on impulse. If you upset his balance slightly, offered a solution and pressed him to make a decision, he would snap up the solution, because he was too busy calming his stormy spirit. 'No question,' Thomas answered. 'As usual, we'll act in full coordination.'

'Anything else?' asked Frenzel, when he saw that Thomas was lingering.

'Just one little matter, something minor. I didn't get enough information about my counterpart in the parade committee. I was forced to make do with an embarrassing paper with a few biographical details. I realise that the parade isn't of prime preference, but the German representative shouldn't be groping in the dark. I'd like you to support my request for a detailed profile of that woman. The embassy in Moscow can supply the information with ease.'

When he went down the stairs and cordially returned the greetings of officers who in the past would not deign to look at him, he felt a freezing tremor in his neck. It was as if every one of his actions in the past few days had been observed by Comrade Weissberg's all-knowing gaze, mocking Thomas's miserable efforts to escape it. He hadn't stayed faithful to his initial decision to cooperate with her and had even worked to remove her from the committee, but ugly shame enveloped all his actions: if he believed she wasn't the right person, the matter would have been easy, but he knew very well that she was the one most appropriate to promote this initiative along with him. At night, lying in his bed, he tried to find some logic in his actions—perhaps there were people whom he shouldn't meet? But that idea sounded to him like one of those groundless statements intended to excuse stupid actions by reference to some world view. 'I have no world view,' he once said proudly. 'I have a view of the project I'm working on.'

In the Foreign Office they didn't even respond to his requests, and finally some clerk reprimanded him. 'We won't talk to the Soviets about the Jewess. After all, in the 1939 parade, the Soviet General who reviewed the parade along with Guderian was also a Jew. The Foreign Office is the home of professional diplomats, not fly-by-nights.'

One day Frenzel informed him that he would receive an envelope containing the most comprehensive information that German intelligence could obtain. 'And after you read it, believe me, nothing mysterious will remain about your Jewess.'

BREST
MARCH 1941

No one understood why she was in such a frenzy, why she was rushing out into the street and returning to the office red-cheeked and panting in a coat white with snow, skipping down the streets that led to the river as if it were summer, and coming back with rolls of paper under her arm, spending days on end in the new archive, dragging packages of books from the post office, books from Leningrad, from Moscow, even a package from the embassy in Berlin.

The first task she set for herself was drawing a new map of Brest. This was the map they would use in their work, and every street on it would get a number. But the numbering wasn't simply geographical. It would reflect their assumptions: for example, 17 September Street, where Guderian and Krivoshein had stood on the little platform in September 1939, would be Street Number 1, and Moscow Avenue, which crossed it, would be marked Number 2. All the remaining streets would now be numbered according to their proximity to one of these central streets. She also numbered the streets that she remembered from the summer: one day she stood at the corner of Spitalna and Kobrin and looked at the river, and a car driving past appeared to be surrounded by a golden halo. If the crowd gathered there in the early morning and faced east, the parade would appear to be sliding down to them out of the sun, and the sight would be breathtaking. Aside from that, the parade should not be limited to straight roads; if you heard the sound of military vehicles from around the corner, and calculated impatiently when they would arrive, and suddenly a giant, glowing swarm flooded the street—the effect would be powerful.

She was close to finishing the numbered street map, wondering whether her plans would please the German representative. Would the general idea of a parade draped in golden mystery appeal to him? Many questions still remained unresolved. For example, it went without saying that part of the parade had to be held in the fortress, but perhaps it would be better to hold a separate event there, a homage to previous wars? She didn't consult anyone, and at night locked the maps and the papers in a cabinet, afraid that if people saw them they would make fun of her plans. When finally she did resolve an issue, she immediately changed her mind: every decision seemed fateful to her.

Nikita Mikhailovich warned her that people were talking about how she was going days without eating. At last she set a date to send the new map to Thomas Heiselberg, along with her main ideas. The night before she didn't shut her eyes. She went over the map and the papers again and again. Monsieur Thomas Heiselberg would be pleased: she remembered his remarks about the numbered streets of New York.

Meanwhile Nikita Mikhailovich made a point of visiting her office in the evening and holding their 'truth workshops'. The first time he assailed her with countless questions. Her answers were embarrassingly forced, and she was scared he would declare that she hadn't kept her part of the bargain and transfer administration of the parade to someone else. At later meetings she decided to speak more freely about certain subjects.

'You understand, Nikita Mikhailovich, a person's consciousness is preoccupied, day and night, awake and in dreams, with just one thing: it makes her arguments, the same arguments again and again. One night,' she told him, 'when everyone was drunk and Father even dared to sit next to his Nadka, they recited a little piece called, "A Poison Potion for Consciousness". The next day I wrote: "As a girl you discover the secrets of consciousness; afterwards you discover there are no secrets, just patterns, I have become aware of my patterns, and with every new pattern a part of me dies." Nadka declared that the end was overly dramatic and whining. She had the ability to insult you, to be cruel and at the same time to strengthen your faith in your abilities.'

How long had it been since she had just chatted enjoyably? She was flooded with amusing memories: 'A critic described Nadka in the paper as "more a muse than a poet". Father was afraid she would commit suicide, but she made an appointment with the critic, and in the end he introduced an edition of her poems. Brodsky claimed that Nadka was a political genius, but then everything changed, the games were over. She didn't understand the thirties.'

'All this is fascinating, Alexandra Andreyevna,' said Nikita Mikhailovich. 'I didn't know that you once dreamed of becoming a poet. Even though it's a rather common dream.'

'Maybe I'll be one yet? Perhaps it seems strange to you, Nikita Mikhailovich, but our house was a railway station for people like that. Malevich sat in the living room one night and kept calling me Zhenya, Vasily Degtyaryov drank tea, licked currant jam and consulted Father about his machine gun. Sergo Ordzhonikidze toyed with my braids and placed a copper bracelet on my wrist. Mandelstam and Akhmatova were guests in our house, and Father told them in secret that Kirov had a General Electric refrigerator in his house.'

Belatedly she discovered she had slipped back into the haughty tone that she once used to tell her friends about the famous people who'd visited her house. Snippets of her girlhood returned, and for the first time in a while she felt she could contain the pain. Yes, there had been good days. Was she trying to arouse his envy of her vibrant childhood home? She was swept along to another story. 'One day somebody told us that Pasternak had quoted a line from a letter he had written: "We're no longer people; we're epochs." I declared that it was the most beautiful line I'd ever heard, and everyone laughed, saying that the girl had to be immunised against pathos. The annoying thing was that we couldn't really be enthusiastic about anything. There was always someone who shouted, "Here it is! The kitsch that's killing Russian poetry."'

Nikita Mikhailovich stared at her in amazement, breathing on his glasses and cleaning them with his sleeve. 'Alexandra Andreyevna, doesn't this story have an ending too? You courageously denied your parents and their actions, and then you extracted confessions from all the members of the Leningrad Group.' His voice grew softer, his daring melted.

'There was no other choice.'

'Comrade Weissberg.' His voice cracked a little. 'I hope the question isn't too intrusive, but I'd like to know: do you regret the things you did?'

'I couldn't have done anything else. I could only be lost with them or survive, for the twins' sake. I'm in agony, Nikita Mikhailovich, not remorseful.'

'Nikolai Andreyevich Weissberg is a soldier in the forty-second division in the twenty-eighth corps of the Fourth Army?'

'Yes. That's him.' How could she have thought it was possible to conceal a fact like that from Nikita Mikhailovich?

'Then he's stationed in the area of the fortress, so close to us,' he crowed, and she was full of gratitude for the ease with which he presented the information she had hidden from him. 'Show him to us. We'll invite him to dinner and drink together until the morning.'

'That would be very kind of you.'

'And the other one is Vladimir Andreyevich Weissberg, who was killed in Finland?'

'Vlada died there.'

'He was a stubborn boy.'

'Maybe a little.'

'I've thought about this more than once, Alexandra Andreyevna,' he said softly. He examined his fingernails and seemed troubled. 'I told you that in our meetings I want to speak only the truth, and I believe it's your right to know about the circumstances of his death.'

She turned away. She felt bound to the chair. Now he was going to tell her something horrible, the little gossip.

'In Finland he made an appointment with the politruk* of the company and told him that he had believed in the Party all his life, he was active in all its institutions, but the things he had seen recently had shocked him. He didn't understand the war, and he wouldn't have believed that the Red Army, which he so admired, could be so cruel to ordinary citizens. He couldn't say that his faith in the Party had remained as firm as before.'

Nikita Mikhailovich leaned towards her as if panicked by the look on her face. 'Don't you want to hear this?'

She nodded yes. Now he remembered to ask? She knew how the story would end.

'The politruk apparently liked him, as everyone did, according to the report. He told him to go back to his companions and not breathe a word. The next day your brother repeated his confession to the company commander. It was a war; there was no time for anything. They made a short investigation and shot him and the politruk. The official version is that they were killed in battle.'

Her nails peeled slivers of wood from the table, and blood showed beneath them. 'I don't understand. Did he want to die?'

'The protocol implies that he had undergone a severe crisis of faith and wanted to say what he really thought.'

'I understand.'

'If you want, I can show you the protocol. I obtained it for you.'

'I don't want to see it.'

'As you wish. My intentions were good.'

---

*   The official responsible for the teaching of party principles.

'I never doubted your intentions.'

They sat in silence for a while. She wanted to get away from there but didn't dare. Nikita Mikhailovich played with two bottles as if they were swords. He looked like a boy who had hoped for praise and instead got a scolding. The childishness of men was so exhausting sometimes.

'I thank you for your efforts, Nikita Mikhailovich.'

It was a week of bad tidings: two days later she got a letter from Maxim with the news that Emma Rykova had committed suicide. Brodsky's soft voice sang in her head: 'The gulag, the cold, the hunger and the work—she overcame them all. But not Nadyezhda Petrovna's release.' You could kill Brodsky, but at least in his death he had bequeathed them his irony.

That day she roamed around the city. Tears choked her. All of her memories of Emma were stirred with the heartwarming movement of life. Emma was always looking for someone—a victim to be conquered with the truth, a poem that had moved her but whose words she had forgotten, a lover who had disappeared.

Sasha struggled to uproot Emma from her heart, to transfer her to the regions of night and nightmares. Wasn't that the deal? Until Nadyezhda's release it had not occurred to her that any of the members of the Leningrad Group might come back. Graves had been dug for all of them, each to be filled in its own time; in her dreams they already appeared in the company of other dead people. And now they came back to life.

There was one thing she hadn't discussed with Nikita Mikhailovich: the committee for the Germano-Soviet parade. When he asked, she put him off with a vague answer and requested more time to consolidate the plans. All the documents connected to the parade were locked away in her office, and she was always sure to seat him with his back to the cabinet, so it wouldn't occur to him to look into it. She lived with the fear that she would find the cabinet broken open. One day he asked her about the fortress, because she had spent a few days there to prepare for the meeting with the German—and what impressions she had of the soldiers' preparedness.

'It was strange to be there,' she answered. 'It's so close to the Germans, and it's run like a small village. Lots of women and children. At nights young couples stroll on the bridges, hide in the corridors or in one of the cellars and cuddle there.'

'It sounds very romantic,' he laughed.

'Not really. I've also heard stories about officers who have sent their wives and children to the east. They say that in case of a German attack the fortress will be like a mousetrap: their artillery will wipe them all out in the first minute.'

Nikita Mikhailovich had shown exactly the degree of fury that she expected: 'Anyone who transfers his family to the east and dares to talk about war will pay dearly! Those are the instructions we received from Moscow. Perhaps you remember the names of the officers?'

'It's my job to remember.'

'Very well. The time has come to shoot some of these panic-spreaders and put a stop to that noise once and for all. In our district there's no pity for subversives.'

'Nikita Mikhailovich, I'm not taking pity on anyone. This kind of talk revolts me, too. It could spoil the parade. Mainly I was ashamed to see officers concentrated on their personal concerns. I agree: there's no avoiding a couple of shootings.'

'Tomorrow I'll issue an order to take care of warmongers!'

'A necessary order,' she encouraged him. 'The talk about war has to stop.'

Warm relief thawed her body: all of Maxim's pestering about removing her from Brest would come to nothing. If there had been a slim chance that Nikita Mikhailovich might approve her transfer from Brest, it had vanished after this exchange.

She reminded Nikita Mikhailovich that she had not yet received the intelligence report from Moscow on the German representative to the parade committee.

'Well, it's not the highest priority,' he said. 'There are more pressing matters.'

'I understand, but the material that I got is embarrassing, and in my estimation some of it is wrong: the American company where he worked for years is mentioned in only one sentence. More than that, at the end of the meeting, the German told me that his father had worked in the factory for military aircraft that Junkers established near Moscow in the early 1920s. The fact that his father built warplanes isn't mentioned in the report!'

'Alexandra Andreyevna,' laughed Nikita Mikhailovich, 'wouldn't it be nice if we could sit together and chat like two intelligent people? With you in the end there's always some practical sting, some request!'

She said nothing. He was so correct that a denial on her part would insult him, and rightly. 'I apologise,' she answered sincerely. 'I'm preoccupied by my work, and everything else seems like a waste of time.'

'Educated people must waste their time occasionally. That's how successful ideas arrive.'

'So you no longer believe in diminishing units of time?' she teased.

'For other people, Alexandra Andreyevna, not for us,' he answered, and he began to talk about the teachers who were enthusiastic about his program, and how in the Ukraine they were even adopting it. When he got tired of that, he started up on his latest favourite: complaints about the laxity of the Red Army and its drunken officers. Once Nikita Mikhailovich embarked on one of his speeches, it was impossible to stop him; you just nodded and thought about other things. His remarks reminded her of Maxim's criticisms on his last visit to Brest. Maxim saw a lot of army people and kept up to date with intelligence estimates. He was disturbed about the weakness of the first strategic level and was furious that the new line of fortifications was too close to the border with the Germans—there was no space to halt any advance, and they had put up concrete boxes with no camouflage. The Germans across the river could study our weaknesses, and an attack would be a death sentence for everyone.

The silence that had fallen upon them was proof that they were both imagining the district going up in flames. She saw ashes in the sky and a wall of fire racing towards the city.

Then Maxim said: 'Enough, dear, let's not talk about depressing subjects. Your skinny brother will bury us both. They've been talking about war for a long time, and nothing has happened.'

He wanted to reassure her. But the result of any German attack was so horrifying that she preferred to give herself over to the protection of his voice. 'Give me proof that there won't be a disaster,' she pleaded. 'Give me proof that nothing will happen to Kolya.'

He hugged her, and from the flutter of his eyelids she understood his surprise at her childish response to such a weighty matter. Maybe he wanted to remember whether he had seen her coddle herself that way in the past. Well, not since their marriage.

Cast the hook of memory further, Maxim.

LUBLIN
MARCH 1941

The square was filled with people, wagons and suitcases. The pigeons had disappeared. It was late, and Thomas was hurrying to the railway station. The last snow had melted, and rain annoyed the city day and night. From alleys, courtyards and small streets emerged men and women loaded down with belongings, teenage boys dragging wagons with ropes, mules bearing burdens, girls lugging suitcases, boys pushing cloth sacks containing silverware that rang on the street like masses of cymbals. A wagon carried a Louis Quinze chair with a high back, paintings, a rococo cupboard, a dusty chandelier, a desk decorated with silvered ornaments.

The Jews had been ordered to leave Lublin. Posters with the order of the district governor had been pasted all over the city: by 15 April the ghetto would be established inside the Jewish quarter, and no more than twenty thousand Jews would be allowed to live there. The others had to find a new place to live within the boundaries of the district—there were enough towns and villages. The Jews' abandoned houses would be given to Poles, 'who might not love us,' Frenzel had laughed the day before, 'but they know how to appreciate us for getting the Jews out of their faces. They've been dreaming about that for hundreds of years.'

Frenzel was as happy as a little kid: his project was working out in perfect order, and it had already earned 'words of esteem and respect' from the commander of the SS and the police, Globocnik. Yesterday evening he had invited Thomas to the Deutsches Haus and shared with him 'a bottle of the most excellent wine in the Lublin district... as you expected. The Judenrat has given us vital assistance, especially the vice-chairman, Dr Alten. Your advice to strengthen cooperation with them and to give them a feeling of partnership proved brilliant. "Unity of aim" was a slightly exaggerated formulation, which I found hard to sell them.'

'Because you didn't leave the salesmanship to me,' Thomas reproached him.

Frenzel, choosing to be magnanimous, nodded. 'The joint work definitely oiled the wheels. The members of the Judenrat were efficient and obedient, and didn't annoy us with all their Eastern European moodiness. What's more, the Judenrat is paying the travel expenses of those leaving and making sure the Jews who remain in the city report for work...You know when I understood that it was a flash of brilliance? The day that the Jewish women raised a commotion when their husbands didn't come back from Belzec. The Judenrat and the Jewish police restored order immediately. We didn't have to lift a finger. That's when I understood their potential. Even the campaign that they announced to clean up their quarter was a success. Evidently the Judenrat kept the people of means in Lublin, those who can pay taxes and finance the Jews here, and that's their business. As for the Jews who voluntarily leave the city, we treat them with respect—I emphasised this order everywhere, as you recommended—and allow them to clear out with property, without a weight limit, and even to travel by train. Within the framework of the Voluntary Transfer we got rid of thousands of Jews in the first two days. I estimate that we'll get to twelve thousand, and without trouble. In a year, at most two, Lublin will be cleansed of Judenrein.'

Thomas crossed the street, making calculations. The previous evening Frenzel was so preoccupied with the matter of the Jews that Thomas didn't have a chance to tell him that a bottle of wine in the Deutsches Haus was an insufficient expression of gratitude. To demonstrate this to his secret adviser, Frenzel would have to throw himself behind the parade.

In the last few weeks the mass of ideas and tasks piling up on the subject of the parade had kept Thomas thinking until the small hours. Countless unresolved matters suggested themselves, sending him into a frenzy. He sometimes compared his thinking to a racing car (he liked the Mercedes-Benz models) that had lost its brakes and was careering through the institutions of the Reich, looking desperately for allies.

This afternoon he was supposed to meet with Rudolf Schumacher in Cracow for a 'drink shared by two old friends'. He would confide in him, boast about his new connections and his distinguished mission, and tell the fat man that he'd decided to make him a trustee of the Germano-Soviet parade in the Ministry of Economics, to help him enlist supporters among the industrialists who influenced the Führer. Regrettably, though, the fate of the parade didn't depend on Schumacher, but on the Foreign Office: didn't that amateur Ribbentrop regard the treaty with the Soviet Union as his greatest achievement? So let him defend it!

He wrote letters to Karl Schnurre and Martin Luther, boasted about the progress achieved at the first parade committee meeting and predicted that the initiative to preserve the peace would be regarded in history as the greatest achievement of the ministry in the twentieth century.

Frenzel claimed that they didn't believe in the parade at the Foreign Office either—but a week later Thomas showed him a personal letter signed by Martin Luther, in which he expressed enthusiasm about the ideas of his friend Thomas Heiselberg, 'in acting tirelessly to promote the parade, which has gained favour among people around the Führer'.

Frenzel was impressed and suspected nothing.

But how was it possible to make progress without strong allies in the army? Thomas had to address high-ranking officers in the Wehrmacht who had learned from history and adamantly opposed a war on two fronts. And the SS? After reading Martin Luther's letter, Frenzel offered his help there. Nevertheless it was possible that he was bothering the young officer in vain. Perhaps he had no access at all to those ranks. He also took steps regarding Göring, and wrote to Kresling about 'a secret matter of great value', stating that he had learned his lesson and that his punishment had been just. As yet he hadn't received an answer.

Sometimes, if he relaxed even briefly, Thomas admitted that with each passing day the chances of holding the parade became slimmer. It was frustrating: an exalted historical event had been entrusted to him, he had been seduced by a project in which he could fulfil his vision undisturbed (except for little Weissberg), without the sacks of lead that people like Weller and Mailer always loaded on his shoulders, and now the bastards had abandoned him. No one in the Reich would respond to his appeals, and the second meeting had been postponed to April. But instead of giving in to despair, Thomas swore he would shake up the system, make a commotion, scatter bait everywhere, spread false rumours; maybe the time had come to take even more extreme measures.

A grey-haired Jewish woman puffed up with tattered sweaters spoke to him in Polish. 'Where does one get a receipt for items deposited in the warehouses?' He wagged his finger to show that he didn't understand. She had caused his whole tower of ideas to collapse. He took a deep breath and looked at the sky. The roofs mingled with the clouds, birds crossed the black chimney smoke, people stood on wooden balconies and held on to rusty iron railings. Two policemen with a drowsy German shepherd lying between them called out to a girl who was supporting the old Jewish woman who had just accosted him.

The girl was tall and broad-shouldered. The policemen ordered her to turn around and come over to them, and her mother pushed her towards them, but she stopped, seated the old woman on the pavement and tightened the scarf around her neck. Everything was done lazily, as if she had all the time in the world. The policemen shouted again, and the dog got up and stretched its rear legs. Even Thomas was on edge: move already!

He passed her. She was well dressed, and wore a bright blue shawl. She walked with her back straight, and didn't even deign to look at them.

One of the policemen shouted to her in Polish: 'Take off your hat. Don't you see a German?'

The young woman answered that, according to recent announcements, it was forbidden to remove one's hat. Her voice had a touch of insolence. Thomas hoped the policemen hadn't noticed.

A baby-faced Polish policeman took a puff on his cigarette and coughed while his two friends laughed, then he straightened up and shouted, 'Rosa Heiler, you're not in the library anymore. Get the hat off your head!' He whispered something to his friends.

'Librarian Rosa Heiler,' shouted another policeman.

Thomas froze.

The young woman looked perplexed, blushed and mumbled in Polish, 'What hat? There is no hat.' She undid the knot in her kerchief. The wind dishevelled her black hair, which hid her face. Grey strands showed in it—she wasn't young.

She raked her hair with her fingers. 'Is this all right?' she called out to the policemen, turning towards her mother and beginning to walk away.

'Are you leaving already?' they laughed. 'We told you to report here, now!'

Unwilling, she turned around and walked towards them.

'The Jewish filth always acts as if she's something special,' shouted the young policeman. 'Rosa Heiler, I want you to recommend a book!'

Thomas approached the old woman who was sitting on the kerb. Her face was wrinkled, ashen. As soon as she understood he wasn't dangerous, she lost interest in him. There was a broken scream behind him. The old woman's eyes widened and her face twisted in dread. With a great effort she pushed her body upwards but couldn't rise. Thomas turned around. Rosa Heiler was lying in the street. The policemen's batons rose and fell. The young one put his boot on her stomach. His hand groped behind him and gripped the iron bars of a window, and then he raised his foot and kicked her in the head. It happened in seconds.

Thomas was roused. He crossed the street and stormed the cluster of policemen, pushed them aside and shouted that he was a personal friend of Globocnik.

They pushed him. A club struck his arm. The pain made him laugh. A sharp smell of vomit filled his nose. The asphalt was blotted with black stains. Rain began to fall.

One of the policemen waved his baton at Thomas's face.

'Hit me, you Polish dog,' shouted Thomas, 'and by this evening you're a dead man!'

People approached them from the direction of the Europa Hotel, headquarters of the Propaganda Ministry. One of them, in an SS uniform, gripped his arms.

'Take your hands off me,' Thomas shouted.

'Calm down, calm down right away. Stop going wild!'

Thomas pulled his identification out of his pocket and almost stuck it on the officer's face. 'Ask Sturmbannführer August Frenzel from Globocnik's office about me!'

'What department are you in?

'I'm not in any department. I'm dealing with matters that someone like you might hear about in another ten years.'

The officer pretended that his words didn't impress him, and examined the identification paper.

'Give the document back, you rogue!' Thomas shouted.

Two policemen gripped Rosa Heiler's mother and shoved her towards the crowd of Jews sitting in the square. A little boy approached her, and his father ran after him.

'I'm the one who devised this plan for removing the Jews,' Thomas shouted. His face was burning. Restraining his body demanded a supreme effort. 'The order was to treat the evacuees with respect! I demand that all of those animals be put on trial!'

'Clearly,' said the officer, and his tone of voice softened. 'You retain the right to submit a report.'

'You're a disgrace to your uniform!' Thomas spat in his face.

The officer leaned forwards. His burst of rage stood in opposition to the strange delay in his movements. It was clear he was waiting for his friends to hold on to him.

One of the policemen grabbed the woman's body by the hair and pulled it towards a wagon. Her head dangled back. The rain was rinsing the blood from her neck, revealing a gash.

The officer's companions restrained him. He twisted as though trying to extricate himself.

'You want to bet you don't dare come close to me?' Thomas muttered, trying to control the tremor that had seized his body.

Lying on the wagon, the woman's body looked like meat hanging in a butcher shop. The wagon rolled away, the body rocked left and right, bumping against the sides. The policemen stood in a huddle with their friends against the wall of a green-steepled church.

The SS officer and Thomas exchanged names almost as an afterthought. The officer reminded Thomas he wasn't connected to the incident and told him that the Polish policemen had heard that in eastern Poland, under Soviet rule, the Jews were cruelly persecuting the Poles, and so it was no wonder they were angry. Thomas said he didn't intend to lodge a complaint. They parted without a word, and the officer disappeared into the square.

A voice burst from a loudspeaker, shouting to the Jews that soon they would be taken to the railway station in wagons, and any Jew who dared to approached the city of Lublin again would be shot.

The sky brightened. Locks were removed from the shutters of shops, lights were turned on in the display windows, a waitress in a white apron served a pot of tea to two young men. One of them lit a cigarette, his friend waved the smoke away and they both laughed.

A woman queued outside the pharmacy. The rain fell harder and washed the sweat from his face. His trouser cuffs were muddied. He missed the train.

BREST
APRIL 1941

A joint flyover above Brest was an excellent idea. People, especially children, love planes.

The peace parade of the armies pleased her so much that sometimes she looked at the pencil sketches she had made for a full hour—soon she would draw the big maps—enjoying their beauty, unable to take her eyes off them.

The armies would take positions on the plain outside the city according to the precedent of the Russian-Austrian parade in front of the two emperors before the battle of Austerlitz. The armies would be arrayed in similar order: the cavalry at the fore, behind it the artillery, and finally the infantry.

The cavalry would, of course, be replaced by tanks, and other adaptations to the spirit of the age would be required, but in general the ceremonial aspect that was absent from the 1939 parade would be a central value in 1941. The soldiers would wear splendid dress uniforms, including their insignia and medals. She always saw something of Kolya in all the boy soldiers standing in the square. Sometimes she saw him erect and elegant, and next to him the shrivelled, mud-stained soldiers from the camp, with thin fuzz on their cheeks. Even though their bodies were tense, they were laughing, slicing the air with their swords. The fear of death had abandoned them.

Maxim, the only one with whom she discussed her plan, was dismissive. In his opinion there would be no parade. War was going to break out as soon as the earth dried, probably in May, and anyone with eyes in his head who observed the movements of the German army would understand that. Soviet intelligence agencies all over the world, from Switzerland to Japan, were flooding the Kremlin with evidence of the Germans' intentions: in the past month Merkulov's men in the NKGB* had collected dozens of signs of the aggressive deployment of German forces. There was even gossip that German operational plans had reached the Red Army. The whole story of the parade was just one of their stupid tricks that we were falling for in the vain hope of preventing war.

Maxim's boldness in writing like this in his letters which, were they to be discovered, though he had taken severe precautions, would undoubtedly lead to his liquidation, was further evidence of his urgent efforts—by turns begging, demanding and petulant—to get her out of Brest. 'All the smart people in your district send their wives and children to the east, and you've fallen in love with some parade. I implore you, dear, listen to my plea!'

As he became more desperate, states of mind that he hadn't dared reveal slipped into his letters:

> I understand: your heart tells you that it's better to die for
> the sake of the thin boy or to die with him than to live. Do
> you think I don't grasp the horrors you've gone through? I
> encouraged you and guided you as best I could to get out of
> the black labyrinth that opened up in your soul—we all

---

* The People's Commissariat for State Security.

wander in a labyrinth like that, every human being, and certainly every NKVD man, but your case is truly dreadful. Even on that night, when I stood in your room and laid out my plan for your survival, I told you: your new self won't be a better person. She will have to do horrible things. Those are the conditions of the deal.

Then you clung to the story that you had actually helped your parents' group, that because of you they received more lenient punishments. I encouraged you and gave you evidence that it was really true. But I always feared it was the first straw you grasped to stop from drowning. A person might feel he is capable of struggling against the will to live, but we aren't able to fathom the different tricks our cunning souls can play on us. We're survival machines, we have to recognise that.

You're too smart, Sasha, I told you that on the day we met in our fourth year of school. I've been horrified to observe the guilt that's draining you of life. I hoped that— before the moment when the veil of your denial was torn away, the moment you understood, with blood-curdling clarity, the meaning of your actions—maybe one of the twins would come back, maybe we'd have children, maybe you'd love me again, maybe your soul would find some other reason to cling to life. I swear to you on my honour: the only reason I pressed you about having children was you, not me.

My dear, remember that I told you, on our vacation in Sochi, that Stepan Kristoforovich had urged us to have children? In fact, the other subject we discussed was your twins. We each made supreme efforts to help them. Though I'm contemptuous of that liar's crimes, and appalled by the filth that people of his kind cast upon our organisation, his endeavours on your behalf were admirable. He desired you feverishly. I saw it in his eyes.

That hypocrite told me that he'd managed, with some difficulty, to have Kolya drafted into the army too. In retrospect we realised that they'd split up the twins the day they arrested them in Leningrad. Everything went easier with Vlada: he was made of choice material, and a small forgery of his documents was enough to draft him. The thin boy, in contrast, was supposed to be locked away in an institution for delinquent youth. His second piece of news was that Vlada had died in Finland.

And because you showed no signs of recovering from the horrible thing that traitor did to you—I won't mention his name here—I fed his body to the dogs with my own hands! We decided to work out how to tell you the news when we returned from holiday—only about the thin kid, of course. But when we got back from Sochi, Stepan Kristoforovich was already in trouble. He knew his story was over, and so he acted to send you far away from the city and to have you meet Kolya. He didn't consult me.

My dear, I'm going back to that night when I came to your house after they were all arrested. A few days went by before I decided to do it. I'll admit it: I was afraid! I knew how much fury had been aroused in the organisation against your parents and the Leningrad Group. Did I kindle the will to live in you that night? Or should I, as someone who loves you, have let you die in your childhood bed? The schoolgirl's bed on which I touched your body so tentatively, choking with desire, and kissed your skin. Do you remember us in your room? One eye on the door, every noise outside making us rush to straighten our clothes and hair. 'Maxim,' you'd laugh. 'Father will lock you up in the freezer at the Institute!'

Maybe I should have waited until you decided by yourself to survive. But I didn't do that, and I risked my neck for us—not for you, for both of us. And now we're still alive, and I'm desperate. Think about your parents. One day they'll be released and return to Leningrad. A lot of people are coming back now. Nadya came back. And what present will they receive when they return? Three graves? As for us: what evidence can I produce that we can have a life together? I swear, we'll have gorgeous children.

The picture that came to her mind when she finished reading was very distant: little Sasha wallowing in deep snow while her father swore to her once again that summer was locked in the cellar, and this time it wouldn't get out. Children believe their parents. She didn't want there to be a child who believed her or her husband. And she didn't understand why Maxim insisted on ignoring the facts: hadn't Nikita Mikhailovich issued an explicit order to deal severely with those who run off to the east? Moreover he had entrusted the planning of the parade to her. So by virtue of exactly what leniency was she supposed to return to Leningrad?

Maxim, you're labouring under an illusion. Love is a noble source of dreams, but in days like these one must avoid both. I forbid you to do the slightest thing to transfer me from here. I won't leave Brest without Kolya. And as for the past—there's no stain on your actions. You showed courage. Your observations are only partially correct. Guilt is not my main motivation. My only request is for your letters to be more practical. I'm concentrated on the mission that was thrust upon me, and memories weaken me. If we grow old, we can share our memories then.

At the end of her letter she added a few lines and then decided to rub them out:

I got an anonymous letter from Leningrad with a poem by Nadyezhda P., in which she extols the imaginary figure of a certain Morozova, the twin of Pavlik Morozov: this Morozova informed on her father, a bespectacled literary critic who incited students against the Party, and her mother, an amiable housewife who didn't understand anything about literature but saw everything and kept silent.

Even now she hasn't stopped pursuing me, and even dares to mortify Mother, as if the catastrophe she brought down on us weren't enough. She roams around all over the place, celebrates, gets drunk, boasts and writes while everybody is dead or in prison. Do you want to defend your wife, Maxim? Do you want to show that you're the man you claim to be? I want that woman dead. Dead! Do you understand? I want that whore dead!

Every time she received a letter from Maxim she hoped he had guessed what she wanted, understood everything and had done what he was supposed to do. The details didn't interest her. She just wanted to hear that the woman had returned to the dead. But whenever she was tempted to look over one of his letters, she was sorry she hadn't burned it. Instead of the report she hoped to find, he only warned her about the war.

Sometimes she woke up terrified. Had something happened while she was asleep? She would hurry to the window and look for movement in the German camp—the silhouettes of planes, tank tracks, a flash of gunfire—and struggle against the urge to put on her coat and rush to the fortress. Barefoot at the window, while the searing cold on her feet ascended her body, she would stare out into the darkness. Only after scraps of dawn were visible would her trembling cease. She would leave her little apartment, sit in the office, still pursued by the visions of the night, and immerse herself in the drawings again.

She stopped wandering in the streets. Brest had become repulsive to her. Every time she went out she encountered signs of the city's agitation. Sacks of flour became scarce in the stores, along with soap and matches, and the financial department reported that the locals had begun to get rid of their rubles. Red Army soldiers complained that tailors, watchmakers and shoemakers gave slow service. 'Future corpses don't need watches,' said one merchant who had been arrested and interrogated. He was shot.

There were rumours every day that the war had already begun, that Germany had invaded the British Isles, that in the Great War the Germans had punished Belgian children by cutting off their hands. Residents reported seeing tall German spies in summer suits. A shoemaker wrote to the city committee that he had sat behind a German spy in the railroad workers' clubhouse. The man had jumped onto a train going to Moscow. It was said that the women of Brest danced with handsome, silent men who wore white gloves, that German agents had poisoned the water in the wells. In the evening, in 1 May Park, there were dance parties, and after a while she realised that it was worth going there sometimes, because the place was swarming with drunken officers who possessed interesting information. One officer whom she danced with told her that his job was to observe European sheep, and that he reported directly to Golikov.

'Don't talk to me in code,' she laughed and pinched his arms.

'I really do observe sheep,' he panted. 'Don't stop pinching, please. It's very simple: if Hitler decides to attack, he'll have to manufacture millions of woollen coats for his soldiers. The price of mutton will plummet, and the price of wool will rise. But there's no sign of that.'

Satisfied, she leaned her head on his shoulder: Maxim certainly didn't know about the sheep.

Nikita Mikhailovich listened to her arguments patiently. As far as he could tell, he said, the city was calm. Wherever there were people, there were bound to be rumours. A surprise attack was not a reasonable prediction. He revealed a great secret to her: intelligence people believed that the deployment of the German army at the border was in preparation for Hitler's demand that we transfer part of the Ukraine and the Caucasus to Germany. He would also ask to use the Soviet navy against England. If the government refused, Germany might declare war. In any event, there would be time to prepare. Sasha answered that she trusted his opinion, but this was not connected to the fact that they had to silence the warmongers.

'Every time we meet you encourage me to make arrests,' he joked, and his face showed he was happy. 'It's lucky you're dealing with the parade now. Otherwise nobody would be left in the city.'

She dictated an article to the editor of the newspaper *Zaria*, making fun of those who spread rumours, who preferred to deal with fears of war between the Soviet Union and her ally Germany than work on behalf of a better society. On the same page they published an interview with a sixteen-year-old girl, who presented her plans for the future under the heading: 'I Will Be an Engineer'. In her last year of school, Sasha had responded to her father's request and was interviewed by a Leningrad newspaper. The headline was: 'I Will Be a Physicist, and in the Evening I Will Write Poetry'.

...

After she sent the new map of the city to Thomas Heiselberg, they exchanged several telegrams. It was decided that at their next meeting each side would present its general program. In his letters the German representative raised fanciful, megalomaniacal ideas: he wanted the parade to look like the World's Fair. He suggested gigantic pavilions should be set up in Brest, and he described the House of the Twentieth Century, which would be 'the throbbing heart of the entire event'. He waxed poetical over a tram that would carry the crowd from pavilion to pavilion, and over a lighting system that would bathe Brest in a huge glow all night long. Sasha believed that, once he realised that his ideas could not be implemented anywhere except in his dreams, he would accept her plan.

Her parade would be a multi-stage event:

1. A military review that would be held in the early morning on a broad field outside the city.

2. A parade that would march through the central streets of Brest.
3. Towards evening a symbolic war game would be held in the fortress. The residents of the city would look at the sky, lit by shells and flares, and the entire event would conclude in an atmosphere of splendour and mystery.

Of course, a historical thread was woven into her plan: in the morning, a homage to the great covenant between Russia, Germany and Austria against Napoleon, and in the evening a gesture towards the peace that both countries had declared in the fortress, ending Russia's part in the Great War. There would be an intervening tribute to the previous parade, which symbolised the treaty and the new spheres of interest of the two states. Wasn't that perfect?

The last letter she had received from the German disturbed her. First, he announced the postponement of the next meeting until the end of April, a delay that jeopardised the entire parade. The appropriate time to hold the event was between June and September, and given how much preparation was required, it was possible they would miss these dates, in which case the parade should be postponed to 1942, world change permitting. And there was another strange thing: the reserved tone that had prevailed at his earlier meeting had been replaced by his determination to influence the parade: 'Imagination, Mademoiselle Weissberg, is a rare commodity among diplomats. With all due modesty, it seems to me that I'm the man who should lead the imagination department of the parade.'

As the date of the meeting drew closer, her faith in her plan deepened, and yet she had made no progress at all in dealing with the German representative. In her work she had frequently encountered people with flexible personalities that they could not control. This wasn't a tactic aimed at the interrogator but rather a sign of their torment. It made the interrogator's work complicated, because they hadn't yet decided whether or not they were guilty. Some believed they could be everything, that every talent or trait they found in somebody else could become theirs. Others, and she felt this might include Thomas Heiselberg, struggled to become the person they wanted to be, but kept one eye fixed on the abyss they always believed was about to swallow them up.

These were dangerous people, because they were like a tiger that pounced on a plant with the same determination as it pounced on prey. Even the slightest gesture could be taken as a threat. They might respond in the most extreme way, as if a sword rested on their neck.

Thomas Heiselberg was in fine control over the cords of his flexible soul. To someone like him, she'd say: You are a magician. When you wave your wand one face disappears and another pops up. Or she might reach for an insult: You act with malice and behave as if there were no such thing as conscience. In either case he wouldn't be bothered at all. As he saw it, you'd acknowledged his power.

BREST
MAY 1941

A fine spring day, Thomas said to himself, but you have to admit that people die on days like this, too. In the morning they wandered the streets and decided on the parade route, the placement of the platforms for the dignitaries and the areas intended for the crowd. They visited 1 May Park and the stadium, and they met pleasant athletes at a training session, preparing with the municipal band for a performance in June. Their decisions were made quickly, but they were both of the opinion that they were excellent decisions, and not even a shadow of doubt passed over them.

'Maybe it just seems that way, but I'm hearing more Russian in the streets than Polish. You work fast,' he observed.

'Monsieur Heiselberg, in the street you hear the will of the people.'

She noted that recently the residents of Brest had been seeing German planes. The Red Army air force was acting responsibly and escorting them out of Soviet air space, but those incursions didn't improve trust.

'Our pilots are young and not fully trained,' he recited. This was the excuse Frenzel had given to him, but a half-smile showed that it seemed weak to him as well. 'Aside from that, they've heard so much about Communism, can you blame them for being curious?'

'The parade will completely satisfy their curiosity.' She leaned towards him, flushed and excited.

Perhaps his elegant appearance at the first meeting had influenced her. This time, instead of wearing an ugly skirt whose edges had yellowed and a faded jacket, an abundance of joyous colours flowed from her body: a skirt with red and white polka dots, a tight coat with a plunging lapel. Her dark hair was combed to the side, and it had a bluish glow. She was all gathered in, *tirée à quatre épingles*. His fear of her eyes had ebbed away; at the railway station he already noticed that the look he remembered was not like the one she was giving him today, and he began to wonder whether the whole thing was a monster he had inflated in his imagination.

They reached the conference room in the afternoon. It was on the ground floor of an old building on a side street. She led him down a corridor that smelled of naphthalene. The hallway arrived at a small office where cobwebs hung over shelves laden with rolls of paper. They went through a doorway into a vaulted room, in the centre of which stood a rectangular wooden table. The brass doorhandles had been polished that morning, and on the floor were patches of white plaster that had been hastily scraped.

She announced with an apologetic smile that this was her new kingdom. She couldn't get the necessary inspiration for planning the parade in a bustling office. This was a lie, of course. Her new office had been created for this meeting; naturally her colleagues were not enthusiastic about having a German diplomat—and a diplomat was really an authorised spy—wandering about their offices.

A large sheet of paper was hung on each wall of the room. Two were maps sketched in charcoal, and the others were bright drawings of lawns and cypresses frozen like dark feathers, soldiers in uniform, behind them a blue river, carrot-topped children on a rose-coloured path cheering for a column of toad-coloured tanks. Where were the women in crinoline, carrying parasols? He stifled a laugh—the children looked like fish in a bouillabaisse.

The sheets of paper hid the windows and blocked the daylight. Two table lamps cast weak beams of light, and their shadows skipped from map to map. She stood in the middle of the room, twirled on her tiptoes as though saying, please be excited! Then she approached him, her face glowing and her bandaged hand behind her back, in a gesture of respect. He couldn't remember whether she had concealed her hand at their first meeting. Now they were hidden away here, she had shaken off her chilly manners, and the professional restraint she had insisted on, even when laughing, vanished.

Doubtless she noticed his slight reservations about the decor, but she apparently had no doubt of her ability to inspire him. An interesting woman, Comrade Weissberg…Did the maps really have an intoxicating effect on her, or was it all an act? How disappointing that both possibilities seemed equally probable.

And there was something else: the parade was her entire world. She would tie a loop at the end of every sentence and, after every friendly exchange, toss the loop in a trice over another sentence, knotting them together into a conclusion involving some aspect of the parade. He found it hard to follow the pace of her loop-tying. When she noticed that his interest was waning, she would quickly present another irresistible idea, like a child feeding a dying bonfire.

She dragged him on a tour of the maps: this was the 1939 parade, and this is where the retinues stood, and this is the route the column took, and this black line represents the belt of people who watched, and here was the new parade: the armies deployed in three rows, grass-green, olive-green and grey tanks with a red star in front and tanks with a swastika, small cannon whose barrels were pointed at the horizon, and here was the parade through the streets of Brest, exactly along the route they had just taken. The gold dots showed the column descending from the bridges over the river, pouring out of the sun and storming the city. She would, of course, include his excellent comments.

She surveyed the maps lovingly, dwelling on the flaws, and when she touched them to emphasise a point her fingers removed invisible specks of dust.

He acknowledged the 'deep impression' made by the design of the maps and the professional work, and was careful not to pass judgment on the ideas. When they stood in front of the last map, he felt a stab of pain in his right knee, which he had tired out on their walk that morning, and he wanted to sink onto one of the chairs. But she remained standing next to the picture of the sky over the fortress, decorated with flashes of fire, and presented her vision of searchlights and flares rising from the cannon. The searchlights reminded him of the light ship from the advertisements for Persil, one of his brilliant ideas at Milton, as well as a slogan that lit the Berlin sky: 'Paul Hindenburg for President of the Reich.'

She smoothed her dress, which soon dotted the room: red and white spots appeared no matter where he looked. For now it was impossible to tell her about his recent actions, to speak reason with her, present his plan. It was too dangerous. She might go wild and destroy everything. He had to gain her confidence so that she would acknowledge the true state of affairs.

In a sympathetic tone he asked how the Ministry of Foreign Affairs had responded to her plan. She spun around to him, hostile, and said that, as he knew, very few people were in on the secret.

He sat down. She detached herself from the maps and seated herself at the head of the table, her eyes open, as in a waking dream. He was prepared to bet his apartment in Berlin that he was the first person to see the maps. Her anticipation of approval was not disappointed—he praised her profusely—but it wasn't enough. Maybe she sensed his artificial tone. Like an actress returning for another curtain call, she asked his opinion of the maps again, and this time he showered her with compliments. That seemed to calm her down.

Then she stood up again and began to describe her multi-stage plan for the parade. She delivered the lecture with panache, and there was infectious power even in her little exaggerations. Comrade

Weissberg could have been an excellent saleswoman, Thomas said to himself.

They went for a walk. The moment they left the map room he felt relief, the visionary film left her eyes, and he hoped that soon he would be able to speak reasonably with her. His mood improved, and in the market he stopped at a stand laden with old things and insisted on buying her a present. She chose an army knife with tweezers and a screwdriver. He gave it to her with a bow: 'If you please, a gift from the German Foreign Office. Just don't use it against us.'

They walked across the bridge and left the city, heading for the woods she wanted to show him. She planned to hold a joint luncheon there for the senior officers of the two armies. Fishermen sat on rocks surrounded by weeds that waved in the wind, boys raced around them and scattered breadcrumbs for the swans, and on the bank across from her a gilded triangle spread and then gathered in the black thicket.

In the forest the city was only a rumour. There was the rushing of the water, the rustling trees, cawing crows, the gaiety of the birds. He loosened his tie, took off his jacket and hung it over his arm. They walked on rustling leaves, passed under a tunnel of vines bent by the wind, and entered a clearing surrounded by birches and oaks. In the morning the sun was hidden by cloud, but now, towards noon, it was spreading its bright glow. The light plunged into Alexandra Weissberg's eyes and wove golden strips in their grey gleam. She pointed at the treetops. 'Look, they're like lions.'

'A poet's imagination,' he teased her. 'From a pointed spire, a bell and a bird, you create architectonic visions.'

She was proud of their achievements, and he agreed with her, and when he felt she was relaxed he told her that indeed they saw the first stage of the parade eye to eye, but as for the subsequent stages, he was sorry to say that the plan didn't seem right to him: clinging to history was, in his eyes, merely an empty quotation. What good would the masses derive from these gestures? Unlike Goethe and Croce, he did not believe that knowledge of history was liberating; it shackled us and restricted our imagination. Instead of describing the future, the parade would force the masses to look backwards. And what landscapes did we want to present to them? A pile of mangled corpses, the treaties that were violated? Two years after your great military parade, Napoleon, against whom the emperors had joined forces, reviewed battalions of the French and Russian army with Czar Alexander, and the Russian army helped its former enemy to fight against the Austrian Kaiser, with whom Alexander had surveyed their splendidly arrayed regiments. Nor did that treaty prevent further deaths a few years later with the French invasion.

'Why shouldn't the parade represent, for example, the history of the movement of merchandise in Europe; we Germans bought some planes from the Americans; other American planes, from the same manufacturers, are now bombing the cities of Germany, and the President of the United States condemns us. But American companies are still trading with us. My father, who worked in the Junkers factory, built planes for you Russians. Advanced models of them might soon kill German boys. Why not show that history in the parade?

'The preoccupation with the past is one huge fixation. History speaks in the primitive language of blood, and it's abuse of school children to force them to study those horrors. After all, history is at everyone's service. That's all well and good, but our parade has to be more elevated. Germany and the Soviet Union stand on the brink. I am sure you know about the forces on the border: four million soldiers on both sides, maybe more. Our goal is to fire everyone's imagination with the opportunities for peace.'

While he was speaking, she grew pale, her shoulders sank and her eyes, which had once terrified him, lost focus. She hugged her coat to her body. Then she stiffened, and stared proudly at him.

'I do not mean to belittle your impressive work,' he said quickly.

Contempt showed on her face. 'There's no need for compliments. We're here to do the best for our shared purpose. These matters aren't personal.'

Indeed, he concurred. They could easily resolve their differences. With her permission, he would like to tell her more about his suggested model of the world's fair. He had been to the one in Spain, in Seville, and in his opinion, if you hadn't seen the splendour of the Iberian fair, you'd missed out on the world at its best. He told her about its fabulous artifice, which contrasted with the faded face of Seville, about the Mexican, Brazilian, Portuguese and Guatemalan pavilions. Wandering around there, he felt that he was walking across a map of the world. He couldn't resist telling her the story about the final Moorish ruler: in 1492, after losing the battle for the last Muslim fortresses on the Iberian peninsula, he had wept in the ship as it sailed away from Granada. His mother reprimanded him: 'Don't cry like a woman for a place that you couldn't defend like a man.'

'When was that fair?'

'In 1929. You must have heard about the other fairs too, which have been held all over the world, in Chicago, New York, Paris.'

'Did you go to the Paris fair?'

'Unfortunately, no.'

'But you've been to Paris?'

'Of course! We had an office there.' Her tone was heartbreaking; she struggled to subdue the longing in her eyes. She was a little girl-woman who had never left the Soviet Union. He cleared his throat. 'In any case, our peace event should not include military stunts or history. It has to charm the people.'

Here was his plan: a ring of eight pavilions to be built around Brest; six of them would represent the armed forces—land, air and sea—and he could imagine children climbing on tanks, pressing buttons in cockpits, clambering around a decommissioned warship.

He leaned wearily against a tree. It felt like the feeling had been cut off in his fingers. This day was exhausting him. The sunlight shattered on the leaves. Grey dust hung in the air, and in some places under the trees the darkness of evening had already fallen.

'You are actually planning a circus,' she said. 'Don't you want a battle of elephants?'

'The details aren't important,' he said, ignoring the provocation. 'I also propose two joint pavilions: one of Germano-Soviet art, and another of peace and fraternity.'

'And what will we exhibit in the pavilion of peace and fraternity?' she asked.

'What a question!' he called out in cheerful surprise. 'Things connected with peace and fraternity.'

He expected to savour the familiar taste of victory, but he realised that his answer didn't reflect his thoughts. The clarity of his words had diverted him from his intention: to present his solution to her sincerely. He was struck by the uselessness of his actions—his pattern of behaviour remained set even when his intentions changed; his behaviour preceded his will.

Had he come to the second meeting and risked what he had risked just to rid himself of the gaze that tortured him? Every morning he had got out of bed to harness all of his abilities, both exalted and contemptible, in service of the parade. This woman was the only other person in the world who believed in it. The problem was that Mademoiselle Weissberg was floating in a dream, hiding in the map room the way his mother and Frau Stein had hidden in the bedroom. He had to bring her back to the world of action. Yet it was hard for him to believe that this young woman would have the courage to be his partner in such a freewheeling plan.

He heard her saying: 'I arrive here in a confused state, and here my doubts are resolved. In the forest the grip of external forces is weakened. Here I came to understand that the parade is my fate.' After a brief silence she added, 'And I hope that it's yours, too.'

An entreaty whose meaning he didn't understand was woven into her words. When he looked up, the city and the sky had disappeared. The sky was tangled with the foliage, and it was already hard to distinguish between them.

'*Gospozha Weissberg, nashi raznoglasya dolzhni bit raznersheni yeshcho svodnya!*'* He had decided to surprise her and speak to her in Russian. Maybe French was keeping them apart; the time had come to get closer

---

* Miss Weissberg, the differences of opinion between us must be resolved today.

to the truth. Her face betrayed nothing. Maybe she had read in some report that he spoke Russian. 'I'll support any reasonable plan for the parade,' he went on. 'In fact, the plan isn't the main thing. We share a common goal, and we might be the only people in the world who believe in this goal, so we have to do everything we can to attain it. My strong recommendation is that, starting from tomorrow, our only goal is for the parade to win over our Foreign Offices. The date that I propose for the Germano-Soviet parade is 1 July 1941. Does that sound good to you?'

'Herr Heiselberg,' she answered, and her voice was distant and cold. 'You've acquired a fine Moscow accent. But I have to say that our differences of opinion about the content of the parade are profound and apparently touch upon deep-rooted differences between the nations we represent. I suggest we schedule another meeting to reach a decision. Until then, let's seek a proposal full of inspiration.'

She was completely ignoring the urgency of his words. The armour that she had donned was impenetrable.

'We have to present our plans for the parade to our superiors immediately,' he protested.

'It's better to present the plans when they're ready.'

'You understand that by then it might be too late!' He lost his composure.

'Why do men talk about war all the time? There's no inspiration in that,' she said with a facetious expression.

There it was, the word 'inspiration' again, as if she were labouring over a work of art. 'Miss Weissberg, we'll make all the decisions today!'

'How will we do that?'

'How will we do that?' he asked bitterly. 'Here's an example: I accept your entire proposal word for word!'

'Mr Heiselberg, is this a game for you?' she shouted. Furious wrinkles formed between her eyebrows. 'Don't you understand that your capricious behaviour is endangering our entire mission?'

Between the trees the violet sky showed, spotted with a few stars, like a cracked glass dome. Time was running out. The second parade meeting was about to end, and it was clear that Weissberg's only goal, the only thing left in her arsenal, was to end on a note of hope.

'Miss Weissberg, I will speak now with the utmost sincerity.' He had no alternative but to threaten a little. 'If we don't decide that within a week we will present our plan for the parade to our superiors, I will have to report to the German Foreign Office that the second parade meeting came to a dead end.'

'You aren't going to do that,' she declared. But her eyes showed fear. 'We have to stay united.'

They climbed up towards the bridge over the black river. Every step demanded an effort. His breath whistled, and the fatigue he had been combating for the past few hours overwhelmed him. Weak light flashed from the windows of the first houses on the edge of the city, and a flame spiralled up from the saw mill. The bridge sloped down to the bank, but the closer they got to the city, the weaker his body became: they were both small, too small, staggering through the sand like two crabs, here was the city before them, and beyond it other cities—Lublin, Moscow, Warsaw, Berlin—fates were decided there, no one remembered them there. He felt like a little pin that was making oversized dreams dance on its head. He wanted to be among the trees again where the world could not pounce on him. He had lost the confidence that protected him at Milton—the company was a bit like that forest—the confidence that he could predict outcomes and plan his future. How could he have known, for example, that the model he had sketched out in Berlin would be used to eliminate the archaeologists in Warsaw and Lublin? It didn't matter how much he mocked his feeling of guilt—in his dreams the archaeology class still taunted him. Sometimes they shouted, as befitted the future generation, and sometimes they mourned, as expected of orphans: 'Teacher Thomas! Remember us, please. We want to see your parade. Orphans like parades too!'

Outside the market, merchants had gathered under the streetlamps. A child was running among them, holding a large fish head against his chest. She broke their silence and told him that the city committee had punished residents who had spread poisonous rumours about war, and expelled them from the Party. 'We deal severely with warmongers.'

'I have no doubt.'

'People find it easier to believe in war than in our peace march.' Her words rang out fondly to him, as if the two of them had been dancing at a ball. 'But I have no doubt they'll come to admit we were right. Every great deed in history has run into naysayers.'

'Well said.'

'Differences of opinion between us are natural,' she said. 'We're both so devoted to the goal that every detail is crucial. I see our discussion as a fertile pathway that will lead us to the truly great idea. I feel it in my bones: we're close.'

'To the truly great idea?'

'To the truly great idea.'

There was an evening breeze. He put on his jacket, but he was immediately awash in sweat. The cloth was too thick. Spring was lurking: the chill had vanished, the sky was brighter at night. It was still raining but it was the last rain. Dread swept through him. Didn't she understand that the earth was ripe for war?

'Miss Weissberg,' he said, renewing his oath for the sake of the parade. If a fool was needed, there was one in front of her. 'In my view, when this is over, in another ten years, or maybe more, people who believe in great ideas will be locked away in padded cells. Maybe it will turn out that our plan only accelerated war and death, but right now, according to my best judgment, the parade might prevent the deaths of millions of our countrymen. If we don't do something exceptional, something that's hard to conceive of, I fear that the only place where the Germano-Soviet parade will happen is on your maps.'

It didn't appear that she intended to answer him.

'This meeting isn't really official. In Germany they've lost interest in the idea. The last two telegrams you received, confirming our appointment, were sent on my own initiative. In fact, they're forgeries.'

He spoke in a rush. He focused on the horizon.

'I don't understand,' she said miserably. 'You're here...'

'I'm here to give you letters from the German Foreign Office confirming the parade and its date, and I want you to circulate them as soon as possible along with the plan of the parade. These letters will create turmoil in both our governments. In the first stage, your Ministry of Foreign Affairs will receive the letters and will announce the march, annoying the Germans. At the same time we'll exploit the confusion reigning in Poland, and certain organisations will receive orders from Berlin to prepare for the parade. In the second stage, your General Pavlov and our Generalfeldmarschall von Bock will receive the plan for the parade along with an urgent order to meet to plan the final details...there are four more stages.'

She sketched faces on the muddy ground with a stick. 'These letters,' she said. 'Are they real?'

'No, Miss Weissberg. I've already told you. I forged them.'

'Can fake documents move armies?' Her voice sounded stable, but something in her eyes made him think she was losing her bearings.

'Miss Weissberg, your disdainful tone is out of place. Let me remind you of the role that forged letters have played in the history of Europe. For hundreds of years the authority of the Catholic Church depended on a forged letter from Constantine the Great to the Pope. Skanderbeg conquered Krujë with a forged letter. The Protocols of the Elders of Zion are also actually a forgery, though the people still believe in them. As usual, the most wonderful example has been contributed to us by the history of the Slavs.' He adopted a triumphant tone. 'I speak of False Dmitry, a forged person who became the czar. When the world loses interest in you and your dreams, there's no alternative but to falsify a more attentive world.'

'You're taking an enormous risk.'

'Not really. I've reached a point where the loss isn't so great.'

'This is the raving of a madman!' She dropped the stick and approached him. Her bandaged hand was no longer behind her back.

'Less mad than sitting in a gloomy room and drawing maps.'

'Your chances are zero.'

'We're a pair of talented forgers. Maybe we'll start something extraordinary. In any case, even if I wouldn't bet my own money on our success, it's the only plan.'

'They'll kill you.'

'Oh, I assume they'll be satisfied with a labour camp.'

'They'll kill me when they discover the fraud.'

'You're also willing to die.'

'How do you know?'

'I'm aware of your situation.'

'But you don't have a reason like that.'

'How do you know?'

'At least I didn't find one in our reports.'

'My reasons are no worse.'

'And they are?'

'Rather mixed-up psychological matters.'

'You're an expert in making things simple.' She sounded exasperated.

Apparently she understood that he found it hard to explain himself even to himself. While he was looking for the right words, black veils shaded the city.

Not now, he begged.

You always say that, laughed the attack.

The black veils drew close, flapping in the wind. The city darkened. Tar dripped from the sky. Once again he had no idea where he was standing or at what angle to hold his body. The houses around him were buried in black nothingness. Maybe he screamed—he heard a shout, strangled by his shortening breath. He pressed his hand to his heart, which seemed to be leaping crazily between his chest and his throat. Here it was: the attack he always feared. He had paid Erika for eight years to prepare for it, silly man. Blades pierced his ribs, slicing deep, he heard them clashing in his gut. His body convulsed—right-left-right. He didn't understand how he hadn't been thrown to the ground. He saw his fingers tremble violently. He curled up like a hedgehog—the main thing was to keep his limbs from being torn away. He saw his fingers scattered through the streets, in the woods, in the river. His fingers touched his throat, looking for air, then plunged into his ribs, holding back the pain. Suddenly he knew they weren't his fingers. Somebody was holding him. His body sank, ready for the blow that would shatter his skull. Now he could understand how it was possible not to be: everything narrowed until only a single slit remained.

Now they were removing his jacket, tearing his shirt, and arms were wrapped around him, gently lowering him. Sprawled out on the moist earth, he leaned his head on her knee. Her polka-dot dress stroked his cheek, and her hands rested on his ribs. How did she know the pain started there? The breeze cooled his chest. His eyes opened to the clouds that took shape as a slope with little terraces on it. Breathe-breathe-breathe, he heard her whisper. I'm alive, he thought.

...

Eyes closed, he lay like a dead man on her bed. His white shirt, which she had torn, hid part of his torso. His breathing was shallow, and there was almost no pulse. His body was pressed against her. When she let go, he whimpered in his mother tongue. Are you your body? The traces of the past gathered around her. The starry night sky, visible from her window, was their only refuge. When it disappeared, there would be nothing to defend them.

You have to wake up, she said softly. You can't lie there and leave me alone. We can still extricate ourselves! We haven't finished anything yet. Do you understand why I couldn't drag you to hospital? They would have discovered that you're German, brought in my superiors, forced me to reveal your identity. Then they would have reported the incident to your embassy, and discovered that your trip was unauthorised. They would have accused you of treason, made you disappear, and our parade would have been dead. I can't help you. You see that as clearly as I do, we are both conspirators who have performed horrors. If you die in my bed, the pair of us are finished, more or less.

Her eyelids drooped. Sleep beckoned her. It would be easy to sleep.

She got up, went to the table, lit the candle and then knelt next to the basin and washed her face. The cold restored her. She dipped her fingers in the water and moistened his swollen lips. The candle spread a golden light in the small room, and she saw how red his face was. His eyes were puffy and his dusty hair clung to his forehead which was bathed in grimy sweat. Spit dribbled from his lips. She dipped a cloth in water and passed it over his face. He quivered as though he had been stung. She withdrew in alarm and leaned over the basin. If she washed his body in cold water, would that help? She started to drag the heavy basin towards him, but changed her mind and left it in the middle of the room. She had no notion of how to treat him.

She remembered Vlada burning with fever in the attic, Grandfather slowly dying in the mirrored parlour, Mother getting sunstroke in Varlamov's courtyard—Father holding her tongue, Kolya burying his face in her lap, Emma exclaiming, 'She has a talent for drama, that woman.'

None of that would help now. Those sick people weren't in her care. Someone else was there to give instructions. Maybe his pants were constricting him? She dared to loosen his belt, loosen the buttons of his trousers and pull them down to his knees. She did it as though committing a conscious sin: she had never met anyone who took the pains he did to make a respectable impression. If he woke up now, he would collapse again with humiliation.

His yellow, waxen thighs and flaccid stomach contrasted with the lively colour of his face. His thighs moved a little, maybe to help her. His naked body wasn't as she had imagined. His clothes filled him out and gave him a sturdy appearance, but they concealed a withered, bony body.

She had to stop staring at him. Where were his shoes? Had they been lost on the bridge or fallen off on the merchant's wagon that brought them here? Even if he got up now, how would he get back to Lublin? His shirt was torn, his trousers were dirty, his shoes were lost. She was already planning how she would go shopping for shoes and a white shirt in the morning so he could respectably report to the railway station as soon as possible. She would explain to the sentry that the committee's discussions had been prolonged, they hadn't paid attention to the time and suddenly it was dawn. But what explanation would he give to the Germans in Lublin?

He had planned to return by the night train. He might have accomplices. He had probably bribed someone. Could he cross the border in the morning and return to Lublin without being caught?

She placed her hand on his chest to make sure that his heart hadn't stopped. Her fingers pressed on the bright tuft of hair, moist from cold sweat. She checked her watch: midnight already. Sometimes, in the depth of the night, there's a moment when the morning will never come, but for days and weeks she had been watching the dawn spread over the city, and it would happen this time, too.

He had been unconscious so long! Seething with anger she slapped him; her envy of the tranquil world he dwelled in strengthened the blow. He groaned and gave out a stifled whine. White saliva spurted onto his chin. She stood next to him, trembling. The strange thing was that she had hit him with her bandaged hand, and she would hit him again, she understood with frightening clarity.

She stepped away from the bed, and paced between the window and the wall, which was covered with green wallpaper and dotted with rusty nails. If you wanted to lean on it, you had to find a smooth section. Newspaper clippings, her research for the parade, were scattered on the floor. Seven steps separated the window and the wall. A line hung with underclothes and socks stretched between the small dressing table and the pine table where the candlestick stood. There were two children's stools painted orange. A clothing cupboard leaned against the wall next to the door, leaving a narrow space you had to squeeze through to avoid being scratched.

The shadow of his body moved on the ceiling. The air smelled of sweat mixed with vomit—she didn't remember him vomiting—and the floral scent of his hair oil. For some reason, as she leaned on the wall between the nails, as far away as she could get from him, the stench grew more intense. His smell was in her dress and on her skin.

Should she air the room? The scraping sound of the window might wake the neighbours. Thomas Heiselberg had taken over her house; his shadows had trapped her. Would he live or die? She put out the candle to kill the shadow, and approached the bed to confront her fear: a real body could never be as dreadful as its shadow. Now she only wanted to comfort him; how was it possible to think of harming a body lying helpless before you?

Don't lie, an inner voice teased. You're being docile because even if he's fatally ill he might still save the parade. You have no choice but to anoint him with the oil of victory. He's your last hope. Him and his grandiose forged plan.

She lay on her back on the bed. Actually, lying beside him, her fear subsided. There was no reason now to resist sleep. One more hour of wakefulness and she'd go mad. She would close her eyes for a minute or two. Maybe the time had come to surrender to fate. The bed was small. Her back pressed against his smooth arm, and her head rested on the hollow between his shoulder and his neck, which shivered at her touch.

Something sharp suddenly pierced her consciousness, a picture of the disaster that sleep would bring down on them. She rolled off the bed, rushed to the door and charged down to the street, spurred on by the urge to put her problem into someone else's hands. She turned right into Valerian Kuybyshev Street. Father had liked Kuybyshev: 'He worked day and night so we could catch up with the West.' At the end of the street, Nikita Mikhailovich's building looked like a huge ship without its sail. She could hear the ticking of cicadas and the yowling of a cat. A figure passed by the window—it seemed to be looking at her.

She went up the stairs and touched the wooden door: this was a horrible mistake. There would be no going back. He was never a friend. Haven't you learned anything? He'll do only what he has to, he won't take your wishes into consideration. She knocked, and heard bare feet approaching. Nikita Mikhailovich stood there blinking, his hair dishevelled. Now, when he wasn't wearing glasses, she saw that his eyes were different in colour and flecked with dull amber.

She told him that the German representative was lying in her bed, hovering between life and death. 'You studied medicine, Nikita Mikhailovich. Maybe you can wake him up.'

'Just send him to the hospital.'

'Impossible.'

'Why?'

'Simply impossible.'

'I order you to send him to the hospital!' His tone was curt, but she could see he was puzzled by her rashness.

'Impossible. The Germans mustn't know he's here.'

An angry shadow crossed his face. She was familiar with it: Why are you involving me in this? Don't you understand, you simpleton: our friendship is limited to matters that involve no danger?

She had anticipated this. In a minute or two, no trace would remain of the friendship between them, of the truth workshops, of his respect for her.

'He came without their permission,' she said.

'Does he want to defect?'

'No, he wants to promote the parade.'

'And did you know about that?'

'Only after he got here.'

'And now you want to collaborate with him?'

'I just want to wake him up.'

'You have to take him to the hospital and inform our Ministry of Foreign Affairs. They'll decide how to deal with this.'

'It's impossible. He doesn't need a hospital. You're a doctor. Save him first, then we'll see.'

She gave him a stubborn look and hoped he understood that he had no choice, that he was already involved. He couldn't slam the door on her and go back to sleep. She had transferred the responsibility to someone more senior and she could always claim that he was the one who had hatched the plot. He had to do as she wished.

'I studied medicine long ago,' he squirmed. 'I don't remember much.'

'You remember enough! We have to hurry,' she ordered.

He registered the tone of command, and frowned.

'You have to come with me, Nikita Mikhailovich,' she whispered. 'Otherwise this thing will blow up and endanger us all.' She looked over his shoulder into the dark hallway. Somewhere in there his wife and children were sleeping. He tried to block her field of vision. Strange guy, suddenly playing the innocent—a man who had deported tens of thousands of children from the district ought to know there was no end to it.

Now he understood the threat in all its fine detail: all their times together, the amusing notes they had exchanged during staff meetings— had she ripped them all up? How soon until she mentioned her husband's connections? He was already anticipating the accusations she'd pin on him if he refused her, and the evidence she'd invent; for the first time he was comprehending that her story had the power of myth: here was a woman who had informed on the people most dear to her and scattered them in labour camps all over the country.

As they stood there face to face, silently engaged in a life and death struggle, it finally became clear to her how other people saw her. How hard she worked to evade that image of herself! But in a fight for survival, she was willing to trade upon Nadyezhda's interpretation of her actions, to hint to Nikita Mikhailovich that perhaps she was indeed that person.

She could tell he was afraid she would pre-empt him and 'expose his true face', as Reznikov did to Styopa. That she would use methods he couldn't even imagine—were there any such?

She brought her face close to his. Her eyes were on the level of his chin. 'It's impossible to leave him alone in the bed,' she whispered into his flushed neck. 'He could die while you're standing here like a lump!'

'Two minutes,' he said. She waited while he dressed, and when he didn't appear she knocked on the door again. He came out in a black military jacket, with a dark scarf around his neck and a small satchel in his left hand.

'Do you have everything?' she asked, and he nodded. She looked him up and down for a pistol or knife hidden in his socks, or shoes, or in his satchel. She should frisk him, but she didn't dare. Aside from that, she needed him and it was better to act as if she trusted him. He had to believe that their friendship could be remade.

They went downstairs. She heard him panting behind her and decided to increase the distance between them. Even if he seemed weak and compliant, she had to remember that this man, unlike her, had killed people with his own hands. Just like her, he was weaving intrigues for the end of the night.

Nikita Mikhailovich continued to lag behind her. She turned around and urged him to hurry. The meaning of what she had done did not escape her: Nikita Mikhailovich wouldn't forgive her threats. He would not rest until he could liquidate her. Maybe not tonight. Maybe in a week—when the crisis had faded, when an opportunity came his way. She mustn't labour under the delusion that it was possible to heal the rift. Thomas Heiselberg, if he woke up, could extricate them from the tangle; it was strange how, even after he was stripped of his tricks, and even when his flaccid body had been laid bare to her, part of her still clung to the way he presented himself to the world. After all, that wasn't a groundless deceit. She still remembered how, a few hours ago, as though in a former life, he had stood smiling beside her in the glade, and toyed with her until her head was spinning.

She pushed the door of her apartment open. In that instant, as she stood between the door and the cupboard, it seemed to her that a body had been moving around the room and immediately sank onto the bed. But the darkness made her doubt her eyes. She approached him. Heiselberg lay in the foetal position, panting. She checked his pulse. It had grown stronger, and in general he seemed more alert. A torrent of relief warmed her body, and she sparked up. When she turned back, by the weak light of the moon she could see Nikita Mikhailovich leaning against the wall and drumming lightly on his belt.

She stood opposite him. 'He's breathing,' she said.

'Very good,' he answered.

She moved to the middle of the room.

Nikita Mikhailovich approached the bed and leaned over Heiselberg. 'The satchel, please,' he ordered.

She laid the satchel at his feet. Control over their fate had passed into his hands. She was afraid he would kill Heiselberg while he was treating him. But there was no logic to that—the death of a German representative in her room would be fatal for both of them. No, Nikita Mikhailovich would wake him up, they would help him obtain clothing and then he would take care of himself. He must have a plan for returning to Lublin, and he knew how to improvise, to make up for the hours he had lost, and to wriggle out safely.

'Nikita Mikhailovich,' she said hoarsely. 'It's still possible to solve all this.'

He heard her conciliatory tone. 'I hope so.'

'Will he be all right?' she asked.

'If he hasn't died by now, he'll live.'

'Can you wake him up?'

'I'm doing that.' He spoke with a note of pride. He was recovering his wits. She slid onto the floor and sat with her back to the wall.

'I'm giving him smelling salts now.' Nikita Mikhailovich was using his doctor's voice.

She closed her eyes. There was no doubt about it: Heiselberg was awake when they arrived. He was pretending to be unconscious to gain time, to find a solution. He would only come to life when he understood exactly what was going on around him and how he should act. She had a sudden insight into his silence.

'Nikita Mikhailovich,' she said. 'I'm sorry that I woke you and urged you to come here against your will. I apologise if, in my emotional state, I said things that could be interpreted as a threat. That was not my intention. I respect your rank and your senior status. I have always admired your decency and your distaste for intrigue. Since my arrival, I've served you and the NKVD to the best of my ability. You have treated me with great generosity.'

'This isn't the time to review our history,' he said. 'Believe me, we'll get to that.'

Did he suspect that she was talking to the German? But it wouldn't occur to Nikita Mikhailovich that the German spoke Russian. French was the language of the committee, so he wouldn't suspect. What else did Heiselberg need to know? Through the window, the moon had been enveloped by dark clouds. It would be morning in two hours. She got to her feet, went to the small table and lit the candle. Then she leaned against the wall again and remembered how on the morning of Morozovsky's interrogation she had floated around the interrogation room, cackling like a silly goose. Instead of grasping his intentions, she had fallen into his plot, approached him even after he dipped his finger in the boiling tea. She thought she understood how the psyche works at times like that—she was somehow absent from the evidence of her senses. The critical moments are usually silent; the scream is only heard after everything is finished. That wouldn't happen this time.

'Please put out the candle, Comrade Weissberg.'

Her body straightened of its own accord, as if she had been yearning for the sound of his voice, emphasising every syllable. She blew out the candle and gave herself over to the relief that flooded her. Had she acted well? From now on, things were in his hands. No doubt he had prepared a perfect plan that would satisfy everyone.

Thomas Heiselberg was sitting up on the bed, looking at his naked feet. Nikita Mikhailovich sat down on one of the orange stools and tapped the floor with his shoes.

Heiselberg pulled up his trousers and disguised the rubbing of the cloth against his skin with a slight cough. Except for these sounds, the silence in the room was absolute. He got off the bed, tightened his belt, brushed away the scraps of his shirt and combed his fingers through his hair again.

'Nikita Mikhailovich Kropotkin'—his voice revealed that he had comprehended everything. There was no doubt: the man had talent. But his strange appearance—he went over to the window, and his naked chest touched the pane—aroused a vague fear in her.

'Comrade Kropotkin!' he called out again.

Nikita Mikhailovich stood up.

'Perhaps you would be willing to lend me your shirt,' Thomas asked in Russian. 'I am sure you'll agree that it's not proper for me to return to Lublin dressed only in my jacket.

Nikita Mikhailovich didn't respond. He was a circumspect man and wouldn't utter a word until he had processed this new information: the German representative knew him by name, he spoke fluent Russian and he dared to ask for his shirt. He looked at Thomas Heiselberg and at Sasha by turns, as if he understood now that he was trapped between the two of them.

'I am sure you know, Comrade Kropotkin, that this little episode has to remain among ourselves. I understand your suspicions. You think that Comrade Weissberg is afraid you'll take revenge against her, and therefore she will attack first and expose your true face—I believe that's the correct expression here. After all, you know our darling Comrade Weissberg well; in the light of her previous actions, it's hard to believe she'll have mercy on anyone, no matter how close they might be to her, or that she will refrain from doing something vicious to neutralise a threat. She doesn't believe you're capable of restraining your thirst for revenge, and you don't believe she'll hesitate to act against you. Am I correct?'

The realisation that he knew everything about her filled her with bitter despair. She felt naked. It was her deeds that shocked people, Russians as well as Germans. She had been judged already, become an example of evil. He had treated her with respect, warmth even, while feeling only disgust for her, telling himself, 'Look how she's made herself pretty for you, the monster who destroyed her parents!'

But less than half an hour ago, outside Nikita Mikhailovich's apartment, she, too, had brandished her reputation to frighten her superior. So why did she feel desecrated when Heiselberg did the same?

Nikita Mikhailovich made a sound that might have been a stifled laugh, but it was swallowed in a cough. He spat onto the floor. He wouldn't agree to any deal, Sasha thought, but nevertheless she still believed that Heiselberg could work some magic.

'Listen to me, Nikita Mikhailovich,' Heiselberg said amiably, brimming with good will, as if promising to get an old friend out of trouble. 'Obviously you are endangering yourself by doing nothing, because Comrade Weissberg might decide to act first. I don't make a habit of lying: this is quite possible. People like us can't trust someone else. But it would be regrettable if you destroyed each other because of this lack of trust. And what if your anger tempts you to get even with your protégée, who was willing to betray you? Come on, Nikita Mikhailovich, our children rebel against us, that's how the world works. And in any case, assuming you can overcome her, what about the power of Maxim Podolsky, her husband? And let's not ignore the German representative: for purely professional reasons, Comrade Weissberg is dear to my heart. Even from Lublin I can harm you by finding evidence, for example, that you spied for Germany. You're surrounded, Comrade Kropotkin, and the only thing you can do is take off your shirt and give it to me. Oh, I'll need shoes too. If I leave now, maybe I can cross the border in time. As you may imagine, I have made the necessary arrangements, but I'm already very late, and the people who are supposed to be satisfied with my flimsy documents will soon lose hope and leave their posts. And that's something we don't want to happen.'

The room was too small for the three of them. One slight movement by any of them might become an invasion of the other's space. Nikita Mikhailovich was pressed between the dressing table and the clothes-line. He needed a drink. If he asked, she would say that she had nothing except water. Vodka would fire his resolve. She felt her legs and discovered they were scratched.

'What guarantee can you give me that she won't act against me?'

His question surprised her. He wasn't the sort to make deals like that. Even his tone sounded false.

'In our dealings, there are no guarantees,' Heiselberg declared cheerfully. He had apparently concluded from the question that Nikita Mikhailovich accepted his account of the situation. 'You know that as well as I do. Logic dictates that you'll serve your own interests, if you can each accept the other's survival.'

Heiselberg walked over to the basin. He knelt one step away from

Nikita Mikhailovich, rinsed his face, splashed water on his chest, then wet his hands and again combed his hair back with his fingers. He did it naturally, as though he were at home. Only a cheerful whistle was missing. Having recovered from the attack that almost killed him, he had found new strength, as if nothing could frighten him now, not even death. Certainly not Nikita Mikhailovich.

He had a rare talent for hope, not only in his smooth talk, but in his very being, in the childish faith he placed in his ideas, which he truly believed were destined to remake the world. She knew why he had won her heart in the glade, and why she was ready to do anything to save him. A part of him—not all, and not all the time—believed that their parade, too, would remake the world in its own image.

But, precisely for that reason, he would never learn what he could not understand. He deciphered people according to his formula of characteristics and motivations, and thought that everyone, except madmen, would accept its validity. He would never understand people like Nikita Mikhailovich who lived solely by their rigid principles. He always felt like offering such people inducements, including ways of enhancing their careers, that he believed it would be perfectly rational to accept. For Nikita Mikhailovich to violate his own tyrannous dictates was like leaping off a bridge.

'I'm not convinced you understand the problem,' said Nikita Mikhailovich, while Heiselberg wiped his dripping chest. 'I'm a gentleman and not a believer, and I am sure you are aware of the difference. But there is one thing that I do believe: every secret will eventually come out. Even if you pressed a knife to my neck, I wouldn't accept your proposal. I didn't come here because I was afraid of young Comrade Weissberg, but because your death in her bed might cause a crisis. In any case, if I can help a sick person, it's my duty to do so. Maybe you'll think I'm self-righteous, but to remove my shirt and give it to you, to be a part of your insane plot, to cooperate—as Comrade Weissberg is—with a German representative who entered the district for which I am responsible with forged papers, is contrary to everything I believe in.'

Fear surged in her: it was over. He wouldn't budge. He was determined to remove her from the district, from the parade committee, and from his orbit. Now she would have to do battle with a man who had shown her warmth and friendship.

'Really, Nikita Mikhailovich.' Heiselberg's voice trembled slightly. He looked out the window. 'You're talking like a Red Cross volunteer. We all know your past.'

'I'm the first one to admit to my deeds,' said Nikita Mikhailovich earnestly. 'I make a spiritual accounting every night, and it isn't always flattering. I am aware that my position enables me to do what I do. In other words I accept the authority of the Party. You might doubt the methods, but all my actions have a purpose. Your plan…it's simply inconceivable. It achieves nothing except my survival, even if I decide to trust a woman whose character you describe so well, and a Nazi official, who is hatching all sorts of cosmopolitan plots with a Jewess against her direct commander.'

'There's no plot,' Heiselberg protested, trying to conceal his despair. 'It's the right action for everyone's good.'

'You really are a gentleman,' bellowed Nikita Mikhailovich. 'It's great to see you concerned for a woman whom you wanted to have replaced on the parade committee.'

'We've already discussed that,' Sasha said at once, 'and resolved our differences of opinion.' When, she thought, had the bastard managed to do that?

A thin strip of light crawled into the room. Heiselberg laughed, and maybe he even winked at her, as if a fraction embarrassed. She smiled at him as though to hint that this was a trivial matter and he should concentrate on the main thing. She wasn't insulted by the news that he had sought to replace her—there was no obligation of loyalty between them, nor could there be. Was she insulted because he, unlike other men, remained indifferent to her charms and intelligence? She remembered something Kolya had said on the plain: 'Nadka says that the NKVD has made a wunderkind out of you again.' Now she understood what Nadka meant: None of us saw you as a poetry wunderkind, so you looked for another way to star, and in your ascent you erased us all. How could that be correct? Was there a place in your soul where all the little ruses melt, where denial caves in and the truth is revealed?

'Nikita Mikhailovich,' she said. 'You don't understand Herr Heiselberg. He's the man who wrote the Model of the Polish People. He gave advice about deportations and arrests, executions, labour camps, the treatment of the Jews. I believe that he's committed to the parade because he sees it as a noble event for peace. Maybe he has a yearning for personal redemption. It's impossible to know how a man feels who was responsible for such criminal behaviour, for persecuting people simply because of the blood that flows in their veins. In any event, good deeds won't clean our hands of the blood. Who knows better than I? If you act against me, you'll jeopardise the parade, and I know you would rather we struggled for peace than war.'

She hoped Heiselberg had missed the pleasure she had taken in condemning his model. Like a beloved song, the accusations had rolled off her tongue, and she regretted she hadn't expounded further about the crimes committed under his inspiration.

'God help us,' declared the German. 'A man has no more secrets.'

She lowered her eyes—she didn't dare look at him once the information they held against each other had been laid bare in ugly sentences, for the benefit of Nikita Mikhailovich.

'I must leave you now,' said Nikita Mikhailovich. 'I have a busy day ahead of me.'

Heiselberg gave him a wild look. Now there was no recourse for him. By the light of dawn she saw his spreading pallor. Perhaps it cost him an effort to stand, and that was why he was leaning against the window. 'You understand that we can't allow that?' he said. 'I've never met anyone so stupid in my life! Do you believe we'll allow a self-righteous nun to endanger the most precious thing of all?'

'You'll allow it,' Nikita Mikhailovich chuckled. 'And how! Comrade Weissberg, you said, I recall, that noble actions won't wipe the blood off your hands. Show us your bleeding hands, please.'

Heiselberg slumped. He appeared to acknowledge his defeat and lose interest in the whole event. She linked her fingers behind her back. 'The only thing you'll find there is the bandage that she never takes off,' Mikhailovich said to the German. 'Did she tell you how it happened? It seems that one of her defendants poured hot tea on her hand. When was that, Comrade Weissberg? Late 1939? A small burn, and since then: the bandage. Our doctor changes it for her every two months. He tells her: It's almost completely healed, Comrade Weissberg. You don't need a bandage at all.' Nikita Mikhailovich took pleasure in imitating Dr Zimyatin's high voice. 'But she stubbornly orders him to change the bandage, and keeps her eyes on the ceiling. A little burn—she can't look at it. So blood? And of dead people?'

'You're exhausted, Nikita Mikhailovich,' said Heiselberg. 'You're talking nonsense. I don't see the connection...'

'You see it very well,' Nikita Mikhailovich interrupted. 'You've never had blood on your hands. Obtaining confessions, writing papers, triggering hidden sequences of events that cause other people to die? That's what gentlefolk like you are so good at. But to give a direct order to kill someone? To kill a man close up, stab him in the heart, break his neck, shoot him in the head and see his brain explode, and then at home discover that brain fragments have splashed onto your ears: you've never done that. We're standing here, and you wish you could bury me. But this time no one will do the dirty work for you. It's almost absurd: you've both caused the death of hundreds, maybe thousands of people, and suddenly, because of one little death, you're helpless.'

Nikita Mikhailovich stood between them as though waiting for some action that would contradict his arguments. After a few seconds he walked to the door and kicked the basin over. Water began to spread over the floor and the clippings.

Sasha looked at Thomas Heiselberg, still at the window, which was glowing with sunlight. He hadn't moved. Really, won't you do anything? Won't you stop him?

Nikita Mikhailovich approached her. His eyes were opaque.

He's going to hit me. She retreated to the wall and tensed. She was expecting Heiselberg to do something, but he stared at them in puzzlement, like a stranger who had arrived by chance. He was paralysed, but underneath he was writhing and screaming. Nikita Mikhailovich's opposition had thrown him headlong into reality. He couldn't even talk anymore.

With an effort she forced herself to look at Nikita Mikhailovich, hoping that his aggression was only a product of her imagination. Through his moist glasses he was looking at her with contempt. 'You are a diminishing unit of time,' he whispered, then squeezed between the cupboard and the wall, and left, slamming the door.

They stood stock-still. There was a flurry of footsteps in the apartment above, and a woman called out to her children to get dressed for school.

'Now we will have to expose his true face,' the German grumbled. But it was too late to say that—they both realised how useless his words were. 'And maybe he won't do anything. After all, he looks like a responsible person.'

Don't talk anymore, her eyes said, just as the ball of the sun burst into the window. You sound like a dead man.

GERMANY
1941

Scanning the horizon lines of the cities he approached, he sometimes yearned to make one great leap back to life, an actor bounding to centre stage, shouting, Here I am! Don't say you weren't looking for me. You need someone to come up with a daring new plan, something inspired!

But afterwards—among winding potholed roads, seaside villages and hamlets with a handful of houses—the surge faded. The lecturing voice that astonished people with flamboyant international plans fell silent.

Towards the end of the summer he went to the village of Heiligendamm, where his mother had spent summer vacations in her youth. In the morning he would pack up a book, a broad-brimmed hat, a towel, sunglasses and a notebook, and sprawl on a beach chair facing the sea. Was Thomas devoting himself to writing? Recording his dreams? Several years too late, was he responding to Erika Gelber's request that he keep a journal? Not exactly. Sometimes when an idea came to mind he was tempted to scrawl it down, principles he once believed in, impressions of a young family walking down to the shore, their hobbies, their origins and the future of their children. An abundance of time led a person to paths that once seemed superfluous.

After a while he stuffed the book and notebook into the towel, and watched the people out among the waves. Should he join them? If he dived into the water, would he feel better?

He felt like a nap. It had become too hot. He was sweating. He tried to brush the sand off his body. There was sand everywhere, even in his privates, making them itch. He rose heavily and returned to his room. People passed by him, flocking to the shore, their faces still sleepy, ready for the pleasure the day had in store for them. He closed the windows, drew the curtains shut and lay down in the darkness. Residual snatches of noise from outside emphasised his isolation. Naked between the sheets, he challenged memory to a duel—do your worst, show us some horrors. Memory spits fire: faces, events, pages of the model, the streets of Berlin, behind which Lublin and Warsaw split off—there were masses of images. He squirmed in the bed, lashed out at the images with his fencing sword from university days, until sleep fell on him.

At noon he woke up, taut with fury, cursing the holiday-makers whose voices rang out like alarm clocks banishing him from the kingdom of sleep as they walked to the dining room. He had no choice but to drag himself to the window, to watch the other guests cheerfully passing the time according to routines established on earlier vacations.

Now, lacking any all-consuming project, he was left with fragments of the past to fill up his days and keep at bay the void, the boredom, the terrifying silence. He jumped from stone to stone: the quicksand around him was all memories. His new mission was to discover strategies for shrinking their influence: 'the Heiselberg technique for no-memory'. He already had a rough idea: since it was impossible to drive the images out of his mind, since he could not make them disappear, he had in fact to summon more and more of them until their colours, dates and contexts all blurred, and he could exile them to a space where they could recur, but with less force. They became like a horror story that you read once, but on second reading wasn't so frightening anymore.

After a week he was nauseated by the smell of the sea and the naked bodies, with their pallid skins, wandering between the shore and the card games in the lobby, and there they were again, eating lunch, drinking beer, retiring for a nap. Wherever he turned, he heard only vanity, fussing, banal chatter about the war in the east, and saw only rich complacent faces closed over with pride. To calm his spirit, he tried to moderate his disgust at these types with their lazy movements, their soft foppish speech. At dinner he was surrounded by dozens of bespectacled, shiftless Wellers, all singing the praises of the Wehrmacht.

He caught a train and decided he would get off at a station close to the Belgian border. Perhaps Aachen. Someone he had met in Lublin was born there. Two hours later the train stopped, and the passengers were told to evacuate. Enemy planes circled, casting shadows on the fields. In panic the passengers clambered down, clutching their belongings, and lay under the carriages. Thomas spread out on the warm earth next to the tracks. His cheek rested on a stone that was as smooth as a pillowcase—he wasn't going to die because of some stupid bomb. He listened to the fading roar and comforted a young mother who was crying, huddled over her infant. He didn't reboard the train, didn't feel like hearing the passengers' frightened whining. He took his suitcase and walked a few kilometres through the fields until he reached a small village near Hanover.

Frau Gruner, whose house was next to the village cemetery, was the first person he met. She offered to rent him her top floor, which was reserved for important city people, and to cook his meals. The only thing she expected in return for her generosity—aside from money, of course—was his learned opinion regarding the future of the war. He would understand it better than the stupid peasants here. Her grandsons Hans and Franz had been sent to the east, and she and her daughter couldn't sleep at night for worry.

'Sleep in peace, Frau Gruner. I am completely certain that Hans and Franz will return by the end of the year.'

For a few days Frau Gruner was satisfied and treated him with the greatest of respect. At six-thirty in the morning she would prepare a rich breakfast for them both. Afterwards she would do her job of tending the cemetery, which she did with the devotion of a peasant working his soil. Every day she asked Thomas for 'the tiniest bit of help'—a little exercise never hurt anyone, and he looked so low. Here were gloves for weeding, it would be nice if he could mix the whitewash for the wooden fence, here's where we want to clear away the rubbish and level the earth. She dreamed about an entrance path strewn with fine gravel and told him there were misers in the village who refused to pay for upkeep of the cemetery—they'd have to look elsewhere to be buried.

In the afternoon, after she had bathed, applied perfume and tied a blue ribbon in her white hair, Frau Gruner served him egg liqueur in his room and pestered him with questions. Why wasn't he married? Had his girlfriend married someone else? It happened to the best people. She too, out of all her suitors, chose the failure; love was blind. She was a cheerful woman, Frau Gruner, even when telling the saddest stories.

At night Thomas would cut across the cemetery and lose himself in the fields beneath a starry sky, going further into the darkness, feeling that he was vanishing along with the world itself, becoming nothing more than an assemblage of memories fading out over Germany. He forgot that Hanover was nearby: darkness now shrouded all the places he had passed through, and the places he had yet to reach.

One day the owner of the beer hall remarked to Thomas that his eyes were red. Apparently he wasn't sleeping well—no wonder, if he was living in the house of that Gruner woman, a terrible person who wandered about the village with her sinister, deathly smile. When Thomas returned home, he made some casual remark about the grim future of the war to Frau Gruner.

All that night he heard panting and snorting, as though of a tired bull, from the ground floor. Finally her shoes pounded on the steps, and she knocked on his door brandishing a smoking candle. She complained that he had promised her grandsons would return safely. Those were exactly the words that had been said to her in 1914, and two years later her husband had been killed.

'I didn't say they would return safely, Frau Gruner. I said they would return.'

He immediately packed and left. Where would he go? To Heidelberg? Perhaps he would sit in the university library, do some research. Aachen? The week before he had planned to take a train to the Belgian border. Now he wandered among the platforms, heading first, as always, for the Berlin train before remembering those regions—far from the bright city lights, which he had always held in a kind of contempt—where he had decided to stay. Maybe you'll learn to enjoy the little things, he sometimes mocked himself: Carlson Mailer, Rudolf Schumacher, Frau Tschammer, Weller all wanted him to have a holiday.

He wondered whether he was being pursued. Was the Foreign Office looking for him? His discharge was the direct consequence of his actions. In the first week of June, Frenzel had summoned him to his office. Adopting an official manner, as though they had only ever been colleagues, he informed him that his delay in presenting the Model of the Belorussian People had aroused great resentment in the Foreign Office.

Thomas replied that he hadn't managed to finish it because of his workload regarding the Germano-Soviet parade.

Frenzel interrupted him and said frostily that to the best of his knowledge it had been two months since anyone had talked to him about the damn parade. The bureaucratic junkyard, as Thomas well knew, was overflowing with initiatives that had come and gone, and his parade was just another one of them. But Thomas insisted on annoying everyone, sending letters, travelling to Warsaw and Cracow to all sorts of questionable meetings, revealing details to people who weren't supposed to know them, arousing anger in the highest circles. 'The party is over,' declared Frenzel. His severe tone sounded forced, as if imposed from above. 'Indeed, in early May they were already urging you to finish the Model of the Belorussian People.'

'Does this mean that war with the Soviet Union is close?'

'No,' said Frenzel. 'The Belorussian model interests us for philo-sophical reasons. Please don't ask me questions that I'm not permitted to answer. All I know is that you have been asked to deliver the model or bear the consequences. The Foreign Office is complaining about your negligence and suggesting you have been deceitful. After all, you received a salary to do a certain job.'

'I was asked to work on the Germano-Soviet parade, too.'

'True, you were asked to do both things together, but, with all due respect, one meeting in Brest-Litovsk and an exchange of letters is not exactly a full-time job.'

Thomas couldn't help admiring Frenzel's official manner, in which no trace of doubt or discomposure was evident. As if he truly believed they had never shared anything but a working relationship.

'There is no Model of the Belorussian People,' said Thomas.

'Do you understand the implications of saying that?' Frenzel asked, and his tone softened. He leaned towards Thomas. 'Look, even if lots of the material still needs to be written up, I have no doubt that within a week you can prepare an excellent report. Maybe it won't be as impres-sive as the Model of the Polish People, but you can easily explain that.'

'You may inform the Foreign Office that I haven't completed the work.'

'Perhaps you should go home and reconsider your reply,' proposed Frenzel, straightening his papers, as though hinting that the meeting was over.

'I've thought about it more than enough.'

'So your answer is final?' asked Frenzel, rising.

'Absolutely final.'

A week later Thomas was discharged, and received a letter ordering him to leave Lublin immediately, advising that the Foreign Office was considering prosecuting him for fraud. He was invited to supply a detailed answer explaining his conduct. He didn't reply and left Lublin in the middle of the night.

Before leaving the apartment he took a last look at his desk, which was piled with typewritten pages. He had come to think of the apartment as a kind of factory for assembling models, but now the machinery had shut down, and whatever left his hands was stunted and ugly, a bloody stump without shape, inspiration or spirit.

The last thing he did in Lublin was send a letter to Viktoria Sovlova, a resident of Brest, in which the writer, Ewa Pushchinska, regretted to inform Viktoria of the death of her beloved aunt: the funeral had already taken place. Everyone was brokenhearted. She urged her dear friend to leave Brest at once, to return home to console her widowed uncle, who, left alone even for a week, might die of sorrow. She must return to him right away!

As soon as he got back to Berlin, he sold his mother's apartment. On the morning of 22 June, when the German invasion of the Soviet Union was announced, he signed the contract. He packed his clothes in two suitcases, having already donated everything else in the apartment to the NSV. He even received a letter of thanks for his generosity.

He didn't see Clarissa. Her parents had gone on holiday, and the concierge, the only acquaintance he met in the city, didn't know where. The concierge had heard from Clarissa that Thomas had received a lofty promotion in the Foreign Office; he congratulated him. It was regrettable that Herr Heiselberg was leaving, but nothing had been the same since Frau Heiselberg had died. 'She's engaged, our little Clarissa,' added the concierge. 'Maybe she's even married by now. Her mother told everyone that she was engaged to a young man with a bright future.'

'And where is that bright future going to be?' Thomas asked.

The concierge didn't remember. The fiancé's father was something in the film industry. He recalled only that Clarissa's mother said the young man was finishing a doctoral dissertation.

Thomas didn't leave a forwarding address. If the Foreign Office decided to take him to court, they'd have to take the trouble of finding him.

The summer passed. He went to Heidelberg (and did indeed spend a few hours in the university library), visited Aachen, too, the Swiss Alps and quite a few villages and towns. He didn't go near Munich, of course. It didn't matter whether he went to the Ruhr district or Bavaria, to Schleswig-Holstein or Hesse. There would always be fields and orchards, tall bushes, a blacksmith shoeing a horse beside a smoking chimney, and a steeple and a church bell, a barn piled with hay, peasants' houses painted yellow, and a forest not far away, as in Rettenberg, for example, where the men used to hunt quail in those lovely days. But now most of them were hunting and being hunted on the Russian front.

He crashed into mornings when everything seemed unreal, and his banishment from life was like a cruel punishment, incomprehensible, a story with no moral. On mornings like that he stayed in bed, prayed not to be, but when his imagination smashed his head against the wall or sent him another unbearable attack, he was so ashamed of such images that he burrowed under the sheets, and the sound of every step from outside made him shudder. When he saw his face reflected in a train window, in a mirror, in a glass bowl of fruit, it seemed expressionless. Something had been laid upon it that would neither expand nor contract. He decided to choose certain expressions, but none of them stuck, there was always a hollow space. He grew a small neat beard, but that only made the situation worse. Like a little demon, the beard jumped on his face and shouted: Look, isn't something missing? Or, after attaching the requisite facial expression, he went out determined to make people pay attention to it, to believe in it so they would ask him: Why, dear fellow, are you so sad, so happy, so tormented?

He didn't feel lonely. Among strangers he was calm, and could chat about ordinary matters or prospects for the war. Contact whose meaning he never understood, loyalty as insubstantial as a soap bubble, the pursuit of vague associations, describing encounters at work in terms of friendship, revealing aspects of his personality that he had never in any case hidden—the demands of social connection finally disappeared.

He didn't try to conceal that he didn't have any schedule, status or position. If people asked him his field or his plans, he answered with total sincerity that he had no notion where he was heading. He was offered ridiculous jobs managing small businesses, supervising a distillery, in a watch factory, and he respectfully refused them all. He didn't intend to settle anywhere. The urge to wander was like a spiritual command that he scrupulously obeyed.

There were no men in the villages he passed through. The fields, gardens and greenhouses were orphaned, unless young women or prisoners of war took the men's places. In the stations he sometimes ran into a group of girls, all from the same village in Poland, Belorussia or Ukraine, who got off the train wrapped in heavy coats lined with cotton, and carrying cardboard cartons on their heads. Representatives of factories or workshops were waiting for them.

One day, for no apparent reason, he offered to translate for the masters of a group of young Polish women. The girls were dispersed in different houses. Thomas mediated between one farmer in particular and a few girls, even demonstrating as the farmer instructed them to thin out his sugar-beet field: you dug a little trench around the strongest plant and weeded out the stragglers. You moved forwards on your knees in a broad line: your knees turned black, but you got over that. You had to keep a straight line, and if someone went too fast, they'd hear the whistle. The farmer's wife scolded Thomas: 'Sir, it is not right to ruin such fine clothing,' and she insisted on laundering his shirt and tie, and even sewed up his trouser cuff.

His sturdy body aroused surprise and drew nasty comments; then an old quarry owner asked him why he hadn't enlisted. The homeland needs her sons. This isn't the time for self-indulgence! Thomas amiably told him (venomous answers, that he would have loved serving up to the old simpleton, bubbled on his tongue) that he had worked in the office of Generaloberst Fromm in Berlin, had volunteered to serve and as proof showed him the document he had received.

Then he deluged the old man with gloomy economic figures: the economies of the Western countries that Germany had conquered were collapsing. We were wasting valuable raw materials on France, Belgium and the other countries, but the end of the war was near. And while the old man listened in awe, Thomas praised the power of the Luftwaffe and predicted that soon all of Moscow would go up in flames, 'and we'll visit the German Kremlin together'. The old man stared at him with bloodshot eyes and groped for a sentence that would stitch the predictions together, but Thomas had already gone away.

As the year drew to a close, the atmosphere grew murkier. Everyone was talking about tragedies: parents who had lost sons, miserable widows, children longing for their fathers or big brothers. The joyous shouts of victory, which he had been absorbed by in Poland, and which he had heard in Germany during the past summer, had disintegrated into little sighs, stammering discontent beneath the cries of faith in the Reich and the Führer.

When he encountered people mourning around a table in an inn, shouting about Germany's righteousness and the cruelty of her enemies, he wanted to tell them about the Jewish woman whose face was smashed between the asphalt and the policemen's boots in Lublin, or about the class of archaeological orphans who in his dreams were still at their studies.

One day he met a doctor who had come back from Ukraine on a short furlough, and who described dead men and women loaded onto wagons, and gigantic pits housing layer after layer of human beings. Only then did it occur to him that he wasn't privy to such a great secret. All the people he met had friends and acquaintances and sons and relatives at the front or in Poland who probably knew much more than he did. It wasn't the information, but how you arranged it.

For example, he had rebelled against the Foreign Office when he refused to give it the Model of the Belorussian People. But a stubborn voice within him argued that, big hero that he was, the real reason he had refused them was his remorse that his Polish model had sentenced so many people to death. Now that voice was mingling with other voices, with memories that, when the dust settled, would form his story. He would consign to some attic the knowledge that he hadn't supplied them with the model because he was unable to write it; nor would he remember that maybe he had refused to finish it in order to defend his honour, because he wasn't going to give another organisation the opportunity to absorb his strength and then vomit him out; and mainly he wouldn't remember that he had refused them because he knew that the price wouldn't be high, that they wouldn't behead him. If they'd put a gun to his temple, would he have left the model unfinished?

Everywhere in the country horror stories were told about soldiers who had frozen to death in light military coats. 'We lost twenty-nine men out of a hundred and twenty-seven in the Great War,' the wife of a village mayor told him. 'This time an even greater disaster will befall us.'

The talk—in the train, in restaurants and inns, in the street—didn't change. Strangely, until now, he hadn't paid attention to idle second-hand chatter of this kind. One day, consumed by pain because he was wasting his life among these miserable souls, Thomas tried something new: he complained with them and consoled them, predicted a smashing victory and hinted at certain defeat, praised the Führer and expressed doubt about future success. At last he had found an amusement that gratified him—playing the role of the ghost who floats all over the country creating confusion. There were fundamental contradictions in everything he said. People heard endless facts and figures, but nothing cohered. That was life, no? In Baden-Baden he terrified a small audience with the vast numbers of the enemy armies, and mocked the Red Army as a rabble; in Dessau a restaurant owner invited his friends to a secret meeting where Herr Heiselberg would lecture about the war; at the end, after the applause, when he had already left the restaurant, he heard them yelling at each other, and every voice offered a different interpretation of his views; at a dinner in the home of a wealthy estate owner in Lübeck, who invited Thomas after he had impressed his daughter in the library, he told them that in Dortmund they had melted down a precious statue because metal was badly needed for the war effort, and the next day someone had put a piece of paper on the empty pedestal. There was a poem on it—'Woe to the nation who chose these men/ Wurm, Spiegelberg, and Franz Mor' (and he explained to the young people that the scum who wrote it was apparently hinting at Göring, Goebbels and Hitler)—but in the same suburb women donated their fur coats to soldiers, and they all composed love letters to the Führer. 'Doesn't this faith in our victory makes one's heart swell? Most regrettably, we can expect ruin,' he declared, leaving an oppressive silence behind him.

The truth was he was saying nothing new, but as if in a nightmare he heard himself declaiming sentences from the past. These ignoramuses might be impressed, but he knew his motor was running on empty.

He wandered in circles around Germany. At the end of the year, on a dull winter day, he found himself in a village in the Saar district. Snow fell and melted. When he approached the church, some girls shouted at him, 'Get out of here, you rotten ghost. We've heard enough fast-talkers from the city in old suits. Our men at the front would have killed you.'

To his astonishment he discovered he had already been in this village. Could he be blamed for not remembering? Red-tiled roofs, two-storey houses, little velvet lampshades, lawns, giant elms, an oak leaning over a muddy path, one or two taverns, fleeting welcome smiles, black nights—everything looked the same. It was possible that he would knock on Frau Gruner's door again.

The people's pride in victory was intertwined with their fear of defeat. He had no delusions—even if it took fifty years he knew how time eats away at the victors, how lethal its destructive power is, even during the exhilarating hours of glory, when it seems that life will always be like this. This awareness was imprinted in him. No one asked him whether he wanted it. To be means to sell your soul, with all you've got, each morning each day. He had no better definition of his life: to make your dreams big enough to let you escape the fear of extinction for a while. A clever man was a true believer in his life's work.

Where was he heading? He was sprawled in a chair on a balcony, cold winds whipped his face and he struggled to dismiss the question. Where was he heading? To places he had already been, where people were still waiting for him to scatter the fog he had left behind? How could he do that? The truth was that he himself was a cloud of fog that invited people in and then swallowed them up. Sometimes he observed himself from outside: what did others see? A grey cloud around the outline of a body and, on the edges, a black suitcase. A moment ago he was here and stunned everyone with his magniloquent performance. Now he was already far away, swallowed up on a train moving through a field among poplars and firs. Maybe he had gone north to the mountains that surrounded the village, and maybe he had turned around and retraced his steps.

BREST
JUNE 1941

Sasha woke up covered with hot dust. Her eyes stung with tears. Her breath was short. It was happening, and she mustn't lose time.

She rushed to put on her boots which for a month now she had been placing next to the door every night, and between them the jackknife. The roar of motors. A plane was diving outside the window, spitting fire. Chunks of plaster fell.

She ran down the steps into the street. Buildings and trees were burning, and fire was licking the grass. Loaded wagons lurched among a line of people snaking its way down the avenue. She leaped into the crowd, entirely focused on the distance between her and Kolya at the fortress. She climbed up onto a truck that had turned over. The driver was still in his seat with his charred hands on the wheel. Next to him lay a small, wrapped-up body; a little girl whose hair looked like a bundle of charred twigs gathered in a bow. Fragments of glass lacerated Sasha's bare arms, a deep breath shook her, the pain passed through her whole body as quick as mercury. Dizzy, Sasha leaped down and raced forwards, clenching her fists to dull the burning. She turned right and went past the building where the map room was. A thin film of brown dust coated her. A curtain on the second floor was slightly open, the way she had left it.

...

In early June, on a fine morning, Maxim had come to visit. It was a holiday and the streets were flooded with young men who were celebrating their graduation from military school. When he got off the train, she brought him to the map room. He stood in astonishment in the middle of the room uttering curses, then started tearing up the large sheets of paper. They tore up the maps, the copies of them, the position papers and the letters she had exchanged with Thomas Heiselberg.

When he learned that she had corresponded with the German representative under a false name, he pushed her up against the wall and slapped her hard. She had paid some woman named Viktoria Sovlova on Devortsovaya Street to receive letters from her close friend in Lublin. The code was her aunt's illness: 'My aunt's illness has got worse. No one is interested in her. Even those who love her are reconciled to her death—in all sincerity I don't know what to do.'

Maxim shouted that she was crazy. At last, she thought, he had learned to detest her. In all the years they had known each other, he raged, he had trusted her good judgment and now he found out that his wife was someone else altogether.

They stuffed all the scraps of paper in an iron box and burned them. Then they burned the ashes. After the Germans attacked, anyone connected to or friendly with them would be condemned as an enemy of the people and executed! Even during war the good old machine would work. People would be arrested, graves would be dug, just as before, but the pace would be accelerated.

Maxim stomped on the ashes and asked whether any other papers remained. Tears choked her throat. A few miniature copies of the parade maps were buried in her mattress. She didn't dare tell him.

Every time she heard a knock on the neighbours' doors, she still hoped it would be representatives from Foreign Affairs who needed her documents to prepare for the parade. She strained to remember whether there was anything in her office cabinet, but her brain was a mist. She recited instructions to herself: now stand, now sit and now drink water.

Maxim suspected that she was indifferent to his fate and wouldn't lift a finger to save him. It wasn't true. It was just that his efforts to hold on to life were too complex. She was amazed she had once made these detailed calculations, designed intricate plans. At night, in bed, she learned that her husband was visiting Brest for another reason: he had heard that Comrade Nikita Mikhailovich Kropotkin was planning his revenge against Sasha for some little episode. Yesterday Maxim had met him and was informed that she had dared to threaten Comrade Kropotkin, her direct superior who nonetheless refused to reveal the circumstances of the incident.

Fortunately, Comrade Kropotkin was a decent and reasonable man. He understood that a gratuitous struggle would harm them all, and they reached a satisfactory agreement.

'What agreement?'

'A satisfactory one.'

'An agreement that I'm to leave the district?'

'Are you crazy?' he hissed. 'I understand that you want to stay here and greet the Germans. A good husband allows his wife to fulfil her dreams.'

After he took off her clothes and sat her down on top of him, then they lay hugging each other, and he declared that it was fine if she wanted to stay. He wouldn't leave Brest without her.

He knew it was a lie. Two days later he was summoned to Leningrad.

'I risked my life when I married you. I did everything I could to save you, and in return you doomed us both,' he reproached her at the station. 'You no longer have the will to live. That's your right.'

To leave her there, on the front line, without guilt or shame, he had to believe she was beyond remedy.

He didn't kiss her, just held her hand and looked in her eyes, as though searching for a remote spark of love. She didn't doubt his courage. If he believed they had any hope, he would have taken enormous risks to stay with her. He was pale, twirling his moustache as though indifferent. 'When you return to Leningrad, we'll talk about our marriage,' he said. 'Maybe we'll see things differently.' He held her but didn't pull her close. 'Maybe we can see things differently.'

A week later Nikita Mikhailovich summoned her. 'At the end of June you're leaving the district and returning to Leningrad.'

She wasn't surprised to hear that he had made this arrangement with Maxim, who had lied to her. Again.

...

The wife of a city official passed her, pushing a wheelbarrow with two or three children in it, curled up like foetuses, a mess of faces and hair, closed eyes, a blue sweater, girls' underpants, pink arms, stretched legs. She turned to Sasha and asked her to push the wheelbarrow for her, 'Just for a minute or two', she had no more strength.

Sasha didn't answer. The distance between her and Kolya remained a vast desert that couldn't be crossed. How much death there was in the chasm of time between them.

A plane dived and she heard the whistle of the bombs. Everybody lay down. The official's wife put her body over the wheelbarrow, and Sasha started to run. She ran down alone and prayed that the people lying down wouldn't get up. Behind her machine-gun fire chattered, screams could be heard, weak moans. She could smell burned skin. A huge brown mushroom of dust—apparently pulverised bricks—spread above her and hid the avenue. Everything was silent, dislocating her senses. Her imagination roamed through the fortress, painting Kolya with the pallor of death, wherever he was: in the meeting room in the winter palace, at the end of the bridge over the river, beneath the tunnel that led to the Kholmsk Gate. She struggled against weakness, twisted her body as though fighting off a ghost and kept running. Maybe he was alive, maybe he was only wounded, there was no certainty he was dead, if she could find him she would get them out of there.

For a few minutes that seemed like an eternity, she ran blindly in the swirl of dust until it settled a little, and at the end of the avenue she could see a column of refugees moving along Pioneer Street towards Moscow Street.

She ran faster and pushed through the tangle of people. She was already close. Figures were bending over plane wreckage and tore hunks of aluminium from the wings. Suddenly, through the smoke, the fortress rose up.

Fire raged above it, explosion after explosion, and in her imagination each bomb pierced his body anew. To her right, from the edge of the field, soldiers in dusty uniforms emerged. She joined them, and together they ran towards the citadel. These men, who looked as if they had risen from the dead, encouraged her. Her body was flooded with lightness and life, his life. Was it an illusion? Could such complete awareness be a lie?

The soldiers knocked on the gate of the citadel again and again. No one opened. She shrieked and banged on it. The minutes passed. She lost the clarity in which she had heard him breathing. She felt pain from the pieces of glass in her arms. She had already lost sensation in her hands, which were still pounding on the gate.

A bearded officer with two barefoot soldiers by his side approached her, raised his rifle and shoved the barrel into her face. For a moment she thought it was all over, and a moan of happiness formed in her throat—she had never understood those who clung to life. He cursed in Ukrainian, wrapped the stock in a rag and hit her in the face. The earth beneath her shoulders was a mound burning like coals.

'I'll burn you along with your wife and children,' she provoked in Ukrainian and gaped at the rifle like a girl looking at a magic wand.

He aimed it at her. One of his escorts approached and placed his bare foot on her lips. 'She's crazy,' he shouted to the bearded officer. 'Don't shoot, don't shoot.'

A shrill girl's voice shouted in Russian, 'Kill the whore! She's NKVD.'

The soldier pressed his foot against her mouth. She tasted dirt and gravel, blood and pain, a tooth breaking. She felt with her tongue and didn't find the tooth. Maybe she'd swallowed it. The earth resounded with thudding earth thrown into the air by a bomb. Death and life had been snatched from her control. The gate was locked. A stubborn voice wheedled, tempting her to faint.

The gate moved. She came to: now to get in. The bearded officer talked to someone. A group of soldiers raced out. 'The telephones are dead. It's a rat-trap here,' the escapees shouted. 'Withdraw to Kobrin!'

'Kobrin?' the bearded officer shouted. 'You can barricade yourselves in here. Outside you're running right into death.'

A perplexed silence enveloped the two small camps. They were trying to understand: where was the trap? Where was life, and where was death?

The soldiers saw the wall of German artillery that was spitting fire. Some of them turned around and began to trample those in front to get back into the citadel. Shells exploded, the earth spun beneath her and a curtain of raging fire spread before them. She felt for the jackknife in her sock, drew it and with a single movement brought it down the back of the soldier's leg. He shook his leg as though trying to chase away a mosquito. She rolled out from under him and spat out dirt and blood.

The soldier leaned over her. He looked like an officer she had danced with the day before in the park, a man in a fine uniform who spoke with a slight accent. Was he Baltic? Then she realised he was German. 'So when are you attacking?' She tightened her grip on his shoulder. 'I won't give you away. Just tell me the secret.' The officer angrily told her she was a madwoman and asked someone else to dance.

About two hours later, at midnight, Nikita Mikhailovich came to the door of her house and asked her to join him. He had promised Comrade Podolsky that he would evacuate her if there was an attack, and he was a man of his word.

She mocked him: 'Don't you understand? Your little schemes won't change anything. I won't stay alive for a second after Kolya. The excuses for not dying are all used up. Besides, why are you clearing out, Nikita Mikhailovich? Are you in a panic? For months you've been swearing to everyone that the Germans won't dare fight on two fronts, and that the army is not anticipating an attack. Where's the TASS story that you were waving around, as though your mother had written it, condemning talk about war and saying that the Western press was sowing discord between Germany and the Soviet Union? Where's the parade you placed in my hands?'

Nikita Mikhailovich had no time for explanations. His wife and children were waiting in the car. He wasn't running away but going to Kobrin to organise the counterattack.

'That's what I always loved about you,' she said bitterly. 'Unlike your friend Styopa and my husband, you're one of the few who still differentiate between truth and lies.'

...

She got up. The soldier grabbed her shoulder and pushed her towards the gate. The stench of burnt flesh, burnt grass, burnt wood. They tripped over piles of stones, wooden beams, fragments of shells, shattered household utensils and corpses in nightgowns, pyjamas, undershirts—the ruins of the living quarters where she had slept when she worked in the citadel.

'We have to hurry,' she shouted. 'My brother is there!' She started coughing. The sour taste of sick was in her mouth. The soldier didn't answer. The main thing was not to stop, to get away from all of this death. They moved away, but the stench grew stronger, wafting up from her skin and nightgown, from his uniform and face. She vomited. The soldier brought a canteen to her lips. The putrid water nauseated her. He grabbed the canteen from her hand and drank greedily.

'We have to hurry!' she shouted again.

'We're hurrying, we're hurrying,' he said, leading her to the central courtyard. Black locust and lilac branches had fallen into the trenches. For a moment their scent filled the air. Pits yawned in the earth, and bodies were scattered between them. From above fierce whistles were heard, and thunder rolled out of the trembling ground. She caught a glimpse of fire in the windows of the castle. A few soldiers stood near cannons and waited.

'They don't have any ammunition,' said the soldier. 'It's an army of shoeless soldiers and whores.'

The dust-covered citadel, full of smoke, and the soldiers standing at the cannon were terribly similar to the map of the war games she had drawn for the parade. He led her through a twisting tunnel with damp walls. There were groups of soldiers, women with unkempt hair, weeping women twirling their hair and wrapping it around rusty nails, men whispering to each other, young people who looked like gypsies, faces like none she had ever seen in the city. A chorus of panting and grunting, the shouts of the wounded and the cries of children.

She pushed in among them, and glanced right and left. Everywhere she looked became a focus of light, and among the hundreds of filthy faces she looked for Kolya. People cursed the officials who had abandoned the city, leaned over radio sets and pleaded for the help that was expected from Kobrin. A few children sat sharpening wooden sticks into knives around a big kerosene lantern in a niche in the wall. They talked about sticking their blades into the necks of German soldiers. 'I'd even stick the blade deep into the throat of a girl soldier like nothing,' one boasted. She stroked the blade of her jackknife and dropped it. Another child grabbed it and the others jumped on him.

The heat was heavy. A stifling cloud crawled down the tunnels. Somebody was shouting after Viktor Nestorovich Kravchuk. Was he dead or a prisoner? The name sounded familiar. A long time ago, when she first came to Brest, she obtained a list of the soldiers in Kolya's unit. Every morning she wondered which of those soldiers were Kolya's friends and which his enemies. Kravchuk was one of the names on that list.

She squeezed her way into the bunch of drunken soldiers who were lying on the ground. She asked them about Kolya and Kravchuk.

'We can't hear. Lean over!' they called to her and laughed. Then they said that Kravchuk was an NKVD border guard, but they didn't know anyone called Nikolai Weissberg. Maybe Nikitin knew.

'Where is he?'

One of them, no more than a boy, put his hand under her dress and pinched her thigh. 'We haven't seen him,' he laughed. 'Probably dead.' His fingers were already inside her vagina. She kicked him and moved away. 'That hurts more than the German,' he groaned, and a boyish laugh rang through the tunnels.

Near the wall people were speaking about women who had been captured by the Germans, about a girl named Valya Zenkina. A small group discussed whether they should break out, but there was nowhere to go. The city was falling. Better to dig in here until reinforcements came. The suggestions came in disgruntled fractured sentences, the desire to cling to illusions. How it had enslaved her in the past.

'Has anyone seen Nikolai Weissberg?' she shouted. 'Did you see the soldiers of the forty-second division?'

'We haven't seen anything,' they roared angrily and shoved her.

Two girls in braids, wearing dresses filthy with dirt and blood, were begging for water. Their strict education showed in their erect posture, their proud tone. They were like small women, and their pleas were like orders. After they drank, happiness spread over their faces.

The soldier appeared again. 'Don't disappear. I'm keeping an eye on you.'

Why didn't he leave her in peace? He gripped her shoulder again and pushed her forwards, steering her right and left like a puppet. She moved away from the girls and wished them a speedy death. When she understood they were going down below, she struggled to escape his grip. It was clear to her that Kolya wasn't there.

The soldier pressed her against the wall. 'Where do you want to go?'

'Upstairs.'

'Outside?'

'Yes.'

'Do you want to die?' He loosened his grip. She removed his hand and went up against the stream of people.

She was outside, running towards the cannon. The soldiers who had been standing beside them were gone, except for one who was curled up, his face smashed and his legs bent in a kind of broken circle. She leaned over him, stroked his hair and asked him if he had seen Private Weissberg, forty-second division. He grunted and was seized by a convulsion. She pushed his hand off her nightgown and went away.

More and more soldiers, some of whom had been stationed in defensive positions around the citadel, crossed the central courtyard—crawling, limping, on stretchers. She whirled among them, grabbing their bodies, howling, begging for information. A few said meaning-less things, pointed in opposite directions. One said Private Weissberg was dead, another had seen his officer slightly wounded.

The dawn rose. A red cover spread over them and columns of smoke rose between earth and sky. A lookout holding binoculars who lay on the roof of the building shouted that columns of the Wehrmacht were marching in the streets of Brest.

People shouted that he was lying.

He insisted: the citadel was surrounded.

Podolsky's calculations had proved to be amazingly exact. The flow of retreating soldiers was now a trickle. Two soldiers stumbled from the western gate and rushed into the tunnels. She fell on them to ask if they had seen Private Nikolai Weissberg of the forty-second division. One of them, a blood-soaked rag wrapped around his arm, looked at her with dreamy eyes, whose thick lashes were burnt. It was Grigorian. Suddenly, as if he understood her intentions, he grabbed her hair in his good arm and dragged her after him into the tunnels.

She obeyed, shouting, 'Is he dead? Tell me whether he's dead!' They squeezed between people, pushed and were pushed, kicked. News spread rapidly that everywhere except this part of the fortress had fallen to the Germans. People in uniform grew scarcer: shirts, hats, belts, epaulettes and Red Army coats were rolled up hastily and stuffed into the water troughs. Some children fished them out and flaunted insignia and caps.

Grigorian didn't let go of her hair, and she held on to his belt. They pushed through secretions and sweat, vomit and blood, among the children's dreams of glory and those of two girls who had fallen asleep on the floor hugging each other, among people shouting orders, those who were encouraging, others who were silent, among those weeping for their imminent deaths, cursing the state and the army, among those whose wide open eyes reflected immeasurable imagined horrors.

'Is he dead?' she asked.

Grigorian nodded.

'Is there any doubt?'

'No. He was sleeping next to me.'

'Did he suffer?'

'We got a direct hit from a shell. I flew into the wall. When I got up, he was dead.'

'Did he talk about us sometimes?'

A voice called to Grigorian. 'The doctor is here!'

He didn't move. 'In the last days, when everyone understood that something big was going to happen, he spoke a bit more.'

'What did he say?'

'I don't know exactly. He spoke with Denislov.'

'Is he dead too?'

'I haven't seen him since this began. I'll look for him.'

'It doesn't matter,' she said and turned away.

Now her memory bore him up and set him before her; she didn't resist, there was no time for that; in a little while the deceitful morning would rise, and offer cunning arguments, it would find proofs, it would enslave her consciousness to staying in this world. 'Even if the thin guy dies,' Maxim said, 'even if everyone you ever knew disappears, you'll still be a survival machine, like everyone: when it happens, you'll see.'

Part of her believed him. Part of her always believed Maxim Podolsky.

Suddenly other voices were heard around her—a battle was taking place near the Terespol Gate that defended the citadel from the west. A few hundred soldiers had dug in there and were repelling the Germans. The soldiers who had been lying on the ground were now loading their rifles and giving out hand grenades. Women and children gathered around and encouraged them. In a single row they rushed up: the boy who had fondled her strode forwards first, and Grigorian, in a new bandage, joined them.

'We need reinforcements near the Kobrin Gate!' Shouts were heard. 'And in hell, too, idiots!' A hoarse voice laughed, and other bitter laughter rolled around.

Hope bubbled up in the tunnels. The joy of action became infectious, tasks were assigned, maps spread out, the smell of despair disappeared.

She surveyed them with horror: even now are you clinging to life? She bent over and stuffed her fingers into her mouth to stifle a scream. The feeling of orphanhood crushed her, and she realised that she was buying time with her wits now, that vital strength was crawling into her body, that life was whirring inside her. Here was the ticking of the survival machine as it woke up. Father and Mother, freed from the gulag, would want at least one daughter, even Boris Godunov, a hint of Pavlik Morozov, but she was still their only daughter. She would give them grandchildren, and, as Maxim said, grandchildren are like children. Wasn't it strange that even while she was in the citadel, bombarded and surrounded, she still believed in her ability to choose to live or die?

She crawled out. Did she hope it would be hard to get out of the tunnels? She was afraid of horrible pain, of immeasurable suffering, but the certainty that her choice had been made long ago made her calm. Everything that had happened to her in the past seemed like a little mishap, sometimes even amusing. There was no reason for pathos. There had been bigger tragedies: for years people had been counting the arrested, the disappeared, the dead. Now corpses would be piled up from here to Kobrin, to Minsk, maybe even to Leningrad, hundreds of thousands, even millions—here was her modest contribution to all that death. Sometimes, for a certain group, things come to an end, the world slams them against the wall; it's not exactly their fault.

But all the things that came to her mind now seemed pointless, little Maupassant ideas. She had only to give her body up to the movement, and she knew where she was heading.

She stood outside. From the west a squadron of German planes was approaching. She stepped to the centre of the courtyard. There wasn't a living soul around her, only bodies. The planes approached, the chatter of their machine-guns like drizzle on house roofs. Behind them the first scraps of sunlight sprayed their wings with all the grey-blue glow of the summer. Preceded by their heat, sparks of fire from the machine-guns were already burning her body. She stopped, threw her shoulders back and looked up at the sky.

'Nadyezhda Petrovna'—she had sneaked a letter for her into her husband's suitcase—'you wrote poems about me, calling me Boris Godunov and the beautiful twin of Pavlik Morozov. Everybody praises the change you underwent, but I understand: you wrote those poems for me, and maybe for the dead and the imprisoned. I only ask you that if I die here, and Kolya lives, take care of him. Your position is stronger now, and you can be a kind of guardian for him.'

The rumble of the machine-guns grew louder. She looked up. A mountain of red dust rose up before her and within it shone the sun and the plane wings. She closed her eyes, and when she opened them black smoke was curling up from the dust and the carved words. She identified Nadia's handwriting:

You won't die without him.

And anyway it doesn't matter, fool that you are.

You call the bundle of lies and baseness that we are 'life'?

Day-night, winter-summer—it's only time, under the heavens of loss, that crouches on top of us.

We're chained to it like dogs to a kennel.

For a long time, as you realised, none of us has been alive.